PRAISE FO

"Populated by ghost l̲ ̲, ̲w̲o̲o̲d̲ sprites, vampires, androids and – above all – queers who survive, *Unthinkable* taps into a rich seam of potential in the Gothic tradition. Like a haunted well in an abandoned churchyard; I felt utterly compelled to throw myself in!"

– Eris Young, author of *They / Them / Their* and *Ace Voices*

"From a monastery in medieval Japan to a hipster bar in Buffalo, *Unthinkable: A Queer Gothic Anthology* is a journey rife with mystery and longing from beginning to end. In *Unthinkable*, Editor Celine Frohn has brought together a diverse collection of evocative stories that reframe the gothic with a queer lens. These are tales of haunted houses and haunted hearts, each story shimmering with its own dark magic. This is an anthology that will leave you shivering – maybe with fear, maybe with desire, or maybe, with a little bit of both."

– Anuja Varghese, author of *Chrysalis*

"A glorious and multi-faceted exploration of how the gothic flourishes at the intersections of queer existence. From the crumbling walls of a monastery in medieval Japan to haunted ancestral homelands, this is a collection that breathes new, expansive life into a genre that has always been about change and shifting powers."

– Heather Parry, author of *Orpheus Builds A Girl*

UNTHINKABLE

A Queer Gothic Anthology

Published by Haunt Publishing
www.hauntpublishing.com
@HauntPublishing

ISBN (Paperback): 978-1-915691-02-6
ISBN (ebook): 978-1-915691-03-3

Edited by Celine Frohn

Cover design by Ashley Hankins: ashleydoesartstuff.com

Typeset by Laura Jones: lauraflojo.com

Printed and bound in Great Britain by Clays Ltd, Elcograf S.p.A.

UNTHINKABLE

A Queer Gothic Anthology

Edited by Celine Frohn

CONTENTS

CONTENT NOTES

The publisher has made every effort to accurately reflect the content in this book. Any omissions are accidental and the publisher's own.

CONTENT NOTES A-Z

Animal Death: It Passed By Morning.

Child abuse: The Wellkeepers.

Classism: All Sweet Souls.

Confinement: The Wellkeepers.

Death: All Sweet Souls; Bess and the Thrasher Bird.

Death of parent: All Sweet Souls.

Depression: An Epitaph, Epistolary.

Grief: Clutching Air; An Epitaph, Epistolary; Ghosts at Haunting's End; Sea Salt and Strawberries.

Gun violence: Bess and the Thrasher Bird.

Incest: Bess and the Thrasher Bird.

Loss of a loved one: All Sweet Souls; Bodies of Water; Clutching Air; An Epitaph, Epistolary; Ghosts at Haunting's End; Reynardine; Sea Salt and Strawberries.

Miscarriage: Vestal.

Misogyny: Vestal.

Murder: Bess and the Thrasher Bird; The Wellkeepers.

Racism: Bess and the Thrasher Bird.

Rape: Bess and the Thrasher Bird.

Sexual assault: Bess and the Thrasher Bird.

Slavery: Bess and the Thrasher Bird.

Suicide: Bess and the Thrasher Bird.

Suicidal thoughts: All Sweet Souls; An Epitaph, Epistolary.

Torture: Raion Kuīn.

Violence: Bess and the Thrasher Bird; Raion Kuīn.

Vomit: All Sweet Souls.

CONTENT NOTES BY STORY

All Sweet Souls: classism; death; death of parent; gore; loss of a loved one; suicidal thoughts; vomit.

Bess and the Thrasher Bird: blood; death; gun violence; incest; murder; racism; rape; sexual assault; slavery; suicide; violence.

Raion Kuīn: blood; torture; violence.

Vestal: miscarriage; misogyny.

Clutching Air: grief; loss of a loved one.

Fun at Parties: blood.

The Dead Space: blood.

It Passed by Morning: animal death.

The Wellkeepers: blood; child abuse; confinement; murder.

Sea Salt and Strawberries: blood; grief; loss of a loved one.

Bodies of Water: blood; grief; loss of a loved one.

Reynardine: gore; loss of a loved one.

Reflections: none.

In Ruins: none.

Blood Play: blood.

An Epitaph, Epistolary: depression; grief; loss of a loved one; suicidal thoughts.

The Ghost at Haunting's End: grief; loss of a loved one.

Q.E.D: none.

INTRODUCTION

S.T. Gibson

The Gothic has always been fertile soil for queer stories to take root in. From its inception as a genre to its proliferation today, the Gothic has been largely concerned with what happens in the shadows, on the edge of reality, and on the margins of society. For much of history, queer life has also happened in liminal spaces, in underground communities or in parallel societies to the one we all live in. It's in these in-between spaces that sexual identities, found families, and queer romances and friendships have flourished. In the Gothic, liminal spaces are where terrors and grotesqueries live, true, but it's also where a brave reader might find magic, mystery, and even true love.

Bringing together these two themes, queer life and the Gothic, makes for a spine-tinglingly inspired marriage. That match made in a haunted house is exactly what this anthology endeavours to highlight.

The stories contained in this book deploy classic Gothic conventions with new twists, and always with a generous helping of queerness. Within this anthology's pages you'll find a gentleman haunted by a lost love, a witch surprised by an unfamiliar visitor, a potion peddler with a secret, a university student wrestling with an undead creature, a forest god in love with a human, a Southern girl witnessing a terrifying magical fox hunt, a nun protecting an injured woman in a 13th century convent, a highwayman avenging their beloved's murder, a strange cultus dedicated to an indescribable force, an android attempting to step outside of the shadow of a dead girl, a modern student stumbling into a vampire in a bar, a woman awaiting the return of her beloved on All Souls' Day, an art student infatuated with a museum statue, two grieving people bonding over their mutual haunting, the son of an eccentric fossil-collector discovering a creature held captive in his mother's estate, two lovers facing down a restless house and the legacy of colonialism, a ghost watching her girlfriend recover from grief, and two neighbours who find each other amidst strange dreams and buried guilt.

The stories featured in *Unthinkable* are love letters to, refutations of, and continuations of classical Gothic tropes, from the haunted house to the vampire, to the family full of secrets to the solitary practitioner of magic. They span time periods, genres, and styles to create a wholly unique reading experience steeped in a deep and abiding love for the Gothic. Many of the stories work to decenter the colonial and western lens through which so many Gothic stories have been told. Moreover, they are an unapologetic celebration of queerness in so many of its forms and permutations, and the ways in which queer people can find community even in the darkest of places, or step up and become the heroes in even the most twisting of tales. They'll appeal to those readers who have always had an affinity for the night, found comfort in shadows, or saw themselves reflected in the monster.

I hope you'll find a story or two that speaks to you in these brutal and beautiful pages. I certainly did.

ALL SWEET SOULS

Antonija Mežnarić

Stella stood by the window, drinking in the spreading view of the green hills, vast vineyards and bright cornfields bathed in the dark orange of the sunset, slowly stroking the skull in her hands. She hummed with a barely restrained thrill, only a touch of trepidation, counting down the moments until nightfall.

On her windowsill, a candle burned. It was just one of the many flickering lights in the villages scattered nearby, where someone was lost to death in the last year. In every house with such a candle, preparations were made after a hard day in the fields. A place was left at the table for the dear dead to find when they came home for the night.

But tonight, they were not the only ones set loose from the underworld. For those *others*, there was not a feast waiting on the table, but a circle of blessed lanterns looping around the village territories, keeping the unholy ones who had risen out. It was a folly, of course. As soon as the first lantern burned to ash, the rotting legs would find their way inside – whether seeking sinful souls to drag to hell, or the simple comfort of the family they'd left behind.

No one wanted to believe their loved ones belonged to the damned. That when they came, they wouldn't be here for a hug and a meal of fat goose meat, but for the living to replace them in the grave. Or at least that was how the folktale went. If an unholy one catches a living soul in the night prior to All Souls' Day, they could barter it for release from death.

Stella hadn't bothered with the dinner. Instead she had bathed until certain her skin was smooth and clear. She had taken her greatest pride out of the chest – her late mother's nightgown, made from rich silk, with an embroidered bodice and ruffled sleeves. When her mother wore it, the nightgown was white, but now it was sickly yellow with age. It had been bought in Vienna and it was the last of her mother's clothes still in Stella's possession. Shrouded in the silk, barefoot, she sat on the moth-eaten divan under the window, where the amber light of the dying sun was like a crown upon her lush black hair, falling freely to the floor in great locks.

Her brother, Ljubomil, was securely locked in his room for the night, while their father was drinking himself to ruin over at their neighbour's, the illustrissimus Batorić, both crying over their lost serfs. Stella had let the manservant – the very last to still stay with them – take the week off, to be certain there would be no one to accidentally stumble upon something they shouldn't see. She meticulously planned for the night, with her hard-sought catch firmly secured in the dried-out wine cellar. Now, it was only a question of patience.

"Soon," she whispered to the skull, before leaving a chaste kiss on the bare bone. Gently, she lowered it into her lap, her body burning with anticipation.

Because, when the night fell and the bony hands broke through the ground, there would be a clear path to her candle atop the hill. No warning lanterns burned in front of the old curia – a home that dreamt of being a palace – which was slowly wasting away.

Where she waited for her beloved to return.

★ ★ ★

It was a rainy day when Barica first came to the old curia nobilitaris Vidovec, years ago, trailing in mud on her modest shoes.

At first, Stella had no interest in the arrival of the new

governess, warning father not to be such a fool. "I can teach Ljubomil everything he needs to know," she had argued, even though she loathed the idea. It wasn't like she didn't care for her little brother, but she would rather her time spent doing something else. Anything else.

Father had, of course, refused. It wasn't even to keep up appearances, because he never cared about that – not since he'd married an Italian opera singer of Indian descent – but because he was acutely aware where Stella's knowledge fell flat, mostly with a bad Hungarian accent. The new governess, he said, was fluent not just in Hungarian, but also German, Italian and French. None of it mattered, since the woman would still die, Stella had replied, but not even that had managed to sway her father's decision.

No matter how indifferent she was, when her eyes fell on Barica for the first time, something in Stella's chest moved in a fluttering rhythm, like a swarm of fruit flies drowning in wine. Stella couldn't stop watching the other girl, from the hem of her puffed-out brown dress, stretched over layers of underskirts, to the golden locks of her corn-yellow hair, fixed under the bonnet.

The other woman excitedly looked around the open hallway, waiting for the servant to fetch Stella's father. She seemed to be in awe, which Stella didn't understand. There was an obvious stench of rot permeating the air in the curia, the dust and the stains permanently settled in the carpet, walls bare of paintings, discoloured patches showing that it hadn't always been like that. It was sort of sweet how the young woman's huge eyes radiated excitement, regardless.

It was all too much. Deep inside of Stella, something awoke. The woman's obvious vivacity broke through the heavy fog which her mind constantly dwelled in, and it urged her legs to move from their hiding place behind the half-opened bedroom doors at the end of the entry hall.

As soon as Barica noticed her, Stella smiled, aware of the awkward pull on her face. It must've looked awful because the other woman's expression turned into a blank mask, belied only by the deep scarlet blooming from her cheeks to her hairline, as if the sun burned through her skin, leaving a cherry smudge. Seeing that, Stella was more than glad she'd inherited her mother's darker complexion.

With that thought came the jolt of reality, bringing her back to her senses. This woman in the hallway, amazed by a sad, decrepit house, was as good as dead as soon as she'd accepted the position of governess in the Vidovec family. Stella adjusted her expectations accordingly.

The woman started to greet her, expressing her shame over dragging mud into the hallway – the carpet was hardly pristine to begin with, but she politely didn't mention *that* – but Stella cut her off.

"You are making a mistake." She didn't bother to hide the harsh tone, hoping the girl would have enough sense to recognise the danger, as would, surely, any serf in front of a fickle master. "Turn around if your life is dear to you."

Barica's mouth moved soundlessly for a blink or two, chewing through replies, probably, searching and discarding words.

"Excuse me? I'm sorry, I'm obviously not as noble as you to know the intricacies of highborn etiquette. Surely, I only misunderstood your words as rude. Because the illustrissima Vidovec would never be that ungraceful." The girl's voice was steely, her granite eyes unflinching. She was *mocking* her. Stella was trying to keep her alive, and the girl was mocking her. Highborn, she'd said, to the face of a daughter of lower nobility, one of the peasants-noblemen, jokingly called noble plumbringers, who were too knee-deep in the dirt to come anywhere close to aristocracy. Above the serfs, but below everyone else in this backyard of the Austro-Hungarian Empire.

Stella should've been insulted. She should've raged. Instead, her lips stretched into a deeper grin, showing off her teeth. In two big strides she was in front of Barica, invading the other woman's space.

"You are funny and have a spine, and I don't know if it's a good or a bad thing to have when your job is to cater to the whims of the *honorable* plumbringers. It would be such a shame for your life to be cut short." She moved closer to Barica's ear, and to the woman's credit, she didn't even flinch. Aware how close she was, almost like a lover ready to kiss a cherished neck, Stella whispered, "You are the fifth governess to grace our halls. What do you think happened to your predecessors?" That caused a reaction; a slight shiver passed through the other girl, right under Stella's eyes. Satisfied, she moved away from the tempting skin, her eyes finding Barica's flaming face. The blushing red glowed so hard it reminded Stella of a furnace, with the strength to warm the room up in the dead of winter. "I will tell you, so you don't need to guess."

She raised her hand, ticking off with fingers. "One, an accidental death in the field. Poor Vilma lost her footing on a hill, while we were checking up on our vineyards. She tumbled down and fell on a raised stake, impaling herself." Barica let out a soft gasp. But that wasn't enough, Stella knew. It could just be explained as a regrettable accident.

"Second, poisoning. She did it herself. We don't know why, there were whispers of sordid affairs, of course, but that is only idle kitchen gossip. My little brother found her in her room, choked on her own vomit." A pause, for dramatic effect, to savour the image of a little boy standing over a puke-covered corpse.

"Third, tuberculosis. That's a bit boring, I must admit. Not to mention it took forever," she added morbidly, hoping to disgust the girl into fleeing with her head intact.

"And, at last, gored by a boar in the woods. She went to pick mushrooms. Don't you see?" Stella asked in the end, showing the four raised fingers. "And now you're here. The fifth governess." To enunciate that, she lifted the pinky, too.

Barica's gravestone eyes were sad, clouding over with compassion. It was not a good look. Stella had high hopes for that animal fear living in all of them, hidden under the frilly dresses and three-piece suits, but ready to burst out with the right incentive. Instead, the girl was sorrowful.

"I understand that a string of unfortunate events has befallen your family, and I'm very sorry to hear that," Barica said, so very polite.

Stella groaned, not even trying to hide her frustration. Why was she even bothering? If the foolish girl was so eager to stroll into an open grave, who was Stella to dissuade her? She should've turned away and gone back to her room; waiting for the day when the old servant would come with more bad news.

"He was born from my mother's corpse," Stella finally said, the words souring on her tongue. This wasn't the way she'd wanted to mention her mother, as if she were just some doll her brother broke, instead of the woman whose voice dazzled the great opera halls of Trieste, Vienna and Paris, ending with the cursed Zagreb, where she met the lowly Croat noble she would eventually marry. Settling for a small rural estate and leaving glory behind.

Barica simply looked confused.

"You must've heard stories about people like that. Born from the dead? Ask any of the servants if you haven't, or any of the villagers, or perhaps a priest, if you're so inclined."

If Barica did that, she would surely hear the gruesome tale of a childbirth gone wrong. How, when Stella's mother's heart stopped beating, her baby brother pushed himself out from the ruined body, on his own, pulling with his small hands at the opening, descending in the pool of blood under her legs. The servants still whispered the tale to each other, believing Stella couldn't hear them. But they always said something else, too, and that part she believed wholeheartedly. How could she not?

"There is something malevolent clinging to my brother. If you stay here, it'll touch you too. The smart thing would be to turn and run, before it's too late."

Stella had said her piece, letting melancholy colour her voice. Barica was looking at her with a thoughtful expression, her eyes dazed. But at that moment an old servant came back to fetch her, breaking the spell between them.

Barica straightened her back, following after him with her head held high and unafraid.

★ ★ ★

Stella decided she would not care for the new governess, keeping away from the other woman, avoiding her brother and his childish games. She had already perfected the life of someone unattainable, gliding through the empty halls and dusty rooms. A disappearing figure in the shadows, a face glimpsed at the window for a heartbeat, before fading away.

If, by chance, Barica managed to catch her unaware, Stella welcomed her with an austere face, carefully curt with her words, before excusing herself. It was a complete reverse to their introduction, leaving the governess in stunned silence at every such brief meeting.

Yet... Stella's heart still ached for contact, for words. She dreamt of Barica, kissing her in the vastness of her creaky bed, nipping the other girl's tender skin. She tried to stifle the flame in her chest, but it was hungrily expanding, consuming her senses. To fight against it, she threw herself into reading bad German novels and even worse Croatian poets, writing her own trivial verses, not even bothering with style.

Their estate was a rusted cage around her; an unmistakable destitution, reflecting the hollowness she felt. The silence of abandoned fields, where the pumpkins and the corn slowly rotted away. Her home, just a sturdy square one-storey palace, its façade the yellow of a runny egg, decaying in the sun. Quietly standing on top of its hill, a crumbling crown on a balding head.

At times, servants and restless serfs – the handful that was still with them – would manage to burst her ghostly act, searching for her while her father was unattainable. While he was spending all his time at their neighbour's, the illustrissimus Batorić, chasing some old dreams of youthful glory, lavish feasts and hunts, Stella was keeping their estate in check. Which meant going through her mother's chests more than once, selling opulent dresses, silk ribbons and gems in secrecy. It was never enough. There was always something to repair, farm equipment to replace, mouths to feed, wages to distribute. No matter what she did, the curia slowly rotted away with their fields in disarray because they didn't have enough people to work them.

One day Stella was in a particularly foul mood, after she had to sell her mother's precious pearls. Barica jumped at her from the moving shadows of the approaching evening, almost giving her a fright. She hadn't expected the girl to just appear before her, the hallways not even properly lit, as some coalesced specter. Stella tried to do what she always did, just sidestep her with a polite nod of the head, but the girl did the unthinkable.

A profound strangeness passed over Stella, raising goose-bumps. For a breath or two, she was frozen in the moment, before her mind finally caught up. Barica's hand had reached for her own, keeping her in a place with a tight grip. A spider's touch in a carefully constructed web.

Ever so slowly, Stella turned towards her captor.

"Do you believe your brother will murder you?"

Stella's heart plummeted, ending up somewhere in the gap of her stomach. Barica's voice was quiet, as if she was afraid someone would overhear them. They were out in the open, but Stella was too afraid of making a move towards her father's study – the closest room – so as not to lose contact with the other girl.

"No, of course not." Stella was fully aware she didn't sound overly confident.

"But you believe he's cursed. Everyone believes that, actually, the cooks, the servants, the villagers," Barica continued on in a strangely calm tone. Her face was half obscured in shadows so Stella had to guess at her expression. "And you are so insistent on shutting him away. You must believe his curse might strike you too, and that's why you avoid him."

Her tone was questioning, curious, more than accusatory. Stella could only laugh bitterly at that, but she bit down the urge to mock the girl.

"I'm not afraid of dying, why would I be?" Stella asked, not really waiting for an answer. Her eyes had already turned inward, toward her festering mind. "To die is to sleep; I'll just exchange my bed for an eternity in the ground."

No, it was not death she feared. Nevertheless, she couldn't say out loud what made her stay away from her little brother. The ugly truth was that when she looked at him, at his chubby pale cheeks and autumn brown hair, she saw their reckless, uncaring father, but no traces of the supposed curse. That made it easy for her mind to wonder. Was he truly cursed, if there were no signs of it? And if not him, then who? What if she was the one who bore it, unknowingly? Or even worse, maybe there was no curse, no rhyme or reason, just an unfairness so boundless she could burst from hurt.

"I'm just tired," Stella settled on half a truth. "So many people I cared about went on to their eternal slumber, and here I am yet. So tiredly awake."

Barica was so quiet, so unmoving, Stella wondered what was going on in her head. Wanted nothing more than to drag the girl in the light, to see her face. She reined in her needs and waited, in turn, to hear what the other woman had to say.

Barica still held her, a warm point anchoring her to the world.

"I understand," Barica finally said. "I would be tired, too. But you have to know, your brother is a lonely ten-year-old." Barica took a deep breath, as if getting ready for some troublesome request. "He misses his father, the mother he never met, all the dead governesses, but mostly, he misses his big sister whose step he can hear, but never sees her face. Will you please think about spending some time with him? If you're not afraid of death, as you claim, can you spare some attention for your starving brother?"

What about you? Stella wanted to ask. *Should I spend some time with you, too?*

"How are you not afraid?" she dared to ask in the end. Even if Barica didn't believe in the curse, there was obviously something amiss in this house.

"We all need to die eventually," Barica said with a teacher's certainty, "but that doesn't mean we can't live our life to the fullest before that. I can't lose these precious days on mindlessly running away from the fear of suddenly dropping dead."

"I will think about your request," Stella said, ignoring the heavy foreboding settling in her lungs, as if it were a growing tuberculosis.

★ ★ ★

After that, Stella's common sense packed its bags and went on vacation, abandoning her completely. Her resolve crumbled; she was so ensnared by the other girl that it was impossible for Stella to refuse Barica anything. Ignoring the sense of doom, she locked it deeply in her chest, in a compartment where she kept scattered memories of songs and dances.

She found happiness again, though. It was so easy to forget that she could laugh at jokes and enjoy other people's company. When one is so accustomed to empty rooms, even dust settling on the old wardrobe is loud. For a long, long time, the world was not a bright place to Stella's eyes. It still wasn't, not truly, but there was something in not having to be alone in that oppressive dimness that it made it easier to just *be*.

Having Barica near was such an endless joy. She shared stories with them at nights, like Scheherazade's. Some of them were tragedies so deep Stella could weep for understanding them to the point of catharsis, some pure comedy that, in turn, brought out tears of laughter. Most of the time Ljubomil was with them, buzzing with energy in a way Stella hadn't seen before, as if brimful with the unexpected joy of having his older sister's company. It was still hard to be near him, to be reminded of the dead as if their shadows were clinging to his back, while his warm brown eyes were completely innocent. Barica's calming presence, though, was like a bridge between the two, helping the siblings to communicate.

Soon, there was not a lot Stella didn't know about the girl. How she had no one in this world, a harsh, unfair life taking away her parents and younger sister before their time. What she liked and disliked, all the shapes her face could make, all the tones of her voice. The more time she spent with Barica, the more she wanted, a need growing bigger and bigger until one day she'd, undoubtedly, spontaneously combust from the heat of her own longing. Barica would look at her with crimson, plump cheeks and Stella would wonder – was that her want reflected back, or was it just wishful thinking? She had to tread carefully, not to put the other woman in a precarious position. This was her job, they were not peers. Stella was a lot of things, but not a monster or a brute, so she firmly kept her feelings to herself, simply enjoying this newfound company.

★ ★ ★

One All Souls' Day found Barica, Ljubomil and Stella spending a lazy afternoon together, carving out the meaty parts out of pumpkins, turning them into lanterns to scare away the undesirable dead. It was usually a chore for their staff, but Barica thought it would be a fun activity and Ljubomil was happy to play with a knife. When he got tired of it, he asked to be excused, leaving the two of them alone. He was always weary of this upcoming night and Stella knew he would retire before the sun got its chance to hide behind hills.

"Do you think this will be enough?" Barica asked, pointing at the seven pumpkin lanterns they'd made on the wobbly kitchen table they really ought to replace. Stella shrugged, popping one salty seed in her mouth. She was elbow-deep in orange juices and seeds, sticky and tired, yet also content. The kitchen's faint, everlasting smell of fat and burning wood in the stove was concealed with the strong stench of butchered pumpkins.

"Who really knows with the pokojniki. The dead have their own ways. I mean, this will be enough to form a loose circle around the curia. It *should* be enough if the glođans decide they don't want to visit villages, but rather creep up the hills."

Barica had that adorable, scrunched-up look that Stella knew meant she wanted to ask something, but struggled with it.

"Did any of the governesses… you know… ever come back?" Barica finally asked. No wonder she'd mulled over the question. Stella took a deep breath, almost rubbing at her face before remembering how dirty her arms were. They should clean up before having conversations like this.

"Some, yes," she finally said. Her voice was dry. This wasn't a topic she wanted to discuss, but Barica deserved to know. "Vilma came back. She had yellow chrysanthemums from the graveyard in her hands and she knocked on the door so politely, we almost missed it." Stella played with the seeds on the kitchen table, her thoughts lost in the past. "Flowers were a sign she was a dušica, not a glođan, so we let her in. Father ordered the seat at the table to be set for her. We sat there, the staff, little Ljubomil, father and I, watching her eat pork left from dinner with her rotted teeth. Her skin pock-marked, foul-smelling, eyes missing. Ljubomil silently cried all the while, and one maid almost fainted when a fat white worm wriggled from an empty eye socket, hanging limply from her blank face." Barica was completely silent, just a shape in Stella's peripheral vision. But she wasn't focusing on the live girl. No, Stella's eyes were turned on Vilma's corpse feasting on their leftovers, while Stella poured her white wine into a tall crystal glass. Her skin alive with the constant squirming of maggots burrowed inside, eating her in turn. Vilma was leaving dirty white fluid over anything she touched with her decaying hands and Stella knew they would probably have to destroy anything she'd held.

"Her family was dead, you see, and her home far away, so she was buried here. That's probably why she'd crawled to us. She didn't have anyone else to visit." The closest she had to a second family. Stella hadn't shed a tear that night, not while Vilma was sitting at the table with them. Instead she'd talked, about how happy they were to see her again, how Ljubomil was doing so great, anything, so Vilma's chewing and slurping wasn't the only thing heard in the silence. A first dušica – an actual blessed soul – was in their house and it was as exciting as it was terrifying.

"The third one came back too. But she wasn't a dušica." At this, Stella blinked away the memories of Vilma and turned towards Barica. The girl was listening to her with arrested breathing. For a moment, the decaying corpse of Vilma, with holes in her body and missing eyes, superimposed over the unblemished, living Barica and Stella had to blink away the images. Barica, unaware of what sort of morbid thoughts were clouding Stella's mind, nodded her head, showing she wanted to hear more.

"She – I'm not going to name a damned soul – came here with some ropes she'd managed to find in the fields. She screeched and banged at the door with her bony hands, and scratched like she was trying to rip apart the wood with her nails." Stella took a pause for a deep breath. This was where the story should've ended. With a pathetic corpse begging to be let inside for the night, before turning away and going back to her grave before the dawn of All Souls' Day. But instead…

"Our illustrissimus neighbour Batorić was here that night. Father and he drank too much, so when the sun set he smartly decided to stay with us." One drunk Stella could handle, two, not so much. "They got into their heads to have some fun with the poor wretched creature." Barica's pretty little mouth opened at that, letting out a quiet gasp.

"They took father's prized flintlocks, went outside and shot at her until they'd riddled the corpse with holes. Until she could move no more." The loud booms of pistols had reverberated in the echoing hills and Stella's bones had vibrated in compassion. A white thick smoke had ominously risen like fog over their curia. "The sound was a beacon for any gloðan nearby. They kept coming all night. Creeping from the shadows, walking on their putrid legs, with clanking chains and ropes intended for us." And God forgive her, but maybe it would've been better if they'd caught her father then and there. "They were drinking, shooting and even chopping at the gloðans with an axe, all night long." Worst of all was their giddy laughter which she was able to hear from her window. It was so joyful, the humour so out of place with what they were doing, as if it were a bright sunny day and they were simply on a hunting trip. Stella had spent a wakeful night at the window, looking at the thick smoke obscuring her view, flinching at the loud booms, screeches and laughter. It was beyond disgraceful towards the dead – damned or not.

"When dawn finally came, it soon became obvious how much of a mess they'd made. It was something out of a nightmare, the whole yard littered with remains. There was so much cleaning to do and a lot of our staff resigned on the spot and left us." And they'd never had a full house after that. "I helped out with the cleaning in the end. It was the least I could do." She would not mention to Barica how hard it was to stop smelling the decay after that, as if the mold had started its growth inside her nostrils, stretching toward her brain, rooting in there forever. Nor that she'd had a rash on her skin for weeks, as a visual reminder of her father's sins.

"I'm sorry," Barica's sweet voice brought her back from morose memories. Her skin still itched, though, in a phantom ache.

"Don't worry, it won't happen again." Her father was either ashamed of what he did, or couldn't handle her contempt, but he made sure that every All Hallows' Day and the subsequent

All Souls' Day he spent at the illustrissimus Batorić's. Whether they'd continued their tradition of shooting at the damned undead, she didn't know. Though, she could not hear shots from the hills, so they'd probably found some other entertainment to pass their time.

"Come, we should clean up before dinner," Barica said, obviously deciding there had been enough of this doom and gloom. Stella was grateful for simple commands, but something held her back, her legs rooted to the mouldering wood of the chair.

Barica's questions brought back other memories, equally disturbing.

The only person she wanted to come back – waited, in fact, for her return – didn't.

If Barica had asked her, would she have told her how a young Stella prepared the table for her deceased mother, searching for the best plates and cutlery, wearing a meticulous dress, her hair done in a low braided bun? Sitting at the table, ignoring her father's drinking or the servants' sad looks, eyes fixed on an empty chair. Only for the night to turn into dawn, welcoming Stella completely alone because, at some point she wasn't even aware of, everyone else had left.

That was her only chance to see her mother again; the dead never rose more than once. And mother hadn't come to them.

Had she passed the night knocking incessantly at someone else's doors, looking for a soul to steal away? Did some lantern halt her steps? Or maybe she didn't want to see them, at all.

Stella looked up at Barica, her eyes full of understanding, like she could hear her thoughts. A quiet sympathy offered instead of words. Who knew what she thought of Stella at that moment, but Barica's cheeks burned crimson. Barica leaned over her, so close she could touch Stella's shoulder. Stella wanted nothing more than to rise from her chair, close that dwindling gap, and kiss the other girl until they both lost their senses. Only the return of the cook, with a fat, headless goose hanging limply from her hands, stopped Stella from acting on that urge.

Stella blanched, before excusing herself to the two women, fleeing from the kitchen like a guilty soul.

★ ★ ★

For most of that night everything was calm. The lanterns burned in a circle, not blessed, because no priest dared to come near their estate. Stella was trying to banish the young governess from her mind and fall asleep when the wailing started.

It was going to be one of *those* nights.

She rolled her eyes and rose from the bed. Her room was dark, only a small candle at the bedside table reflecting dancing lights at the walls. Checking her own flintlock in the drawer, just in case, she came to the window, peeking from between the dense curtains. It was a clear night, the silvery shine from the moon illuminating the moaning hills. The undead wails were still far away, and who knew, mayhap the dead wouldn't even come closer. Maybe their fetid remains would drag themselves elsewhere.

The knock behind her back was faint, yet it recoiled so loud in her head that she turned over so fast she almost fell among the curtains. Her beating heart leapt to her throat and she could not breathe out of fear that the dead would hear her. *Calm down*, she said to herself, grasping at the light material of her night-gown. It couldn't have been the pokojniki – not the damned glođans or the blessed dušicas – without someone letting them in the house.

Another restrained sound from the thick wooden doors. She hadn't moved from her spot, still frozen, but aware of the flint-lock in her drawer. So close, she just needed to be quiet, it was already loaded with gunpowder and…

"Stella? It's me," the voice was muffled, but her heart recognised it in an instant. She opened the door.

"Are you mad, I was getting ready to shoot you!" Stella hissed, dragging Barica inside and closing the door. Only then did her brain catch up to the impropriety of it all. Of the way Barica's own nightgown clung tightly to her body. It revealed her shape, usually hidden under layers of skirts. Her long blonde hair looked like spilled white wine over her shoulders and back. Standing closely, she could see Barica tremble.

"What is it, is it the wailing? It'll stop, they'll go away—" Stella started, faintly aware of the dead rustling in the forest, when Barica disrupted her sentence, thoughts and sense with an abrupt kiss.

Whatever reserve she had shattered under that simple taste of lips, shocking her to her core. Barica's hands were in her hair, grasping tightly at her scalp, the pain mingling with the desire, driving Stella to move. She took the girl in her arms, deepening the kiss, searching with her palms for bare skin to touch. Her mind was on fire, engulfing her whole body. She should stop, say that this was a mistake, remind Barica who Stella was to her, before doing something the other girl would regret. This was a folly fueled by fear, perchance, a wish to have comfort while corpses walked outside. For a moment she broke the kiss to say just that, only to see the way Barica was looking at her, with palpable desire, her nails digging into the skin where she clung to Stella's arms. What was wise or not, and all other worries and questions, were cast away, like bones for the glođans to gnaw on.

She didn't want there to be a distance between her and Barica, not even for a candle light to pass through, kissing her again with such an ardour she broke her lip and drew blood. Barica only gasped and deepened the kiss, dragging them fiercely towards Stella's bed. In a frenzy they managed to fall on it, to a locked mess of limbs and tangled hairs.

All while the dead bemoaned, first from afar, then at her window, their clawed fingers scratching at the walls and glass, begging for entrance.

★ ★ ★

In the subsequent months, Barica and Stella lived as if they were married, sharing Stella's room, dining together, walking hand in hand all over the estate, uncaring if any of the remaining staff would find it inappropriate. Stella had concerns about their arrangement, knowing fully well her family was slinking in the deeper wreckage from which they would not recover. Fearing that, when the money dried out completely, and the honorable family Vidovec finally crumpled into nothingness, Barica would cling to them instead of saving herself. Stella warned her of that, showing her the empty fields and coffins, the angry serfs and decaying yellow not-quite-palace. Barica, in turn, waved it all away with her hand, unconcerned.

"While we have each other, we will find a way, don't you think?" she would whisper to Stella while they lay in bed, tangled together under the sheets. It was so easy to believe. Stella would stomp down any worry, promising to the girl while she slept that she would do anything for her. To care, to love, to keep safe against all odds. Forever. She would daydream of selling the last of her mother's possessions, taking Barica and running as far as possible. They would get away from Zagorje, its muddy hills and unruly peasants and collapsing Croatian nobility, to the glorious streets of Vienna, or Budapest, or maybe all the way to India, where Stella still had some relatives she'd never met.

It was such a sweet dream that it covered the sense of a pendulum swinging wildly above her head. She refused to listen to its swooshing, to the persistent *tick, tick, tick,* of a clock coming to the midnight strike. With Barica at her hand, everything was as it should be.

★ ★ ★

Everything changed that wretched day, when news came to them that there would be no more serfdom, by the proclamation of the Croatian Parliament and the great Ban Jelačić. Stella accepted it like a wounded animal would a merciful strike with an axe, but her father raged. They would lose it all, he screamed, for once at home. They already had, she wanted to reply. But he still lived in the past and refused to acknowledge how the world had already changed, leaving them behind in the dust.

In the midst of her father's shouts, Barica's eyes found Stella's, some strange shine to them. Ljubomil was at her side, his eyes burning with tears, grasping at her dress like a child possessed.

Stella's heart skipped a beat, her head swaying with certain foreboding. Her mind was suddenly aflame, as if with a fever, so she rushed towards the other girl, unsure what she should do, but knowing, feeling, the inevitable doom. Just as she neared her, Barica collapsed into Stella's open arms. Ljubomil swayed with her, confused.

"Let go of her!" Stella screamed at his trepid form, repeatedly, until he moved from his unconscious governess.

The heavy burden of the deadweight body overtook her and she fell to her knees, hugging the other woman to her chest. She searched for wounds, for breath and a heartbeat, screaming for help.

It was too late, though. It had been too late as soon as Barica joined their blighted family.

★ ★ ★

The only thing Stella could do was to stand in front of the grave, her eyes full of tears, heart stupefied. Her mind was jumbled, so tired. She jumped in the open hole, ready to fall asleep in her beloved's final resting place, just like they usually slept together in Stella's bed. They could stay like that, dreaming together, for the whole of eternity. But someone grabbed her and dragged her screeching, fighting form away from the grave, from her love.

They locked her in her room, completely alone, abandoned, her mind in disarray. Without Barica, nothing mattered – not her drunk of a father, nor useless brother, least of all the worries about her home and lost serfs. For a moment, she contemplated hanging herself with her sheets when Barica's soft voice broke through her grief. The question she'd so shyly asked that day while the pokojniki groaned under her window to the rhythm of the different sort of soft moans, coming from her room.

A plan formed then and there. Through a fevered mind, she came to an idea so brazen it was surely destined to fail. Yet in her anguish she didn't care for reason or logic, she only wanted Barica back. They were young, had their whole life ahead to live with full hearts, as two souls joined. She would not let this greedy curse win, not this time.

No one knew who would rise from the grave on All Souls' Day and in which way. And she would not let herself relive her childhood heartbreak when her mother refused to come back home. There should be a way for the dead to be compelled to go where they were needed. For them to lose something so important that they wouldn't have a choice.

So one night, when the moon was hidden behind dark clouds, with a full purse after another sold gem, with a dagger at her belt, she bribed the cemetery keepers to dig up Barica's grave. This time, no one held her back when she jumped on the wooden coffin, a dagger ready in her hand.

* * *

Here she sat, cradling the skull in her hands, watching out the window. The candle had almost burned out when the knock sounded at her bedroom door. Just like it did a year ago when Barica first came to her room. Stella's breath caught, her eyes watering. A scratching sound of nails trailing on wood, pleading with her. If she'd been wrong, and this wasn't Barica on the other side, but a random glođan searching for someone to take his place, this would be the end of her. She stroked the clean skull in her lap, gathering her strength. The knock repeated and a loud bang of the clock striking midnight responded.

There was no point in dragging this out. Stella stood, with dignity and grace, the skull safely in her right hand. She moved in silently fluid steps and grasped the cold doorknob with her left palm. With a deep breath and a mind that was everything but calm, she opened the door to a headless corpse slightly swaying, one hand poised to knock again.

The corpse was almost naked, the white dress Stella remembered seeing when she squatted over the opened grave – severing the head with her father's dagger – mostly wasted away. The rags hung loosely from the dried-out, sickly gray skin, resembling parchment stretched over bone. Where she'd hacked Barica's head off, her dagger had left jagged edges. She held no flora or bondage in her claw-like hands, nothing to hint whether she was a soul damned for all eternity or an exalted dead in a painless slumber, wishing for some company on this sacred night. Maybe Barica had rushed towards her, without any thought of why she had risen from her grave, simply in a hurry to reunite with her love. Or maybe it was only her stolen head she was after.

She prayed her brother would stay behind the locked doors, like he always did, hidden in his room from the pokojniki. How could she ever explain this to him?

"Barica, beloved," she whispered to the corpse. Barica hadn't moved, didn't reach for her or the skull, her hands useless at her side. Waiting. Unknowing what else to do, Stella offered the sickly gray body the skull. "I'm sorry, my love, for stealing your head. I had to be sure you'd come."

Barica's mushy, decomposing hands moved, taking the offering. Stella's breath caught in her neck, like a trapped goose fluttering wildly with its wings. What if it was all Barica had come to take with her, leaving Stella behind for the second time in as many months?

Would her heart be able to stand there uselessly, watching Barica's retreating form, returning to her grave, forever this time, not even saying goodbye? Dread closed around her lungs, choking her. The thought that Barica could attack her, break her skin in half with her bony fingers, tear away at the flesh, wasn't nearly as terrifying as her simply turning her back.

Barica's hands moved and she stuck the skull on her shoulders. It shouldn't have worked, but this was a night when the dead ruled, and if she wanted her head back, she would have it. Tendrils rose from the severed neck, like vines growing over bone, hooking it to the spine. In an anatomical mockery, it somehow held together. But that was all. The skull remained cleaned of meat and nerves, without eyeballs or a tongue, hair or lips, everything that Stella had boiled away to preserve it. Yet, there was still expression there, in the naked bone, shining under the candlelight. Profound sorrow played on her featureless skull, so much so that Stella's heart ached, and she took the other woman's decaying arms in her own. A tear broke on her face, sliding down her cheek.

"It's all right, everything will be alright. I have a plan," she promised, leaning over and peppering Barica with soft kisses, all over the frontal bone, following the arching orbits of the eyes, down the cheeks, stopping at the jaw. Barica's palms firmly grasped Stella's hands, holding onto her as if her death depended on it, angling at her face. Lightly, she touched Stella's forehead with her own skull.

"Come," Stella commanded her lovely sweet girl in a way she couldn't even in life, and how unfair was it that now Barica listened? Following her in Stella's old room, the smell of the unsympathetic passage of time mingling with the odour of the living corpse. To Stella, though, Barica smelled of sunlight hidden behind fog, of violets glistening with dew, of warm cornbread left cooling in the air.

There was no amount of pus or wriggling maggots that could ever erase the dear image she held of the other girl. And after they were sated from each other's company, Stella would take her by the hand and bring her to the cellar where a gift – bound and drugged senseless, but still alive – waited. She only hoped that Barica would forgive her for kidnapping a living soul for her to use, that she'd understand what was necessary for them to be together again, for Barica to gain her life back.

If needed, she would force Barica to accept the gift and take it to the grave, to offer the unfortunate upstart who'd crossed Stella's path instead of herself. Stella didn't know if it would work, not truly. Maybe the dead would simply feast on the living meat when Barica brought her boon with her to her grave. In that case, this would've all been for nothing, and she would have to face the day wrecked, unable to handle her father's mood, when he finally returned from the illustrissimus Batorić's, or a sullen brother clinging to her company.

Or maybe, just maybe, the priests were right, and the grave would accept a new sleeper on its eternal bed. A soul for a soul.

Maybe Barica would be released from death. Maybe she would return to Stella, waiting for her at the top of the hill, in front of a dying curia illuminated by the rising sun of an All Souls' Day.

BESS AND THE
THRASHER BIRD

Arden Powell

PART ONE:
THE BALLAD OF BESS THRASHER

They lay wrapped around each other like a braid, legs tangled on the rough pallet as the moon painted their skin in blocks of silver and blue. The night was still, the sweat that slicked their skin minutes earlier turning sticky. Through the open window, frogs chirped from the grass. Merleau walked her fingers up her lover's arm to the shoulder, and Bess leaned forward to capture her mouth in a kiss.

Merleau was tanned brown like the dust on the roads. Any white folk tried to crawl their way into Bess' bed, she'd've met them with a knife between their ribs before facing her mama's fate, but Merleau only looked white. Though her blood was as Black as any slave, she could slip through white crowds without them being any the wiser. Dressed in her fine velvets and doe-skin, sat on the fastest horse in the South with her spurs and pistols glinting under the stars, bright as her eyes and the flash of her teeth – if anybody out there could rob them plantation masters blind, put a bullet between their eyes, and ride away clean, it was Merleau.

Not forever, Mama Thrash sang. *If she acts like a wild dog, she gonna be put down like one.*

Merleau stilled, her lips at Bess' throat, warm against the pulse. "You hear that?"

"It ain't dawn yet," Bess murmured. "My mama ain't around to sing me lullabies, so I got the sweetest-voiced bird in all of Georgia instead."

"I've heard that birdsong before."

"Folks call her a brown thrasher. They say she's not the prettiest thing in the world, but I think she's as nice to look at as any of them fancy songbirds."

"What's she sing about?"

Dead girls walking.

"All kinds of stuff. In the evening time when she comes to see me, she tells me how the fields look from way up high. How the land's all squared off like architecture, and how it didn't used to look like that before the devil got his claws in things."

"She must be real old, if she can remember that far back."

"Oh, for sure. And she knows stuff from the future, too. Just last week she told me Old Bill was gonna die out in them fields, and the very next morning, his heart gave out and he dropped dead on the spot."

Merleau let out a long whistle.

"And she told me about you, too," Bess teased, one finger pressed to Merleau's chest. "A whole year before you came around, she sang me a song all about you."

"What'd she say?"

She'll come to you by moonlight, though hell should bar the way.

"Well." Bess broke into a slow smile. "She told me I was gonna meet somebody, and I should keep an eye out for a rider on a black horse. A real silver-tongued rogue, with jewels on her fingers and gold in her pockets."

"And what'd you think about that?"

"I thought, that sounds like a real interesting kind of person."

"Do I live up to your expectations?"

"Every single time I see you, you meet them, and then you go barrelling right on by."

Merleau kissed her again, lazy and sweet.

"But that ain't the most interesting thing she ever told me," Bess confided in a low voice.

"More interesting than me?"

"Mm-hm. But don't be jealous. You're gonna like this one."

"You think so?"

You watch for your love in the moonlight, blank and bare in the moonlight, but she's dead like a dog on the highway, dead in her blood on the highway...

"Yeah. Because my little bird told me what this place is gonna look like when it all burns down."

★ ★ ★

Wingbeats like a funeral march, like hooves pounding the packed red dirt of the plantation road. Like gunshots. Bess shuddered awake in the blue haze of pre-dawn and stared at the rafters. Merleau was gone. She was always gone before sunrise, but the sheets still smelled like her. Bess should get rid of them before anyone came by and poked their nose in where it didn't belong. She should torch this whole goddamn place, light a fire right in the heart of that big white manor house and fan the flames. That house whose floors she scrubbed on hands and knees, with its columned porches and windows like weeping sores. The one built with blood money dragged out of the Black bodies slaving in the cotton fields, the bodies she wasn't allowed to slave alongside or talk to, like keeping her separate could make her less Black than them. She imagined how the cotton fields would burn away to ash, smoke blocking out the sun and smothering the cicadas till the screaming stopped and everything went quiet. She'd walk the ruins after, barefoot in the dust, clinging soot turning her lighter skin coal-black.

Bess knew how she was gonna die. Not on account of Mama Thrash's prophesies so much as the fact that she knew how everybody on the plantation was gonna die: worked to death or beaten or shot. A million indignities adding up to an unmarked grave and nobody but the birds and the frogs and the wailing cicadas to sing over it. Merleau was the only one who had the time and privilege to ever promise her something better.

"I'm gonna steal you a ring fit for a queen," Merleau had told her, one knee pressed to the dirt floor at the edge of Bess' bed as she held Bess' hands between hers like she was ready to slip the ring on then and there. "Deck you out in silks and diamonds so nobody will ever believe you were a slave. They'll be so busy hunting down a runaway and a highwayman that they won't look twice at us. I'll buy us land up north across the border, and we'll be happy there." She kissed the underside of Bess' wrist where the skin was thin and delicate. "They'll never catch us."

"You gonna give up all these gunpoint robberies once we're up there?"

"Sure I am. We're gonna live like real ladies, Bess."

"Real ladies," Bess murmured under her laugh. "I never seen you in a dress before. You gonna be wearing them silks and diamonds, too?"

"Yeah, if you want me to." Merleau came in closer, still down on her knees, to wrap her arms around Bess' middle and press her face into the hollow of Bess' throat. "I'll wear all those fancy dresses and brocades, if that's what you want. Or, if you want me to keep the boots and breeches and live like a man, I can do that, too. We can get married and call ourselves husband and wife, or we can be girls and call ourselves spinsters or sisters. Doesn't matter to me, so long as I got you."

"I'd marry you as a man or a woman or both or neither, if they'd let me."

"Then let's do it." Merleau pulled back to look her in the face, her hands on Bess' shoulders and her eyes fierce. "I've got just about enough money. One more job tonight, and when I come back at dawn, we'll leave together. If not dawn, then next midnight. Just you and me and all the money we'll ever need."

It was a real nice promise, but Bess knew it wasn't gonna happen. Not with Mama Thrash singing about dead dogs the way she did. And once Merleau was killed, Bess knew her own death wouldn't be far off either, one way or another. Tuck Johnson kept too close an eye on her for Bess to grieve her lover's death when it happened, never mind escape on her own.

That was the worst part of it. The way Johnson watched her, his greed almost strong enough to hide his disgust. Pleased with himself for doing what he did to her mama, and mad as hell that Bess turned out prettier than any one of his white babies with their straw hair and soft, useless hands that had never done a day's work in their lives.

When it all burns down, he'll burn with it.

"You promise?"

Your girl's not the only mad dog that's gonna get put down.

★ ★ ★

Merleau didn't come back at dawn, and the prophecy Bess carried behind her ribs turned hard and sharp like flint. Merleau could still come that night, sweep her into the saddle and make for their new life like they'd talked about, but Mama Thrash stared at Bess with bright yellow eyes that told her it wasn't gonna play out that way at all.

It'd been a long time coming, that prophecy. Mama Thrash had been singing it since Bess was a babe, screaming her lungs out for justice, for fire, for somebody to hold her and give a damn about her life as something more than kindling. Bess wasn't a fool; she knew there wasn't no way to cheat fate. As Merleau took up more of her nights and started featuring in more and more lines of Mama Thrash's songs, Bess constructed the story in her head until she thought she had figured out how things were gonna go. Not exactly, but enough that she could see the signs coming from miles off. So, when Merleau whispered those hot runaway promises against her skin, both of them sliding against each other and panting each other's names into the heavy air, Bess took the knife she kept hidden under her pallet and sawed off one of her locs, the one wound up with red ribbon like a love letter, and she pressed it into Merleau's hand. Bess curled her fingers over it, a promise of her own, and once they were dressed again, tucked it into Merleau's breast pocket to sit coiled over her heart.

"Ain't saying I belong to you," Bess whispered, one palm pressed to the lapel of Merleau's velvet coat when she turned to slink back into the night like a coyote.

"I belong to *you*," Merleau said back to her, catching that hand to kiss her knuckles like some kind of gentleman prince.

"Nobody belongs to anybody else," Bess countered. "Ain't no ownership happening here. But you go on and keep that part of me safe with you, and maybe later I can keep some part of you safe, too."

Merleau didn't understand nothing about prophecies or work songs or birds singing eulogies over mass graves, but she nodded all the same, real serious, and pressed her face into Bess' hair like she could breathe her in and take her away just like that, in her memory. Then she disappeared into the black-blue-bruise of the cotton fields to mount up her horse, the one that ran like quicksilver, but not even quicksilver could outrun a bullet.

Bess kept one eye on the windows as she cleaned the house that day, watching the sun climb, peak, fall. The air was hot with anticipation as the nerves built in her guts. The sun turned from noontime white to yellow to fiery red as it set, the dusk sky like a hellscape, all burning streaks of clouds like bloody slashes. Cicadas screamed from the treetops, giving voice to her anxiety.

Once they went quiet, the moon would start its climb, and everything would turn blue and silver again. Merleau would come back for her, hoofbeats drumming the red roads between the fields, and Bess…

Would be dead.

★ ★ ★

The full moon hung like a skull, its craters empty eye sockets staring down at her, when Johnson and his men came to her hut that night. Pale as corpses, all shuffling to the tune of his commands like the walking dead, not a mind of their own between them. Guns standing stiff and straight at the ready. They strung her up to the bedpost like a masthead on one of those wretched ships that had dragged her ancestors to America, wooden women with painted eyes forced to witness a hundred thousand atrocities, silent bystanders to all those bodies tossed into the waves.

"I know that highwayman's been coming to see you," Tuck Johnson said as he pulled the ropes around her tight. "I know you'll warn him off, given the chance. So I'm going to keep you right here, just like this, till that son of a bitch comes back. And then I'm going to put him down like the animal he is."

Men like Johnson couldn't conceive of a woman taking what she wanted the way Merleau did. Couldn't imagine a woman causing them the kind of pain Bess was gonna inflict. Men like Johnson liked things either or. Man or woman. Slave or master. Dead or alive.

From the rooftop, Mama Thrash sang with the voice of a million murdered souls, *Look for your love by the moonlight, watch for your love in the moonlight,* and Bess did.

"You should be begging for your life," Johnson sneered.

"You think I'm some lapdog like them spaniels you keep around," she said evenly. "You kick me and beat me and still expect me to sit pretty for you, and come when you call? Fawn over you like I'm no better than some idiot pet and call you my master? I ain't begging for a goddamn thing."

He stared at her before forcing a laugh. "The bitch can bark!"

"Go on and kill my highwayman. Kill me, too. I ain't afraid of that. Because once we're dead, this whole place is gonna burn." She bared her teeth and he stepped back a pace. "You ain't never experienced a consequence for your actions, Mister Johnson. But you will. My little songbird told me so."

He hauled his rifle up and she gritted her teeth – not from fear of dying, just of dying too soon. But he didn't shoot her. He hit her across the face, the rifle butt connecting with her temple hard enough to crack bone, but that didn't matter. A skull fracture wouldn't kill her before she did what she needed to get done.

"There's no consequence for hunting wild animals," he told her, his voice real low and his breath hot and fetid against her face, "and there's no consequence for owning chattel."

She snarled when he kissed her, his mouth pressed rough to hers, one hand knotted in her hair. The same way he'd kissed her mother, once, with a rotten touch that put her in the ground before she ever got the chance to hold the baby girl who'd come of it.

"That highwayman of yours is nothing but a coyote for me to shoot dead, and you're nothing but livestock. You understand me, girl?"

"You got a reckoning coming your way, Mister," she whispered. "All of you do. It's been building a long time."

He spat in her face, his expression distorted in rage that made her feel powerful, even as his spittle drooled down her cheek to hang off the line of her jaw. If she could've killed him with her glare, she would have. For her mother, for the people he worked to the bone every day. For the skin he flayed open, and the babies born screaming into this ruin of a life. For every time he held her name in his filthy mouth, or looked at her like he looked at the other women out there, like she was meat, like she was *his*.

For Merleau.

He jammed the rifle up against her ribs, the muzzle pointing to her breast as he roped the stock to the bedframe and the side of her thigh. Angled so that if she shifted and the bullet missed her breast, it would still shatter the underside of her jaw and blow half her face off. They were coming to the end of Mama Thrash's song, the part where the music swelled like it was gathering itself for one last burst of energy. Through the window, the red road was grey in the moonlight, winding through the slaves' quarters out to the fields and beyond, where Merleau would ride.

"You keep watch, now," Johnson said, and patted her cheek all condescending-like, laughing when she snapped her teeth at his hand. Like she wouldn't take his finger off if he lingered too near. He didn't give her the chance, leaving his men with sharp instructions and stalking out to the front of the hut where he settled into the shadows to wait, pistol drawn.

Her hands were tied behind her, fingers slippery with sweat as she twisted them against the ropes. They dug into her skin, and soon the sweat turned to blood as she rubbed herself raw. Johnson's men crouched under the window, watching her with cruel smirks slashed across their faces, but they couldn't see her hands. Couldn't see that she had loosened the ropes just enough to reach the rifle's trigger. If she had more time, she could've worked them loose altogether, and it was real tempting to try. Her survival instinct reared up to fight that prophecy like it was just a nursery rhyme instead of the stone-cold future. But by the time she freed herself, Merleau would be in Johnson's sights, and Bess would be caught in seconds anyhow. The prophecy had a better plan for them than that. The metal was cool against Bess' fingertip, and she shut her eyes for just a second. She couldn't give the game away too soon.

The slavers by the window shifted restlessly, talking to each other under their breath. Rifle noses poking out over the sill, ready to fire at the first sign of her love's return. Curling her finger around the trigger, ropes digging tight around her ribs, she hummed a tune that mingled with the crickets and the frog song and the low, drumming rhythm that lived in her blood and always had done, no matter how Johnson tried to beat it out of her.

"One kiss, my dark-eyed sweetheart," she whispered, Merleau's goodbye entwined with Mama Thrash's prophecy. "I'm after a prize tonight, but I'll be back with the yellow gold before the morning light. But if they press me sharply, and harry me through the day, then look for me by moonlight, watch for me by moonlight, I'll come to you by moonlight, though hell should bar the way."

"Shut your mouth," one of the slavers said to her, the same way he'd tell a dog to knock off its barking.

"She came not in the dawning; she did not come at noon," Bess sang louder, voice lilting to the cadence of the work songs she wasn't supposed to know. "And out of the tawny sunset, before the rise of the moon, when the road was a lover's ribbon winding past my door, the slaver's men came marching–marching–marching–Johnson's men came marching, to pace upon my floor."

Up on the rooftop, Mama Thrash dug her pinprick claws into the thatching, keeping time with Bess' words.

"They said no word to the slave girl, like I were a dog instead, and they beat my body and bound me to the foot of my narrow bed. Two of them knelt at the casement, with rifles at their side. There was death at every window, and hell at one dark window; for I could see through my casement the road my love would ride."

One of them got up to club her, his rifle cracking against her skull in the same place Johnson had hit her, and she screamed – not out of pain or fear but sheer unadulterated fury, and the man staggered back with his hands clutched to his bleeding ears when he couldn't handle the repercussions of what he dished out.

Bess took a deep breath, holding the air in her lungs. Blood ran down her wrists to coat her hands, hot and tacky against the trigger. The same blood pounded in her ears like a war drum, like a work song, urging her to throw off her bonds and turn the rifle on the devil himself and make him pay for what he done to her and to everybody else. It pounded like hoofbeats. Gunshots. When she swallowed, she tasted metal. Blood or flint, she couldn't tell.

"The road lay bare in the moonlight," she said hoarsely, her throat in tatters. "Blank and bare in the moonlight; and the blood of my veins in the moonlight throbbed to my love's refrain."

The road was still empty, laid out like a ghost under the full moon, but Merleau would come for her. She always came. And Bess only had one way to warn her off before she rode straight into Johnson's trap.

"Down the ribbon of moonlight, over the brow of the hill, my highwayman comes riding, riding, riding." Hoofbeats echoed from the cotton fields and Bess shut her eyes a final time. "She'll come to me by moonlight, though hell should bar her way."

The shot rang clear at the stroke of midnight, loud enough to shatter the still air and blow a fresh crater clean through that skull-faced moon.

PART TWO:
MERLEAU AND MAMA THRASH

Merleau was dead the instant she heard that rifle crack. A gunshot could mean any manner of things, but the dread coiling sick and hot in her stomach told her exactly what had happened.

"Mama Thrash!" Merleau's voice tore out of her and all she could taste was iron, like that bullet had hit her instead of Bess.

A single bird shivered in the trees, a flash of copper on the wing as it darted down to earth. Yellow eyes stared up at her and Merleau stared back, she and her horse both panting and shivering with sweat. The thrasher bird stretched tall, all the way up into a woman's shape.

"So. They finally killed my baby girl."

Mama Thrash didn't look completely human, let alone like Bess' mother. She was all hard angles and sharp bones and large, round eyes that shone in the night. In her first life, Mama Thrash had skin so dark it looked violet, echoed in Bess' jewel undertones. Now Mama Thrash's skin was the same rusty orange-brown as her feathers, speckled through with cream and umber.

Wordlessly, Merleau drew out that red-ribboned loc. It lay coiled in her palm like a foetus waiting to be born or buried. Mama Thrash took it up real gentle, precious as that newborn she never got to hold, and folded it into a new shape. Almost bird-like, if Merleau looked at it just right.

"She knew it was gonna happen, didn't she?" Merleau's voice was wrecked, a rasp of broken metal to Mama Thrash's music. "She knew they were gonna kill her."

"They always do, sooner or later. Ain't no other end for folks like us."

Merleau steeled herself, swallowing a mouthful of blood. "You told her it was all gonna burn. I want to be the one to set that fire."

Mama Thrash looked speculative, head cocked to one side as she sized her up. Merleau held her chin high like she was facing down a mark on the highway, all arrogance with her weapons glinting in the starlight. She'd taken on bigger men than some plantation owner who only ever roughed up girls, and hired other folks to beat his slaves. Johnson had built his life on blood and sweat that wasn't his. Without those slaves, he was nothing. Just an infection waiting to get lanced and drained and cut away.

Merleau could already smell the smoke, choking her lungs and making her eyes sting. Mama Thrash held up that little bird made out of Bess' hair, still soft and smelling like those flowers Bess used to wear tucked behind her ear.

"Open up," Mama Thrash ordered, and Merleau leaned down against her horse's neck and opened her mouth obediently for Mama Thrash to place the loc on her tongue. When she swallowed, it slipped right down her throat like water. "You keep that inside you, now. Keep it safe till she's ready."

"Will I see her again?"

Mama Thrash didn't answer. Just shrugged off her body like dropping a dress to the floor, and streaked back into those tall black trees to disappear. Inside Merleau's breast, something trembled and tapped against the shell of her heart.

PART THREE: THE DEAD DOG AND THE FLEDGLING

Bess stretched her wings and came up against meat and bone, enveloping her and keeping her warm like an embryo. Tempting to curl up and savour that safety, but it wouldn't last, and besides, Bess had a prophecy to finish. So, she pushed against Merleau's ribs and quickened her heart, urging her away from Mama Thrash's crossroads and back to the plantation where all that cotton was waiting for their fury to light it up and burn it down.

Merleau rode hard. Her horse's hooves tore chunks from the red earth, thundering through the night. The plantation sprawled across the land like a disease: endless cotton fields, and behind them, the manor house, white as a ghost, lined with chestnut and magnolia trees all trailing Spanish moss like fingers reaching down to grasp at anybody who came near. Merleau torched the fields as she passed them, the dry summer grass taking the fire like a matchstick, cracking and snapping at her heels like a starving dog as she galloped on. Her rapier, the one with the jewels in the hilt that had always been more for show than fighting, was lit up all aflame like it had been dipped in oil.

Bess felt the fire from inside Merleau's body, and she dug her claws into the backs of her ribs like the rungs of a ladder and climbed up to sit in her throat, right where Merleau wore that bunch of cream-coloured lace that burst from her collar. Up there, Bess could feel Merleau's voice when she talked, a low vibration that rattled her hollow bones. Couldn't make out the words like that, but words were never the point with Merleau. She was all action and intent, always had been, and Bess would know how to read those parts of her if she were blind and deaf. And right now, Merleau was intent on burning the whole world down.

Men scattered from the house like ants, rifles swinging up to catch Merleau in their sights. Bess clawed her way into Merleau's mouth, poking her beak over Merleau's tongue to stare out from between her teeth. Thrashers weren't small birds and she was already too big to emerge from Merleau's mouth the way she'd gone in – soon she'd be too big to stay inside Merleau at all – but it was enough to see the flames licking bright and deadly into the night sky, sparks jumping to mingle with the stars. Merleau rode for the slave quarters, eyes locked with the master of the miserable little ant hill. Johnson's face was white and peaked, his eyes hollows of madness reflecting the fire, and Merleau galloped straight up to him in a thunder of hooves and velvet tails, her sword point angled for his gut.

It promised an agonizing death and it was what Johnson deserved, but they didn't have that kind of time. Johnson could take hours or days to die like that, and he wasn't the only one they needed to lay low. Flinging out one wing, Bess jostled Merleau's arm from the inside, and the sword came up to shove that burning rapier clean through Johnson's throat. He screamed – choked – gurgled – as the fire caught, dropping to his knees. He'd burn and bleed out, then crumble into ash like he'd never existed at all.

Merleau reined in her horse as she stared wild-eyed at the char surrounding her. The fields were burning, but there were too many guns between her and the house to light it up the same way. Shouts rang out as the slaves were dragged from their beds to run lines of water to the cotton fields – too little too late to save the crops, but burning the cotton and killing Johnson wasn't enough. Merleau hadn't thought past avenging Bess' death, too wild with grief. But Bess needed to free her fellow slaves and then raze the whole place to the ground till there was nothing left but an ashen memory, and Merleau couldn't do all that single-handed. Couldn't do it at all, truth be told, because tangled up in it as she might be, it wasn't her prophecy. It was time for Bess to be reborn.

Bess didn't see who fired the shot. The bullet hit Merleau in the back and streaked straight through her, blood blooming against her cravat where its ends ruffled over her chest. She pitched forward over her horse's neck, reins falling from nerveless fingers. Shot down like a dog, she was dead before she lost her seat in the saddle, body slumping to the packed red earth, red velvet all dusty with blood drops clinging to it like rubies. Bess felt Merleau's heart stop, her lungs still, the rush of hot night air flood in through the open wound and out the other side, and she followed it, bursting out in a flurry of grief and brown feathers. Keen-eyed, she took to the sky, shaking off the mat of blood and gore that clung to her, a red ribbon clutched between her claws.

From way up high, she could see the whole plantation, just as Mama Thrash described, with the land divided all neat into sections. The manor house sat like a child's toy with the slaver men scrambling around like desperate insects trying to put out the flames, and Johnson no more than a speck lying dead down there, face down in the dirt where he belonged. A glistening mass of maggots and flies squirmed weakly from the gash in his throat, one last grasp at life, before going limp. No resurrections for men like that.

Bess flew to the ragged line of slaves, Black bodies glinting with sweat in the firelight. There weren't enough of them to stop the flames from eating up the cotton, but the slavers were still willing to kill them in the effort. Flying low, Bess brushed her wingtips against the slaves' skin – all these people who looked like her mama, like her ancestors, that she'd never been allowed to talk to or learn from, the same Black skin Johnson would've kept her from claiming as her birth right – and with every touch, they shook off the trappings of clothes and earth to take up feathers and fling themselves into the stars. Mama Thrash had tried to free them a thousand times since Bess'd been born, but she was the keeper and speaker of the prophecy, not its enactor. They all had their separate roles to play. The freed slaves shed sparks with every wingbeat, fanning the flames as they raised their voices all together, a chorus of loss and survival, joy and mourning, redemption and revenge.

When the plantation was emptied of slaves, Bess angled for the house, darting over the panicked slavers' heads to swoop in through an open window and carry her sparks right into the festering heart of the place. She set fire to the master bedroom and watched the bedsheets curl up like beetle legs until the roar of heat got too much and the windows rained shattered glass to the scorched ground below. It felt good, felt vindictive and righteous, laying out violence like that, even if it didn't take back the bullets and the beatings and the bodies Johnson left in his wake. Bess was still dead, slumped against that bedpost and going cold, and Merleau was dead, too.

Every single room in that house, Bess burned. She shredded the wallpaper with her claws and struck her flint beak against the floors, trailing embers and coals until every inch of that rotten place was on fire. Only then did she fly out the front door, through the columned porch, and out the other side of that billowing smoke engulfing the drive.

Merleau lay where she had fallen, red velvet splayed like a bloodstain. Heart torn open in her chest, bled out and turning the dust under her to mud, and her horse long since fled. Bess pressed her beak to Merleau's lips, parted in a final gasp, her eyes open too and staring blankly into the night, the fires reflected in her pupils that were slowly going dull.

Blood-red were her spurs in the red firelight, wine-red was her velvet coat, Mama Thrash sang, *when they shot her down on the highway, down like a dog on the highway, and she lay in her blood on the highway, with a bunch of lace at her throat.*

Bess pecked at the ruffles, tentatively at first, the way she used to curl her fingers in them before she got to undressing Merleau, and then desperately, tearing the lace away from the dead flesh like she wanted to burrow back inside and pretend Merleau was still warm and breathing. She'd known this was coming, known it since before she'd ever met Merleau. Bess had thought their deaths would be easy to take, knowing what she did. Having all that time to prepare. She couldn't even cry, not with her eyes gone all round and yellow like they were. No tears for thrasher birds.

Something shifted behind the lace, and Bess stilled her frantic struggle. Out of the ragged bullet hole pushed a snout, black-tipped and wet, slick with blood as it emerged into the crackling heat. Merleau's skin tore wide, velvet and doe-skin pulling away from her body to make room for the slender coyote that slunk out of her corpse. She was brown and red like the roads, grey like smoke, the ruff of fur at her throat all creamy and soft under the blood. Their eyes met – the bright, staring yellow of a brown thrasher and the clear, cold gold of a wild dog – and Bess held out the tangle of red ribbon pierced through by her claws. Hesitantly, the coyote pressed her nose to it, gold eyes sliding shut as she inhaled. Coyote noses, so much stronger than human ones. Bess knew the ribbon still held the perfume from her hair in its fibres. Closing her teeth around it, the coyote gingerly tugged the ribbon free from Bess' claws, then paused, letting it hang like she wasn't sure what to do next.

Around them, the plantation burned. Dead white bodies heaped up like refuse, Black bodies all flown into the night. The frogs and insects gone quiet, fled from the smoke. They'd done it, her and Merleau. They'd brought Mama Thrash's prophecy home to roost. And now the song was done for the plantation: no more lines about either of them, for good or bad. No more bullets, no more dead dogs.

Bess stretched her wings, head tilted to the side like she used to do when she was inviting Merleau to come closer. The coyote grinned, eyes flashing in the dark, and together they lit off through the burning cotton fields, heading north under the light of the full moon. The smoky air was thick and hot under Bess' wings, lifting her above the plantation's ruins. She kept her gaze fixed on the dusty red ribbon of road stretching ahead of them, not looking at the destruction to either side. The prophecy was finished. She had better things to look to, now.

RAION KUĪN

Hunter Liguore

Japan, 1206 CE

The night hours were the hardest for Sister Catherine.

She sat in a wooden chair near the front door, now locked and barred. It was only last month when the Prioress called her into the den and assigned her the task of the night watch. Sister Catherine knew this meant she was trusted. It meant she had finally moved into the senior ranks, despite being only twenty, the youngest of all the matrons. If she did her duty without infraction, the inner mysteries of the convent would be shared with her.

She especially wished to see the corpse of Saint Pavel, a Russian monk who died a few years ago, the same year she'd left her village in Kitayama, where her eyes had once dazzled-up at Mt. Fiji as a child; she'd arrived by boat in the Kurils, forging her own way to the convent, trusting it was the right decision. Something inexplicable had led her, an inner-knowing, the same way when a cough comes and signals haien, and won't leave one's chest for weeks.

It was a good decision, Sister Catherine kept telling herself, though the fated reason, her inner chokkan had yet to prove reliable. *Soon,* she thought. *One day.* Maybe too, she'd be lucky and look upon the corpse; it was meant to bring miracles, she was told. Rumours abounded that the convent was still in operation by selling off his sacred fingers, one by one, and she hoped to discover the truth.

Just after midnight, Sister Catherine began a thorough walk-through of the stone corridors. She usually started in the west wing, by the chapel, then took the spiral steps to the outlook, an open terrace, which offered a view of the Okhotsk Sea, and on a clear day one or two of the fifty-six islands known as the Kurils. From there she went into the dorms, and then back down again towards the washrooms, the bath, the kitchen, the prayer rooms, the enclosed gardens, the tool sheds, ending at the shrine of Our Lady of Grace, before returning to her post at the front gate.

Her duty was to look for any misdeeds. She had a list of offenses to use as a guide, and ranged from the Lesser Ills, like remaining awake or eating in one's room, to the Greater Ills, which usually came with severe punishment. Passion and desire topped the Great Ill list. Her mother used to call it, *jaakuna kōi*, and beat her with an iron mallet used to pound the seeds in the earth if she was found to have transgressed. Passion and desire were the Devil's tools to bring a woman to Hell – Jigoku – the place she feared ending up, where the fires rolled over you like a waterfall. Forever. And then some more.

For this reason, Sister Catherine needed to be vigilant, with both ears and eyes, if she was to find someone committing an Ill. It usually occurred in the dorms, her least favourite area during the walkthrough. If she found a man smuggled into a nun's bed, or if she heard the suppressed excitement of two nuns fornicating, she'd have to report it. Sister Catherine had seen other sisters divulge misconduct, and while the Prioress was pleased to have someone stamping out the Ills, the rest of the convent saw it as a betrayal. If she was accused of betrayal, Sister Catherine knew she'd come to know an even deeper isolation, and wondered if she could bear it.

She started the first leg of the dorms and found little move-ment behind closed doors down the dimly lit corridor. Sister Catherine had been instructed to lay an ear upon each unlocked door, in order to be sure. Locking or barricading one's door was forbidden, and it was in her jurisdiction to test the door, and enter any room, should she suspect wrongdoing.

During these times, Sister Catherine tried to think about the women inside the rooms, to find a redeeming quality, rather than a premeditated judgement. She considered moments from earlier that day when she witnessed them at work in the garden or singing hymns in the church. Women just like her. Mostly. More often, her mind went to something askew, a secret meeting of two nuns, the secret glances or whispers through vespers; her skill had improved; she knew what to look for. It was at those nuns' rooms that she lingered longer, listened harder, and returned to, out of turn, to ensure the commandments were being kept.

Through the second wing, Sister Catherine discovered a newly arrived sister humming in her dark room.

"You should be in bed, Sister Deborah."

"But I can't sleep. I'm so frightfully alone in here."

"Do you not keep the commandments?" Sister Catherine helped the nun into bed. "Lay me down in sleep, for thou, Lord, cause me to dwell in safety." She blew out the candle, the room darkening, as she closed the door.

Further along, Sister Catherine noticed light bleeding out of the door crack. Inside she found Sister Gertrude, an old veteran of the convent, knitting by candlelight.

"Now, now, sister, you know the rules." Sister Catherine noticed the blanket she wove looked to be the length of three beds.

"Не гони лошадей, Кетрин! You know I don't like to be rushed. It's the only time I can work without interruption."

"Remember," began Sister Catherine, "adherence to the rules is like shepherding your soul for Christ. To bed at once, or I shall have to report you."

The old nun sighed, grumbling, but made an effort.

Sister Catherine continued into the south wing, pleased at her ability to handle the night's minor impediments. As she made the last sweep of the dorms, she delighted in the quietude, the artful appearance of the bold stones that looked like gold when the candlelight hit them.

She had three doors left. Upon placing an ear to the last, her stomach tightened. *Had she heard whispers?* Whispers held the implication of two sisters together in the room. She placed her hand on the doorknob and waited.

Several minutes passed, and then it began: the muffled, restrained sounds of passion.

Sister Catherine cupped a hand to her mouth, dismayed, and backed away. She trembled, unsure what she should do.

"Give me strength, Lord," she whispered.

She reluctantly put her ear back against the door, sure she'd hear wrong, and holding her own breath, as if that would help her hear better. The strained groans grew louder, interspersed with heavy respiration, and two distinct voices, whispering, as if praying vigorously under their breath.

She backed away. What nun lived here? Sister Catherine consulted the chart tucked under her gown, which also saved the page to her prayer book. The room belonged to Sister Lybianka, a Russian girl of fifteen, who had not yet completed her first year at the convent. But who was she with? Who had she coerced with her serpent tongue?

A flurry of decisions passed through Sister Catherine's crowded mind. She didn't want to enter the room, for fear of seeing what they were doing, to confirm or disconfirm, to rebuke or consent. But she was bound by duty. The Prioress told her she might be tempted or weakened, maybe even persuaded to turn the other way. To allow the effects of jaakuna kōi to infiltrate their home was to damn the soul to an eternal fire. The firefalls of Jigoku flashed in her mind, legs quavering. The Prioress's message turned in her head, striking like the chapel bell, louder and louder, until it finally gave her the courage to open the door.

The nun's voices stilled inside the room when the door squealed ajar. With the handle turned in her hand, her senses became aware of a noise elsewhere. Distantly, she could hear knocking. She identified the sharp, repetitive sound as the iron doorknocker on the main gate. But who was knocking at this hour?

Sister Catherine cleared her throat, ready to go in, but the knocking continued. It was her responsibility to keep watch of the front gate, especially to greet weary travellers who might need a room for the night. If found absent, someone could perceive it as shirking her duties, nor could she risk waking the nuns, let alone the Prioress, with the incessant banging.

She let the door go and hurried toward the stairs, stopping only for a moment to see the two nuns crowd in the hallway, then splitting apart; the ring of two separate doors closing.

As she hurried to the gate, Catherine felt vexed that they had escaped punishment. She would have to report it in the morning, though she realised an accusation of this degree would result in severe punishment, usually a public whipping in the courtyard. The last two nuns accused of a Great Ill later hanged themselves on separate occasions.

By the time she reached the door, the knocking had stopped. When she looked, no one else was present. No one had awoken. Sister Catherine calmed her breath, pleased nothing would come of her neglect. She sat in the chair and opened her prayer book. Her eyes trailed over the words, but her mind was elsewhere, circling on her dilemma to report the two nuns or not. She tried to push the episode out of her mind completely, focusing harder on the prayer – *Evil shall slay the wicked, for none that trust in Him shall be desolate.*

Then came a scratching from the other side of the thick, wooden door. Sister Catherine had read about in the convent histories; it was inherited from a Zen Buddhist monastery that had been destroyed in 1180 by Russian marauders. She often tried to read the faded Japanese caricatures etched into the wood, while she sat there waiting for morning to arrive.

There were precautions to take when opening the front gate at night. Sister Catherine should've called for a second nun, so in the event of an attack one could go for help, or raise the alarm to awaken the others. She disregarded the rules, hoping for a welcome distraction.

After releasing the three heavy locks, Sister Catherine slid the gate open. To her surprise, no one stood in front of it. She brought the candle nearer. Lying idle on the ground was a bloodied hand. She drew closer.

Hunched against the wall, like a sack of dirty robes, was a Japanese woman. Her wildly-thistled hair clung to the frame of her face with sweat and blood; bruises confounded the left side, her neck, and her dress had been torn. Her feet were bare and muddy, swollen and hurt.

"Help me, please." The woman spoke in patois to Sister Catherine, a mixture of Russian-Japanese.

"What has happened to you?" She lifted the woman best she could, dragging her inside, fearful that whatever did this still lurked nearby. As she closed the gate, she noticed the trail of blood on the ground. She knelt over the woman, who fought to keep conscious. It was not uncommon for local women to take refuge at the convent, but in all her ten years, she'd never seen someone so brutally wounded. Who had done this? And what would happen if they came looking for her?

There was no time to waste. Sister Catherine had learned to care for the sick during a feudal war, when the convent took in soldiers. She went for a knife, cut the woman's robe off, and tied off the worst gashes. Next, she dragged her to the bath – returning later with a bucket and pail to clean the blood trail. Later, she would reopen the gate and clean the stoop, to remove any suspicion that a visitor had been taken in.

In her mind, she calculated how long it would take to boil the hot water, how long to bathe and tend to her cuts. Would a doctor be needed? A doctor meant someone from the outside, one who would have allegiances elsewhere, and could easily, for a handsome fee, turn the woman back to her oppressor. It had happened before. In Sister Catherine's second year, a woman betrothed to a wealthy man ran away after being beaten and took refuge at the convent, only to be returned to her husband-to-be, and was put to death.

No, she thought, a doctor will be a last resort. She kneeled on the cold floor and began to sew the woman's gashes; soon, the water would be hot enough to draw a bath. More than once, she thought the stranger might've died. But the woman's chest continued to rise, and the occasional blue eye opened and gazed up at her. She stopped very briefly to fetch the sacred wine from the chapel, forcing the woman to drink in order to dull the pain. She worked quickly, accidentally pricking her own fingers from time to time.

The woman no longer bled. Sister Catherine burned the woman's clothes in the fire that heated the water, and lifted her, with much effort, into the wooden tub. She couldn't help but notice – startled more like – to see the red tattoo on the woman's back. Tattoos were considered a desecration of the flesh. The image was of a fire-breathing lion with a savage serpent tail. It frightened her. It was something that would live in Jigoku. The shaking in her body came but she bit her tongue, a trained response.

When the wounds were cleaned, Sister Catherine hoped her effort had made the woman more sightly, so there was less risk she would be turned out. Sister Catherine understood there were all sorts of reasons to cast a woman out. *Trouble* was chief among them. If someone wanted the stranger bad enough, the convent walls wouldn't stop them, and if the law was against her, there was even less to keep her protected.

Right now, only *she* stood in the way.

The first tendrils of light bled in through the window.

Sister Catherine was soaked and soiled. She was fatigued, but knew there was more work to do. With haste she pulled the woman from the tub, dried and dressed her in a clean robe. She put her in a chair by the fire, while she refreshed her own clothes, and cleared all evidence of the night. One drop of blood left behind would tell all, she thought, as she went over the floor and tub a second and third time.

The woman was still very weak, but Sister Catherine begged her to walk. Slowly, she carried her to one of the guest beds, tucked her in, just as the morning bells rang.

As the sun poured through the window, footsteps were heard in the hall, along with hushed voices. Sister Catherine glanced at her appearance once more. She would have to account for the missing robes, pay for them even, but there were more pressing issues at hand. She still needed to tell the Prioress the woman was here. What then?

Sister Catherine sat on the stool beside the woman's bed. Her body felt numb, tired. She closed her eyes, knowing she could drift off to sleep so easily...

A gentle touch upon her skin jarred her. She looked down to see the woman's one blue eye glancing up at her, the other still swollen shut.

"You don't need to pray for me," the woman whispered. "I will live, as will my baby. You have assured this."

Sister Catherine glanced to the woman's abdomen, where the pregnancy did not quite yet show. Two lives were at stake then, she thought. In the hall, someone called for her, most likely the nun on day-watch.

"Sleep," she comforted, pulling up the blanket. "I will be back shortly."

★ ★ ★

The Prioress, a Russian woman whose face looked as creviced as the damaged mortar between the brick wall, expected a full report of the night's event each morning in the garden where she took her tea. Sister Catherine found her resting on a bench, sorting flowers into a bouquet, one she would dry and later put out near the shrine. Sister Catherine bowed, and remained kneeling until the Prioress bid her to sit with her on the bench; she asked for her report.

"There is little to tell." Sister Catherine blushed slightly. She tried to look away, but the Prioress caught sight of her face, and questioned her further. She mustered, "A woman has taken refuge in the convent."

"What woman?"

"A Japanese woman. I'm not sure if she is from the islands or the mainland. I only know she's hurt and needs our help."

"I will decide who we will help and who we won't."

Sister Catherine bowed her head. She had learned from her predecessor that there was a particular way to address the Prioress. Always, she had to be made to feel she was in control.

The Prioress continued. "Another mouth to feed could be a burden with the end of summer so near, the crops being stunted from lack of rain as they are."

Sister Catherine knew that once the Prioress made a decision, it was final. She needed to distract her, to keep her from sending the woman away. Helping her, in Sister Catherine's eyes, was an opportunity to do the Christ's work.

"The night held an indiscretion, Prioress." Sister Catharine blushed further, her head dizzy with fatigue.

"Oh, one more pressing than a refugee?"

"The woman will surely recover and move on, permitted your gracious acceptance that she remain among us." Sister Catherine hardly stopped for air. "But this other matter may not go away, unless it's brought to the attention of someone with your calibre of correction, your heavenly wisdom."

"Out with it, Sister Catherine," said the Prioress. "I warned you about protecting your sisters. It was in the Christ's singularity that the Almighty delivered him from the heathen."

"I cannot say that I'm qualified to make this judgment, and since I saw nothing, I will leave it for you to interpret." Sister Catherine proceeded to make mention of her suspicions of Sister Lybianka acting on desire, and thereby partaking in the Greatest Ill. The Prioress questioned Sister Catherine about specifics, for which she denied knowing anything more than she'd already related.

"I've suspected her for some time," said the Prioress. "I suspected her of colluding with your predecessor. My suspicions were correct about you." She smiled. "I knew you would do your duty."

Sister Catherine stood with the Prioress, her head bowed reverently.

"You have done well. I'm very pleased."

Sister Catherine stiffened when the Prioress placed a finger under her chin and lifted her face upward. The Prioress had a way of making the nuns believe she could see into their soul and see if they were lying. The long gaze was just that, a perusal of Sister Catherine's soul. Could she see her fate ending in Jigoku, like her predecessor?

She assumed the Prioress found nothing, as she let her chin drop, and began to depart.

"About the woman?" Sister Catherine spoke up.

"Yes." The Prioress paused in her step, picking at a dead leaf in her bouquet. "She may stay. She will be your responsibility. Make sure she obeys our laws. If she strays, you will bear the brunt of correction. Don't let her be an excuse for your failure, not after you have proved yourself so well today."

"Yes, Prioress."

★ ★ ★

The morning meal was quieter than usual, especially when Sister Lybianka and Sister Elizabeth were escorted to the den of the Prioress. Whispers spread with assumptions as to the offense. Soon all eyes fell upon her, the last one on night watch.

"It could've only been her," whispered one nun.

The conversation at her own table stopped, and one by one the nuns picked up their dishes and left her. Outcast. It happened faster than she had imagined. She tried to make herself feel better by rationalising her isolation was worth the life of the Japanese woman and her child, or so she'd hoped.

In her room, Sister Catherine crawled under the blankets and fell fast into sleep. Her mind swirled with images of the night, of the woman and the fire-breathing lion tattoo and then to the fiery realm of Jigoku, always there under the surface, like an eternal eye watching her.

It wasn't long before her door was flung open, and a nun yelled, "Get up, get up now, and come to the courtyard."

Sister Catherine had no intention of going. She could tell by the sun's shadow on the wall that only a few hours had passed. She was still tired, and hid her head beneath the pillow. But two nuns rushed in and pulled her from the bed, roughly, dropping her to the floor, demanding that she come to the courtyard. When Sister Catherine still refused, they dragged her.

A crowd gathered at the edge of the garden, where both Sister Lybianka and Sister Elizabeth were tied to the chastisement pole, a place reserved for the most severe punishments. Sister Catherine had missed the decree and statement delivered by the Prioress, arriving only in time to see their cloaks stripped off their backs.

A tall nun held the whip, her face masked. Lybianka was first and was whipped eight times before she passed out. When it came Sister Elizabeth's turn, she braved twelve. Each time the whip struck their flesh, Sister Catherine grew faint. She had caused this agony upon them.

When it was over, she silently disappeared into the convent, crying. She had nowhere to hide where she wouldn't be found. Each corridor held an angry nun's rebuke. Finally, she took refuge with the Japanese woman in the guest room. She wished she could've locked the door, but there was no lock, nor anything to barricade the door.

She fell asleep in the stool and awoke to the woman's touch against her hand. The woman asked for water, which she fetched promptly. Night had rolled around again, and soon, she would need to take up her post outside. She busied herself with bringing the woman a meal. Afterwards, she read to her from her prayer book, until she sensed the woman was fast asleep. Before leaving, Sister Catherine checked her wounds, and was pleased to find they were healing well.

★ ★ ★

To the nuns of the convent, Sister Catherine was as good as dead. No one spoke to her, but the Prioress. The Prioress told her not to give into the desire for acceptance. For Sister Catherine, she longed to find a way back to her old life. Upon finding no evident path to her old life, she made her way toward the new.

Each night, in the quietude and dark, Sister Catherine made her usual rounds through the convent. Alone and neglected, she soon sought the company of the Japanese woman, whom she learned was named Taira. Sister Catherine brought her back to health with nourishment, both of the stomach and of the mind. She relished reading to Taira and looked forward to the questions she asked afterwards. Every night before leaving, Taira would take Sister Catherine's hand and place it on her belly.

"How much has she grown today?" Taira would ask.

"She has grown much," Sister Catherine would answer.

★ ★ ★

On the eighth day after Taira's arrival, Sister Catherine was called to the den of the Prioress after her morning rest. The Prioress sat at her desk, writing in her ledger, which she put aside, giving her full attention to Sister Catherine.

"A reliable source has told me you're spending all of your time with our Japanese visitor."

Sister Catherine rose from her chair ready to deliver a rebuttal, but the Prioress stopped her with a raised hand.

"I know that it was only brought to my attention because there's still opposition to your perceived disloyalty toward your fellow sisters. Still, your actions could be misconstrued. We need to ensure that a... special friendship isn't manifesting. I've decided Sister Elizabeth will share the duty of care-giving with you. The two of you may begin incorporating her into our daily activities, if she is able. She is able?"

The question took Sister Catherine off guard. "Yes, she is healing well."

"Who is she, then? Where is she from, and why did she come here seeking refuge?"

"Refuge was my word, Prioress." Sister Catherine bowed her head. "I'm not sure of the answers to your questions."

"Then find out." The Prioress hesitated for a moment. "I'm told that she's an escaped prisoner from a merchant vessel bound for Japan. If this is true, someone will come – pirates, Sister Catherine. And when that happens, I won't hesitate to turn her over, to keep the convent from ruin."

"Of course, Prioress. I will discover the facts at once."

Sister Catherine was excused from the den, without further debate regarding Sister Elizabeth's taking over of her caring duties. Wasn't she providing adequate care on her own? Weren't Taira's wounds drying up? Nothing had greened, and her appetite had blossomed.

I'll need to be wary of Sister Elizabeth, she thought.

Already Sister Catherine found Sister Elizabeth taking Taira to the baths. Sister Elizabeth was older by a few years, she guessed. Together, they helped Taira undress and step into the tub. Sister Catherine watched Sister Elizabeth's eyes drop to the fire-breathing lion tattoo; then their eyes locked. She knew Sister Elizabeth must be thinking: here is one of the Great Ills, but you have not reported it.

Sister Elizabeth excused herself, leaving Taira and Sister Catherine alone.

"She does not approve of my lion?" said Taira. "It's not my fault it's there. I was born with it."

"Born with it?" Sister Catherine questioned. "What does it mean?"

"It means born of the lion."

"I don't understand." Sister Catherine soaped a cloth and washed her back.

"Your kind doesn't know of our legends?" Taira shook her head. "Too bad."

"Tell me." She was pleased to have a distraction, as her hands shook with worry. Any moment the Prioress would come and rebuke her for not reporting the tattoo. A heavy heatwave rippled her body, like Jigoku's door had opened behind her. She tried to ignore it and listen.

"My people are descendants of the Great Raion Kuīn – the Lion Queen," Taira began. "She was the first and last of her kind. A red menace, powerful, brave. She was not human."

"Not human?"

"Not like you're thinking. No, she was superhuman – the first. She was lion. She breathed fire. She saw future and past. She ruled with balance. To each of her descendants she gave a gift. To the first daughter she granted the gift of sight, to the second the gift of armoured skin, to the third the gift of flight, to the fourth the gift of fire. I'm a descendant of the fourth daughter of the Lion Queen."

Taira turned to her, taking hold of her wrist, gripping tightly. "To each of her daughters the Great Lion Queen sent three acolytes to ensure her well-being. To each were given a lover, a protector, and a midwife." Taira pulled Sister Catherine closer, gazing at her, much like the Prioress did when she tried to see into her soul – was she doing the same? What did she see? "I have been wondering this whole time which one you are, the lover, the protector, or the midwife."

Sister Catherine felt Taira's grip slacken. "Perhaps I'm none of them."

"No, there is a bond between us. I know you can feel it. It's what gave you the strength to do all that you have for me." Sister Catherine had dropped the cloth rag, and waited as Taira fished it from the hot water.

"If you're here long enough, surely I may help deliver your baby, but I'm no midwife."

"I have a midwife waiting for me on the mainland," said Taira. "She prepares a home for me and my baby, and will deliver the next heir, as her mother has done before her."

Sister Catherine was quiet for a moment, believing for a moment she heard footsteps in the hallway approaching.

"Surely, then I'm your protector, since through the grace of the Christ, I've interceded to keep you from being cast out of the convent." Though for how long, she wondered.

"Yes, yes," began Taira, "I've considered this. But a samurai warrior watches over me. He was the one who rescued me from the ship bound for my homeland. A death ship that would've delivered me back to the brother of my deceased husband, a warlord bent on enslaving the Lion Queen."

Sister Catherine turned away, blushing. "Your husband, was he not your lover?" Sister Catherine offered Taira a towel and helped her dress.

"My husband forced himself upon me, then sold me. For this, I gave him fire. I burned him alive, and destroyed his kingdom. Now his brother seeks revenge. But he'll not have it. Not now. I'm stronger than ever." Taira cupped Sister Catherine's face in her hand, causing Sister Catherine to freeze. "Finally, I have before me what I have longed the most for. Come with me. When the moon is full, my samurai will return for me. Say you will come with me, lover."

The door swung open. For a moment Sister Catherine was certain it was the Prioress, but it was merely Sister Elizabeth returning. Sister Catherine jerked away from Taira. Sister Elizabeth might misconstrue their closeness, or would even exaggerate it and relate it to the Prioress.

"We are nearly finished," she said.

"I see." Sister Elizabeth handed over a jar of brown cream. "For the covering up of the Ill." Before Sister Catherine could thank her, she left.

★ ★ ★

Several days of rain brought a gloomy atmosphere to the convent. Sister Catherine was in her room praying for her soul to be upright in the eyes of the Almighty. Although she believed her Saviour knew all, she kept secret her new feelings for Taira, ones she couldn't quite articulate. In fact, she resolved that until she admitted them, she was not in any danger. Her prayer was interrupted by Sister Lybianka, who barged in unannounced and thrust a note into her hands.

Without hesitation, Sister Catherine dashed from the room to the kitchen, as the note requested. Sister Elizabeth was waiting for her.

"I overheard the Prioress speaking to the pirates." Sister Elizabeth's voice quavered. "They're looking for Taira."

"I must go to her."

"No need." She stopped Sister Catherine. "I sent her away, and she's not far. I called you, so you could go to her and offer the further help she needs, since her walk is still impaired and she'll not get too far on her own." Sister Elizabeth led Sister Catherine through the pantry and unlocked a secret door that Catherine had never seen before. "Follow the stone path to the crypt. Beyond that, a door will lead you outside to a small lake. Stay away until they've gone."

Before Sister Catherine could thank her, Sister Elizabeth closed the door behind her. With a lit candle, she followed the tunnel. She sensed the incline, imagining she was far beneath the convent – or maybe she'd been lured to descend into Jigoku, willingly... She grew hot all over as she entered a dusky alcove with an open casket. To her surprise, she stood over a decomposed body. His face was cavernous, and his regal clothes were dusty and aged. Carefully, she cast the light over his hands.

Eight fingers were missing.

"Sister Catherine," a voice called. Turning, she found an open door behind her, leading outside. The grey sky blinded her, momentarily, and there, beside a tranquil lake, framed and hidden by foliage, she found Taira. She ran to meet her, embracing her tightly, pleased to see her safe.

"They've come for me. I fear my time has run out. I cannot hide here much longer without causing harm to you or your sisters. I have only to wait for the full moon to rise, and my samurai will come," Taira said.

"When they don't find you at the convent, they will leave."

"You'll see."

"You have a greater faith than me, despite all my years of praying."

Sister Catherine noticed a flat, balled up canvas sack in the grass, when it suddenly moved on its own. Frightened, she backed away. Taira investigated, unafraid.

She untied the rope, and revealed two kittens, one orange and one white.

"They are half-starved."

"Who would do such a thing?" Sister Catherine took one in her hand, forgetting her fear, delighting in the gentleness of its fur.

"Someone who doesn't know what wonderful creatures they are," said Taira, sitting down on the damp grass. "There is one for you and one for Sister Elizabeth."

At Sister Elizabeth's name, Sister Catherine felt paralysed, and a strange feeling overcame her.

"Why not one for each of us?" she asked.

Taira placed both kittens in Sister Catherine's lap. "You're jealous of Sister Elizabeth, especially the time she has taken from you."

Embarrassed, Sister Catherine turned away.

"You have no reason to be." Taira reached for Sister Catherine's hand. "You're the one I yearn for. Didn't you know?"

Sister Catherine shook her head. She started to cry. Taira touched her tears as they ran down her cheeks. Sister Catherine pulled away, leaving her, and brought the kittens to the lake to drink.

Taira said, "They were failed to be drowned, were they not? We've given them half a chance to live."

"That's more than some people are given." Her back was facing Taira. Avoidance. The words played over in her head, and before she could think, or tighten her lips to keep from talking, she said, "If only you knew how hard it was to keep away from you. I try. I truly want to be good. I find excuses to be near you, or close to where I know you'll be, even if it is Sister Elizabeth who's tending to you. I can't keep away. But I must. Even now. I shouldn't be here." She broke into a sob.

Taira sat beside her at the edge of the water, the ends of both their robes soiled. The kittens tumbled into their laps, vying for attention.

"Are you so miserable when you're with me?" Taira laced her hands around Sister Catherine's.

"It hurts in here when I'm with you." She pointed to the centre of her chest. "And even greater when we've parted."

Taira leaned to kiss her, but Sister Catherine turned away. "No. I can't. It's one of the Greatest Ills. I'll be condemned to Jigoku. My mother warned me…"

"Ah, yes, the great pollution of the soul. I see." Taira folded her hands, prayer-like in front of her. "The only vice I see is the denial of the Great Love."

"I'm subservient to love only Christ."

"You're bound to love only he, while he loved many. Such a strange faith."

"It's getting late." Sister Catherine retreated to the door. "Surely, the pirates have gone."

"And if not, I'll go with them. I don't want to cause anyone any more suffering."

They walked back to the convent slowly, neither speaking a word. They passed St. Pavel without so much as a glance at his benevolence. Once inside the pantry, Sister Catherine waited, allowing Taira to go out first. Her heart pounded, wanting to say something, but she couldn't articulate the constant churning in her heart into words. After collecting herself for a minute, she followed, watching the swinging door come to a full stop before entering the corridor. Sister Elizabeth, eyes wide with fear, greeted her. Sister Catherine caught a glimpse of Taira. Two pirates, armed with swords, escorted by the Prioress, were taking her away.

"No," she cried out, struggling against Sister Elizabeth's strong grip. "You tricked me!"

"Never." Sister Elizabeth wrapped her arms tighter. "You can't go out there. She'll know. The Prioress will know." Sister Elizabeth pressed Sister Catherine up against the wall and held her as she fought to get free.

"There is nothing to know! They can't just take her."

"The Prioress will see that you love her."

The words jolted Sister Catherine. She held her breath. She felt a heartbeat in her ears, and a touch of faint.

"I know you love her," Sister Elizabeth continued. "I can see it every time you look at her."

"They'll take her away." Sister Catherine worried.

"No. They're looking for a woman with a lion tattoo. They won't find it, and she'll be free of suspicion. It's the best way. I should've realised it sooner."

Sister Catherine took Sister Elizabeth's hand for support. "How do you know what I myself refuse to admit?"

"It's the same as what I feel for Sister Lybianka."

"I'm sorry for what I did to you."

"No matter. I'm all the stronger for it." Sister Elizabeth offered Sister Catherine a drink of water. "I've done what's necessary to protect Sister Lybianka. I've told her I don't love her, and though it hurts right now, she's young, and will heal."

"And what about you?" For the first time Sister Catherine saw the deeper side of Sister Elizabeth, her redeeming qualities overflowing.

"I'll leave this place soon enough. Either I'll force the Prioress's hand to cast me out, or I'll find other means."

Sister Catherine assumed this to mean she'd take her own life, and grabbed hold of her, pleading for her to reconsider. The door swung open. A nun reported to Sister Elizabeth that Taira was safe, and alone in her room.

"I must go to her," said Sister Catherine.

"And I to the Prioress to find out when the pirates are leaving."

The guest room door was partly open. On the bed with a shredded robe was Taira. Her naked back revealed, though the lion stayed hidden. Weary with worry, and strangled by her emotions, Sister Catherine slipped onto the bed, and wrapped her arms around Taira. Soon, their breathing synchronised, and they fell into slumber. Sister Catherine awoke to screaming. In the courtyard, terrified nuns ran past. Several pirates, with swords drawn, were stopping nuns at will, ripping their robes, searching for the lion tattoo.

"Stay here, Taira." Sister Catherine rushed to the den of the Prioress to warn her, evading the pirates stalking the hallways. They had to send for help, evacuate the monastery. But the Prioress wasn't there. Sister Catherine retreated to the main gate. Beside a nun, back to her, shackled at the wrists, stood the Prioress. Sister Catherine was just in time to see the Prioress hand over the shackled nun to the pirate in exchange for a handful of silver coins.

When the nun turned, Sister Catherine saw the slit in the robe, the naked back, and the fire-breathing lion. She screamed, catching the Prioress's attention. The pirates dragged the nun outside through the front gate. Sister Catherine tried to follow, but the Prioress ordered the gates closed. The last thing Sister Catherine saw was the frail body of her beloved tossed into a metal cage on the pirate's wagon.

"It's best this way, Sister Catherine," said the Prioress. "If we didn't cooperate, they would've pillaged the convent. One woman is not worth the lives of many."

Sister Catherine wanted to say that Christ's one life was

given for the lives of all, but knew it wasn't the time, as Sister Lybianka appeared and led her away.

They went to the kitchen. Sister Catherine noticed the sister's tear-stained face, and wondered the cause, since her robes were still intact, unlike many of the other nuns.

Sister Lybianka handed Sister Catherine a handwritten note, and said, "She's gone."

"Who's gone?"

"Sister Elizabeth." Sister Lybianka's face turned red with tears. "She told me she would find a way to leave, but I didn't believe her. She came to me, asking me to paint a red lion on her skin. I didn't know what I was doing. I thought she'd forgiven me for getting us into trouble. But it was a trick, and she's left me." Sister Lybianka flopped into the chair, lifeless, sobbing. "They'll kill her. I can feel it. They'll kill her."

Sister Catherine read the note signed by Sister Elizabeth. *She is waiting for you by the lake.* One small message held so much weight. She wouldn't believe the truth of its words until she saw Taira, untouched and safe. "I must go," she said, and tore open the secret hatch, not caring who saw, or if they would ask why. She hurried along the path, past the crypt, and flung open the last door. Standing at the water's edge was Taira. A slight breeze pushed her long tresses over her shoulders.

The thought of losing her had filled the chasm between them, and in one long stride, Sister Catherine met Taira, cupping her hands to her face and kissing her deeply. All of her longing and desire swelled, as her body filled with fire. At their feet, the kittens danced.

"Come with me," said Taira. "The moon will be full tomorrow, and we'll have safe passage to the mainland." She pointed. "We can take this path away from here, and wait till then."

Sister Catherine felt hope, she felt fear, then excitement, even, and said, "I hadn't thought past this moment, and I can't think past anything more than knowing you're safe."

"It's not over yet. Sister Elizabeth gave her life for me."

Sister Catherine nodded. "I'm shamed for believing she was anything less than a friend."

Voices neared them. Someone must have followed Sister Catherine in her mad dash to reach Taira. The Prioress and several nuns appeared in the doorway. "Seize them!" the Prioress yelled when she spotted Taira and Sister Catherine in their embrace by the water.

"Run!" Sister Catherine screamed, as she pushed Taira away and tried to stop the nuns from following her. "Go now or all will be in vain."

As Sister Catherine was subdued and her hands restrained, she watched Taira disappear into the brush.

"She won't get far," said the Prioress. "I've sent a messenger after the pirates explaining they have the wrong girl. They'll be back soon enough."

Back at the convent, Sister Catherine found she'd been locked in her room. When she tried to leave, the handle hammed; the window was too small to climb out, leading her forced to remain. When morning came, soup and bread was brought to her. "Your punishment will come soon enough," said the attending nun.

She tried to persuade her to let her out, but the door was closed fast upon her.

At night, through her window, she watched the movement of the full moon across the blue-black sky. She imagined Taira rendezvousing with her samurai protector and traveling across land and sea, until she arrived at the home prepared by her midwife.

She considered if she was ever truly Taira's lover, doubting if such good could come to her, that all the steps she'd taken in life, had led to *her* being the one promised by the Great Raion Kuīn.

After midnight, as she lay quietly on the bed, the door to her room was cast open abruptly. Two nuns ascended upon her and dragged her out. She was dragged to the garden, where the Prioress and nuns, including Sister Lybianka, waited in attendance, Sister Catherine was tied to the chastisement pole, the back of her garment ripped.

"Twenty lashes, and not one less," said the Prioress, listing off her transgressions of betraying the convent, and especially the Great Ill of Desire. "I don't care if she faints. Twenty lashes, and tomorrow the same."

Sister Catherine wondered if the Christ, when he had found himself in a similar position, had lamented the road he'd taken to get there. Had she found a different path to follow, Sister Catherine knew then and there that she wouldn't have taken it.

This was it, the reason she'd left her home and the safety of the Fuji Mountain, this was always in her future, waiting...

The count was on six, when she no longer felt the blood dripping, though the sting and the cut grew more intense. As the Prioress called seven, Sister Catherine saw a great flash of light, as if the stars and the moon had dropped from the heavens and exploded into liquid light across the garden.

Fire swept from the shed, to the crops, to the benches, like a gust of wind. As the flames rose, Sister Catherine noticed the whip had stopped. Someone had untied her hands. She fell into the embrace of two arms. She fought to stay conscious. Two other arms grabbed her and helped her across the blaze. Sister Elizabeth and Sister Lybianka. The last thing she saw, before passing through the gates, was the small frame of Taira casting out flames from her open mouth, like a fire-breathing lion, and the Prioress consumed in the waterfall inferno – Jigoku was no longer a thing to imagine.

Nor something to fear.

* * *

Somewhere on the western mainland of Russia, Catherine walked hand-in-hand with her lover. In front of them walked a small girl child, naked; a small lion tattoo covering her back. Two cats, one orange and one white, followed them, as the sun eclipsed the dawn of a new day.

VESTAL

Dee Holloway

The potions peddler arrived in Vestal on a fine September day, when the trees were just beginning to blush with autumn's chill. Capucine didn't hear of it, being occupied on her rounds, but word of his local competition reached Wilhelm Gleiber soon enough, and she was pointed out to him striding across the main square. She was as tall as a man, cloaked and hooded, an undyed veil obscuring her features and gloved hands swinging a black bag.

Capucine Lenox, yes sir, she's our physician, the wives of Vestal told Gleiber smugly, even if *physician* wasn't quite accurate to Capucine's history, nor her position in town. At this Gleiber's ears perked up. He loved nothing more than competition, and the besting of such. He'd take this spinster Lenox's custom, he would, and every cent Vestal had to spare, and not a few they didn't. He'd see what was what, in the remote Lenox estate on Vestal's northern rim, and smash Miss Lenox's business accordingly. He loved to know that a town would miss him, when he rolled away – loved to leave them pining, grasping for promises of his swift return tossed over his shoulder like spring posies.

His assistant, Annie, kept her own counsel as they approached the Lenox property.

The place was a rambling wreck, half grown over in vines. A stone wall crumbled around its borders; an orange cat sat upon the blocks sunning itself. It hissed when Gleiber passed through the gate, Annie some steps behind. Where the house was tumbledown, its land was planted up thickly, the remnants of summer bounty creating a green corridor on either side.

The door endured the peddler's fist upon it once, twice and more, until he rubbed his knuckles.

"Where in the blazes can this woman be?" he demanded of Annie, who maintained her quiet.

Further knocking produced Capucine Lenox from the house's depths. Wilhelm Gleiber surveyed her with distaste. She was dirt-smudged top to toe, her gown the texture and tint of a flour sack. Beneath it her feet were bare, though the air outside and within the hallway was chill. The veil she'd worn into Vestal was nowhere to be seen, and her hair was bright brown.

"Miss Lenox," said Gleiber, who didn't deign to ask questions of women.

"Are you in some need?" said Capucine.

She spoke dimly, as though she'd been sleeping. Annie observed that the state of her suggested Capucine had instead been gardening. A thready twist of grapevine wound through her hair at the temples, a woodland crown that Annie beheld with surprised, distant delight.

"I should say not," Gleiber returned. Then, not liking to show hot emotion to women either, he found some inner well of slyness and set to his task. "I am Wilhelm Gleiber, crafter of remedies and tonics for body and blood. Your townsfolk say you are the doctor of these parts, and know such potions as no man can match."

Capucine bent to scoop up the cat from where it twisted around her ankles. When she straightened, she was smiling. "They're very generous."

"Perhaps we are a meeting of minds," Gleiber suggested. He intended to woo her with compliments and flattery of her craft, lulling her into a sense of superiority and then setting his traps. "Perhaps you might show me something of your remedies. I've several patents. I would pay you for such secrets as you care to impart."

He bowed, extending his hand. Capucine's own hands were folded around the cat, making no move to shake. Annie, watching the proceedings, noted a strangeness: gloved hands and bare feet. Dirty, plain garb and a vivid figure beneath, generous as Vestal's populace. A title of physician but no airs of one, and – Annie's eyes swept the property – no notes of grandeur to affirm the position. The Lenox house was in disrepair and its mistress, though lovely, was humble.

Wilhelm Gleiber gestured, and Capucine busied her hands with the cat.

"I'm no true scientist," she said, still smiling. "My father studied plants and gave me some knowledge of them – my mother all the more. If I can help the townspeople, I do." A tendril of deep chestnut hair curled over her forehead like a grace note. "I doubt I'd enrich the coffers of your learning, Mr. Gleiber."

With this mild admonition, the door shut. Annie bit the inside of her cheek to stem laughter. Wilhelm Gleiber didn't permit anyone's laughter in his vicinity. But when she looked at him, she saw his eyes starry and dazed. He stared at the sturdy oak door as though he could penetrate it with his gaze, reach beyond its solid opacity and follow the woman within about her business, whatever it was. Annie's view of her master wasn't rosy, but she was a fair woman and admitted he was no rogue of the road. He'd never taken up with village women, if only because of his high opinion of himself, his adherence to the reformers knitting bodily health to spiritual. But as his wagon carried him away from the Lenox house and its gentle goddess, each roll of its wheels plunged him further into the well of desire.

"By God," he announced to Annie over the horses' hoofbeats, "I will have that woman's secrets."

★ ★ ★

Capucine had but one secret.

Annie was in the business of secrets. During the War of Independence she'd ferried messages to Boston, and knew the value of silence. Gleiber thought his recipes unknown to all save himself, never mind that the majority of his knowledge was gleaned from Annie's mother's people – but Annie memorised each as it was concocted, a hoard to be dipped into at will should the day come that the man admitted she'd paid her so-called debts to him. A fine irony, Annie thought, how Gleiber held himself pious for honoring his uncle's will, which had freed Annie and her brothers, and in the same breath reminded her of what was still owed for her schooling, what seemed to be eternally owed. Her bitterness, too, her righteous anger were more secrets, frigid furies beneath a serene surface. Her anger would be waiting, when the time came to call upon it.

It was fed and watered lovingly, her anger, the only crop which he could not harvest from her.

"Acadian French," a Vestal wife confided in a busybody way, counting coins into Annie's palm one morning. "A fur trapper's daughter. They say her mother's mother was of the Huron people." Annie hadn't asked, but that was one of silence's values. An open face and calm manner made people want to tell her things. "Real woodsfolk, the Lenoxes. Miss Capucine's grandmother – well, it must be true, for there's no one in these parts can match Miss Capucine's way with plants."

Clearly that wasn't a secret, true or not.

Annie stored away note of the Huron grandmother, the French fox-trapping father. She slipped other fragments of gossip into the jewel-box of her mind as they came. Capucine Lenox had no book-learning, said Mrs. McLendon. Miss Capucine hadn't set foot off her father's property except to see to the sick in over ten years, said Mr. Larsen. The town boys spied Capucine dancing in the pines at the spring's turning, wreathed all around in larkspur. Capucine didn't receive visitors, but everyone called her friend. Capucine had given birth to a baby by an itinerant preacher and lost it in childbirth, buried it on the sloping southern lawn of the Lenox property beside her parents' headstones. Alternately, Capucine had never known a man's touch (this tidbit imparted with a saucy titter), but then whither the origins of the third headstone visible from the Vestal road?

Meantime, Wilhelm Gleiber hadn't been successful at his game. He visited the Lenox property daily, telling Capucine of his sales, the townsfolk's appreciation, of certain new ideas and experiments. She didn't rise to his bait. She spoke sweetly, but with firm distance. She never shook his hand, and Annie knew that this stoked Gleiber's blood to lust and annoyance. She watched him rub his own hands together and set them on the horses' traces to drive away again, unsatisfied.

"Take this as an offering," he declared after they'd been in Vestal two weeks, thrusting a flask at Annie. "I'm sure she'll never have seen such efficacy."

"Do Miss Lenox's courses require adjustment?" Annie inquired. The flask housed a purifier which Gleiber prescribed to settle women's cycles and calm nerves.

"I wouldn't wager so," someone else laughed. Annie turned to see a village elder, Mr. Bredar, leaning on the wagon's window ledge. "Why, Mr. Gleiber, it's well known Miss Capucine is barren."

Annie's chest twinged. It was sad, the way Vestal talked of Capucine Lenox: proud and yet possessive, profligate with their gossip, as though she wasn't real, or lived only in their heads, existed only at their need.

Wilhelm Gleiber harrumphed. "Then the story of her illicit babe is untrue!"

"Oh no," said Mr. Bredar, "it's quite true. Miss Capucine got a babe, the father's name we gave to the road, and 'twas stillborn." He nodded gravely. "The third headstone on the hill belongs to the infant. She buried it herself with no ceremony. Didn't allow Reverend Allston to baptise the poor thing, but then," – a finger laid beside Mr. Bredar's nose – "ever a pagan clan, the Lenoxes."

"My purifying tonic has brought more than one woman into fruitfulness," Wilhelm Gleiber said modestly, but his eyes gleamed. "I might be of service to Miss Lenox yet. Take that up the hill, Annie. I have business with Mr. Bredar."

The business likely involved the fruits of Mr. Bredar's vineyard. Annie took her leave and gladly.

★ ★ ★

Capucine didn't often invite folk into her house, but the peddler's quiet assistant was disarming.

"Up the hill in this rain," she said to the woman – Annie Ten Hove, a Dutch surname that must've come from white owners – as she held the door open. "Won't you have some tea for your trouble?"

"It's no trouble," Annie said. "Mr. Gleiber sends his regards." She held out a flask, a label identifying it as GLEIBER'S HARDIEST BLOOD PURIFIER pasted across the belly. "If you will."

Capucine's blood needed no purifying. "I suppose you aren't to return without delivering this into my hands."

Annie nodded.

"A switch, then. I'll take this flask if you take tea with me."

The woman's eyes lit on Capucine's and then dropped. "You're very kind."

"No kindness to offer warmth on an evening such as this." At Capucine's words, the rain outside thickened, pelting down emphatically. "Let me dry your wraps."

To her credit, Annie didn't stare at the house's interior as she followed Capucine into the kitchen. Capucine wasn't much of a housekeeper; her father had never demanded it of her, used as he was to wood camps and trappers' fires, and after his death the place had fallen into disuse, Capucine spending most of her time among her plants. The greenhouse pulsed on her periphery, a verdant jewel visible through the kitchen's Dutch door. She longed to be back inside its steamy glass, to lie down amid the honeysuckle and study the droplets gathering on the roof – but Annie's presence kept her in the kitchen. Annie's calm brown face above her teacup begged careful inquiry. Annie's sober blue dress at the table kept Capucine's attention… distracted her, in fact, into nearly spilling tea on the woman's arm.

"Beg pardon," Capucine said, settling the teapot. "I don't often have guests."

"And you're not curious about outsiders," Annie said. "About my well-traveled master. About your fellow townspeople?" She sipped, looking pleased by the tea. "They're curious about you."

"How should they be? They know me well."

Annie hummed.

"And I know them," Capucine said. A defensive prickle grew along her spine. "Too well, perhaps. Familiarity breeds contempt. It might amuse you to hear that Mrs. Larsen seeks poultices for her husband's back, to remove the hair. Like a bear's pelt, says she! Then there's Mrs. Cvetkovic – oh, such a family as was never so cursed by the Catholic faith. Monthly she steals up my hill with her hand out, seeking fennel and rue – all this to prevent her husband's seed from taking root again. And the Engel twins," Capucine rushed on, "they've been trying to poison one another for an inheritance going on ten years, and the girls, the town girls, poor things, Miss Capucine, they say! Miss Capucine, give us a sachet to bring us husbands. Miss Capucine, give us a paste to make us lovely. Miss Capucine, oh Capucine, so familiar they are with my name, as though the mere repetition will cure them of their ills!"

In her rising temper, Capucine lost herself. She loosened hold of herself, of the seeds and rootlets and twining branches which grew deep within her chest and belly and lay coiled in her veins. Briars latched into the wooden tabletop when she lifted her hands. A strange flush lay across her cheeks: not red but dull green, turning the green-black of lime skins where the flush stemmed from veins in her throat. Those veins lit her countenance like a will o'the wisp, a withy network glowing beneath her skin.

This was Capucine's secret.

Annie was silent. She sipped her tea and didn't shift from her chair, even as the kitchen plants in their windowsill pots unfurled new growth and reached leafy fingers toward Capucine. Finally Annie said, voice low and startled, "Violets in autumn?"

Capucine gazed at the now-lush tabletop, where a clump of violets tangled with a blackberry bush sprouting through the hardwood.

"In the village you wear your cloak and veil. What times Mr. Gleiber has come to see you, you've kept your gloves." Annie looked at Capucine's hands on the table, at the broken nails hard and curved like rose thorns. "Just as well for him, I suppose."

Capucine's heart strained against its bone cage.

"He fears a woman's influence," Annie said, the inflection of her voice turning *influence* into innuendo. "Never heard him admit it, but I know him. He's jealous of your stature."

"He may have it," Capucine murmured. "Does your employer plan to stay? Is Vestal your new home?"

She nearly wished it. If Gleiber stayed, Annie would too: Annie, this woman who looked so calmly at Capucine. She reached for the teapot, again handling it clumsily, and Annie caught her wrist. Capucine froze, horror seeping through her. Gleiber might fear her influence, but for the wrong reasons: men looked to their custom and their reputations when their very lives might be at stake. But Annie only took the teapot, refilled their cups, and set it down. The fingers that had grasped Capucine's wrist flexed, then subsided.

Capucine breathed out in a gentle gust. The brambles twining in the thicket of her hair relaxed their tight-knotted buds.

"He doesn't like to stay put," Annie said. "But this place intrigues him."

She meant Capucine intrigued him. It had always been thus. Capucine dreaded it.

"For as long as you're in Vestal, you are welcome," Capucine said. "Please – do come again." She wanted more time with Annie, without Gleiber. "I'll show you the greenhouse."

Perhaps Annie would like that. Perhaps, since Capucine's nature hadn't startled her, Capucine among her plants wouldn't, either. Perhaps they could garden together and talk of recipes, clay vessels and glass, planting methods, moons.

Annie nodded. She smiled at the cat, Walter, as he bolted into the kitchen, and a small hopeful tendril grew around Capucine's heart.

★ ★ ★

When Annie returned to Gleiber's camp, she found him roaring drunk. Drunkenness went against the high-minded ideals of his health crusade, he indulged occasionally. In the morning he'd claim it'd been part of his experiments with a new tonic for headaches and flux, which he was testing on himself first. For now, in the night's cold cloak, he danced Annie around the fire, singing "All Creatures of Our God and King" out of tune.

"Annie, my faithful," he called to her, "such news as never man did hear. Mr. Bredar is possessed of a wild imagination, or else he imbibes too deeply of his own vintage! I have heard–"

Annie's head spun not with his motion but with her own fresh knowledge. Capucine's image lay in her mind, gravid and heavy, the emotions she inspired ready to burst forth. Annie wanted to be snug in her bedroll, where she could pore over what she'd learned at the Lenox house – if anything. Of Capucine's fey-touched complexion and the heat of her skin beneath Annie's fingers, and the sudden, fervent growth, greenery spiraling through the kitchen, enclosing the woman at the table protectively, lovingly. Annie's hand had stung in that moment, as though one of the thorns growing into the table pricked her.

Even now vague numbness lingered in her palm.

"What tales this village tells of its physician," Gleiber huffed. He released Annie and sank beside the fire. "What am I, a man of science, to make of this? The very idea goes against every sound theory undergirding my practice. A woman is a woman and can be naught else."

Annie paused in her circuit of the fire.

"There is a tale that Miss Lenox is a hothouse flower," Gleiber said. His voice grew sonorous, puffed-up and important. "They say the merest touch of her skin is a poison, that she secretes death in her lips, her very veins."

"That belies her position as a doctor," Annie said carefully. Dread slipped icicles into her blood.

"A mystery indeed. I shall unravel it. Did I not say I'd have her secrets? Well, this is one – and no doubt, if there is some scrap of truth in it, her familiarity with plants is explained by it. Her prowess…" He fell quiet, glaring into the fire while Annie banked it. "It's witchery. I wonder that the people trust her, if they believe such strange villainy of her."

Capucine was no villain, in Annie's view. She'd been so careful in her gloves, not shaking Gleiber's hand. She'd gone stonestill when Annie touched her hand, withdrawn it immediately. Those were not the actions of someone bent on harm.

"This must be the source of her shyness," Gleiber mused. "Do you recall, how she did not even dare to give me her hand in greeting? Nor has she since, and her demeanor all hushed up, her eyes low. I don't doubt she fears her effect, should she grow close to – a man."

Annie had her own doubts on the subject of Gleiber's influence over women, and Capucine's interest in men.

"I will cure her," he said, the total confidence in his voice stealing Annie's breath. "I shall make a study of the region's poisonous plants and concoct a cure. If she's native to these environs, so must be her poison. Whatever its source, I shall drown it in wholesome water and dilute its bite. I shall tear it out at the roots!" This pronouncement seemed to sap his energy, and his shoulders drooped.

Once he was laid snoring in his cot, Annie curled into her own blankets and stared at the sliver of sky visible through her tent. A worrisome heat thrust her heart against her ribs. Her hand – her right hand, the hand with which she wrote and sewed and ground herbs, the hand with which she'd touched Capucine – tingled and jerked. Her pulse beat in her fingertips. Warmth spread up her arm, pouring through her chest and belly, until her brain was dazed. Was she fevered? Wild concerns and tall tales spun in her mind. If Capucine's touch was poisonous, then surely Annie was infected, as surely as her brother Nathan had stepped on a nail and his foot rotted off.

She rolled over, readjusting her blankets with a violent wrench. These were the stories of children! She'd learned, in bondage and in war and in every interaction with Wilhelm Gleiber, not to put stock in fairy tales. There was no strength in them. They led a person astray.

When she closed her eyes, Capucine was there, foxfire-bright.

★ ★ ★

Gleiber didn't prevent Annie from going to the Lenox house. As Annie told it, he was preoccupied with his new project and saw no harm in her visits, provided she tended to their customers in a manner timely and respectful. Capucine thought it likely that neither did the man consider Annie's visits a threat – to Annie herself or to his custom. Why should he have any notion of Annie in danger? The thought that Capucine might touch Annie – might have already touched Annie – might *want* to touch Annie would not enter his mind. If Capucine presented her hands to Wilhelm Gleiber gloved, never would she show them bare to his mere assistant.

Capucine's hands were bare with Annie in the house, and the garden, and the greenhouse; her hands and her arms bare to the elbow with gown-sleeves rolled; her throat above the neckline of her dress, shamelessly bare. Her doe-brown skin took on the tint of the plants with which she worked: she grew rosy as she tied back an enthusiastic tumble of tearoses, and her green veins made themselves known when she tucked a fat-leafed aloe vera into a pot. She ate grapes one by one, standing with Annie beneath the muscadine vines in the back garden, and as the firm globes passed her lips a ruddy bloom grew, darkening to claret, burgundy, near-black.

She pointed out each tree and vine in the greenhouse to Annie, whose knowledge of plants was limited to northeastern natives. The glass dome stayed warm as the days turned chillier, perfumed air and wet-streaked walls close as a lover's embrace. She didn't touch Annie again, accidentally or with purpose.

"Is it true?" Annie said one afternoon at Capucine's potting table, planting stoneware vessels with vervain and lavender. "The people in Vestal, they say…"

"What do they say?" Capucine tamped soil atop the seeds. "Last I was down to the village to deliver Sarah Fremont's baby, I heard them say quite a few things of your employer."

She didn't repeat for Annie words from the man's own lips – the insinuations and promises that chilled her blood like sap freezing in the maples. She didn't tell Annie of Wilhelm Gleiber's further visits to the Lenox house, on mornings when Annie was with customers, nor did she mention his forthright commentary on her person, her very being. She thrust these thoughts away. There was no substance in the man, she thought, nothing in him but pomp wedded to fear, and if there was hunger in his face when he looked at her, well –

"They say a poison lives in you," Annie said. "As long as you don't lay hands on them or their loved ones, all is well."

"It's true enough," Capucine said. "I learned long ago – oh, not to touch skin to skin, not even to breathe too heavy on delicate constitutions. The glover in town laughs at the volume of my orders for the finest kidskin." She thought of her father in his last years, his disease nothing either of their crafts could counter and his death too swift, the veil shrouding his mouth before he could warn her. "What's mine is blessing and curse."

Annie was quiet with her pots. Capucine liked to watch her hands at work. They were clever, longer and more elegant than Capucine's, though Annie was delicately built and but half Capucine's height, a braided crown adding a few more inches. The greenhouse hummed around them, concerned with its own business.

"The baby," Annie said. "I'm sorry. I don't know why I pry like this. With everyone else I'm only listening, but you…"

The baby. *The baby.* Word had rushed through Vestal that Gerard Lenox's girl-cub was with child and no mother in the house to teach her daughter the ways of men, to prevent her destruction. Yet what had come of it but a blue corpse… poison-blue, death-blue, blue as pokeweed on the stalk… What had come of it but a grave with two bodies, a young man and a baby dead by its mother's hand?

"The town might've rid themselves of me then," Capucine said. Her voice roughened. A climbing sprig of honeysuckle twined around her calf sympathetically. "But they don't fear me. I've proven myself. I like helping them. It's more difficult to help with plants than harm, and worthier." She examined her fingers, staring at her palms' pink skin with a sharp eye. "Do you fear me?"

"No," said Annie.

"Do you fear Mr. Gleiber?"

Annie laughed. "No."

"Then why do you stay with him?"

"He holds a debt over me," Annie said. She gazed past the greenhouse walls to the blur of autumn leaves beyond. "And yet – it's safer, still. People don't like a free woman of colour."

There was nothing Capucine could say to that.

★ ★ ★

Wilhelm Gleiber held himself to strictness in all things: the severity of his dress, the veracity of his remedies, the discipline of his diet, firm rigor when he had a medicine to refine. As the days passed, his grand goal inched into view – mixture by mixture, a pinch more of this and a measure less of that. The mice he used as subjects withered under his ministrations, until at last one small mammal sneezed, blinked its black bead eyes at him, and went about its business in the cage.

"Hm!" said Gleiber.

He restrained his excitement; he admitted to himself that this success was the natural course of things – that his quest for a cure could never have ended in defeat, for defeat was but the meager ashes of scientific method applied too listlessly. He was a conqueror as the Spanish had been on this continent centuries before, an explorer like Hudson, breaking new trails through wilderness and bringing modern medicine to the benighted.

He labeled his success with a painstaking hand and stoppered the bottle, then called for Annie.

"Have you any ribbons?"

Annie regarded him with eyes narrowed. "I'm sure I could find one at the milliner's, sir."

He chuckled. Of course Annie wasn't a woman to keep ribbons about her person. She was modest and plain, not given to vanity or fripperies. He'd seen her wear violets pinned to her dress once, in their younger days at his uncle's Watervliet homestead. To his mind he was generous with this praise. A woman's virtue reflected in her demeanor, and his Annie was a good woman. Yet it struck him that his cure was not only a beneficence, but Cupid's tool. A woman like Capucine, now; he considered Capucine Lenox a sort of woman whose eye might be softened by a ribbon.

"If you would," he said. "Quickly. A green ribbon, I think."

The ribbon was procured and then secured about the bottle's neck. Gleiber tucked this into his vest. He bid Annie remain with the wagon against customer need, and took a horse up the hill to the estate. He had some idea that gallantry was more obvious on horseback, and wanted Capucine to have full warning of his arrival.

For all his ostentatious warning, Capucine materialised belatedly. She appeared at the door in her usual smutched state, which Gleiber regarded with mild derision and growing fondness. She was unsullied despite the dirt. If the tale of her baby was true, it had been youthful folly – or more likely she had been taken advantage of, perhaps ravished, no more her fault than a lightning strike.

She met his eyes frankly, not dipping into a curtsy of greeting. "Mr. Gleiber. Annie isn't here, I'm afraid."

"Well I know it," he said. "I've come on my promised errand. The cure of which I spoke has been found." He amended himself. "Rather it has been created, with no small effort on my part."

Quiet met this statement. She looked pale, her skin faded and dull. What proof more was required that his cure was welcome – necessary?

"Shall I tell you of its contents?"

"If you will."

"May I be permitted inside?" Gleiber inspected the sky with a critical glance. "Rain seems imminent."

Capucine turned aside silently and he went into the hall, stamping his boots free of mud. He withdrew the bottle from his pocket. "The base is sumac," he said, eager to tell her of his success, "suspended in mineral oil with a compound of antimony, manchineel, and belladonna. Ah! I see you are wary."

"You've named only poisons, sir. How should I be anything but?"

"Poison is best combated with poison," he returned. Capucine moved past him in the hall, her skirts brushing his leg, and a thrill shot through him. Soon enough he would know not just the whisper of cloth against cloth, but the exact weight of her hand in his, the warmth and texture of her skin. "A poison's effects are effectively canceled by another poison, given opposite reactions in the body. In your case, Miss Lenox, *you* are the poison. A powerful poison, if the town is to be believed! A small army must be deployed to battle this poison on its native ground."

Capucine turned to him, framed in the threshold between corridor and kitchen. Her lovely face was somber beneath its smudges. "I suppose you've tested this cure."

Her voice broke, turning *cure* into a breathy note of funereal anguish.

"But of course. You must have no concern for its efficacy."

"You've tested it on yourself?"

Gleiber laughed. "Good gracious, Miss Lenox. It would have no effect but a deleterious one on a normal human. There is no poison in *me* which needs excising."

Capucine twisted her hands in her apron. Then she dropped the garment and drew her gloves off slowly. Heat blossomed in Gleiber's head. He didn't like to look on women with a hungry eye, but neither had he beheld a sight so erotic as the simple unveiling of a pair of hands. They were small hands, with callused fingertips. They didn't look as though they went about gloved and hidden from sunlight every day.

"Mr. Gleiber," Capucine said. She stepped closer. There was a heady scent in the hall, perhaps stemming from something she was cooking, or leaking into the house from that flagrant conservatory. He had a vision of Capucine growing up in the greenhouse, some tropical plant brightly coloured to warn birds it was deadly. She said again, "Mr. Gleiber. I can't trust this fluid's effects, not knowing how it might react with the human body. Won't you partake in this experiment with me?"

Gleiber frowned. Perhaps she was correct that, mice or no, his scientific process was lacking.

"I'll give you a kiss," said Capucine. She smiled at him, shyly, and took the bottle from his hand. He ached to grasp her fingers in his, but permitted her modesty for the moment. "And then the cure will have its effects upon both of us, for there will be a poison in your system needful of curing."

Horror mingled in his belly with avid interest. It stoked his fascination and desire, not least his thirst for knowledge, this idea of hers; her request was delivered humbly, but had the effect of a devilish dare.

"I think this village well-named," he said. "You are its vestal priestess, its virgin goddess. You are an anchorite in her cell, and I–" A powerful urge gripped him, to kneel and bury his face in her apron, clutch her bare hands to his face and breathe the intoxicating floral aroma of her skin. "I am blessed in this undertaking."

She tilted her head, faint green lacework illuminated beneath her skin like a leaf's veins. Gleiber imagined he could track the lethal flow of her blood. He'd done well suggesting a green ribbon for his cure. When the bottle was drained, he would thread the ribbon in Capucine's hair, displacing the stem of bluebottle tucked behind her ear. No more need for her cloaks and veils, her gloves and long sleeves; she would be gowned in the finest linen and silk, exquisite as a rose in his lapel.

He took her hand. At the first touch his own palm tingled. Her poison was swift-acting, communicable by the barest of brushes, but he would be bold. This endeavour couldn't be completed by halves; his success would be complete, his triumph undeniable, Capucine herself the living proof.

He crushed her against him in a desperate embrace and kissed her fully, probing and hungry, seeking the poison roiling beneath her skin.

★ ★ ★

On that gray and empty morning, Annie couldn't bear the thought of Capucine in her house with Wilhelm Gleiber advancing like a plague ship. When she arrived at the estate and slipped through the front door, she believed she was too late – for there they were, her master and Capucine, twined together in the hall. Gleiber bent Capucine as though she were a flower battered by rain. Her hair tumbled loose, and her lips were turned to his, sealed, their breath a private exchange and, it seemed to Annie, a promise.

She fainted.

The soft thud of Annie's body broke Capucine from Gleiber's embrace. Dismay surged in her veins at the sight: Annie crumpled, her plain blue skirts twisted about her ankles and her head limp against the floor. Capucine strained forward, Gleiber's grasp already slackening. As she moved, he staggered; her firm stature had become a bulwark.

"This poison," he gasped. His hands groped for her, fumbling at her wrists. "Such swiftness, such–"

He had grown pale about the nostrils, Capucine noted. She was torn between rushing to Annie's side immediately, and seeing Gleiber through to his end.

"Ah, but such sweetness." His voice was wet and choked, his eyes shot with red. "Capucine. My Capucine. What you will be when – when you–"

Disgust wrenched Capucine's viscera. She had not hesitated to kiss this man, for whom she held neither affection nor interest. She hesitated less to take him in her arms again, brace him upright as his limbs stiffened with death's approach, and cup his livid face in one palm. She saw, then, the poison roiling beneath his skin, and it was not *her* poison. Rather it was the poison of greed, arrogance, grasping theft and unrighteous dominion; it was a potent brew, one that had been stewing in Gleiber's veins for a long time. Its corrosive effect was only hastened by her skin and her kiss.

When his cheek had turned cool beneath her palm and his stale breath drawn one last time, Capucine let him fall. She smashed his cursed bottle on the floor beside him, its cure oozing forth fruitlessly. The world held nothing more for Wilhelm Gleiber, and no more would Capucine pay him mind.

There were other matters – blue-skirted, slowly stirring matters – worthier of her attention.

★ ★ ★

When Annie woke, there was nothing above her but sky. She tilted her head, confused. How was it that rain fell, yet she was dry and warm? Warm, so warm, encircled by comfort, softness beyond any blanket she'd known. A scrap of silk tickled her forehead, and a face swam above hers.

"Don't move," Capucine said. "You hit your head when you fell."

It wasn't silk that brushed Annie's skin, but a strand of Capucine's hair. Capucine didn't smile, but all her attention was directed at Annie. The strangeness of her bare hand stroking Annie's cheek set in only belatedly.

"Am I dead?"

"No, dear one," said Capucine. "I think you're impervious."

Annie had never felt more vulnerable.

The soft movement of Capucine's fingers repeated. "You see? All this time you've come to see me, and I've been so careful – but you must have no reaction to me. Otherwise how might I touch you with no harm?"

There was a reaction, Annie registered, but indeed it was not one of pain or paralysis.

"Perhaps I'm full of you," she said. She reached to cover Capucine's fingers with her own, remembering their work in the kitchen and their close movements in the greenhouse, that dome of secret heat which cradled life. "Perhaps I've taken so much of you into me that where there might once have been harm, there's now only…"

Now Capucine did smile. "Only?"

"There are diseases and poisons to which a body can develop resistance," Annie said. "Through exposure. The Chinese call it inoculation."

"Yet you've never been exposed to me," Capucine teased.

Annie laughed. A flush spread through her face, delightful warmth originating with Capucine's hand. Then she remembered. "Gleiber?"

"I didn't mean to distress you," Capucine whispered. She bent close, cradling Annie's head in her lap. The greenhouse flowers encircled them in a bower, their petals and leaves burgeoning with Capucine's nearness. "I could think of no other way."

"Then he's dead."

"Yes," said Capucine. "By his own hand, fairly. It's well known in the village that he tests his medicines before selling them. A good practice, until it isn't."

Annie searched for guilt or distress in her soul, and found neither.

"You ought to take over his business," Capucine continued. "The townsfolk like you. I'm sure the other towns you've visited liked you, too. It seems you did a great deal of Mr. Gleiber's work, anyway. I'll tell them what happened. That he tested a cure and it went wrong. And then..."

And then Annie could do as she liked. She could hitch up the horses and take the wagon east to New York City, south to Philadelphia, anywhere she pleased.

She moved her hand to touch Capucine's face. Capucine sighed, a surprised noise, and a curl of delight fluttered in Annie's stomach. Heady colour returned to Capucine's face; her cheeks blushed with roses and her eyes gleamed like forest pools. Annie sat up slowly, noting a mild ache at the back of her head. Her free hand caught Capucine's, nestling them both together in her lap. Capucine's eyes widened, unblinking, as Annie kissed her.

"I think I'm done traveling," Annie murmured. "I think the village of Vestal has snared another virgin."

Capucine laughed, deep in her throat. Her hand twined around Annie's, and her lips opened to Annie's lips, and in the midst of laughter and sweetness, in the fragment of space between their breaths, a violet bloomed.

CLUTCHING AIR

Jillian Bost

I struggled to climb the stairs, which moved like wooden waves. The sconces seemed to have vanished from the walls. I ought to have brought a candle.

I had just reached the top of the steps when a hand reached out to grab me. "Robert," a voice whispered.

With a cry I jerked away, for the hand was not the warm, pink flesh of a human hand.

It was a skeleton hand, white and blinding.

"Get away!" I cried. "Leave me be!"

The skeleton emerged from the shadows, and I whimpered as its empty eye sockets glowered at me, shining unnaturally in the dark.

The skeleton's jawbone chattered as if it were cold. "Robert," it whispered. "Robert, come to me."

The voice struck me with its familiarity, and I trembled. "Henry?"

The skeleton lunged at me, and I fell back down the stairs with a shout.

★ ★ ★

"Robert! Stop it!"

I thrashed about, certain the skeleton was coming for me. It would mash my flesh between its teeth until I was pink paste. "No! Get away from me!"

"Robert!"

I thrashed again, and a feminine shriek wrenched my eyes open.

I gasped in horror when I saw Elizabeth shrinking away from me, clutching her face. "My darling, did I…? Oh, no. I am so sorry, my love. Please forgive me."

She glared at me, but seemed to calm herself a moment later. "I forgive you, dear. You were having a dreadful nightmare."

I pulled her close to me, and ran my trembling fingers down her lush chestnut hair, so long it went to the small of her back. I settled back against the pillows. "It was indeed a horrible nightmare. I dare not tell you about it, it pains me so."

Henry, reaching out, nought but cold bone and those blank eye sockets, glowing as if from the pits of hell.

"Robert, my love…" Elizabeth pulled away from me and took my hand. "This isn't the first nightmare you've had of late." She drew in a deep breath. "This is in truth the first time I've been able to wake you."

"Why have you not mentioned this to me before?" I stroked her arm, for she'd begun to tremble. "Elizabeth, you need not fear to tell me anything."

"I didn't want to trouble you. You kept – you…" Her face reddened. "You often called for Henry," she said at last.

My heart sank. I wondered how I had slept so fitfully the past few days, and not known when I had called out the name of my dearest friend.

"Yes. I did dream of him," I said at last. "Though, not as he was. Something much worse."

Elizabeth nodded, her expression now stony. "He has been dead for some time, I understand?"

"Yes." I swallowed. "Four years, nearly."

"I have been very concerned for you of late, Robert. We've been married these six months, and–"

"The happiest six months of my life," I interjected.

Her lips turned up, but it was no smile. "I wish I could believe you."

I drew her to me again, and enfolded her in my arms. "Elizabeth, I would never lie to you."

She shook her head, her face pale in the sliver of moonlight that had escaped through the brocade curtains. "I'm certain you would never lie to me. But I also have no doubt you are unhappy, and have been for some time."

My heart plummeted to my stomach. "My love, I have no other wish than to be with you, and to make a life together." I kissed her hands and hair. "Let's forget this until the morning, at least. We both need sleep."

Elizabeth looked away for a moment, then sighed. "I suppose you're right." She burrowed back down into the sheets, turning away from me. "Goodnight, Robert."

"Goodnight, my darling." I lay on my back and closed my eyes, but I didn't sleep until the sun began to rise.

★ ★ ★

Elizabeth said nothing of our disturbed night as we breakfasted together. I couldn't say I had much desire to speak of it myself.

I'd just begun my second cup of coffee when Elizabeth delicately cleared her throat. She looked luminous in her pale blue silk gown. "I would like to speak to you about something."

I tried to keep my posture neat yet relaxed. "Yes?"

"Your nightmares," she began, but I waved her off.

"I slept very well last night after that little hiccough. You needn't worry about me." I poured bright cheer into my voice, belied by the cloud of the late morning.

"Nonsense," she snapped. "We both lay awake until the sun rose."

I hadn't fooled her, then. "Nevertheless—"

"I must insist on you listening to me, Robert," she said.

I folded my hands in front of me. "Very well. Say what you will."

"You should leave this house," my wife said, looking me straight in the eye.

"What—" I shook my head and laughed. "My darling, if I have been robbing you of your rest, I would happily sleep in a different room to ease your discomfort. I have no need to leave this house. I can't abandon my work—"

"You will not complete anything if you don't exorcise your demons!" she burst out, slamming her hands on the table.

I gaped at her. Since I had met her at a dinner party two years earlier, Elizabeth had never been anything but polite, sweet, and intelligent, with a thoughtfulness that could make a person believe anything she told them.

But not I. Not always.

I rose, and held out my hands. "It's out of the question, Elizabeth. I have no wish to be a tyrant to you, but you won't order me out of my own home."

Elizabeth frowned. "As you wish. You are the man of the house, after all."

Shame coloured my face. "Darling—"

"No. You know best." Elizabeth sank back into her chair, and took a sip of coffee. "I have a headache. I think I shall rest this afternoon."

"As you — yes, of course, my dear. Rest well. I shall be in my office should you need me." I withdrew from the breakfast table and headed toward my study, though I suspected I wouldn't do much but smoke and brood.

I settled at my desk and began to leaf through letters from my clients. A gentleman had written me, begging for help regarding the loud, obnoxious neighbours who were making his life hell.

My papers suddenly flew about the room, as if I had just opened the window.

With a curse, I raced over to the window to shut it, vowing that I would have words with our maid Betty for having meddled with my study.

But the window was shut tight. And my papers were still fluttering about on my desk.

My inkwell fell over, the darkness spreading with an ooze that threatened to pull me in.

"Robert."

I whirled around.

No one was there.

I gripped my hair. "The lack of sleep must be affecting me greatly. Or I am going mad." I ought to go upstairs and rest like Elizabeth, though not in the same room as she. My face burned as I thought of her rejection.

But how could I blame her? She'd been an angel to me since our courtship began over a year ago, ever patient and kind while I struggled through my mourning like a bereft widower, though I should have borne it with dignity. I ought to be giving her more care, and pay more attention to my own health, so that I could be the husband Elizabeth deserved.

I resolved to take my own rest upstairs (though I would respect my wife's space) and with luck and time, render myself of some use for the rest of the day.

I headed toward the unused bedroom at the back of the hallway, where I was determined to nap.

The door was unlocked, to my relief, and I pushed it open, wincing in irritation at the heavy creak.

A pile of bedsheets rose like a wave from the bed. I staggered back. "What the devil?"

I took a deep, gulping breath, and ran my hand over my eyes.

When I dared to look again, the sheets lay dormant on the bed. It looked as if Betty had just made it this morning. My heart continued to pound as I struggled to control my breathing. All was well. I was not losing my mind. I merely needed sleep.

"Stay where you are," I ordered the sheets, and flung myself onto the bed. Sleep soon took me.

★ ★ ★

When I awoke, it was dark. "I must have slept the afternoon away," I murmured, fumbling for my pocket watch. It was nowhere to be found.

I could ring for a servant. If I could remember where the bell was, I could call Williams and he would set me to rights.

"Robert," someone whispered, and my bones chilled. I felt as if I were floating out of my body for a moment, could even see myself convulsing in terror, and then with a jolt I was staring at nothing again.

Someone meant to drain me of my sanity.

"Who's–" I swallowed – "Who's there? I need a light."

"Robert," the voice whispered again. "Come to me."

I swallowed a moan. "Henry?"

"Come to me, Robert."

I couldn't go anywhere. I was trapped in a void. Who was this faceless formless being to demand anything of me?

And yet I would do anything for him, whatever spark or morsel of Henry that might be left, would follow the trail of the most meagre breadcrumbs to get to him. "Henry," I repeated. "Help me."

Suddenly I felt something bony grab my wrist and yank me into the abyss. I cried out in terror.

And fell into sunlight, poking through a dusty window and curtains.

It was still afternoon. I'd only slept a few hours at most.

My cursed brain had fooled me again. Though my muscles soon relaxed, I could not help but want to return to the dream. Perhaps it would have ended differently.

Or perhaps I would not care if it ended badly.

"Robert."

I jumped, then threw myself back onto the bed. "Elizabeth."

She walked into the room, her buttoned boots clacking against the floor. "I trust you've slept?"

I rubbed my face and discreetly wiped away the crust from my eyes. "Yes, I think I slept a few hours. Have you?"

She nodded. Her face remained cold, stony like a statue. "Will you walk with me? We've had too much rain the past few days, but now that it's settled…"

"Yes, of course. Let me make myself more presentable, and I'll join you shortly."

She nodded again and left the room.

I ran my fingers through my rumpled hair and sighed. I must appear as a complete madman to her, unshaven, with eyes more red than blue. What would convince her I was still the man she'd married?

A nagging thought pushed itself into my mind: perhaps she wanted me to be the husband I had yet to be.

Though we'd been married six months, we had only performed the conjugal act three times. Once on our honeymoon, and the other two times at her instigation. How could I refuse her? And Elizabeth was no displeasure to look upon, with her flowing chestnut locks and earnest hazel eyes. Her skin was luminous like moonlight, and her figure was soft.

And yet, and yet.

I squeezed my eyes shut until it hurt. "I must try for her, Henry. I'm sorry," I whispered.

★ ★ ★

Elizabeth's voluminous blue sleeve continuously brushed mine as we walked through the garden, though she declined to take my arm.

"My mind cannot help but be drawn again to what we spoke of at breakfast," she said, and I groaned.

"Elizabeth, please let the subject die." I flinched at my poor choice of words. "I would not leave you here alone with the servants, in the vague hope of convalescing somewhere far from home."

"Then perhaps we ought to consult Doctor Redmond."

I halted. "We will do no such thing."

She stared at me in surprise. "But he is a mere few miles away. You wouldn't have to travel far."

"I know that," I snapped, and pinched the bridge of my nose. "I feel better now that I've had some rest, and I'll see to it that I go to bed early tonight. All will be well tomorrow."

"Doctor Redmond," was all she said.

It was all I could do not to stomp away from her like a recalcitrant child. "I shall not." I would not be told I was unwell, or mad.

And I did not want to risk him seeing the pain in my eyes, and somehow guess its true cause.

Elizabeth regarded me with pure ice, and strode away from me.

★ ★ ★

That night, she declined to sleep in the same room with me, claiming another headache. So I promised to take a guest bedroom (though not the one I'd napped in earlier). I settled on the one next to our room, and tried not to think of my wife on the other side of the wall, of being robbed of her warmth, her gentle, floral scent, and her beating heart next to me, that I might know she was safe, and I was safe, and I had done what was right and proper in cleaving to her instead of the past.

I didn't want to be alone to stare at the blackness of the night, not lightened even by a sliver of moonlight, it seemed. I didn't want to be shivering in the cold, for a fire hadn't been lit in the room for months. I didn't want to hear that dreaded whisper of my name.

Except I did want it, more desperately than I craved water during a fever or chicken soup during a cold.

I heard footsteps creak in the hallway outside the room, and held my breath. Any moment now, I was certain, I would hear that scratchy whisper, like leaves come to life, say my name.

The doorknob rattled, and I bit back a moan. "Go away," I whispered, though I longed for him to come to me, to lie with me, to tell me he had always been near me and always would be, and he forgave me for all my transgressions before and after his death.

The door creaked open, and I could not hold back a whimper. His outline seemed to glow with something otherworldly, and I had a hysterical thought that I was in a cave, or a tunnel, and he had captured me, and I wanted to be his victim. I could see the shape of his collar-length hair, the shadow of his form, the strong muscles of his arms and legs. He'd always been stronger than me.

"Robbie," came the whisper, and I sucked in a breath.

No one called me Robbie but Henry. He had returned to me.

"Henry," I said, the lump in my throat threatening to block my windpipe. "What – what do you want of me?"

"Robbie... you forget me."

I shook my head, reaching out my hands to him, but unable to move from the bed. "I have never forgotten you. I never will."

The room shook. I must be dreaming. I must be.

"You lie with her..." the dry rasp accused me.

"She – she could never replace you," I cried, heart hammering in my chest. I knew nothing but him at this moment. "You were everything to me."

"You lie," he repeated, and the words that I should not have heard on this side of the grave cut me to the bone.

"Come to me," I blurted out, though I wanted to curse him, for speaking beyond the grave could not be natural. Yet I wanted only to hold him, to clasp his cold form with its unmoving heart against mine.

But Henry, whoever or whatever he was now, did not come to me.

I must be asleep. I wrenched my heavy arm and slapped my cheek; it stung.

This was not a dream.

But Henry had vanished.

The next morning, Elizabeth gave me no greeting but a raised eyebrow. I poured brandy in my coffee, not caring if it made me look like a drunkard.

I wiped my brow as I gave my wife a tremulous smile. "I have given your proposal more consideration, my dear. I don't think Doctor Redmond can help me. But I know who can."

★ ★ ★

I received a letter from Thomas Collins four days later, assuring me I was most welcome at Greydon Hall, and could stay as long as I wished.

I took leave of Elizabeth, who kissed me on the cheek, and wished me "a productive visit." Before she turned away, she briefly clutched my hand, a momentary touch that brought me flashes of our wedding night.

The coach alighted at the Red Lion Inn, where Mr. Collins had sent a servant to wait for my arrival. I was relieved to see Parsons, who I remembered from my previous visits. He tipped his hat to me, red-cheeked and cheerful. After we had an ale, we set off, and arrived at Henry's home just before nightfall.

My heart tremored as I gazed up at the stone, ivy-covered manse. It had never looked so cold, and I thought of tombs rather than homes, mouldering, half-eaten bodies instead of warm hearths. I pulled my greatcoat tight against me.

The door burst open before we'd even reached it, and Henry's father beamed at me.

"Mr. Elliot! Lovely to see you again," Mr. Collins said as he pumped my hand with vigour. "Your journey went well, I trust?"

I bowed my assent after he'd released me. "Please, sir, call me Robert. And may I thank you most heartily for allowing me to visit your family."

"Think nothing of it, my dear man. We're glad to have you. If I can be of any use to you during your stay, you must say the word immediately."

As we went into the drawing room, still as green and gilded as ever, my heart danced up to my mouth. It had been so long since I'd been here. I thought of the time Henry and I had tiptoed downstairs well past midnight, and drank brandy while whispering and giggling until the sun rose. His father had not been pleased that we'd slept through breakfast.

"Would you care for some brandy, Robert?" Mr. Collins asked, seemingly unaware of my agitation.

I sucked in a breath, and turned it into a polite cough. "Yes, that would be very kind." I folded my hands in my lap as we settled on the sofa. Mr. Collins signalled for drinks to be brought, and we rested by the fire, for the spring night was still cold.

"May I ask after Miss Collins? I hope she fares well," I said, fiddling with my hands.

"Poor Sarah took ill earlier today. But she will recover by tomorrow, and be glad to greet you, no doubt," Mr. Collins said.

"I hope her recovery is swift and smooth," I replied, not allowing myself to think of Henry's illness. His sister had a mere cold, no doubt.

The rest of the evening passed easily enough; I compelled myself to make pleasant conversation with Mr. Collins. Henry was spoken of only once, when Mr. Collins said, "I hope you won't mind – we've had trouble with leaking and all sorts of problems throughout the house. It's the strangest thing. So we've put you in Henry's room."

My jaw must have dropped, for Mr. Collins frowned. "If you're not amenable to–"

"No. I beg your pardon for interrupting, sir, but I would not trouble you any more on my account. I will stay in Henry's room." My heart began to beat against my tongue, and I was sure both organs would explode.

After a quick supper of beef and vegetables, we parted ways

until the morrow. I went to Henry's room with no small sense of trepidation. My hand shook as I opened the door, as if Henry's ghost would burst out and throttle me.

Before I could step over the threshold, a hefty form blocked my path. "Good evening, sir."

"Good Lo—" I stopped my exclamation when a glimmer of recognition struck my eye. "Mrs. Landon?"

The stout grey-haired woman gave me a lopsided smile. "Young Master Robert! How kind of you to remember an old lady like me."

She had been Henry and Sarah's nurse. I wondered why they kept her on, and what she'd been doing in Henry's room. "How very kind of you to remember me also," I said. "I haven't been to visit for... some time."

"You were Master Henry's greatest friend! He spoke of you much when he deigned to visit his old nurse."

I smiled. "It does my heart good to hear it, dear lady."

Mrs. Landon blinked slowly as a shadow passed over her face. "But Master Henry is here. Why does he not come to visit me? He used to read to me when I felt poorly. Such a lovely lad he was."

My heart lodged in my throat. I struggled to clear it. "Mrs. Landon, do you not remember Henry passed – passed away four years ago?"

Her face fell, then she straightened her wobbling chin. "Oh yes, the poor dear. Do not look at me so affright, good sir. I have not lost all my wits. I remember now. But." She clutched my hand. "But, you know..."

"Yes?" I said, croaking like a frog.

"I am not wrong. Henry is here." Mrs. Landon's eyes burned into mine. "You must find him."

"And then what?" I asked, feeling faint.

"You must send him back. The earth craves him. Master Henry must rest."

My eyes stung as I tried to process her strange words. "Yes, you're right. I promise I will help him."

"See that you do. He was always such a good, kind boy."

I turned away, lest she see my watery eyes. "Yes, madam."

I helped her up the stairs to her room, and made my unsteady way back to Henry's. I took a deep breath. If anything else leapt out at me, it would not be human.

I saw the room as it had always been, though it had been lately cleaned. Henry's toy soldiers from his childhood remained, along with all his books. And the bed of course had been freshly made. I wondered if anyone else had slept in here since his death. I hoped not. At least the counterpane was different. I didn't want to think of what we'd done on top of the last one.

My luggage had been placed at the foot of the bed. I took out the things I would need for bed, and wandered over to his bookshelf, my heart twitching more than beating.

I ran my fingers over the spines of the books, thinking of dust and skeletons. I suppressed a shudder.

My thumb caught on one thin volume, and I pulled the book out. It was blue, with gold lettering on the cover. A copy of *Aurora Floyd*, by Mrs. Henry Braddon.

I opened it to the front page, and read the inscription. A lump formed in my throat.

> *Dear Robert,*
> *I know you have a love for the fiction of Mrs. Braddon. I hope you will enjoy this little gift from me.*
> *In the meantime, my dearest friend, I am yours forever.*
> *Henry*

I cradled the book as if it were a newborn babe. Henry had purchased this book for me. He must have intended to give it to me, before his sudden death.

A gust of wind fluttered the pages of the book, though I still held it close to my chest. I wrapped my arms around it as if it were his body. "If you are here, Henry, come to me not as an angry wraith, but as my truest friend."

The doorknob rattled, and my heart strangled my throat. My lips formed his name, and I sank back onto the bed.

The door creaked open, and I held my breath.

Sarah swept into the room, her gown trailing along the carpet.

I sat up. "Sarah? What are you doing in here? Are you unwell?"

She turned to stare at me. Her eyes were glassy; she seemed to be focusing behind me.

Slowly I got to my feet, holding my hands up in front of me. "Sarah. I am Robert Elliot, Henry's friend. I'm staying with your family for a few days."

"Robert," she said, her voice raspy like scraping leaves. It made me shiver.

"Sarah, you ought to be in bed. Go back to your room, please."

"Robert," she whispered, holding out her arms. "Robert, come to me."

My heart clenched. "Sarah, you must go back to your room. You are tired. You can't be in here. This is my room for the next few days. It's not proper for you to be here."

She continued to stare at me, or rather, through me.

I had no choice. I gently took her by the arm. "Come along, now."

She gripped my wrist with iron force. "You've come back to me, Robert," she said, her voice suddenly deep, rich, smooth.

I sucked in a breath. "Henry." I tasted bile as my heart fluttered. What kind of trickery was this? Why should he do this to me?

She smiled. "You sound surprised."

"Henry," I said, smoothing back Sarah's hair. "I want to see you as you were. Not in the form of your sister. Please, won't you come to me as yourself?"

A shudder passed through Sarah, and she went limp in my arms.

I cursed under my breath. What was I to do now?

"Sarah," I whispered, laying her down on the bed, praying that no one in the house would stir. I patted her face gently, but she remained still.

There was an unconscious woman on my bed in the middle of the night. There was no way I would emerge from this unscathed.

"Please, for the love of God, woman, wake up," I whispered.

"Let the poor dear rest, she's had much to endure. My fault, I'm afraid."

I reared back in shock, and stared at the door.

But no one had come in.

"Over here, darling."

My head snapped in the direction of the window.

And there, at last, glorious, resplendent, and heavy with death, was my beloved Henry. I took in his collar-length wavy brown hair, and his eyes, oh, his eyes! Not empty bony sockets but shining green, green like the sea in a storm, and the tide had called him to me, and I to him. He was dressed as I remembered him, in slim-fitting dark trousers and a white buttoned shirt, with the top button left undone as he'd always left it when we were alone. He looked the same, though my brain screamed that this must be an illusion, a farce, a devilment.

We were mere feet from each other. God help me.

My limbs were shaking like jelly. I sank onto the edge of the bed, willing him to end my suffering.

When he made no move, I groaned like a dying bear, and held out my arms. "You've haunted me," was all I managed to say.

Henry shook his head. "You've been haunting me."

"How could I?" I said. "I have ached to catch even a glimpse of you, Henry."

He smiled sadly. "And you don't see? You anchor me to this world." He took a step toward me, and I melted. How I longed to hold him in my arms, as I had in the nights when I'd stayed here, and the lightning had cracked and thunder rumbled, and I'd snuck into his room, and we'd kissed and embraced under the covers. Yet I couldn't bring myself to move.

Henry moved toward me, and I shrank back, for all my desperation to have him near me. "Would you harm me?"

"Never," I whispered.

I felt a warm current of air waft near my face as he loomed closer, and I clutched at it. "You must choose one of us," he said. "Life or death."

I stared up at him, mute.

"On this side of the veil, we cannot be friends as we were. I would see you live again, and be content to wait for you, my darling."

I'd waited a thousand lifetimes for him after he'd died. Could I give him up again?

"Your stares, your aches and wants hold me fast like an iron grip," Henry said, penetrating me with his eyes. "Do you understand, Robbie?"

I shook my head, my body shivering at the lie. "You're not real."

"Would that that were true."

I sucked in a breath. "I really cause you pain? I cling to you and make you stay, when it is unnatural for you to do so?"

He nodded. His ethereal eyes seemed to shine. "I'm afraid so, my dearest."

"Can there be no happy reunion between the dead and their loved ones?"

"I don't know. I only know what I see before me, and that is you."

I blinked hard, and tried to steady myself, for my body very much wanted to fall. "So then you're saying I have no choice. I must let you go." How could I survive without him? Even if I should let him go, I would die.

What would that mean for us both? What would that mean for Elizabeth?

He took my hands, and I relished the strange, staticky feel of them. "I want you to live a full life." His gaze lingered on my wedding ring. "Wherever you may find it. And you cannot do that with me trailing you like a wraith. One of us must make the sacrifice."

I drew in a deep breath even as every part of me threatened to howl like a wolf. The love I bore him threatened to tear me up, and I was a whisper away from welcoming it. "Then let it be me. I will release you from your ghostly, ghastly bonds."

God help me.

"One moment," he whispered, and glided forward to press his wispy lips against mine. I held my breath so he could have my own breath. Nothing could be more of a treasure to me, even if I were given all the jewels of the world.

"Goodbye, Robbie." Henry caressed my cheek, and I closed my eyes, letting the hot tears drip down my flushed face.

"Goodbye, Henry. Go now and rest." I stifled a sob as I gazed upon his soul one last time.

He gave me a faint smile, and turned toward the window.

Then, mercifully quickly, he faded into the night. I could have convinced myself I was hallucinating, and for a moment I did, until my heart seized in indignation.

I touched my face where he'd caressed me. It burned.

My heart crackled oddly. I went to the mirror, and saw the traces of his fingers, red on white.

★ ★ ★

"You look as handsome as ever, Robert," Elizabeth said, as she settled next to me on the sofa. It had grown cold in the months since my return, and we spent more time sitting close in the evenings.

"You don't think I ought to cover it with powder?" I teased.

She smiled; her eyes were soft as she caressed the traces of Henry's fingers on my face. "No. I know what those marks mean to you."

I took her hand in mine and kissed it. "I hope you know what you mean to me," I told her, and watched her sudden, happy tears sparkle like diamonds.

"I do."

FUN AT PARTIES

K. Blair

My haunting began with a parlour game. I believe Lottie herself suggested the game, having grown tired of cards and idle gossip. A room full of unmarried women lends itself to delight in superstition, a giddy fearfulness at tempting fate. I didn't want to play; had no interest in divination or summoning of spirits or determining future husbands. But it would have been rude to decline the host's invitation — and it was her birthday after all. Lottie pressed the hand-mirror into my hand, malicious delight in the taut corners of her smile as she pushed me into the dark hallway. My only accompaniment was muffled giggles and the flickering candle flame.

You have to walk backwards up a staircase for it to work. I have heard some say that they believe the dead walk backwards or that the future is always at our backs, pressing itself against us. I went into that future with wax-wrapped knuckles. A noticeable chill came over me, my skin breaking out in goose-flesh as a shiver went down my spine. My reflection changed between the fourth and fifth step. I saw a blood-kissed maiden, jawline sharper than my own soft face. Mouth a moue of disappointment as if I should know better than to partake in silly parlour games. Her name came to my lips unbidden.

I fled, clattering down the stairs and out the old oak doors of Lottie's estate. Sprawling onto the lawn, wet from the rain, and taking deep, heaving breaths, I threw the mirror as far as I could. The darkness swallowed it up, a temporary comfort. I knew she was not so easily lost when I took my leave that night. Her hungry gaze reflected in the windows of my carriage.

From then on she followed in the only way she could. In the backs of spoons, the bottom of glasses. How delicate she appeared in crystal, murmuring my name as if she sought to conjure me. I covered every mirror to escape her gaze, cringing away from how it pierced through to the core of me. But at night I dreamed of that crimson visage, hands outstretched, always reaching, always pressing.

After months of this – months of wooden cutlery and opaque glasses, of drawn curtains and blindfolded bathing – my maid, whilst cleaning my bedroom, forgot to replace the fabric with which I had covered the floor-length mirror opposite my bed. A gift from my late father, sentiment prevented me from removing it from my chambers completely. I returned late that night from a social engagement, where I pretended to all that I was perfectly fine. As I struck the match to light the candle wick, I realised the cover was missing.

She stood, hands pressed against the glass, dressed in a tattered lace nightgown to match my own. I was bewitched, frozen in place like a butterfly pinned to a display board. Both of us stared at one another, breath held as if waiting for the other to speak. The maid's knock upon my door broke the spell. I hurried to hide my spectre from view. As she helped me dress for breakfast, I realised that the night had slipped away from us.

I lost my face in the curve of hers. I started to worry that I was always bloody, a stain where a woman once breathed. I thought of us as two beings moving in tandem. When I was taking tea in the drawing room, was she similarly lifting a cup to her lips? When I was in the library, running my fingers along the spines, I imagined her doing the same, a light touch so as not to leave a mark. I felt a companionship in this assumed parallel life, a strange kind of intimacy. I found myself removing the coverings, seeking something I could not name, something that felt raw and fevered.

I left the cover on the bedroom mirror. That night, I wore my best dress, eager to make a good impression. I told my maid to prepare me for a social engagement I wasn't planning on attending. This time I refused to flinch away from her sight and accept all that she was, as I should have done when I took that first step backwards. She was there, waiting for me, with a bloody smile. I pressed myself against that cool glass and when she reached for me, I reached back.

THE DEAD SPACE

Stewart Horn

I began my university education in the first year of the new century, a year to be filled with events variously wonderful, exciting and tragic. It was far from my first visit to Glasgow, not even my first encounter with the university, and I felt in my youthful arrogance that I had nothing to fear in the noisy and bustling city.

I arrived, somewhat ostentatiously, by motor car, my father having made all the arrangements as was his wont in most matters. I rode in the back and my valet, Johnstone, rode beside our driver. The journey would frankly have been faster and more comfortable by train but Father could never resist an opportunity to flaunt his wealth.

Glasgow was an odd mixture then: filthy slums, industrial areas and busy docks all blackened with soot, yet with the grand houses of wealthy merchants a short walk away. Many of the mansions rivalled the grandeur of my own family home, despite being mere pieds-a-terre for gentlemen with larger estates outside the city.

My father had arranged lodgings for me in Park Circus, a quiet area of the city close to the university. The owner of the splendid four-storey town house in an oval terrace rented out single floors to travelling merchants or students from respectable families.

When we pulled up outside, a small plump lady rushed out to greet us as I stepped gratefully from the car.

"Alexander Duncan," I offered. "Delighted to meet you." She spoke for several gushing seconds and I'm embarrassed to admit that I understood barely a word of her patois. I had dealt with the Glaswegian working class before but this seemed an extreme example.

Johnstone, however, conversed with apparent ease and in a very short time we were ensconced in our apartments. The driver brought up my luggage and, under strict orders from home, returned the car to the country.

For a single floor of a town house, our lodgings were grand: four principal apartments that served as reception room, a bedroom each for Johnstone and myself, and one that served as both dining room and study. There was also a small but functional kitchen and a luxurious and fully plumbed bathroom. It was adequately furnished in a modern style, with some touches of art nouveaux that I rather liked: a refreshing change to the ancient and much reupholstered furniture of my family pile.

The university building was thirty years old then, but in a neo-Gothic style with cloisters and a great baroque tower copied from older and grander establishments. I felt at home immediately. On the first day, along with a few other undergraduates, I was given a tour and a reception in the rector's rooms. I rather feel that the recipients of this honour were chosen based on family wealth rather than merit, but I was at an age when I took such privilege for granted.

Lunch was an informal affair, with perhaps twenty students largely in tweeds and only the rector in full gown. It would scarcely be worth mentioning, had it not been the day I first encountered Fraser.

Perhaps his bearing first drew my attention: he was more erect than the other servants, with none of the subservience expected of the serving classes in those times. He was slight in build, with neatly oiled light-brown hair and a strong face. He returned my look with a directness that might be considered impudent, but his eyes were such a striking blue, his features so regular and beautiful, that in truth I was already smitten.

I confess here that my intentions at that moment were less than honourable: I knew from my boarding school days that adequate money will entice working class boys as easily as girls to a stranger's bed, and I hatched a plan to seduce him. It mainly involved making sure I made eye contact as he served each course, holding his gaze infinitesimally longer than would be appropriate, and anticipating a less subtle advance when the time came to depart, but as he passed me my coat I faltered.

"Thank you," I managed, oddly delighted that he still looked me straight in the eye, though he did not return the smile. "What's your name?"

"Fraser, sir," he replied.

"Very good, Fraser," I said, and we parted. I was not a little confused by my reticence but put it down to my being in new surroundings.

Little of interest happened in the following weeks. I settled into my studies of philosophy and religion and ate well, gaining a little weight. The meals at the university were rather heavy, but were served by Fraser every day except Wednesday. We exchanged few words but many meaningful looks, though that may have been only in my imagination. I made a point of leaving a cash gratuity when Fraser served, though my bills were paid by Johnston, to whom my father had allocated charge of my resources. When I required funds he dispensed freely, and I wondered how large a sum would trigger a question of how I intended to spend it, or a letter home to Father.

★ ★ ★

One cold morning in November I awoke in daylight in a chilled room and immediately knew something was amiss, as Johnstone should have been up hours before stacking coal on the fires, and woken me with tea at seven, at which time it would have been still dark.

I confess, I was a little the worse for drink and had slept later than usual and was in need of fluids. My customary pot of tea would have been welcome. I arose, donned a dressing gown and stoked and added coal to the fire before looking for Johnstone.

He was not in the public rooms so I knocked on the door of his chamber.

"Johnstone," I said, quite loudly and firmly. "Are you quite well?"

I knocked and hailed him again with no response before trying the door, which was not locked and opened easily.

The room was smaller than mine but generous for a servant, and very dark. There was a smell, sweet and sulphurous yet not entirely unpleasing, like seaweed. I crossed the room and pulled the curtains wide, eliciting a moan from the bed. Johnstone pulled a blanket over his head and I speculated unkindly that he too had imbibed on the previous evening.

"Are you ill, man?" I asked, but the response was only a laboured wheezing. I leaned closer, but not too close lest it be influenza, or consumption. I have seen strong men taken from this world by these and had no wish to succumb myself. I attempted to tease the blankets from over his head but he held on desperately.

"No light," he gasped, in a voice that sounded like he spoke through sand.

"As you wish," I said, and closed the curtains and lit a candle, ignoring the electric light to which I was still not quite accustomed.

"There," I said in a soothing tone. "Shall I fetch a doctor for you?"

He pulled the blanket from his face with a great effort and looked at me from sunken eyes.

"I'm sorry, Master Xander," he croaked. "I tried to rise but my legs would not support me."

"I shall send for a doctor at once." A brief word with the landlady, and sixpence for a boy to run the errand, and a doctor appeared and locked himself in the room with Johnstone for almost half an hour.

"He is severely dehydrated," he said on emerging. "I have not seen a case so bad since my time in the desert." I have noticed that men who have seen action in any conflict are apt to bring it up at the slightest excuse. He waited a moment, perhaps expecting me to enquire further about his service, before continuing.

"He is to drink clean boiled water, and tea, and to be kept warm. Give him soup if he will take it, and I'm afraid he will be unable to resume his duties for some days."

I thanked the doctor and saw him out, apologising for the coldness of the rooms as I had still not set all the fires. I composed a note to the university asking for a temporary servant, since I had little skill in the kitchen, or anywhere else for that matter. I also wrote to my father to appraise him of the situation and posted both missives.

A scant two hours later the landlady knocked at my door and I opened to see her, accompanied by none other than my beautiful waiter, Fraser, neatly dressed for work, blue eyes twinkling and a smile on his lips. The landlady mistook my expression.

"I know he's scrawny but it's what the university sent."

"Oh no, he'll be perfect. Please come in." The landlady stepped aside and Fraser walked into my apartment, a moment that had played a large part in my fantasies since that first meeting. The culmination of that fantasy is not fit for print.

I showed him round the rooms and discussed his duties: all of Johnstone's normal tasks plus a little nursing of Johnstone himself. I realised as I showed him the kitchen that I had not eaten at all that day, and I said so.

"Shall I make the preparation of lunch my first task, sir?" he asked.

"Excellent idea. The doctor suggested soup for Johnstone, and that would rather suit me too."

"Certainly, sir," he said, and began to search the larder and cupboards.

I settled myself in a chair by the fire to warm myself a little and tried to do some reading to make some use of the time. I struggled to concentrate, however, aware of the man I had known and respected my whole life, lying in his sickbed in a darkened room, and also of the beautiful young man in my kitchen. I pictured him removing his jacket and bending over the range and, once again, my thoughts took a turn that I would hesitate to put to paper even in this enlightened age.

Presently, he brought a tray of bread, cheese and cold cuts and a decanter of wine, explaining that the soup would take an hour to prepare and he did not want me hungry. He said this with a smile that stirred my heart and made me wonder if he were being wilfully coquettish. The soup, when it came, was very good: more richly seasoned than I was used to with a hint of something like cayenne.

Later, I looked into Johnstone's room and found him looking a little better, though still in bed. His skin was less pale but still not a healthy hue and his eyes had regained a little of their customary fire. I would say he looked happier though I have never in my life seen the man smile. There was a sour smell in the room too but he refused to have the window or curtains opened.

"Has Fraser been seeing to your needs?" I asked.

"He has been most attentive, sir," he replied. "Though the soup was rather peppery." I smiled, partly because Johnstone complaining was a sign that he was returning to his normal self, and partly because the thought of Fraser attending to a man's needs had conjured a very different scenario in my mind. I really was distracted, but happily so, and pleased to find Fraser waiting for me in the sitting room.

"With your permission, sir, I shall make a bed up for myself on the sofa, until Johnstone is fit to resume his duties." I scanned his face for any sign of guile – perhaps he was expecting...

"I think it prudent for me to remain on the sofa, sir," he said, as if reading my mind.

"Of course. If you would draw me a bath I shall retire immediately afterwards. I like tea at seven a.m. and breakfast a half hour later."

"Yes, sir."

* * *

That night I dreamed oddly: of fields of the most beautiful roses whose scent dulled all care. The field was strewn with terribly mutilated corpses, some dismembered, yet I accepted that everything was as it should be – such was the effect of the flowers' perfume. Some of the corpses were less dead than others and twitched with energy, and I felt they might come at me had they power of movement, though I felt no fear.

I was dragged from the dream by a terrible crashing and a man shouting. I leapt from my bed and rushed to the hall in time to see Fraser in his nightclothes enter Johnstone's room, the source of the commotion. I rushed in behind and my senses were assailed. The smell hit first: the flowers from my dream but overlaid with the much stronger and more terrible stench of dead things and decay. I could hear Johnstone's cries of terror and thought I saw a figure crouched on his bed, arms beneath the prone form as if in embrace. It was a pale and featureless thing, yet I had the impression of black eyes turning towards me. I may have swooned for a moment for I came to my sense to see Johnstone's room brightly lit, Johnstone flailing his arms weakly as at an invisible attacker and Fraser pounding on the wall at the foot of the bed.

I went to Johnstone first, pushing his arms down and talking soothingly. His breathing was quick and shallow as if in a panic.

"Hush man," I said. "We're here to look after you. Everything is fine." His arms were icy. Fraser returned to the bed.

"How is he?" he asked.

"Cold," I replied. "Fetch some brandy." He was gone and back in a moment, and the fiery liquid had the calming effect I had hoped for when I pressed it between Johnstone's cold lips. Fraser had extinguished the electric light and lit some candles so the room felt less like a tomb, and was examining the section of wall he had been attacking earlier.

"What are you doing?" I asked.

"It went through the wall here," he said, frowning as if worrying over a difficult puzzle. "I got a punch in. It was like punching a pillow, if pillows were stuffed with ice, and ice were soft as feathers." He was as confused as I, but I realised at that moment a vital difference between us: faced with an inexplicable and perhaps supernatural threat my reaction was to freeze and disbelieve my own senses; Fraser's first instinct was to punch the thing.

* * *

The doctor's visit the following morning was similar to the first, though he declared that Johnstone's condition had deteriorated. We were to keep him warm and encourage him to drink water. He offered no likely cause, and despite my interest in folklore and myth, I had no explanation. What creature can move through solid walls yet cause harm to a strong man?

I left Fraser to care for the poor man and walked to the university. I had no intention of attending my scheduled lectures; rather I sought out a man I thought may be of help.

Professor Summers lectured in Eastern and European folklore and his lectures were always entertaining, if not always credible. He taught that an open mind was an academic's greatest asset, tempered with critical and sceptical thought, never ruling out a supernatural explanation but investigating all more likely avenues first. He cut an imposing figure with his barrel chest and mighty beard. I recounted faithfully all that had occurred and he listened intently, occasionally stroking his beard. When I finished he looked at me closely.

"This is all true?"

"On my word, professor." He gazed at me deeply for another long moment then stood up abruptly.

"I think we both know what we're dealing with," he said. "I never expected to see one here." He moved to a bookcase and began to browse.

"Never expected to see what?"

"A vampire, of course!"

I couldn't help it; a laugh escaped my lips before I could stop it. The steely gaze he turned on me silenced me at once.

"If you didn't believe such things you would not have come to me. You would now be standing before one of my colleagues in the faculty of medicine. So give up the pretence, boy, and show me some respect!"

I stood and bowed my head. "You are absolutely right, professor. I apologise." He selected three books from the shelf and sat down again.

"It's difficult to say anything definitive about vampires; there are hundreds of legends from all over the world. There are similarities and common themes, but a great deal of variation. There could be a hundred species of the blighters, or each folk tradition may have modified their experiences to accommodate local beliefs. Give me an hour to refresh myself on the subject then I shall accompany you and examine the victim. You may wait in the outer chamber and read this." He passed me a slim volume. "It's hardly an academic work but will give you an idea of what we're facing."

He opened and began to peruse one of the larger volumes, dismissing me. I settled myself in his reception room and opened the little book. It was called *Accounts of Vampirism in Europe*, and comprised short chapters, each detailing the author's visit to a locale and hearing a tale of relevant experience.

There were none of the articulate high-born gentlemen I expected having recently read Bram Stoker's diverting fairy tale; instead most stories described pitiful hungry creatures, clinging to life by preying on the weak. I read around fifteen chapters and only one described an attack on a healthy adult: they seemed to target children, the elderly, or those already afflicted with some weakness. The methods of dispatch were varied: decapitation was common, as were penetration with stakes or iron nails. It was all rather grisly.

The professor's door burst open and he emerged as energised as a child at the beach. I wondered if he was enjoying Johnstone's unfortunate situation, and this led me to question my own feelings: was I secretly pleased? Did I wish Johnstone permanently disabled so that I may have the pleasure of Fraser as a permanent valet?

"No time to waste!" the professor said, collecting hat and coat from the stand. "We have a demonic menace to deal with." I barely had time to collect my own outerwear before following him.

After a brief stop at an ironmongers to collect some steel posts (with no explanation), we arrived breathless at the apartment, the professor having insisted that walking was healthier and just as quick. I struggled to keep up as he strode up the staircase and barged inside. My heart was beating fast: certainly from physical exertion, but also from the excitement of being in a real adventure, and perhaps a little at the thought of seeing Fraser again. He really had gotten under my skin.

"Where's the victim?" the professor demanded as Fraser emerged from the kitchen. I hurried behind, giving Fraser an apologetic smile.

"This way," I said, and showed the professor to Johnstone's little room at the back of the building.

"Open the curtains!" he bellowed, rushing to the bed and laying a hand on Johnstone's forehead. Fraser obeyed and the room was flooded with brilliant sunlight. Johnstone moaned and tried feebly to pull the covers over his head but Summers pulled them back roughly.

"No nonsense, man," he said. "I'm going to save your life

if you let me." He turned Johnstone's head from side to side, examining his neck closely, and pulled the covers down to reveal a sweat-damp nightshirt. Johnstone must have sunk yet further; he barely managed a whimper as Summers pulled the garment up and examined his limbs and torso.

It was a matter of mere seconds before he covered Johnstone up again and said, "Good." He turned to Fraser. "Where did the creature disappear?" Fraser showed him the patch of wall just beyond the foot of the bed.

"It's just as solid as the rest, sir," he said, tapping it. The professor knocked all over the wall with his fists before concurring. He looked out the window, opened it and stuck his head out, looking from side to side then turning back with a frown.

"I have a theory," he said. "How well do you know the neighbours?"

"Not at all, I'm afraid," I replied.

"Then it's high time for introductions. I believe you have a dead space, but I should like to see next door to be certain." He measured the floor in paces and made some notes in his pocket book, then turned to me. "You best stay here. I shall go and measure the room in the next house. If I have to be rude it won't reflect badly on you." With that he rushed out of the room and downstairs.

Fraser and I looked at each other, dumbfounded, for a moment.

"I think a sherry would be in order, don't you?" I finally ventured.

"As you wish, sir."

Damn his professionalism, I thought.

★ ★ ★

A short time later as I settled in the sitting room with a glass of sherry, there was a commotion outside, raised voices and someone quite clearly threatening to call for a constable. This was swiftly followed by the professor's unmistakeable heavy tread on the stairs. He burst into the room.

"There is a dead space!" he announced. "Your terrace is curved, so the room should be wider at the back. It's not: in fact it narrows a little, so there is a wedge of empty space between these two houses. I bet that's where the blighter is hiding." He checked his pocket watch and turned to Fraser. "We have two hours till sunset. Find us a sledgehammer and a pickaxe; we'll go down to the cellar and break through the wall."

I interrupted. "We really must ask the landlady's permission before we start knocking down walls."

"If you don't care about your man dying! He won't survive another night, and moving him will do no good – the beast has his scent now."

"Sorry to interrupt, sirs," Fraser said, "but might it not be quicker to break in from the attic? We can break through pine floorboards more easily than stone walls."

The professor took him roughly by the shoulders and said, "Bright lad. Well done. In that case, fetch hammers and chisels and a good saw. And two lengths of stout climbing rope."

I fetched the landlady and explained our intention, which sparked a short but quite heated debate: I agreed to pay for any subsequent repairs, and to deal directly with the owner of the building if necessary. I think our exchange was more detailed but I only managed to catch about one word in three of the woman's dialect.

A short time later the four of us were in the loft, which as expected was sheeted in pine floorboards. The professor measured the area out in paces and drew a chalk circle on the floor.

"There," he said, and stepped back, wordlessly inviting Fraser and me to commence the destruction. He started doing something complicated with the ropes while Fraser and I each took a hammer and chisel to the first board, which was up in a very short time, releasing a terrible smell.

"My word," I exclaimed. "It's the very same smell from my dream."

"Of course it is," Summers replied. "It's how this kind of blighter operates. I suspect he has his eye on you as his next meal when your man is exhausted. We must get him earthed as soon as possible."

"Earthed?"

"I'll explain while you're sawing! Get that bloody hole made."

In a few minutes we had created a hole large enough for a man to fall through into sixty feet of darkness, while the professor talked of the importance of earth to certain vampires: they need soil to sustain them but can be robbed of their power by being pinned to the earth, just like grounding an electrical current. He came and inspected the hole.

"Perfect," he said. "Duncan, you're nominated."

"Why me?" I protested.

"Look at us, man. You are the slightest of us. Even your man here has a bit more muscle about him, and I'm the weight of the two of you combined!"

He proceeded to tie a knot round both my thighs, up between my legs and round my waist several times, the rope emerging like an umbilical cord from near my bellybutton, over a rafter directly above the hole and twice round an adjacent rafter. I was thoroughly trussed.

They first lowered another rope with one of the hammers, several steel posts and a burning lamp. We watched it descend until it hit the ground, looking very small and distant. So when I stepped off the edge and allowed the rope to support all my weight it was not a completely black chasm into which I was lowered, merely a very dark one.

I clung to the rope for dear life as Fraser lowered me. I looked around but the walls were invisible, or black. Though I could not see them I felt them press in, as if they would snap shut and crush me. It was a foolish fancy, but tenacious. I tried closing my eyes but that helped not at all. I also expected the rope to snap at any moment and plunge me to my death. As I descended, however, the lamplight grew brighter and I began to make out the texture of the brickwork, reassuringly inanimate and solid, though still somewhat imposing in its closeness.

At last I landed. Fraser cleverly fed a bit more rope so I could move around without untying myself. The floor was a long thin wedge, very roughly littered with rubble and broken bricks, and I scanned, unsure of exactly what I was looking for. I kicked the rubble about, holding the lamp above my head, but there was nothing to see. I suppose I had expected a coffin, or a stone sarcophagus containing a bloated corpse I could easily impale and solve the problem in an instant.

I looked up to the little square of light in the distance. "There's nothing here," I called.

The professor's voice echoed down. "The blighter is in there somewhere. Look harder; he could be in a small space."

I moved as close as I could to the narrowest point but could still see only rubble, nowhere even a child could hide. I looked up and the square of light that was my contact with the world was gone. I panicked momentarily, thinking that my colleagues had abandoned me to darkness before realising what it meant. I took a step back and the hatch came back into view.

"There's something above me. It may be a shelf where the creature can roost."

"Good show!" shouted the professor. "We'll lift you up!"

"Not yet." I attached the lamp to the rope above my head and picked up two of the steel poles and a hammer. "I'm ready." The slack in the rope began to rise, lifting the lamp with it and I had a moment of vertigo when my feet left the ground. I was pulled slowly upwards, rotating gently but uncontrollably; I suspect I was level with the ground floor when I saw the first section of floorboards.

"Stop," I called. My ascent halted and I swung and rotated gently.

"What do you see?"

At the narrowest section of the wedge was a small area of ordinary floorboards. "There's a shelf. I'm going to investigate." I shifted my weight and began to swing. A simple back and forth motion was impossible and I couldn't help going round in circles, bumping into the walls several times before gaining a foothold.

It was a thin triangle of floorboards, thickly coated with dust. I scraped at the floor and walls with a steel pole as far as I could reach into the corner, but there was nothing. Not even a spider moved.

"Pull me up further," I called. I realised as my feet once again left solid ground that the next shelf would be level with my own lodgings and therefore the creature's most likely roost. I spun and bounced off walls again but was learning to accept and roll with the motion and stay relaxed. A few moments later I saw the next shelf and in the dim lamplight could make out what looked like a crumpled blanket pushed towards the narrowest point.

"Stop," I called.

I swung again, punishing already bruised shoulders on the unyielding brick walls until my feet planted themselves on the shelf. The sad little pile of fabric, a size one might leave as bedding for a cat, took on a sinister aspect up close. It was so small and innocuous, but filled with the promise of horror. I poked gingerly at it with a pole and dust rose like smoke. Further inspection revealed a pile of clothes: britches, shirt, jacket and leather shoes. They were fusty but more or less intact, and must have been here since the building was completed four decades previously. I couldn't help but wonder whether the clothes had been occupied when deposited here, and what had become of the wearer. A corpse could not have rotted away fully in so short a time.

"What have you found?" came the professor's voice.

"An empty suit of clothes, covered in dust."

"No remains?"

"Not a thing."

"Damn."

There was a little conversation and Fraser's voice drifted down. "Professor Summers has gone to check on Johnstone. He says you should remain vigilant."

"I wasn't planning to take a nap."

"The sun has gone down, sir. A good half hour ago."

"Does that mean the creature is at large?"

"The professor seems to think so."

I panicked a little, I confess. The small triangle of floor on which I perched was lit well enough but most of the space was in darkness, and a bloodthirsty beast could be watching, stalking, as good as invisible. I pictured it clinging to the wall like a monstrous insect, beady eyes on its prey: the slight young man on a tiny wooden shelf.

My fearful reverie was interrupted by shouting from through the wall. Though I could not make out the words, Summers' deep and gruff tones were unmistakeable. The shouting continued for several seconds, increasing in ferocity, then silence fell like the collective hushed breath of a crowd waiting for the guillotine to fall.

"I'm still here, sir," Fraser called gently, as if reading my need for reassurance in the darkness.

"Thank you, Fraser," I almost whispered, certain he could not hear me.

I looked all round and up and down the dead space and back into the inner corner of the wedge, and gasped in terror. A hand was emerging from the wall.

Slowly, as if pulling itself through mud, more of the arm followed, another arm, a bony elbow, a shoulder, and the face! Oh God, the face: little more than grey leathery skin stretched over a skull, eyes black as anthracite with no trace of pupils, lips drawn back from yellowed teeth that gnashed and snapped like a mad dog.

I have read of men frozen with fear and thought it a foolish notion, but now I understood. My limbs refused to move;

my mind failed to make sense of a man-shaped thing *crawling through a brick wall*. The terrible eyes fixed on me as an owl's eye fixes on a mouse.

As soon as it was free of the wall it pounced, knocking me from the shelf so we both swung uncontrollably. Its arms clamped round me, pinning my own arms to my side, broken teeth snapping at my face. I managed to get a good headbutt or two in and the grip relaxed so I could once again move my arms and keep the terrible jaws from my face. At the same time I felt a sudden rapid descent – had Fraser been unable to hold our combined weight?

It was a matter of a few seconds until we landed and I managed to push the creature from me. It had little weight to it, like a child, but it was on its haunches again in a moment and sprang once more, knocking me off my feet. There was no tension at all in the rope now. Surely Fraser had not abandoned me! I fought as well as I could with fists, elbows and feet but the creature was strong, so fast, and I felt a sharp pain on my fore-arm. It had gashed me with sharp fingernails and now lunged its head at the wound as if to lap at the dripping blood. I spun and lashed out with another elbow but its mouth found the wound and bit deeper. I screamed, and I silently cursed my life, my family, and Fraser for leaving me alone with this terrible foe.

Then the sucking mouth was gone from me; there was a flurry of movement and Fraser was there. He had coiled a rope round the creature's neck and was hauling at it, trying to wrestle it to the ground. My eyes were starting to dim and I feared I would lose consciousness, but I swung a foot under the creature's leg and it tumbled to the ground, allowing Fraser to straddle it as if on horseback.

"Sir, the posts! Impale the thing! Nail it to the ground!" The room spun so I could hardly tell brick wall from dirt floor, but my eyes fixed on one of the steel posts and I grabbed at it. I swung the pole overhead and fell over with it, my own bodyweight giving it the momentum necessary to pierce the creature's stomach. For the first time, a sound escaped its lips, a gasp that could have been pain or fury, and there was a gush of dark blood. I sprawled on the ground, dizzy and nauseous now, but Fraser called to me. "The hammer, sir! Drive the post right through! Over there."

I followed his gesturing head and saw the hammer, managed to pick it up and with the last of my strength struck the free end of the steel post, pinning the creature like a moth on a board. It went still at last and Fraser relaxed, standing up and coming to me, inspecting the wound.

"Nothing to worry about, sir," he said soothingly. He extracted a pocket handkerchief and tied a quick and efficient tourniquet, slowing the bleeding. He was gone from my sight for a moment.

I looked at the creature again, a small, sad and emaciated thing, and felt something like pity. I still knew little about its nature, but had it once been human? Had it been cursed to this life?

I had the further thought, even as my consciousness began to waver, that I had killed something, or someone, just for following its nature. There were those who would kill me without a qualm if they found out about my Uranian tendencies.

Fraser reappeared holding all the other poles and the hammer. He set to work and in a minute or two there were six steel posts through various parts of the beast's corpse, then he returned to my side.

Face to face, he examined my wounded arm and I closed my eyes, more than anything desiring the solace of sleep. The brisk slap on my face revived me and my eyes snapped open.

"Stay with me, sir. I have been through quite enough today and I will not allow you to die. Do you understand?"

I nodded and smiled at him, noticing a tear-streak down one of his cheeks. "I will do anything you ask," I said. He leaned in and kissed me full on the lips.

His head jerked back, shocked by his own action.

"Sorry, sir, I meant no..."

I chuckled weakly. "Don't worry." I paused a moment. "I'm thirsty."

"I'll have to leave you for a short while," he said, and started to climb the rope. He was up astonishingly quickly and I thought that he must be much stronger than he looked and that I should like to see him shirtless and admire the muscles more closely. A minute later my own rope grew taught and I began to levitate.

I do not believe I lost consciousness during my ascent and the journey back to my chamber, though the memory is hazy. I have a recollection of walking, albeit supported and guided by Fraser's strong arms. He patiently undressed me, helped me to bed, and gave me several drinks of water. My mind drifted but started awake when I felt the pain on my arm; Fraser was using gauze to apply liquid to the wound. That was only a moment, however, then I slept.

★ ★ ★

I awoke late next morning, hungry, thirsty and somewhat disorientated, as if after too much Claret. The sunlight was trying to push between the heavy velvet curtains. I reached to the bedside and rung the bell to summon Johnstone, remembering as the sound tinkled through the apartment that Johnstone had been ill, and the rest of the adventure came rushing back like a terrible nightmare. Fraser entered, looking serious.

"Fraser," I said, "you're okay?" He nodded. "Where's Johnstone? And Professor Summers?" His eyes flicked to the floor for a moment and he fixed his gaze on me again.

"I'm afraid Johnstone died in the night," he said. I nodded, half-expecting this news. "The professor took a blow to the head but has fully recovered and is, I believe, back at his desk this morning."

"What of... the creature?"

"The professor considers it adequately earthed to pose no further threat. He has arranged to have cement poured over it, which he says will hold it for a century or two."

I digested all this news for a long moment. "Poor Johnstone," I said, surprised at how little sadness I felt.

"Sir," Fraser said, "I shall arrange a short-term replacement valet for you until a message can be sent to your father. I shall return to my duties at the university." He stared at the floor and looked shrunken, like a schoolboy awaiting punishment.

"Do you not wish to remain in my service?"

He did not look up. "I overstepped the mark last night, sir." His eyes flicked up for a moment and returned to contemplation of his shoes. "I believe that, in the heat of action, I forgot my place."

"Are you referring to the kiss?" He winced at the word.

"Yes, sir. I would consider it a great service if you were not to mention it to anybody at the university."

"Look at me." He obeyed, and the fear in those beautiful blue eyes tugged at my heart. I stood, steadying myself a little on the bedside table, and took the few steps necessary to reach him and put a hand on his shoulder, noting him flinch a little.

Many fine words and inspiring speeches rushed through my mind in the seconds we stood in silence. I wanted to confess all my lustful thoughts, tell him how my admiration for him had grown as we faced the terror of the dead space together, marvel at his courage in the face of mortal danger. All words felt trite and inadequate and in the end I simply kissed him exactly as he had me. We stayed unmoving for a moment then I felt a hand on my back and the kiss became more intense. It was the first time I have felt such passion, perhaps even love, in a kiss, and it was perhaps the most pleasurable experience of my life.

When we finally drew apart the look on his face had transformed from fear to cautious joy. I had read the word radiant to describe a face but never until that moment understood what it meant. I expect my expression was similar.

"Should I take it that you wish me to remain in your employ, sir?" he asked through smiling lips.

"I should accept no-one else in the world."

* * *

I wrote to my father recounting the whole adventure, highlighting Fraser's courage and heroism, and enclosing an affidavit from Professor Summers confirming my tale, lest my father suspect the whole story a product of opium. I expected a visit but instead received a missive from a local solicitor, inviting Fraser to meet and discuss the matter. When he returned he looked grave.

"What on Earth transpired, man?" I demanded.

"I'm afraid, sir" he said, "I am no longer in your employ." My face must have told its own story, and Fraser suppressed a laugh. "I am henceforth in the employ of Mr. Duncan Senior, my principal duties being as manservant to your good self, to keep control of your finances and keep my employer informed of your conduct and academic progress. If you have any additional duties I shall be happy to negotiate."

His smile had gradually broadened as he delivered his speech, and my heart almost burst from my chest.

"I have several ideas for additional duties," I said, "though I do not feel I could demand such things."

Fraser's smile became positively salacious. "Perhaps we could discuss the details in your bedchamber," he said.

"Excellent idea," I said. "Follow me." I took him by the hand.

IT PASSED BY MORNING

Adriana C. Grigore

Nairn expected any number of things when they prised open the door of the hut with gloved hands and booted feet. From woodland animals hiding from the imminent snowstorm, to errant thieves or ghasts or whatever else lived in the midst of these frozen trees they'd been traipsing through for days.

They gave one final kick to the rusty lockset, then pulled back as the door swung open, and let their eyes adjust to the darkness waiting inside. The hut was empty. They were alone in this abysmally towering forest. Had they taken this journey in summer, there might have been others, but at the time they'd assumed their bones would heal on their own. They hadn't.

Inside, the sharp tang of the storm mingled with the musty smell of wood and dust and the underlying odour of smoke that never truly left the walls in these parts. A couple of candles, lit in a hurry, showed an old stone hearth, a bed and a table and shelves that only stored a few clay pots. There was a small stack of logs by the hearth, the ashes fresher than the grime on the walls. A single mug was placed upside-down on a corner of the table.

Fresh air poured in like mist when Nairn reached for the window shutters and opened them outward to the ever-darkening forest. The candles flickered. Nairn fixed their eyes on the high arch of the canopy.

No sign of the sky, no stars, no clouds, just the blackly green needles that cared not for day or night, but kept all those wandering below them lighting their lanterns again and again, until the oil ran out. Nairn's had, a few days before, but that was not what had bothered them.

What was unsettling was the wind. It was not supposed to reach this deep into the forest, and yet it had. It had been keeping pace with them for days, making their walk into a trudge, their days' journey to the mountains into an endless fool's quest. A couple more days, and Nairn would have reached the mountain path, would have left this forest behind them. But the snow had been knee-high and forbidding when they'd woken up this morning.

It had been with an unwitting breath of relief that Nairn had found the hut. Yet, now, as they drew the shutters closed and fastened them with their last piece of warding string, something inside them recoiled. At coming to a halt, at settling in a house that was not their own, at prolonging this journey that had already stretched too long.

They were so far away from home.

They were far away from home, but there was rot in their bones, the wind had been howling in their ears for days, and they needed to rest.

Their hands trembled as they removed their gloves and set a few logs in the ashy hearth, but they weren't about to get themself buried in the snow just because they wanted to go back sooner. Had they been that eager to meet a slow death, they would have just stayed home and waited for the rot to eat them from the inside, not gone hunting for greybells on the other side of the kingdom.

★ ★ ★

On the second day, the forest was quiet, and the snow no thicker than before, but Nairn was old enough to know not to trust any of it. Places like this liked to test the strangers that walked through them. Their own home was the same.

So, instead of leaving, Nairn spent the rest of the day putting the house to rights. They gathered twigs and filled pots and pails with water from the nearby stream. They found more oil for their lantern, and enough shrivelled roots under one of the floorboards to boil into the semblance of a soup.

And in the evening, when they were sure that their wards were holding, and the wind was staying firmly on the outside, they reached into their bag and took out the wych elm sapling they'd brought from home. It trembled feebly in their hands as they set it in a bowl, its three leaves soft and bruised, and Nairn watched it as they warmed by the fire.

A night's sleep had made the thoughts at the back of their mind louder. The insistent voice that urged them to go, to leave, to never have left at all. It tired a part of themself that no amount of rest could assuage. There was a reason witches hardly ever left their cottages. It was not in their veins and bones to be this far away from their woods. It was like swimming upstream, with ropes tied to every joint.

But seeing their sapling barely grasp at soil with rot-blackened roots, they were reminded of why they'd had to go. For they were wood, and their home was wood, and they would not risk bringing back with them the same sickness that had made them pull up their roots and leave. They'd wait another day, they decided.

And it was good they did.

Come morning, the storm swallowed the woods whole.

★ ★ ★

The stranger came in the evening of the fourth day.

Hunched low, Nairn watched through the shutters as he stumbled through the snow that reached up to his middle, sleeves of embossed leather shielding his eyes, hood pushed back by the gale, the hilt of what might have been an axe peeking over his shoulder.

The knock came a bit later than they'd expected, so their hand was already hovering over the handle when the door thudded softly. They waited another moment, then opened it with some effort, their wards groaning against the wind that tried to make its way in.

Dark eyes red-rimmed and wide with disbelief, the stranger stared back at them. He was younger than he'd seemed from afar, face not quite cleanly shaven and long, dark hair strangely streaked with grey and coated with snow. Woodsman, he might have been, judging from his garb. His voice was faint against the raging storm.

"I'm sorry," he said. "Please. I saw the light, and I've met no one else on the way. Can I – please." He drew in a breath. "Can I please share your fire?"

Nairn stepped aside, wrists creaking as they opened the door more widely before letting it clatter shut once the man was inside. With its last clang, the world was suddenly quieter. Nairn turned around.

The stranger had trailed in a path of snow in the shape of his steps, and more was raining down from his clothes as he trembled.

"Sit by the fire," Nairn said. "I'll bring you something to eat."

He nodded, unbuttoning his overcoat with fingers made clumsy by the cold. Next came a leather vest, half-frozen too, a thick woollen scarf and, lastly, his boots. Nairn warmed up a bowl of soup as they watched him collapse on the rug before the fire, cracked and reddened hands combing the snow out of his hair.

They did not expect him to look up when he did. "Thank you," he said. "I feared I would not see morning. The gale caught me unawares."

Nairn nodded, and pressed the bowl in his hands.

It was nothing more than the tasteless broth they'd made days before, but the stranger ate it with a relish Nairn envied. Some days, they imagined they could taste the rot at the back of their throat.

"Have you been walking long?"

"About a week," the stranger said, chasing the scanty vegetables with the spoon. "I was down to the villages when the snows started, but I hoped it would not reach me if I walked deep enough. I got separated from my brothers. They must have taken another path owing to the weather, but I realised it too late."

"Can you find them again?"

"Yes," he said, cold-burnt face scrunched in a grimace. "But not until the storm passes."

Whenever that may be, Nairn thought bitterly.

The stranger's gaze swept over the small enclosure of the hut, and Nairn saw him gradually reach the conclusion that there was no one else there but them. His breathing had calmed as he finished scraping the bowl clean. There was something vulnerable in his eyes as he looked back at them.

"Are you lost too?"

It hurt their jaw to smile. "No," they lied. "The snow caught me in. I wish I had a blanket to give you."

The stranger shook his head. "No, it's alright, I have my cloak, and—"

"What is your name?"

They gazed at each other for a moment. This was a precarious path to take. But the weather was revolting, and their bones hurt, and Nairn needed a distraction.

"Havel," the stranger said carefully.

They smiled. "Mine is Nairn."

★ ★ ★

Contrary to what most believed of witches, Nairn did not need human souls. They didn't feed on them, didn't steal them and keep them in jars, did not, even, sell them in exchange for hexes. In fact, they had never even so much as held a soul in their hand.

A witch was of their wood inasmuch as they did not need anything outside of it to keep alive. They might have had their own soul once, back when they were flesh and bones, the human half of a changeling exchange that had no place in the woods and soon melted to mosses and mushrooms. But there was only the forest now.

Nairn had grown from and with their woods like a sapling from a tree. The reason, perhaps, why they hadn't just torn out the wych elm when they'd seen their rot stretch to it.

They loved witching, though.

Witching was like running your hands through a box full of trinkets at the market, without buying anything. Only, the box was someone's soul. Nairn, personally, took and broke nothing, but they might have left the place in a bit of disarray on a couple of occasions. Nothing one couldn't recover from, however.

It was a bit like weaving a waking dream, fine as gossamer, broken at any sudden sound. And like with dreaming, whether it was pleasant or terrifying depended on a thousand small thoughts. Depended on the witch, really.

Then they let them go. Unlike those witches that did prefer to eat them.

There were always exceptions.

★ ★ ★

"It's not letting up," Havel said the next morning, peering through the shutters while Nairn stirred half a spoonful of herbs into a pot of water. "I think we need to make a path outside, before it gets to the roof. You said there's a river nearby?"

Nairn nodded, waving a hand in the vague direction of the door. "Yes, just… straight ahead past the outhouse."

Delusively optimistic, they'd only brought one pouch of plants from their home forest on their journey, and its contents were dwindling by the day, especially since the pain had worsened. But there was no point in being frugal if it meant risking not seeing another morning.

"Are you alright?"

"Fine," they said, pressing their face into their palms. "Just a headache. I'll be right over."

"Don't be daft," Havel said, and seemed to catch himself at the same moment Nairn cracked an eye open in his direction. "Sor–sorry. I'll do it myself. I'm used to these things."

He slipped out of the hut before Nairn could say anything else. *Small blessings*, they thought. Their skin was pulled taut just with keeping the hut from breaking apart. They didn't think they could have mustered persuasion on top of it.

At least the wind was staying out for now, even if Nairn felt it prodding at every crack and splinter, of which the hut had many. The storm drummed its fingers impatiently on the thin walls. Had they not found shelter before now, Nairn had no doubts they would have already been dead, frozen through and cracked down the middle, for the rot to thaw and bloom again come spring.

And as they slurped through their weak decoction, they gazed at their sapling, and thought about greybells, wilting only days away from them somewhere in an unreachable mountain cave, while here they were, wilting too.

★ ★ ★

Havel brought them water on the first day and firewood on the second, and then, most bafflingly, an entire rabbit on the third. He said he could make small treks outside every once in a while, even if the storm wasn't letting up, and Nairn didn't know enough about woodsmen to know if this was admirable or simply expected. They mostly tried to ignore the smell of wet fur whenever he returned.

"Better to put in the effort now, in case it gets any worse later," he said, and his face told them he caught their grimace at the idea of even more days spent stuck here.

"I'd help, if you'd let me," they said.

"I'm the guest here," he said, wringing ice out of his hair before the sputtering fire. "And also–" He didn't finish.

With one swift, practiced movement, Nairn pulled the rabbit's skin off and tried not to be annoyed by it.

Once somewhat dry, Havel seated himself across from them and started chopping the handful of frostbitten vegetables he'd brought with him. There were fresher reddish cracks over his cheeks where the wind had gnawed at him during his forays, but he seemed less frantic than the night before. Nairn broke another leg bone in their hands, and tentatively reached out to him.

Witching was a craft of concentration, of digging in a sack and picking up only the grains you wished to look at.

But Nairn couldn't get anything clear out of him. Just flashes of what they'd already expected: exhaustion, worry, caution. A hint of something they could not put their finger on. When they tried to prod a bit harder at it, Havel looked up with a furrow in his brow. Nairn pulled their hand back from the proverbial grain sack of his soul.

They were out of practice, they told themself.

"I'm sorry," Havel said.

Nairn stilled, fingers deep in an incision. "What for?"

"I never asked." The turn of Havel's mouth turned bitter, and he looked away. "Whether I could stay here this long, I mean. I just… I got out of practice of staying with people outside my family. I'm sorry."

Even with the smell of blood and wet clothes in their nostrils, Nairn felt oddly touched. Politeness was not something they'd had much of in the wildness of their forest.

"I'm not a woodsman," they thus said, and smiled when Havel looked confused. "I don't actually enjoy being alone in the woods." Well, alone with the wych elm, but he hadn't seemed to notice it yet.

"Ah," Havel laughed at their lie. "We don't either, really. We're rarely on our own. That's the reason I'm now like this… all over the place."

They barely suppressed raising an eyebrow. If this was

someone all over the place, they could not imagine what he would have made of their situation. But they understood.

"Being away from home is hard," they said, throwing the rabbit into the pot and pushing it towards his small mound of vegetables.

"It is," he said, his smile a bit sad.

As if it heard them, and Nairn had begun to suspect it might have, in a perverse way, the storm keened a bit more loudly outside the door.

★ ★ ★

"What is it you fear most?" Havel asked five days into their mutual stay, when the wind woke them up with a raucous wail that didn't cease till evening.

They'd settled themselves again on the rug before the fire, with a concoction made of steeped bark instead of Nairn's last reserves. Havel's eyes were wide and his face open, like he really wanted to hear the answer. So Nairn thought a half-truth would not do any harm, just this once. They needed a distraction from the pain, the creaking, and the restlessness anyway.

"Wolves," they said.

It made him laugh. "What? Why?"

"They stick their noses where they're not wanted, and it's never just one of them."

"Not the most blood-curdling reason, but not untrue," Havel conceded, amusement lingering in his grin. "Have they given you many troubles?"

"Enough," Nairn said, stretching their legs before the fire. "What about you?"

"What do I fear?"

"Yes."

"Wood shades." He said it with a nervous smile, drawing closer to the fire too. If Nairn were to turn a bit, their ankle would have touched his foot. "Once you see too many, you think they're everywhere. It makes you sloppy, and that's dangerous while hunting."

"I see." Their ankle touched his foot. "And *have* you seen too many?"

Another, more nervous chuckle. He ran a hand through his hair. "I hope not."

Nairn looked at the fresh scratches on his hands, wondering idly whether a few drops of blood mixed with their herbs would appease their creaking bones more than all the sleeping they'd been doing. He hadn't moved his foot away. That emboldened them. They reached out.

Nothing. Whispers and colours. It was as if there was a heavy drape pulled before them, with a roaring fire behind it. They could not brush it away, their mind was slipping off it like water off oilskin. And suddenly the distraction was not enough.

Nairn drew their legs back and got to their feet. Havel looked up in what appeared like genuine surprise, as if he hadn't felt anyone scratching at the edges of his soul.

"I need some air," they said, and stepped outside with their cloak haphazardly thrown over their shoulders.

The door clattered on its hinges behind them. The cold was bitter and instantaneous, washing over them before Nairn managed to take a single breath. Better like that. Otherwise, they would have screamed.

If witching didn't work, then they'd walked into this whole situation unprepared. They had no idea what was still in their power to do, if push came to shove. They knew, however, that axes worked on most kinds of wood.

The air seemed to congeal down their throat, clotting in their chest. Nairn forced more of it down. If the sickness had reached deep enough to take their witching from them, then it must have reached very deep indeed. They would have to bury their sapling in this wretched place.

The vast canopy shuddered with the snowfall, its wide branches bending and whining at all hours, as the snow pressed its way down. And for a moment, Nairn thought they saw something moving against the wind, far above. Yet, when they blinked against the frost catching on their lashes, the darkness was as complete as ever.

★ ★ ★

Perhaps it was a charm.

If Havel had a charm on him, something to protect him from whoever might have been tempted by his soul in the woods, then that would have explained it. He was a woodman, it stood to reason that he would have something to keep him safe. Not that Nairn had ever seen him touch or pray over anything.

So maybe they were losing their touch. Maybe their impatience was showing. Maybe the people around here were too different from the ones back home. Or maybe it was the rot affecting them. Maybe they would simply die in this world-forsaken hovel, with the storm raging around them. Anything was possible, really.

"Are you alright?"

Nairn looked up to see Havel frowning in quiet concern. His gaze lowered briefly, and they realised they'd been rubbing and massaging their hands for a rather long while and with rather a lot of force.

"I'm fine," they said. It went unheard.

"I didn't want to pry earlier." Havel took a few careful steps closer. "But you seem… in pain? At times. Is there anything I can–"

"Don't pry."

They couldn't even be bothered by the look they got for it. If they were to decompose, their mask would have come down anyway, sooner or later. They sat down on the bed, pressing their fingers viciously between their swollen knuckles.

"Can I try?"

Havel's face was so earnest that whatever smouldering annoyance might have tried to catch flame inside Nairn's chest was stifled to smoking embers. *Oh, well*, they thought. It would help nothing, but it couldn't possibly do them any harm either.

At least Havel didn't seem about to hack them to pieces anytime soon, even though Nairn sometimes caught him staring quietly from across the room. They had an inkling that expressed a different kind of hunger.

They motioned for him to sit beside them, and proffered one of their hands. Havel moved slowly, from their wrist to the base of their fingers, thumbs moving in steady rolling motions. It seemed no different than what Nairn had been doing, but they felt the pain subside, ever so slightly, and couldn't hold back a sound of surprise.

"One of my brothers had something like this too," Havel said.

Rot eating away at his wooden bones? Nairn wondered idly.

"How did he pass?" they asked instead, and their dry tone somehow made Havel laugh.

"He's fine," he said. "Probably wondering where in the world I am and if winter ghouls have eaten me yet."

"There's still time."

A deliberate pull on one of their fingers, and a months-old bead of tension dissolved like salt in water. Havel gave them a serious look.

"Knock on wood."

Nairn barely resisted tapping their own leg. They rapped their knuckles against the wall instead, and Havel averted his gaze as a small smile pulled at his lips.

Then he pressed both thumbs in the centre of their palm, and something cracked.

Nairn jerked forward, nausea rising almost instantly in their throat, while Havel leant backward as if burnt, hands held up.

"I'm sorry! I didn't mean, I didn't think I would… is it bad?"

Gritting their teeth, Nairn pressed their fingers, just slightly, over the point where they'd felt the crack, and there it was.

Slight, much slighter than it had felt. A splinter. It pushed slightly against their skin from the inside, but they could tell it would crumble before piercing it.

Slowly, they counted their breaths back to normal, focusing on the rapidly chilling sweat at their temples. Havel was still babbling, so perhaps he hadn't felt the wood break against his fingers.

"It's fine," Nairn said, between two gulps of air. "Old sore. It does that sometimes." They really hoped these last words would remain a lie.

"Is there anything I can do? I didn't realise I pressed that hard, I…"

Closing their eyes against the remnant throb of pain, Nairn raised their other hand and placed it in his. That shut him up. It took another few moments before he started massaging it too, touches almost laughably light.

And as he worked, Nairn thought once more about greybells, and imagined the cold gnawing at their bulbs too, rot climbing up their bluish stems, as nobody got to pick them this year.

★ ★ ★

On the eleventh day, Havel came back from one of his short forays with remarkably little snow on his clothes, and a wide grin on his face.

"I think I saw a patch of sky."

He shed his clothes, untied his hair, and came to sit beside them at the table. A moment later, he grimaced.

"It might have been ice."

"I didn't say anything."

"Yes," Havel let out an amused breath. "But you have a knack for being remarkably pessimistic without ever saying much."

"The feeling is not unfounded," Nairn muttered, peeling a weary-looking celery.

"Of course not. But look!"

After searching his pockets for a while, Havel set a handful of frozen acorns on the table between them. Nairn's eyes travelled from them to him.

"What did you do, dive in the snow for them?"

"Close enough." Havel smiled. "It can't go on for much longer. The air felt different today."

"Felt the same to me," Nairn said under their breath. Angry, always angry. The wind had subsided, but not the pressure on their skin. It felt dangerous to hope against it. "But if you're right, I guess you'll part ways with my pessimism soon enough."

Havel didn't say anything. Nairn had given up trying to guess at what was really going on in his mind. Their waking days were filled with thoughts of how they could trek the canopy, slipping from branch to branch so as to avoid the sea of snow below. They could still make it to the mountains. They forced themself to believe that.

As soon as the storm drew back just enough, they would be out. They would be away. They would be nearly on their way home. How was that for pessimism?

Havel kicked a single acorn towards them. Nairn ignored it, but when a second one joined it, they found themself looking up. He wasn't smiling anymore.

"Is there anyone…"

His voice petered out, left only the crackle of the hearth in its wake.

Nairn frowned. "Anyone…?"

He closed his hands into fists. "Anyone waiting for you? Out there?"

"Of course," Nairn said, the lie at once easy and flat on their tongue.

Havel looked at them. Through their lie and into what lay beneath it, as easy as their witching should've been. His hair spilled freely on his shoulders, and Nairn wondered, yet again, where someone so young could have got so many grey streaks. There was that hunger in his eyes again, the kind that no food or fire could satiate, a dark hollow that only grew. The only glimpse at his soul they could get.

A few nights before, Nairn had dreamt of teeth sinking into their shoulder, a maw closing around it as sap trickled down their arm.

They didn't think of axes tearing into their bones when they finally asked what they'd been unable to glean all this while. They too were good at seeing through lies. "What really brought you here?"

Which was when the hut shuddered from every corner as something slammed into it.

They both got up just as another crash shook the floor, and only the wards Nairn had put up kept the wood from splintering around them. Something banged into the roof too, dust and clay pattering down. They were on the verge of pulling their wards more tightly when they noticed the string around the shutters coming undone.

It spurned Nairn into action, and they dashed to the window, unwinding the string faster than it was being unwound. Always better to untie a ward than let it break.

It was as it came undone in their hands that they finally heard Havel speak, quick and frantic. "No, no, stay back, you don't know what it–"

Nairn opened the shutters before they could be pulled away, and stared into the dark forest, speckled with a scattered flurry. They glared into the darkness, breathing hard, arms freezing, until they saw, there, just at the edge of the light from the hut, a hundred eyes staring back at them.

Then the air was knocked out of them as they were struck down to the floor. There was something wild in Havel's eyes as he held them down, and it only grew when he picked himself up and went to frantically push at the shutters. There was a yowling noise from outside, as whatever it was they'd seen rushed towards the window.

He would never have been able to keep it closed against another blow. Gritting their teeth, Nairn waved their arm towards it and pulled, and new branches grew lightning-fast from that old wood, twisting around the shutters and shuddering violently against the hit. But not breaking apart.

So they could still do that. That was good.

For good measure, they kicked Havel's legs from under him before getting up. He went down like a sack of stones, which Nairn quietly delighted in before catching his eye with a glare.

"Never push me again," they said, and went to open the door.

"You're a *woodghast*? No, don't let them in, they've been prowling around for days!"

"Witch," Nairn said simply. Then, hand on the knob, they looked over their shoulder. "How many days?"

The sudden tint of guilt over his face was answer enough. Nairn wrenched the door open before he could pick himself up again. The shadows they'd seen days before were circling round the canopy, seemingly preoccupied before the candle-light caught their eyes.

Witching wasn't often practiced between shades, but Nairn reached out anyway. Tentatively, the closest thing to politeness they could offer. There were patches and shards of emotion, the murky thoughts of those not used to getting out of their cycles, and one prevalent fact.

They turned on their heels and came face-to-face with Havel. "What did you take?"

He almost took a step back, but stopped himself. "What?"

Thief, thief, thief, the shades outside whispered in their woodland tongue.

"*What did you take?*" Nairn gritted out.

His gaze flitted to his coat before he could stop it, and in a moment they were both lunging for it, pushing and kicking at each other, ripping seams in their frenzy. Nairn felt hands on their arms, grip tight enough to break their blighted bones, and slipped free just before that could happen. They caught fistfuls of cloth as claws ripped through their sleeves, but they still dragged themself over the threshold, into the freezing night.

They pulled and yanked at the coat until it ripped between them, and Nairn fell down in the snow with half of it in their arms. And when they looked up, they did not see Havel panting in the doorway, but a great grey-wolf, almost blocking out the light, the other half of the coat dangling from its maw.

Nairn laughed. *Of all things.*

They saw the softest glint through a tear in the cloth in Havel's jaw. He must have realised it too, the moment their eyes met, but it was already too late, as Nairn pulled forth and twisted the wood from the door around his frame.

He growled when they came closer and dug into his coat, and they couldn't help grinning. *Thief*, they mouthed too, delighted.

Their fingers closed around something smooth and cold, and when they pulled their hand out, they found themself holding a black stone lined with golden-grey. A *moonrock*. Of course their witching had had no effect. And they'd thought they were dying.

Everything, from the storm, to the wind, to the growing anger in the air started to make sense. And, along with it, an idea came to them, giddily, like a ray of sunlight through the leaves.

They turned back to the shades and held up the stone, ignoring Havel's wordless whine. "You lost this."

A dark tendril reached out towards them, and they pulled their hand back.

"You lost it because you did not take care of it," they said, pointedly. "And I won it from your thief. If you want it, you have to give me something back. It's of no use to me."

Even Havel quietened behind them, listening. Nairn could barely refrain from smiling before their next words.

"I want a weeping greybell," they said. "I know you have them somewhere in your mountains. I just want one, cleanly uprooted."

The shadows edged closer, squinting at them, while they stood perfectly still. Then the shades glared at Havel, and back to Nairn, and looked yearningly at the stone in their hand.

Nairn closed their fist tightly around the moonstone, and it disappeared from their hand when they next opened it. "Agreed?"

Wretch, the shades whispered. With another glare, however, they turned away, plunging into the canopy and dashing, Nairn was pleased to see, towards the mountains. It would only take them a day to get up there and back again. So Nairn turned around too, eager to get out of the cold at last.

"Up you go," they told Havel on their way back inside, patting his fur before letting the wood release him.

They heard him scramble in after them, but ignored it as they threw more wood over the dying fire.

"I still need that stone," Havel said, in his more usual, if scratched, form. At least the grey hair made more sense now.

"Why?"

"I broke the last one, so I was sent to get another," he said, brushing woodchips off his arms. "We keep one in our home, for praying."

"Shame," Nairn said. They got back to their feet. "*Those* were woodgasts, you know? The real kind. They come if strangers abuse their forest in any way."

"It was *unguarded.*"

"I never said they're smart."

Havel glared, and got glared at back. "It was unguarded. I didn't think they'd pay any mind to it."

"Yes, you did."

"Yes, fine," he groaned. "I hoped I would be far away from here before they noticed."

"But then the storm came," Nairn said. "Because of you."

It seemed to pain him to admit it. "Yes."

They regarded each other in silence for another moment. Then Nairn sighed. They pulled the stone out again, closed their hands around it, and broke it cleanly down the middle. They offered one half to Havel.

"They're not smart, so they won't notice it's smaller than before. But try not to linger, anyway."

Somehow, this seemed to confuse him. He took the stone from them as if it would burst into flames at any moment. "Thank you," he eventually said, still dubious.

Nairn rolled their eyes. "You're welcome."

They sat down before the growing fire, feeling their bones groan within them. While it was good to know their witching still worked, it didn't mean their body wouldn't protest the extra effort of wood-crafting. They closed their eyes and waited for the creaking of the door, but it never came.

Instead, after a moment, Havel joined them on the rug, stone still cradled in his hands. He didn't seem to notice Nairn staring at him in open perplexity, nor realise the fact that he should've been bounding away before the shades returned.

"Why do you need a greybell?" he asked.

The confusion turned to a withering glare and they reached out underneath the bed to retrieve their sapling. Its half-blackened stem was leaning precariously in its bowl, leaves barely holding on.

"Why do you think?"

Havel gazed at it and said nothing. Yet, after a moment, he held his hand out, and Nairn couldn't tell why, but they hardly hesitated before passing it over to him. He turned the bowl in his hands, looking at the decaying roots, the moulding skin. Then he set it on his knee and untied his hair. His gaze found Nairn's.

"I can do something to strengthen it, before you get the greybell." His fingers twisted around a single strand of grey hair, and plucked it out.

Nairn didn't say anything.

"We take care of our forest too," Havel went on, voice harder. "We might not be able to talk to it at our whim, but we know how to look after it."

Relenting took almost as much self-control as holding the hut together had. Nairn sighed, rubbing at their face. "Do what you know."

They watched as Havel wrapped the strand around the length of the wych elm, carefully coaxing it back to an upright position.

"Pity you can't do that to me too," they said, earning an unsettled glance. "Too many bones, too deep in. Would give you a bald patch *and* make a mess of me."

Havel huffed, focusing back on the elm. "I'm not good with shades anyway."

"I noticed."

The glare slid off them rather quickly, especially when they saw their sapling looking almost on the way back to health. A fingertip of greybell mashed with wood ash would push it the rest of the way, and hopefully them too. Soon, so soon, they might be on their way home at last.

Havel set it aside out of the stronger firelight, and then his gaze drifted to Nairn's own hands, resting on the rug. They didn't notice him reaching out until his fingertips were against theirs. Strangely warm, expectedly bruised. He took their hand in his with the same care with which he'd handled the stone, the elm.

His thumb was quick to find the place where their bone had cracked days before, and Nairn kept their breathing steady as he pressed softly over the splinter.

He was quiet for a while before choosing his words. "Were you trying to bewitch me? I sometimes thought I could feel… something."

"Just for a bit. It didn't work," Nairn admitted, relishing his scandalised face. "Were you trying to eat me?"

A huff. "No."

"You sure? You looked pretty hungry for a while there."

Havel gazed back at them. Nairn smiled.

"Yes, like that."

He pressed a bit harder on their bone, but they didn't let their smile falter. And when his gaze flitted down, when it stayed there, they slipped their fingers in his hair and pulled him to them. They wondered whether he too could taste the rot on their tongue, or if it was just sap, waiting to spill at the first bite.

It was probably not very auspicious that the hut chose that moment to groan on all of its hinges, reminding Nairn that most of their wards were down. The ceiling did not fall on them, but more dust floated down, and the towering trees outside creaked in a near derisive manner.

Havel pressed his face into their neck. "World, I hate this forest."

"You and me both."

"What did you do with the previous owner?"

"Ate him and buried his bones so that they could grow another for next year," Nairn said blandly. "It was abandoned, can't you smell the mould?"

Havel laughed, forehead now on their shoulder. "Alright."

They looked up at the cracked ceiling, trying to ascertain whether the hut would hold for one more night. "You know you should probably leave before they return, right?"

"I'm not you," Havel mumbled. "I don't actually enjoy being alone in the woods. I'll wait for you."

His breath was fire-warm against their shirt. Nairn closed their eyes, and kicked his ankle.

"Alright. Then let's hope the worst of it will pass by morning."

THE WELLKEEPERS

Sydney Meeker

There were some fossils in my mother's collection that we never spoke about. Her obsession was older than the family. As far back as blood could be traced, her mother and her mother before her had sifted dead things from the Pacific Ocean like gold. The Pacific Northwest borders one of the deepest undersea trenches in the world. Even primordial stone churns to the surface under the right conditions, and there are some ancient things in the depths that never die.

Though my mother was ancient and cruel, she was not undying. The manor house she left behind lay on a flat strand peppered with bone-white driftwood and towering juts of water-eaten cliffs. There was no one left for a funeral. Only me, and the rocks, and the wellkeepers.

When the estate passed to me, I figured I'd fire the two wellkeepers immediately, organise the fossils and books and furniture (what else is a house?) and sell it all away. These old manors, with sitting and dining and tea and mud rooms, eat up so much more than just resources. The well stood inland, all cracked stones caulked with moss, lilies and roses spreading wildly all around it. The pale beach grasses avoided it by some twenty feet, content to whip and whistle at a safe distance.

When I first beheld it as an adult, luggage in tow, I imagined I had seen it in a painting. With the gentle accompaniment of the low grey sea, I daydreamt a mistaken turn in some dark museum, housing artifacts bought in blood. The stone older than any of us or our nations, the crudely-rendered iron rings the remnant of some long-forgotten star.

The wellkeepers were part scullery maids and part research assistants, artifacts of imagination themselves. They doted on that well. When I arrived, they doted on me, they acted like I had forgotten what they had done. I could hardly blame them – they had never seen me as an adult, this man they had never met.

How the unpredictability of a child disturbed the plans they shared with my mother. How they had treated me then: another case to be measured. Another case to be controlled, emotionally, intellectually, physically.

The two were sisters. The older bore long lines that stretched from her mouth to her eyes. She chattered and gave orders ceaselessly to her sister. The younger, brown-haired, had spent much of her fifty-four years silent. She was content with simple tasks; carrying trays and transcribing and taking my luggage from my hands. I insisted against it, but she nearly wrenched my property away. When she touched my hand, I remembered that she was the one who carried out *make her sit down* or *put her in her place* or *bind her mouth if she cries again.* She followed the orders her older sister gave her without question. Her silence frightened me as a child. How afraid I was of becoming like her.

I had been frightened of so many things, the well a pinnacle among them. Faint reflections of starlight twirled within the well. There was little to be seen. "I don't think I was allowed within fifty feet of this thing when Mother was alive."

"And for good reason," the older sister, Gabrielle, said. "Children are crafty in their recklessness."

"Was I?"

"You were a child, weren't you? Not some little goblin creature?" She walked off down the beach path towards the house.

"I was allowed in the ocean and the rivers, on the roof, on the balconies of the highest floors, at the very top of the stairs. How strange this is the one thing Mother didn't allow." When

Gabrielle went silent, I addressed Rachel – the younger sister. "Don't you agree?"

Rachel dropped my suitcase, paling and shuddering. "I-I don't – we – the mistress was–" The sea breeze whipped a few strands of hair from her bun.

Gabrielle spoke over her. "We weren't there to question your mother's decisions. We came here for the library and that was our greatest priority."

I had tucked away the memory of the library deeper than the memory of the people. There were countless yellowed diagrams along the walls documenting every sea monster to have ever existed, from pygmy seahorses to megalodons, the great shark's skeleton laid out with its jaws gaping along the walls. Beneath these diagrams were horizontal archives. In a typical library, they might've held dusty newspapers or crumbling ledgers, testaments to humanity. But these flaking stone sheets were embedded with bone and the outline of flesh, documenting the ancestral arthropod *anomalocaris* and the mostly-mythical sea serpent *cadborosaurus*, long thought to be merely decaying whale spines. These archives of the once-alive were testaments to the inhuman.

When night fell, I dug through the ledgers and bills by candlelight, the rhythm of the sea ever-turning on the shore. My mother's desk had always made me shudder a bit, for nothing good ever came of approaching it, but now I was at liberty to work with its guts. On her office wall were several large pin boards that she, assumedly, used to keep photos for study. Old schedules, receipts, museum ticket stubs. The pin boards' primarily real estate was given over to yellowed photographs of dead sea eels, whales, dolphins, sharks, cadys, and so forth. The empty skull eye-holes gawked from sunrise to sunset.

The matters of money puzzled me. The house operated at a loss; I initially figured the heating, electricity, ice, and water would be our biggest costs. Yet, my mother hadn't turned on the furnace for years. Her comfort, and the sisters' by extension, were afterthoughts to the fossils. The sisters worked for next to nothing. (When I floated the possibility of raising their pay to meet more modern standards, Gabrielle insisted that the only thing they'd do with extra money is give it back to the house. I put off the decision.) The receipts showed the sisters bought food cheaply and in bulk, leaving me to wonder how much three old women could eat. Scant food investment, the basics for stews and home-baked breads, in all but one category: raw meat. How much could our icebox even hold?

Without bothering to change out of my nightgown and slippers, I took my candle holder downstairs. A heavy, metallic rattling echoed out of the library. There was light coming from beneath the door. It was best to assume one of the sisters had continued her documentation late into the night.

Our icebox housed only some yogurts mid-cultivation. But there was a trail of water and ice snaking its way out the door, which I tracked to the beach path. There, the darkness and the sand hid any sign of a dripping trail, but there were two sets of footprints. The sea wind immediately blew out my candle, so I continued by the light of the library that bled out onto the sand.

Two dark forms moved through the night, a dim, trembling lantern between them. The sisters did not speak to one another as they dragged a cart of meat through the sand. I hid myself in the long grasses, watching. They laid out pound after pound of meat on the rip of the well with wet slaps. Several minutes passed as I watched half in awe and half in bafflement.

A singing voice came over the waves, gentle and haunting. It climbed a few notes then descended. The sisters merely kept at their task as though they could not hear it. I thought I'd fallen asleep, caught in a dream. But the wind stung, my feet sank into the sand, all very real sensations.

I pushed further toward the voice, careful to keep myself low and quiet. Slowly the voice transformed into long, hissing, harmonic wails. A dark lump lay along the surf. It heaved, shaking, the cries growing ever louder.

Laying in the moonlight, the surf pounding against it, was a long, horse-like creature, screaming with that horrible fang-filled mouth. It had no back legs, only a long tail and a fin that desperately flung itself back and forth along the shore. Slick and dripping, its hooves desperately paddled against the sand, crying out in misery. It even craned its head to push itself back towards the sea, stuffing its long snout into the sand to shove itself away. Two moons that shimmered with grey and yellow irises lay embedded in its head, unmovable, glossy, stretched in agony. Yellowed anatomical diagrams in the house portrayed several familiar creatures: I assumed it to be *Equus auqerus,* a hippocampus or a kelpie, depending where in the world you find it.

There were fossils of this creature inside the house; how old was this specimen? How old was its species? I remembered the hippocampus section of the "undocumented species" room, and its exceptionally complete skeleton. How strange to see a full specimen, so different than how my nightmares had rendered it. How did this mythical creature find itself on this shore? Why did it face the house even while it struggled to return to the sea?

I looked back towards the sisters; they were gone. Then, the house; just as I looked, I saw the lights turn off. Now it was me and this creature beneath the moonlight, a few feet of sand separating us. I did not think of science, or safety, but only what it was like to experience pain, and the instinct to comfort. I watched its hooves; it pulled itself towards the ocean with such desperation that I could not help but mourn the hippocampus' plight. It threw its head back and forth, shooting long plumes of saltwater into the night air. The gills along its neck opened and closed, blowing out air and water and sand. Was it dying?

Without thinking, I nudged the creature toward the sea with a heavy piece of driftwood. I rammed the log into the sand beneath its chest, giving it just enough leverage to face the sea. It took great advantage of this, pushing back into the surf to breathe. It lay there for a minute, gills shuddering, its fish eyes fixed on me. It struggled further in, the hooves dragging it deeper and deeper, and finally it descended.

I stood alone on the beach in the middle of the night. How strong is the land and the sea; how gossamer is the strand between them. The rhythm of the waves revealed nothing more that night.

How much of it was a dream I could not say; I thought I followed the creature into the waves.

The ocean was speaking, and children like me must always listen and follow directions. A shark swims by as the light softly fractals over its grey head. I pass it on my way below, darkness ever growing. A whale, a flock of tuna, all of our expected sea creatures. In the pitch, all at once I'm surrounded by ancient things. A *mosasaurus* circles above me in a darkening halo.

A hippocampus follows a menacing leviathan, a plesiosaur, an ichthyosaur, coelacanths all circle me as my mind drifts away. They swam heavy and slow, occasionally giving off a roar or a whinny that rings warped through the water. This great mobile of time and memory and monsters lulled me to sleep in its deep cold.

★ ★ ★

The next day, something had eaten the meat the sisters had left on the well. Sopping, putrid strips of it lay strewn all among the roses and wild lilies. The well and I watched one another for a while. I hiked further to the river that fed the well.

The river's mouth flowed a little further inland, just out of sight of the shore, and just before the water turned salty. A wide but tame river intersected a brittle grass field. In the river stood a few large stones, dug up by a glacier years and years before.

I cleared away reeds to examine the water's edge. A shimmer caught my eye. Upon a flat rock in the centre of the river a woman lounged. Her skin was greyish-silver, her eyes magnificently emerald. But she had no pupils or whites, only an iris with a slew of green dashes in a yellow-veined globe. She sunned herself nude in the shallows, her silver hair stuck to her back and shoulders. She waved her hand towards me, welcoming my approach.

After my initial shock, I stood among the reeds, unmoving, watching cautiously. Many years previous, I had read of shape-shifters and their attempts at deceit, in the library. "If you are trying to deceive me, then you have failed. What you claim to offer is of no interest to me."

She glared at me for several minutes like a tiger in a menagerie. The light scattered when she sank beneath the water. I thought I saw a glimmer upstream, and I followed it, always keeping a generous berth.

For nearly an hour, I peacefully made observations and notes of the amount of fish, river snails, dragonflies, and tadpoles. If there was a carnivorous, shape-shifting monster here, it didn't disturb the ecosystem in a way I could detect.

The creature reappeared in a tree-darkened part of the river as a silver-toned man. The eyes were a glorious kaleidoscope of blues and purples now, still with no pupil or whites, just yellow veins at the edge of the globes. He, too, waved me forward.

"I don't appreciate you making assumptions," I told it. "You misunderstand my nature. As I said before, what you claim to offer is of no interest to me."

The pupilless eyes moved a bit, considering mine. He dove back under the river's surface, kicking up an underwater cloud of powdery soil. The tawny cloud hid the creature entirely for several minutes.

The overcast dyed the air grey and gentle. For a while, wind lapped at the water's surface.

A slick, dark-green horse's head appeared above water, its twisted fangs poking from its mouth. It slid towards the shore, towards me. Instinctually I withdrew from the water.

It whinnied at the edge of the river, as clear as any scoff uttered by a human.

"If you think I'm foolish enough to get close to you, you're mistaken."

The great fish eyes, moon-yellow slits set in obsidian globes, blinked and narrowed. It slunk to a patch of sand nearby, where the river's waves met the meager shore. The creature fished up several sunken branches and laid them out in a purposeful pattern on the bank; one piece was halfway between river and shore, the other was stuck upright in the sand. Then the third was a much smaller stick, which the creature gently edged between the other two with its terrible maw. It slapped the sand with its hoof, twice. The most reliable communication is performance.

"Is that us, last night?"

It crudely shoved one stick with the other, as I had pushed it into the ocean. It floated off downstream.

"I thought I had dreamt you last night. If you can shapeshift, why didn't you walk to shore?"

It let out a mournful, harmonic hiss like the one I had heard the night before. It flopped around its fish tail, its second half heavy in the water. The tip of each fin stretched further from itself, the wet seal's skin stretching agonizingly taunt. With an excruciating pop, the fin split, and the tips bent, clefting further into toes. The flesh ran like stockings, turning into ladders of sinew and then into crude mimicries of legs. Gasping, I backed away. Witnessing such a branching of flesh sent prickling pain through my toes and fingers, how terrible to imagine such a transformation.

Its hooves smoothed and stretched, fingerless hands moulded from cartilage. Its elbows and hips largely remained the same; I covered my eyes when its face shifted.

It lay sideways in the water for a moment in its mock-human form. Great uncertainty tempered its movements. Sinking a faux-hand into the sand, it gently pressed a leg against a ground. It trembled like a fawn, giving me far too much time to approach. I held it up, perhaps foolishly. The cold touch of water soaked through my coat, and the smell returned me to the fish market in Seattle. Novel and anxious steps, ever little weight put on each soft foot. Then it pulled itself away and crawled back into the water, jamming the ball of its hands into the dirt, expecting the hardness of hooves but only meeting a thin layer of skin over bone. Water overtook the body.

After a few moments, the equine head surfaced again, gazing towards the manor.

"I think I understand. You can't walk without help. But why do you want to go to the house?"

It flopped to the shore, despondent, a pale half-body writhing with sand and torn grasses stuck to its skin. Soon, it ran its hooves along the sand. It made a cross shape, and a squiggly oblong circle.

"I don't know what you're drawing."

Another harmonised hiss, half-growl, made in indignation.

"Is that a zero?"

It flopped over.

"It does frustrate me to no end that you understand me perfectly and I don't understand you. How about this? Tonight, I'll bring some crutches and some rope, and we'll get you walking into the manor. Will that satisfy you?"

Though it lay sideways on the ground, it whinnied in a way that seemed satisfied.

"I really am trying to understand as best as possible. One hoof pound for yes, two hoof pounds for no. Will you meet me on the beach tonight so we can walk you back to the house?"

Still despondent, one hoof struck the sand.

★ ★ ★

The sun had just peaked in the sky, yellow haze pushing through the clouds in haphazard pockets. I ate an early dinner with the sisters in one of the dining rooms, low-lit in the afternoon.

They avoided my eyes and I avoided theirs.

161

"Were either of you working late last night in the library? I saw that the light was on and heard some movement in there, I asked.

"I was looking for something." Gabrielle jabbed her fork into an asparagus.

"What were you looking for? Was it anything to do with the meat you put on the well?"

The clinking of their utensils stopped. Rachel trembled as she looked to Gabrielle for assurance.

Clearing her throat, Garbielle declared, "I was looking for some records. I assure you, it's of no interest to you. Do not speak of it anymore."

If I am to live in this house, I thought, *I'm going to feel safe.* Her frightening tone worked on Rachel, who returned to pecking, and it would have worked on me when I was a child. How the cruel feed on fear. "That library was my mother's, and now it's mine. I'm certain I would be interested."

Gabrielle scowled. "You cannot truly be saying that you'd be interested in the minutia of our daily tasks, can you?" In her voice was all matter of bitterness, something I was used to hearing from her. She was the same as she had always been.

"Greatly interested. I'm also interested in why you're avoiding the matter of the well and the meat."

Gabrielle raised her voice. "I wasn't avoiding it!"

I had the deepest desire to run away and hide in my room, crawl under my bed and cry for the rest of the afternoon. But I was grown now, and mother was gone, and so I was freer than I had ever been. "If you weren't avoiding it, then tell me, what were the two of you doing last night while you were stacking meat on the well? And why do the receipts say you've been doing this for years?"

The *go to your room* echoed in my mind, but didn't come out of her mouth. "We were conducting adult business, Maddie."

"That's Matthew. And as an adult, I feel I'm privy to adult business."

When Rachel started speaking, both Gabrielle and I snapped our heads towards her, stunned. "W-We were throwing away the meat," she muttered quietly at her plate. "It had gone bad."

Then, I realised how to get the truth. "Gabrielle, you're excused."

Her white hair bun bobbed as she stood. "How *dare* you! You know our arrangement. She is not to leave my side! Your mother promised us that!" She primed her trembling hands.

I stood, setting a napkin on my plate. "What's one private chat at the end of dinner going to matter if you two are going to be together forever?"

"Insolent brat! You don't know what you ask!"

"Would you have done what my mother said?" I asked, careful to sound composed.

"Your mother I respected! Your mother I loved!" She flung her plate, narrowly missing my head, and it shattered on the wall. "She was a woman of science and strength and you are her perverted whelp! Your mother earned her authority!"

Rachel hid her quiet sobs behind her hands. How afraid I was of all this, all this again.

There is nothing to do in these situations but keep one's head. People cry for themselves.

"And I have inherited it. If you are so incensed by that, take it up with estate law. Now leave or I'll choose to acknowledge your threat of violence upon your employer."

A glob of yellow saliva splattered against my face, then the old woman marched from the room, fuming and cursing all the while.

The room quieted as I wiped my face. It was only me and Rachel, now. We had been in the same room, the same house, the same life, for eighteen years and this was the first time it had only been the two of us alone. The weak are only so when they are separated.

"What is it that makes her like that?"

She spoke with trembling lips. "D-Do you really mean to ask? The only other person who knew was your mother."

"I do."

Rachel breathed slowly, gently. "We were locked away together when we were young. As soon as I was born I was put in there with her. I suppose it was the first power she ever had, power over me. I do not blame her for making life easier under our parents by..." Her lips trembled.

"By taking advantage of you? There is no need to forgive."

She didn't move, didn't speak, didn't breath.

"But I will not push you further. I understand you, and I'm sorry. If it's alright with you, can you tell me why you put the meat on the well?"

She swallowed, pausing her tears. "It had gone bad. It stank."

"Indeed, it was putrid. But if it fell in, would it not contaminate the water?"

"It would. We don't get water from the well anymore."

"And why not?"

She stared coldly at the wallpaper. The words spilled from her mouth all at once. "There's a creature in it." The sun dipped past the tracery.

"Do not be afraid of retribution from me. I merely want answers. What kind of creature is it?"

"*Equus auqerus.*"

My nerves burned with fear. Is this what the creature in the sea was after? "And why is it kept in the well?"

Still, she could not look at me. "Your mother and Gabby captured one. Many decades ago now, when she was heavily pregnant with you. It didn't stop her from running into the ocean and snapping the door shut on an iron cage. We had documented a family of kelpie that sometimes left the undersea trench. They travel in tight pods, but form intergenerational family units. And we finally caught one, after years and years. We had lured it with meat. Your mother was going to keep it, to study it, but the logistics were difficult. We wanted a tank in the library, but the ongoing costs, even with her fortune, were impossible. So she thought she'd merely keep it in the ocean, but it was not to be so.

"We saw another trying to free the captive. It gnawed at the bars night after night, but it never managed to make an opening large enough to get the captive out. At night the two sang whale song to the stars. It enraged Gabrielle and your mother, but I thought they were mourning. I almost knew it. Maybe your mother and Gabrielle did, too. Maybe the mourning of their subjects enrages them."

The light in the room quietly dimmed. Night approached.

"Your mother nearly leapt from the mezzanine when she first saw the baby in the cage. It was a terrifying thing, this half-horse, half-fish thing, eyes bulging. It… It…" She breathed heavily, chest shaking with fear, and only when I took her hand and kneeled beside her did she calm. "I saw it turn into a human child. Several times. It didn't know what a human child looked like. It was a disfigured hunk of flesh floating in the ocean, like a scrap of whale meat. But after a while, it stopped doing it. Lord knows why. Your mother would've killed any one of us to capture that thing.

"Whether the creature gave birth in the cage or if the baby had come up from the undersea trench, we couldn't say. Your mother shot the non-captive with a harpoon gun and harvested its organs, bones, and skin for study. She placed the skeleton in the undocumented species room. Gabby caught the baby, lord knows how. We kept it in a tank in your mother's study but day and night it screeched so loud the windows shook. It was meant for the open sea." Her eyes quivered. "When I let it go, she beat me. Gabby did, and your mother watched. She said she'd have joined in if she weren't pregnant. I remember her looking at me…" A deep, breathy pause. "The one in the cage we transferred to the well. It lived there for many years, but I think it's dead now. Gabby won't let us check. Gabby only makes us go to the store. She doesn't let me talk to anyone but her."

I squeezed her hand. How suffering daisy-chains, how trauma has matrixes. There is nothing to say to these people other than what will comfort them. Nothing else matters. "I can see now that you've always been very brave. You can talk to me now. We were both in pain, here. But you don't have to be afraid of her anymore. If you want money to leave, you can have it. You've done nothing wrong. Don't leave anything unsaid."

The old woman wept with her hands pressed to her wet face. To think that it was the same medium that these ancient creatures swam in. "Don't you dare go into the library at night, Matthew. Don't you dare. There are things in there that should've never been pulled from the sea. There are some ancient things that never die."

I stopped in the doorway. I intended to leave, to gather the bandages and crutches for the creature, but the shattered plate and grease from Gabrielle's meal lay on the floor. I had made Rachel confess terrible things; to ask more of her insulted me. I gathered the porcelain pieces in my hands like it was a ritual, like a priest was praying beside me, like a congregation studied my performance. There are things that can never mend.

★ ★ ★

Moonlight illuminated the tide. The bandages and scraps of cloth in my arms whipped beside the beach grasses. Two crutches lay pressed beneath my arm.

The ocean deceives the eyes no matter how long one looks at it; I thought each wave an equine head emerging from the deep. How terrible to look at something, unconvinced of its terrible identity, only to realise that it had watched you since you arrived.

The moss-green head eyed me from the sea, dripping languid drops. A low whistle emerged from its gills, quiet whale song.

"It's not far to the house," I said. "You need legs if you want crutches to work."

The horse-eyes centered on the front of its stretched face, its mouth flattening and shrinking. A few pops rang out as its jaw receded somewhere into its chest, leaving just a few remaining incisors to mimic human teeth. The eyes centered, but the colours couldn't change even as the pupils shrunk. The rest the sea hid from me.

It wasn't much of a person, but it had legs, and more importantly, it understood me and had thoughts and feelings, so I treated it gently. I wrapped the crutches and legs together with bandages, making it barely capable of wobbling its half-horse, half-human body. The wooden end of the crutches and fleshy stubs, nearly feet, sank into the sand with every step. But soon we found a good rhythm, me carrying the monster beneath the arms and its own legs perilously shuddering.

Two massive staircases and two towering doors flanked the house's central foray, the several floors visible all the way up to a towering mezzanine with a round window at the very top. It made the house deeply cold, and deeply dark; it was as though we were looking up from a hole in the ground. The door to the left led to the kitchens, and the library to the right. Neither were lit up.

I sat the creature in the light of the round window as it heaved. The glow of its eyes dashed from door to staircase, from the moonlit window to the stairs.

The library light flicked on, a thin line illuminated beneath the door. A low shuddering began, metal banging against wood. Gently leaving that pinkish-green half-human wrapped in bandages, I carefully opened the door to the library. I was too nervous to look in.

"Rachel?" I asked. No response. The shaking only grew louder. "Gabrielle?"

The kelpie wobbled, and I rushed to help it stand, leaving the door open. Transfixed with the light, it took one anxious step after the other. There was not much human emotion in its eyes, but there was recognition. *Has it been here before?* I wondered. The thought made me tremble.

"Alright, I've shown you inside. Let's get back to the water, friend." I tried to switch its direction, but it pulled against me.

There was a heavy thump on the mezzanine three floors above. Shouts came into earshot, the slamming of doors. Both the creature and I looked up at it as I moved a little quicker towards the library.

The shouts from above became screams. Something sounded like a table falling, a dresser slamming. I heard Gabrielle cursing as Rachel wailed and cried.

Perhaps I had been too rash in telling Rachel she could leave. I was distracted looking up there for too long; the creature's weight shifted beside me. One of the crutches fell, then the other. A wet stump shoved me aside. Squelching footsteps scurried away as the deception became clear.

That creature ran to the library!

Gasping, I watched it sprint away, my insult growing. But it could walk on its own two feet; I needed to get above and stop whatever in the world was going on. I made it up halfway past the first stairwell when I heard the agonizing ripping of hair, and Rachel whimpering.

"*Gabrielle!*" My voice rang out loud and harsh against the stairwell. "*What in the hell is going on up there?!*"

She appeared over the mezzanine handrail in her white sleeping gown, a wad of Rachel's hair crushed beneath her hand and the burnished wood. "You are cruel to make her speak to you! You have no idea what you've done to her!" A shadow appeared behind her.

"This is not my mother's house anymore! Please, stop this. We'll talk."

Rachel appeared in the moonlight; for the first time I saw no fear in her eyes. Time moved slowly. She took hold of Gabrielle by the arms and flung her from the mezzanine. Her nightgown billowed in the moonlight, all the way down the hole made by the staircase. When I caught sight of the whites of her eyes as she fell past me, she didn't even seem scared, only surprised. She didn't even scream. It was the quietest she'd been in days.

She broke against the parquetry tile, a sound like the closing of a faraway door. There was no movement.

Rachel stood in her place. There was no longer a need to go upstairs. How commonly had I imagined this, how this was always the shadow of every act in the house; someone would die, and now someone had. The jittering in the library continued. Perhaps there were many things that died here.

Blood spread along the tile below. The moon rose, unhurried. The sound of the thump against the tile quieted from our minds.

"Rachel. You're free to do as you want, to go where you like. Take a few month's salary from my mother's office. Hell, take a year. Just know that you have no obligations here. The time you have left is yours. I'll take care of the mess."

Rachel watched me, uncertain.

"It won't be any different than picking up a plate and mopping up grease, I promise."

For the first time in my life, I saw Rachel smile. She ran off to her room, and soon I heard dressers open and close.

I ran back to the library, avoiding the corpse all the while. The lights in the library illuminated a trail of water. The rows and rows of fossils, the cabinets filled with stone and bones, all shook violently. The rattling overwhelmed the mournful whale-song.

I followed the melodic cries and the water trail to the undocumented species room, where the *Equus auqerus* skeleton was kept. A naked half-person lay at its base, dripping saltwater and tearlessly weeping with a sound like a contrabassoon, hissing and resonant. It was laid out like it was when it had come ashore.

Suspended with wire, this sea creature's skeleton was hoisted like so many reassembled *mosasaur* and *basilasour*, with its hideous horse-maw open and crying out. Hooves ready to kick at an enemy, tail twisted mid-leap. Every skeleton stood locked in a battle of our own genesis, the ones we imagined all the creatures before us fought.

My mother's hastily-written notes were pinned to the wall. *The Equus auqerus are viciously bonded by brood. Females give live birth in salt water; from an early age they express the ability to rear-range bones and organs to take on different visages for the purposes of avoiding predators or hiding among prey. Yet, their transformations are sometimes unprompted, purposeless; this seems to be some manner of self-expression. Their songs are complex and grating. Observed trans-forming into whales, sharks, dolphins, eels, humans. They live in under-sea trenches; pods rarely surface.*

The creature discarded its human form and lay there, its equine head disproportionate to its own body, to the fingers that coated themselves in cartilage. It stared at the black eye-holes of the other skull, crying out in clicking vocalisations as though the other could hear it.

Footsteps rang out from the stairs. Rachel appeared in the doorway beside me, suitcase in hand. When she saw the creature, she didn't wince, or even seem particularly surprised. It imme-diately snapped its head towards her, so much more offended by her presence than mine.

She stared for a long moment. Her whisper, barely audible over the rattling of cases, distracted it from its pain for only a moment. "I'm sorry for what we did to you."

I couldn't say if she was speaking to me or the creature. The creature looked away, sated. Did it understand who she was?

She touched her hand to my cheek, almost like an apology, as though this one touch could heal everything away. Her palm still stung; my skin remembered the slaps, the binding of cloth over my mouth. How often the body understands better than the mind; when she withdrew her hand, it knew it would be for the last time. She rushed out the door.

The creature lay whimpering at the skeleton.

From the window in my mother's office, I watched Rachel leave. The receipts from the meat were still laid out on the desk. I sat at that desk for a long time, listening to the creature's melodic cries. Lights appeared along the road. Rachel stood over the well, her suitcase in one hand. She slipped into the car and the lights faded.

My mother's cash remained untouched in one of the compartments in the drawers. I was almost angry at her for not taking the money; it told me that she would ask for nothing for the rest of her life.

I looked again to the pinboard filled with old schedules, receipts, yellowed photographs. All these dead sea creatures again; sea snakes and eels, whales and dolphins and sharks. She must've kept them there for reference while writing. There were no photos of people, or of my mother's family. The only picture that portrayed anything of human make was her father's grave, somewhere in Eastern Oregon, where he had been born, and where he had wished to be buried. A cross and a long oval plot in the desert. It was hard to imagine her mourning, but then it was hard to imagine her at all.

A cross and a long oval plot. A cross-shape, and a squiggled circle.

The trail of water in the library had nearly dried in the midnight drafts. The creature still lay dramatically on the cold tile. "You showed me a grave," I told it. "In the sand, you drew a grave. I didn't understand how you knew us so deeply. But now I know: my mother kept you in her office. You were the baby. And you were surrounded by photos of dead creatures, and you understood what a grave was."

By now, it had fully transformed into what I assumed to be its base form: the hippocampus with its hooved legs and *basilosaurus* tail, its moss-green mane laying as formless as water over its neck. For the first time, it looked at me, understanding me as part of the environment. It had heard what I said before.

"Is this your father?" I already knew the answer. "Do you know what's in the well?" After a swallow, I looked at the rattling chests. "And do you know what's in these?"

Growling, the creature dilated its fins, tensing its jaw and eyes. With one hoof in front of the other, it slowly clawed its way towards the foray. I picked up its tail like a heavy fish, help-ing it along. The tip of its tail fin whipped back and struck me, leaving a red mark along my face and neck. Dropping it abruptly, I cried, "Excuse me! You don't get to manipulate me to do something and then hit me when I do it for you!"

As though to counter me, the fin stretched and snapped just as it had when transforming into human legs; but two horse-legs sprouted, the bones shivering and the muscles shifting into place. A clear insult. The clip-clop against the tile echoed in from the foray.

"Christ in heaven! You *act* like no one raised you!"

The constant sound from the shaking cabinets did nothing for my mood. I flung open a specimen drawer and immedi-ately my rage was quelled; the fossil of an infant *diplocaulus,* the bones of an ancient, three-foot salamander with a wide skull in a thin sheet of tannish rock, shook on its own. Rushing to a work desk, I fumbled for a chisel-headed rock hammer and chipped away. The shaking grew stronger, only aiding my attempts to peel the rock off like scales. Finally the hammer broke through, revealing the entire skull. For a moment, it stopped shaking.

The dark within an eyehole shifted.

I have never done anything faster than throwing it in the tide. How many years had these laid in cupboards, how many years buried in the dunes, and how many in the sea? And how many hundreds more were in the library?

As I dashed between the cabinets and the tide, with so many more rooms yet to exhaust, the creature stood between me and the library. It seemed to show concern. A low, sputtering hiss, just to ensure I was watching as it walked to Gabrielle's body.

Its teeth pressed into the pale flesh of her arm until it burst with red, then dragged her out face-down to the tide. She was so much more dead than the fossils I flung into the ocean. Without the slightest pause, it trotted into the ocean with the body. The final ripples of her nightgown disappeared where the undersea bar dipped off. I knew that limit well; I had swam to it a hundred thousand times.

A trail of light from the open foray doors interlaced with the moonlight on the sea. When the creature reemerged, it remained in its four-legged form. It stood watching me for several moments.

"All the wellkeepers are gone," I told it. "I refuse to keep the well. I will ask you again; do you know what's in there?"

It trotted off towards the well, and I followed. There were still bits of rotted meat all around the lilies and roses. "Did you do this?" I asked.

A single hoof pound.

The well's rim lay ominous and open, like it could stutter away and open up beneath us. Over the edge I saw water gently rippling below, the moon illuminating a dark silhouette within.

Claw marks, hoof marks, handprints stained the mossy interior. Hundreds of them, all around the rocks. And the variety was so great; on some stones it looked like a wet snake had attempted to crawl up it a hundred times, others showed where fingers had hopelessly dug out the calk for decades.

The fish-tail, only partially bone, still floated, and wet hair still lay on its back. If my mother had died a year sooner, it could have been saved. How fresh it all was. Its equine skull was missing the bottom half of the jaw, but it still pointed towards the stars.

How hard it was to pull my eyes away, how hard to keep looking.

The beach trail shook as the creature galloped toward the well and brutally rammed it, one side of the wall crumbling. Another hit; the rocks fell into the water below. It slammed into the well over and over at full speed, until there was nothing left but a hole in the ground covered in rubble. Already the wind blew sand over it.

Without waiting for me, the creature returned to the tide. Then it faced me with its gleaming black eyes, demanding my attention. Two hoof pounds on the beach, one in the surf. It was time for a decision.

"I don't understand what you want from me. I cannot follow you into your world." The sea lapped against the dune. "Though I wish I could know the world beneath, more deeply than anything. And I wish I knew how you could understand me so precisely."

The creature approached me, lowering its head, as though inviting me towards its mane. The webbed spines on its back relaxed, flattening. With a pair of gentle whinnies, it convinced me it was safe. Reaching out my hand towards its mane, it suddenly snapped at me with its hideous fangs, leaving a few deep, bloody slices on my hand.

I withdrew with a scream, clutching my hand to my chest.

"What is it you want from me! You deceived me into opening the doors for you to see the bodies of your parents and still you attack me? You have sentience and emotion and still you lash out!"

The creature trotted away into the sea.

No matter how many surgical spirits I poured on the wound, I could not feel the telltale sting.

★ ★ ★

The wound did not heal, not in the way we think of healing. Slick brownish-green hair, like a seal's, sprouted in the cuts. The fingernails withdrew.

And every day I felt more and more different. I was suddenly more limber, the decades spent in a school chair or a work desk evaporated. Some days, I woke up with taller cheekbones than I remembered, with longer legs. My mind changed, too; nothing about it frightened me.

My bones popped every time I moved, my legs crackled as I walked from sea to library, methodically removing the fossils day and night, undoing everything my mother and her mother had done.

As the sun set on the fourth day, I heard whale-song, almost like a howl, over the ocean. In the sea, the creature's head appeared, and suddenly the shape of the sonar clicking, the bow of the guttural hissing, the resonant chirps and squeaks burst from noise into vocalisation, from abstraction to meaning. The voice came muddled in my mind, the voice of the creature, at first formless noise. A new instinct told me the meaning with greater precision than any words I'd ever heard in my native tongue.

"I confess now, I remembered you." The creature pulled me by my ankles into the sea, and I eagerly followed. Once beneath the surface, water filled my lungs and my body welcomed it. I choked when I tried to speak, but the hippocampus merely gave a delicate press of its hoof against my side, shoving me deeper into the dark. The stinging I expected from opening my eyes was gone – instead, it was comfortable, like the new layer of mucus on my eyes had a purpose. My webbed hands had me unlearning how to swim as a human. I was back to being a toddler in the ocean for the first time, flailing my open palms. Mother, Gabrielle, or Rachel never swam with me. But I had always been a strong swimmer, always knew how to stay safe. Did someone teach that to me?

The hippocampus flipped, a flurry of bubbles left in its wake. *"Oh what fun we had! Don't you remember? You were always by the rivers playing. I loved to see you. I tutored you, remember? I was a baby, too."* The whale-song echoed in my mind.

Now it was my turn to be unable to communicate. I smiled, shook my head, tried to speak, but only bubbles spewed from my mouth.

"Worry not. A day shall come that your garish mouth will be gone and you will be free to gab your time away. Perhaps now do you understand my frustration? Eons have I to tell you of, tales told to me in desperation by my caged mother, histories so vast that even my lifetime is not enough! Every human language to have ever been uttered and all those that have let their final whispers ring into the night are the mere squealing of non-sentient crabs to us. How much a crude mimicry of our

vast richness is your land, a hollow echo of what the world laid out for you. I will regard you as a companion, if you will have it. I have never felt as one of my pod; I am unique in that I spent time above, in that dwelling. They call me dramatic for being among you, for my sentimentality toward the rivers and your kind. I am the only one of us among the rivers. So are you the only one of you among the waters.

"There have been others like you, but they are beyond recognition now. They look like me, or however they choose to appear; the ocean is rich with species you can never know, and we can be any one of them. That is what it means to be a half-sea beast, half-land beast; we are a bridge. Come below with me, when you are ready, and all these things will be told to you."

I wanted more than anything to tell it yes, to tell it to please tell me, to give me all the knowledge my mother lacked, that science could not squeeze out of rocks and bones. The language was low and stretched, with sounds I could not have possibly duplicated with my human mouth.

A week later, there is so little of a human mouth left. I have to purposely shape it, to imagine what it is I want to look like, and then do it, but the human palette is delicate and precise. Speech is not what it was, though my hands, even as I move freely between forms, still allow me the use of a pen. Walking is tedious now, and swimming is freeing. But I decided to keep the house, once the fossils were gone. I decided that it was mine, and I could live a life above and below.

When I first encountered the mysterious things in this house, I thought I'd have to write a warning to anyone who came across it. I thought I'd tell them to be wary of the well. To be wary of the house, the sea, the river, to always be afraid. There are ravenous monsters, I would say, and ancient things that never die.

But that is not the way of transformation, of change.

I am a half-monster living in a decaying manor. Some days I am more human than others; but that never makes me less a resident to the land and sea both. If I am found, I will not let people take my home from me. Let them try to take the sea from us. Nothing is theirs that was not taken. And first they must know this: there are some ancient things that can never be killed.

SEA SALT AND

STRAWBERRIES

Solstice Lamarre

The first time we met I had already been ancient for forever and a day, but you were wild and carefree, radiating the light that only newly born souls knew how to shine.

It was an accident, really. You were not supposed to see me. I would let mortals enter my forest, pick berries from my bushes, drink and bathe in my rivers and lake, hunt my children to feed themselves. But I would not let them see me. Even gods get distracted sometimes, though. Humans would run back to their tribe and tell stories about the forest monster, the forest god, the forest's soul. The tales spoke of a lean, giant body covered in bark and moss, of the most intricate antlers ever witnessed, of bugs making their home in long muddy hair, of a face like a human or a stag or like nothing they had ever seen. Humans would hear the stories and they would be more careful for a while. I would receive offerings I did not need. I accepted them nonetheless.

You were different, though. Unafraid.

You ran into me and saw my height, saw my harsh skin and my antlers, the moss and mushrooms that covered me, and the bugs crawling over me and yet you did not run. You smiled like you had found a secret treasure, and for a second I was scared you would unsheathe your sword and try to kill me. Not that you ever could. Instead you tilted your head to the side, long dark hair following the movement, and you offered me your body.

It caught me by surprise so completely that I did not react for a long, long time. Most mortals would not have waited so long for an answer, but you did. A proud warrior boy, with a brand-new sword at your hip, the smooth brown skin of your jaw a testament of your youth. I was sure that many had already accepted the offer you made me, that your confidence was not faked.

I could not say yes. I would not say yes.

But it meant I had to say no.

I had not used my voice for so many ages that I was not sure it had not turned wild, not sure it would still obey me.

When I spoke, it sounded like creaking wood in a wildfire.

"I am afraid I will have to say no."

For a heartbeat, your grin widened. Then it slipped and crashed and died and suddenly you were pouting like a child.

"I can't have that. Is it because of anything I could change? Do you not want me? Do forest gods have lifelong partners? Is it another god, maybe a river deity?"

You almost made me laugh. You were frowning, focused, searching for a solution you would not find.

I simply did not care about what you were seeking from me. All kinds of beasts, humans included, had had sex on my soil and under my branches. Yet it still seemed like something that did not touch me, something I had never wanted to take part in. It did not disgust me, it did not interest me. Still, how much you cared made me smile.

"I do not want to, that is all."

You sighed. "It's not because of me, though, is it?"

"No, it is not."

You sighed again, louder. "Well, I guess it can't be helped, then."

I thought our encounter was over, but when I turned to leave, you followed me deeper into my forest, pestering me with questions I would not answer. You did not seem to mind.

You talked and talked until it was dark and I had to show you the way out of my depths.

You could not see it but your soul shone in the darkness. You were a star; small, bright light breaking against the cool comfort of the night.

You said goodbye. For no reason I could comprehend, it hurt to let you go.

I thought it was the end.

If I had been paying more attention, I would have noticed the night tasted of sea salt and strawberries. The taste of beginnings.

★ ★ ★

You came back. At first, I thought you might have simply been hunting on my soil. You were focused, eyes searching the depths of my woods. Too focused, maybe. A hare ran right before your feet and you did nothing. A bird flew right above your head and you ignored it. You were not searching for prey.

You were searching for me.

You were young, from your body to your soul, and your patience ran out long before mine.

"Where are you? I know you're here! You must be here, *somewhere*."

I smiled, hidden to human eyes, because the forest was me and I was the forest. You would have never found me if I wanted to hide from you.

"I don't even know your name! Do gods have names? Are you even a god? A spirit? I have so many questions, you can't possibly expect me to just let my curiosity die! Come *on*, I promise I won't ask about sex anymore, I just want to see *you*. You don't even have to answer the questions! I just… I don't know, I want to be friends?"

You hesitated on the last word, like you were afraid it would bite you. Or that the forest would burst into mocking laughter. It did not. My forest and I grew quiet, plunged into a thoughtful silence, until I realised you might mistake my silence for rejection.

I did not understand you. I did not understand why your light drew me in so intensely. I did not understand why you wanted my company this fiercely. But you were curious, and this I understood.

Because for the first time in an age, I was curious too.

You were on the verge of giving up when I let you see me. It felt to me like I had made my decision quickly, oddly so. To you, however, it might have felt like an eternity. My hours passed in the blink of an eye, but yours had stretched your patience to its limits. Still you waited for me.

Your face lit up with delight, awe, and mischief when you saw me.

"Ha! I knew you wouldn't resist me!"

You did not know that at all. A heartbeat ago, your face had been sad and resigned.

"So, are you a god? Am I friends with a god? Do you have a name?"

I scoffed. I sounded like a dry branch breaking under a human's weight.

"I am whatever you make me out to be. I only have the names people give me."

You laughed, like this was hilarious. I did not understand, but the loud, strange sound of your human laughter felt like the summer sun.

"Wow, that's pretentious. Though it's not on purpose, is it? You're just *like this*. Incredible. I'll just call you 'Leaf.'"

I let out a low, confused groan. Humans called me names that spoke of nature, strength, and glory. Ancient names, names with power nested at their core. They did not call me 'Leaf'. It was both ridiculous and absurd. 'Moss' or 'Bark' or 'Antlers' would have made more sense than 'Leaf', considering what my body looked like to you.

You were ridiculous.

I let you be.

★ ★ ★

I kept letting you see me. I could find no explanation for my own behaviour, and after a while, it did not matter anymore. I enjoyed your light, your voice, your laugh. Sometimes, you would join me many days in a row, and it would feel like you were always by my side, chattering like a bird during spring. Sometimes you would disappear for a full moon cycle, or even more, to live your own life, the one that did not involve me. I did not mind, but it made me all the more delighted when I heard you call my name again.

You would never get tired of talking: about your new sword, about that girl or that boy, about people whose name I did not care to remember. I would never get tired of listening to you.

You almost made me care. About the world outside my boundaries, about the lives of those who hunted my children or picked all the berries from my bushes.

Almost.

In the end, the only one I cared about was you.

I loved you boundlessly, for no logical reason.

I loved you like a child or a sibling or a friend or a soulmate.

I loved you like I did not know I could, and it filled me with terror and joy.

I loved you so intensely that for a heartbeat of my life, and years of yours, I forgot it would end.

★ ★ ★

I was not used to my reason being so utterly altered. I did not even realise that it had happened, that logic did not matter anymore when it came to you.

I thought I loved you enough that I would know if something happened to you. I thought I would know the end was close, if there even was an end. I thought if you were to die, you would do it here, peacefully and in my arms.

I was wrong.

I only knew because your son visited me, days after your death in battle. You had told him stories about me, like you had told me stories about him. He told me about your glorious death with tears in his eyes. His body looked like yours, but his soul did not. He was not you. Even when he begged me to, I could not bring myself to let him see me.

I loved you so brightly, and it still was not enough to keep you mine forever. To keep you safe from the outside world, to keep you safe from your own mortality.

I did not get to say goodbye. I did not get to see your light one last time. I did not get to hear your strange human laugh again.

I felt odd. Hurt. I knew more than anyone that death was part of life. My animal children came to the world and died every day and I accepted this as truth.

You were different, though. You had chosen to be mine, and it felt wrong that I could not protect you from death, or at the very least help you through your last breath.

My unbreakable heart broke that day.

It was the end.

The following night tasted like sea salt and strawberries, but I did not care if this was supposed to be a new beginning. If it took you to end for something new to start, then it was not a good enough trade to me.

★ ★ ★

For centuries, I buried my love and my pain and my memories of you deep inside me, far under the roots of my trees. I did not want to think of what loving you had done to me. It was far easier to love my trees and my springs and my children, because they all followed rules I had always known. In the short time it took you to live and die, you had managed to turn my eternal existence upside down.

So I pretended I had forgotten you. I pretended I did not need to mourn, because your death should have been insignificant to a god.

For a while, it worked. I would feel the crack left in my heart at your disappearance start to burn again, and I would drown it under all the love I had left, a love that was not for you but for my own kind.

It was easy enough to ignore that the crack was not healing. It was easy enough to think myself invincible. Yes. Pretending worked for a few centuries.

Until it stopped.

★ ★ ★

You had returned.

I could not believe it. I am a practical being. I believe what I see and sense. I believe it because I am a seasoned guardian, and I have steadily withstood the harshest seasons. My feelings *serve* me, they do not *deceive* me.

Of course, none of this mattered when it concerned you.

I saw you, and your body looked nothing like it had in the first of your lives.

You were so young, barely on the verge of adulthood. Blond hair, pale skin, storm grey eyes, white tunic. From a civilisation that had, centuries ago, trampled over the one you used to belong to. I did not feel any anger at this. Even from my static point of view, I knew, like every immortal being in the world, how amazingly good humans were at being terrible to each other.

You were not bright, or joyful, or luminous. You were skulking around, angry and hurt, muttering dark words to yourself.

But your soul.

Oh, love, your soul.

It was still shining like it was new. Its edges were slightly blurred from centuries of use, but its light had not dimmed in the slightest.

Your soul was a miracle. Right there, walking before my eyes, above my roots, under my branches. The wound in my heart cracked open, pain rushing inside my body, spreading to my trees and my streams and my children.

The forest screamed, quietly. Wind rushed between my leaves, wood made cracking sounds inaudible to your ears, deer and hares and foxes whined and ran to try and escape my pain, but they could not, because it was everywhere.

I did not show myself to you. I knew that the joy of being with you again would not outweigh the pain of losing you a second time, either because you would not want me in this life, or because you would eventually die again.

I would not be caught by surprise again.

You took walks on my soil regularly. You often muttered to yourself unhappily. I wanted to hold you and heal you as much as I knew I could not.

Seeing you hurt me. Seeing you healed me, too. Bit by bit until the crack in my heart became a thick, solid scar. Then, I could start to heal you, too.

I made myself, my forest, a refuge for you. I made sure you always stumbled on the best fruits I had to offer, the clearest and calmest streams, the most beautiful clearings. I made myself stunning so you would come back again. So you would have a place to heal yourself under my caring gaze.

You did.

As time went on and you grew into yourself, I could see the difference I had made on your body. Your shoulders relaxed, your frown lightened, and your dark muttered words turned into soft sweet whispers.

In a way, you were still talking to me.

And I was still talking to you. Only I did not use words.

The day I had to admit that you would not come back, that it had been too long since your last visit, hurt.

But it hurt in a quiet, warm way, and the scar on my heart did not split.

The night smelled like sea salt and strawberries, and I knew that if I waited for you long enough, you would come back to me.

★ ★ ★

There was a time when centuries passed quickly for me. Before, time did not matter. Everything was a simple cycle, and preserving this eternal pattern fulfilled my soul.

There was a time when I did not know what *waiting* felt like. When you suddenly *made me wait*, it changed everything. The changes of my heart are not fast. But you had changed that, too.

I did not notice at first when the waiting, the ever-growing impatience, made its nest above my heart and grew and grew and grew. So slowly it was barely there.

It was, though. And it was there to stay.

★ ★ ★

The next time I met you, you were only a child.

There was a sense of relief, seeing your soul again, feeling it brush against the bark of my trees as you climbed them. One of my children, a part of my forest, had come home after a long absence.

Your mother ran after you and told you to be more careful and hugged you and kissed your bruises. Something inside me burned to be her, to hold you like she did.

Instead, I made juicy berries and medicinal plants appear on her way home. I wanted so badly to have some importance in all of your lives here. After some time, I became less and less subtle. Your mother would find the exact herbs she needed for this night's dinner, look over her shoulder, and smile at the forest. At me. To show gratitude, whenever she sent you to play on my ground, she would give you some handmade trinket to tie to one of my tree's branches.

It did not protect you from your own human fragility. Your mother came and begged me to help and heal you.

And I tried. I promise you I tried. Every herb I knew would help a sick child grew under your mother's feet. She did not know what to do with them, but I am sure she tried, too. Then you were gone again.

The hurt was quiet but restless. The air smelled of sea salt and strawberries and the waiting began again.

★ ★ ★

You were a woman and a warrior.

You looked so much like the first time I met you that the entire forest let out a quiet sob when you smiled. The clothes, the armour, and the language were all different, but your long black hair and your wild smile were as dangerous as they had been all those millennia ago.

You did not live here, but you made me your battleground. You and your fighters spent many days getting to know me and all my twists and corners, and I offered my secrets to you without hesitation.

When your enemies arrived to defeat you, you knew how to trick them with my help. And maybe, maybe a few of them tripped on mysterious moving roots, maybe they were attacked by angry foxes, maybe their wounds rotted instantly.

I could only see you. Fierce and dangerous and beautiful. I did not want you to go, but I knew the only way to keep you here would have been to let you lose and die.

You won and celebrated under my canopy. My streams cleaned your wounds, my bushes and children fed you. I politely looked away when the celebrating started to involve naked skin and breathy moans.

I smiled to myself. You had not changed at all.

Then you left, and all of my forest stretched itself towards you in a silent plea for you to stay.

You turned around and showed me that wild, dangerous smile of yours one last time. You must have felt my call, because you briefly came back, pressed your forehead against the bark of one of my trees. You thanked me under your breath. You said you knew the favour I had done for you. You said you would be eternally grateful.

You called me a part of your soul.

I cried softly when you left me alone with the smell of sea salt and strawberries. It was almost entirely swallowed by the stench of blood and rot.

The only things you were leaving me to remember you by were a few healing words and three hundred corpses.

★ ★ ★

I never stopped wondering. Was it the waiting? Was it your absence that made the rest of humanity pale in comparison? Was it your shine that made them all feel like voids that would engulf a part of me if I let them get too close? Or was the seed of weariness there since I met the first of your kind, growing beneath my heart imperceptibly?

Maybe it was both. Maybe your absence helped the seed grow.

I grew weary of anyone that did not wear your soul stepping on my soil. Your kind was getting worse, hungrier, needier, greedier. I used to offer everything I had without restraint. But as the centuries passed, every human standing beneath my branches made me more and more resentful.

Your kind used to be, if not friends, at least another Earthen creature I granted passage or asylum to. Then you entered my life, and time went on, and as humanity grew disproportionately, they started eating at my patience and at my forest like a divine plague.

Humanity started to feel like millions of thieves pretending they were gods.

★ ★ ★

You appeared right when I was about to tear myself apart to avoid destroying the next unfortunate humans who would walk on my soil.

You were a tall, white, spindly woman with hair like a wildfire. You took a step inside me and I recognised your soul instantly. All of me trembled with relief. Your eyes went wide with surprise, and your hand touched the bark of one of my trees with a deference no one had paid me for centuries.

"Do I know you?"

The wind rustled my leaves, shock coursing from my roots to my treetops.

"Well, this seems as good a place as any for a witch to hide, doesn't it?"

I watched you make your home deep inside my forest. You were entirely alone, but you never seemed lonely. You were frail, but you rolled up your sleeves and figured out how to build a house all on your own.

Well, almost on your own.

You always found what you needed quickly, as long as it was something I could provide. You thanked me loudly every time, as if I was a kindly neighbour lending you a hand in the construction of the building.

I did not have the carefreeness and the trust I had back when I met you, and it took you years to tame me. At sunset, you would sit cross-legged in the little garden you had tended to with infinite love, braiding your bright orange hair. You would talk to me, like I was sitting behind the treeline, just out of your line of sight. Close, but invisible.

You were right, of course.

You talked about flowers and fruits and the Earth and how much you loved it. You talked about your day, the animals and plants you had seen, and how beautiful and peaceful all of me was. You talked about the witch hunt and the friends you had

lost and the relationships that had been broken. You talked about
the lives you saved with your medicine and your witchcraft, and
how even that was not enough for anyone to stand up between
you and hanging.

You talked about me, too.

You talked about that feeling of coming home you had when
you stepped inside my forest for the first time. You stared at the
treeline, with a smug smile on your lips, and you told me you
could feel me there. You told me I felt like a long-lost sibling.
Maybe even a soulmate.

One day – I do not know what made that day special – I
stepped into the light. I had become smaller, skinnier since I
first met you. Humans treating the forest like it was disposable
affected me, too. I was still taller than you, and the antlers were
almost enough to still make me feel godlike.

You did not flinch. You smiled, as if welcoming a relative
you had not seen in a while, and I sat next to you. You did not
expect me to talk, which I was grateful for.

And as the years passed and as you grew old, I sat there with
you every night. Sometimes, when I was feeling bold, I would
sit next to your open window in the middle of the day to watch
you cook.

Every year, you carved a small animal bone into a protective
trinket, and braided it into my hair.

"So that I'll never leave you, love."

I knew it was a lie. A comforting one, nonetheless.

One day, you slipped away in your sleep, quietly. I watched
your shine, that used to illuminate your small house from the
inside, disappear.

I wished I could have been as unafraid of your death as you
had been.

I felt small, and empty, and alone, and not even carved bones
and sea salt and strawberries could prevent my shaking sob from
making the forest creak and tremble.

★ ★ ★

There had been wars before. I had witnessed more battles than I would have liked to. Centuries ago, I had even indulged yours, had almost taken part in it myself. I could not have known that after your small, harmless victory other battles would come, and they would not be so kind to me. Many destroyed parts of me, trampled my children, uprooted my trees. I did not like it, but I had made my peace with humanity's belligerent nature. I could always grow new trees, or care for newly born children.

Humanity was childish and violent, but they did not present any danger to my safety.

But your kind was greedy and arrogant, and I failed to notice that that was the real threat they represented.

They grew and grew and grew. They never had enough. They strived to outgrow their natural condition. They wanted to leash the world and drown it under cement and blood.

Their death machines did not only leave corpses in their wake, they injured me and all of the living things that were a part of my system. They burned parts of me to the ground, or left explosions in their wake, leaving my soil spoilt and unable to grow anything ever again.

I watched, powerless, as my forest shrank, and as I shrank with it. I became as short as any human. My bark itched and peeled. My antlers became fragile, fell for the very first time, and never grew again.

I came to hate them all. I could not even muster the empathy I used to have as they died on my soil. I only felt disgust and hatred and, deep down, a nervousness I did not recognise.

When I saw you again, I hated you, too. I wished you were not here. For the very first time, I saw you as part of the rest of humanity. Young, and beautiful, and violent, and disgusting, and doomed to die here. You still shined so brightly. Your soul sang to mine and it sang a war song and I hated it.

You were killing me as much as any other.

Your wars had made my heart swell with resentment, and it was hard to let that resentment die the way you were dying at the hands of a man fighting on the other side of your hateful, nonsensical war.

I had to let that feeling die. If only for a second. I did not want to feel glee as your life left you right in front of me.

I could see you were all doomed to die and rot on what was left of my soil, so I left the darkness to come and embrace you. You were lying in the mud, covered in blood, your breathing laborious. You kissed the picture of a beautiful man you knew you would never get to kiss again.

I held you there, and I let the resentment go. I replaced it with the image of all of the people that had worn your soul and I felt better, but the acidic nervousness I could not identify still sat there, heavy in my chest.

As you died, you looked at me and touched my face, smearing it with your own blood.

"I... I know you, right?"

I did not answer. I brushed my harsh lips against your forehead as you let out your last breath. You lay in my arms, cold and dead. I had wished to hold you as you died so many times, but now I was happy I had not, because the pain was unbearable.

After cradling your dead body for I did not know how long, I realised that the acidic nervousness was fear. Fear of death. Fear that you and your kind were killing me. Fear that my immortality was a mere mirage. Fear of what was to come.

Fear of the end. Because there would be an end.

I knew death more intimately than anyone and anything in the world. I had seen it in all of its glory and pain and ugliness. The idea of *my* death, however, had never touched my thoughts.

I pretended that the smell of sea salt and strawberries was hidden by all the blood, and the mud, and the rot. But the idea that there was no new beginning, that *I* might die before I ever saw your soul shine again, would not leave me.

* * *

You stare right in front of you, fixedly, as I end the story of your soul. It is a hot summer day, and it has not rained for weeks. Birds are chirping in what is left of my trees. I used to be a magnificent forest, full of beautiful secrets and dreadful dark corners. I am barely a patch of trees in the middle of humanity's grey delusion. It does not matter. I have had time to come to terms with the fact that I am dying. It still hurts, though.

We are sitting shoulder to shoulder, the dry bark of mine scratching the soft dark brown skin of yours. We stare at the big publicity board in front of us, a stone's throw away from my last rows of trees, visible from the ugly, loud grey human road.

New shopping mall opening next autumn! Construction soon to be started.

"Well, shit," you say.

* * *

You come see me every day. Your dedication is unmatched. None of your other selves went through this much trouble to join me this often. I think it is because of the unspoken sense of urgency we both feel, almost buzzing in the air.

Perhaps it is because of your guilt, too. I would be lying if I said I did not enjoy hearing it in your voice. I have grown resentful of humanity, and despite centuries of convincing myself otherwise, you are just another human being. A product of your greedy, disgusting kind. I will not get apologies and guilt from anyone else, so I will take yours.

"I'm really sorry," you say for the hundredth time. "I'd never thought my dad's job would do this much damage. I mean, I *know* he's a capitalist piece of shit who doesn't care about the environment, I just didn't think a dumb shopping mall would end up killing a millennia-old forest god."

"It is fine," I say as I refuse your daily orange juice.

You have been trying to share it with me for weeks. Your constant trivial acts of kindness are useless, but they make me happy nonetheless.

"Is god fine by the way?" you ask, your dark brown eyes inquisitive behind your glasses.

I stare silently.

"Like, you're non-binary, right? I mean, I assumed because of how you talked about yourself a few times. Would, I dunno, goddex be more fitting?"

I blink once. Twice. You have been so many different people, but you have always been stubborn and talkative. I am strangely happy that the last of you I will know does not stray away from this unspoken rule.

"I think humanity's conception of 'gender' is foolish and convoluted. Your kind is good at building rigid walls and even more rigid rules. However, god is fine."

"Right. Smart thinking. Cis people are less cool than us anyway."

There is silence for a while. You throw your empty carton of orange juice at the publicity board. It does not fall remotely close to it.

"It's the wind," you say. "I would've hit that stupid thing without the wind."

"You're throwing your junk on my soil," I reply.

"Yeah. Shit. Sorry."

You get up, fetch the bright white and orange carton, and sit back next to me. Closer. I tense when you rest your head against my shoulder, but I almost hiss when you try to get away.

You chuckle, and it quickly turns into a sad sigh.

"One week left."

"Just a moment," I whisper back, barely more than the sound of wind rustling leaves.

"I could call an association. Something. Greenpeace or whatever."

It is my turn to sigh. "What will you say? Save these few trees because a fallen god inhabits them?"

"I'd find something."

Your desperation echoes mine. But I also realise I absolutely refuse to prolong my agony.

I am dying. The scent of sea salt and strawberries will never envelop me again. If it is not in this moment, it will be in the next. I have barely more than the blink of an eye left. I will not birth another child, grow another tree, or see another of you ever again. What is the point, then? This is the last time I get to see you shining next to me.

In a way, you will have outlasted me. I would never have thought.

"Do not. Please," I say. No, I plead. "I would rather go away knowing you are near."

"This is shit."

"I know," I say softly. "But there is nothing you can do."

* * *

Apparently, you do not think so. The next week, while I agonise and scream in silence and die under the machines uprooting me, you sneak on the construction site with a friend. She knows which bit of me you can take back home. You are both very careful and very loving, but I already lost all of my body, and most of my self. You speak to me while you replant me, put me on your windowsill, and water me into health.

You speak to me every day. I do not understand what you say. I lost my full consciousness long ago.

For a while, I am angry at you for not letting me die my violent, quick death.

But your voice, even when speaking nonsense, soothes me. The light of your soul nourishes me more than the sun ever could. Your care and love warm me from my roots to the tip of my leaves.

I have loved you so intensely. It feels good to be loved in return.

I live on the sunniest windowsill of all the apartments and houses you inhabit. I become your most cherished possession, the first thing you would save from a catastrophe. Every night, you talk to me, and I understand nothing, but your words sustain me, and they compel me to live another day.

In the end though, all life decays. You grow old fast, your life close to its end in the blink of an eye. You start to forget things. First, inconsequential tasks, and then, you start forgetting about caring for me. I know you do not intend to. But you are old, and your joints ache, and your mind lets you down.

Slowly, accidentally, you let me die.

It does not matter, love. When I die, I die while you are asleep in your bed. I die next to you.

And I could have wished for so much more time, and I have, but in this instant, when the blurry world turns completely dark, you are with me.

It is enough.

BODIES OF WATER

Valentin Narziss

The sky is wider than in the city, endless and heavy with rain, fading into the dark sea. Sanchul tugs his collar tight against the December wind. It whips over the barren landscape, here, far from any foreigners. Rough volcanic stone carves out the coastline with caves that echo and sing. Many have gotten lost there; many remain undiscovered and unburied, children playing mid moon, and bones of fugitives, hiding from prosecution decades ago. This is his mother's land. Her mother's soil. Island of women divers, burnt brown by the summer sun, faces old and bodies strong. Here, the gods are all around them.

It's been a mile since the bus stop, and no other will appear henceforward. No taxis, and few own a car in the village ahead. He can easily imagine those small, grey houses. Houses that time has bereaved of any charm they might've had when they'd still been decked with straw. Sanchul chews his lip, tongues at where the skin is ripe for splitting. The cold has already seeped inside him and he feels it everywhere, just as he remembers from his childhood. He stares ahead. The island opens before him like an ache he had forgotten.

★ ★ ★

It's dark when he arrives. The winds have softened, drizzle knocks against the house's windows and drips from low-hanging telephone lines. Sanchul swipes his wet hair from his eyes,

shivering, limbs leaden with exhaustion. A groan escapes him.
He shifts his backpack to fumble the keys out.

"No stars."

Sanchul drops the keys. His heartbeat races as he snaps around
to the voice. Someone stands under the narrow awning of the
house next door. The house is shrouded in darkness, and the
streetlamp is too far to illumine more than a silhouette.

"Too many rain clouds for stars. Unusual this time of year."
Laughter swings in each syllable, airy and musical, no hint of the
island's harsh dialect.

What the hell. Sanchul's mouth twists into a grimace, cheeks
hot. He picks up the keys and unlocks the door. He glances
back at the figure, shorter than him, strong, perhaps pretty.

"You're Park's grandson." The person seems to need no invitation to speak; and informal, too.

"Do we know each other?"

The figure takes a step forward and light catches on golden
skin. Strong jaw, a wide smile, dazzling and befitting of the
high-pitched voice.

"I think we might." The person smiles, eyes slitted in amusement. Sanchul can't help feeling it's at his expense. "I'm Lee
Junso. We played together. Why don't you drop in for tea?"

Sanchul squints, trying to tie memory to the features before
him. None comes.

"I think not."

He pushes the door open and once inside, shuts it firmly.

★ ★ ★

The house still smells of her. He barely registers he's crying.
He doesn't feel anything. Anything at all. He wipes his cheeks
roughly. He hadn't cried at the funeral, so why now? Sanchul
lets his backpack fall, doesn't turn on the light though he knows
it works. His mother keeps this place supplied with electricity,
water and gas, but that's it. God knows why, she has not been

here in years, could not stay here even for the funeral and had rented a hotel room the next city over.

The place feels different without his grandmother, smaller somehow, rotten in a way he never felt before.

Drowned, they'd said. Not an uncommon death for a diver. Six months ago in the heat of summer, not even her age would've kept her close to shore. She'd say, the ocean is my true home, these are the fields I know, here you harvest abalone or, if you're careful, catch an octopus. She did not harvest anymore, but she would dive. Of course she would. The foolish old woman. Sanchul had not believed it when his mother had sent the letter telling him in her messy scrawl what had happened. Suddenly he wishes he would've lingered outside and shared a cup of tea with Junso for whom he holds no trace of recognition.

★ ★ ★

The lightbulb stutters and dirty orange flicks over the bathroom walls, the cracked tiles, the bathtub in which Sanchul sits, cold now like lake water. His clothes are heaped on the floor, damp and discarded in a hurry. He can't remember taking them off. He's losing time again. It's been happening since his grandmother's death. He leans back, glances at his bruised knees, wishes he could at least hold – anyone. The light flickers, once, twice. The bathroom is smaller than he remembers, as is everything around him. He's too big for these rooms. He'd hoped leaving the city would…would what? Loosen the snare of daymares? He tilts his head back, sees himself reflected in the tarnished mirror, how even now his face seems calm. You feel nothing, he tells himself. Nothing at all.

The lightbulb cuts out.

Exhaustion sweeps over him in waves and pulls him under. He feels the dream coming before he even closes his eyes.

The ocean roars. No seagulls but crows flutter and crowd before the waxing moon. All is shadow beneath the vault of firmament, blue and black, fish stench, sea salt on his tongue and, overwhelming it all, the rot and warmth of a body cut open. Gigantic, like a dead god it lies on the sands, half hidden in the flood. The whale. On the side its flesh cleaves asunder, sliced to part and spill its steaming guts. And from them comes the man. Tall, wiry. Slicked wet, newborn by death, only his hands are bloodless and golden even in the moonlight. Sun-touched.

He's seen him before. Dreamt him.

The stench of dead meat follows Sanchul into waking, fills his lungs as he opens his eyes and slides his hands under water.

He's dreamt the dream every night since his grandmother's death. Fear is a cup of water he drinks as he's come to expect it. Any moment he closes his eyes he sees the bloodless hands and hears the ocean, now echoed by the sea a stone's throw away from the house. Bad omen, his grandmother would've said. He'd gone to the shaman before the funeral, while his mother had stayed in the city. Next year he will perform the ancestor ritual, as is his duty, and leave offerings for her at an altar. He does not believe his gifts will reach her in the underworld, but his grandmother had been adamant about ancestor worship, as have many of her age, especially here on the island.

He turns the light back on and is drying his hair in front of the mirror when a sudden movement catches his eye. His pulse quickens. He braces himself on the window pane to gaze down into the twilight. Something shifts on the beach. White cloth flutters and billows and falls from shadowed shoulders. Someone walks into the waves. Sanchul blinks, rubs sleep from his eyes. Wind soughs, and when he looks again –

Nothing.

Sanchul swallows. Of course not. It's too cold to swim. He puts down the towel and drains the water from the tub before tugging a t-shirt and loose trousers from his backpack. The lightbulb merely flickers when he tries to turn it on, so he uses his phone to light the way to his old bedroom. It's only a few steps but his heart drums loudly in his chest, and the murk feels fuller somehow. As if it is listening to his every breath.

★ ★ ★

Sanchul wakes with a start. A noise rattles through him. Then a low thud, further away. He sits upright in bed, heaving air, groping for his phone in a panic. Dawn reddens the horizon, bleeding through the window, but it's too red and *smeared*.

He finds his phone. It's dead.

"Okay. You're okay." He tries to breathe calmly as he's practiced so many times. No-one's in the room. He's safe. He's safe. He blinks but the smudge on the window does not clear. It's blood. He stumbles out of bed to the window, opens it and looks down.

Black feathers. Shiny like oil, red blood in red shadows, white bone. A crow.

A curse leaves him. Just a bird.

"Quite the start."

Sanchul curses again, this time more colourfully.

"Can you fucking not," he says, turning to Junso, who watches him idly from his porch, cigarette elegant in a small hand. Junso blows out smoke.

"Not what?"

"Not be a fucking creep." Sanchul's eyes follow the low cut of Junso's shirt, the expanse of flat, golden skin. Junso laughs. Sanchul is about to retort when a flutter and strangled caw pierces the air. The crow's still alive. It jerks, desperate, caws again. Junso lowers his eyes and Sanchul watches as he walks to the crow.

"What…"

Junso kneels, eyes glazed with an emotion Sanchul cannot name. He grabs the crow.

A crack echoes. The bird moves no more.

Junso looks up at him and for a moment that's all there is to the world. Silence and Junso's cheerless eyes.

"Do you want a cup of tea?" Junso's voice is soft, almost as if he's afraid.

Sanchul counts his heartbeats. Wants to say no.

"Yes."

★ ★ ★

"The houses look empty."

Sanchul is sat on the floor next to the tea table. Junso pours tea. The cup steams and the strong scent of lily fills the air between them, clinging to Junso. Would his skin smell of it? Taste like a funeral flower? But as Junso passes him by, Sanchul catches a soupçon of something more solid and earthen, dark, cold.

"Many people have left," Junso says. "Something killed the cattle. Many dead fish in the water." He looks at Sanchul, quiet and intent. "An illness."

"An illness," he echoes, shivers and picks up the cup for warmth. He drinks and watches Junso watch him. "And you? Do you live here?"

"No." Hesitant. "Perhaps."

"Must be... lonely." Embarrassment rushes through Sanchul the second he says it, but it's wafting between them now.

"Yes."

The honesty of the answer surprises Sanchul. Junso does not take his eyes off him as he says it, eyelashes casting long shadows over his cheeks. It's been... a long time since Sanchul's talked this way to someone. Never to a stranger. Unless it's true and they had known each other as children. Who can say? The years blur, and he remembers only the bright blue sky and rush of waves cresting against shore, something like freedom when grandmother had taken him into the bulteok with the other women, where they'd washed and gossiped and bragged about their catches.

Junso straightens his shirt, a nervous expression flitting over his features and Sanchul realises he hasn't replied. He sips his tea, burns his tongue and then stands.

"Thank you for the tea."

Something in Sanchul wishes Junso would stop him. He doesn't want to stay. He feels untethered on this soil, doesn't quite know who he is here.

They look at each other more keenly than strangers.

★ ★ ★

Froth splashes against basalt and seagulls circle in flight. The sea rushes. Sanchul stares at the waves, clutching the straps of his backpack. He's bought and placed offerings at her altar, half a year early and not the right vegetables or wine, no meat, but some things she'd enjoyed in life: grapes and white rice, plum soju. Afterwards he'd walked here, staring at the body that took her, the thing she called home. He searches for rage or sadness, but finds himself hollow. The horizon dims. A shiver runs down Sanchul's spine and he is suddenly very aware that there are no lanterns around and that when night comes, it comes all at once. He turns briskly and walks, feeling silly for his quickening pulse and the rapt attention of his senses. Sweat pools on his temples, and his stomach turns. Every step on the stony path echoes loudly in his ears. He holds his breath to hear *something* but the rush of water engulfs him more fully as the world dwindles to a vibrant blue. A gibbous moon rises in the east, fever yellow. He's alone. He is. Then a step echoes after his own. He freezes, heartbeat so loud it should shake the ground. He runs. It's stupid, he tells himself but some animal instinct takes over. The world flies by and he almost wants to laugh. He thinks of the crow. Of Junso's glinting eyes, the whites in them so prominent against the black of his iris.

He reaches the village with a thumping heart and hands trembling with left-over adrenaline. It's then that he does laugh, sudden and shrill even to his own ears. A hand clutches over his mouth and he needs a second to register it's his own. Slow breaths. In and out. He climbs the small path that leads up the slope to the houses, scattered like rotten teeth in the landscape. He reaches the street. All the houses are lightless, except one. Junso's.

He walks to it like in a trance, and where before fear had trembled through him, everything lulls into stillness. What's that smell? Putrid. Is he awake or adream? He follows the glow to an open window. Inside –

Junso sits at the table, face tilted upwards tenderly. Before him stands the man. Golden, bloodless hands. Such delicate features, hair black and loose. A lightbulb flickers above and sea water reflects off the walls. A murmur between them. Junso sighs like a lover.

Then the man looks at Sanchul.

★ ★ ★

Sanchul wakes in the living room. He's curled on the sofa, cold without a blanket. No light falls through the shutters. He sits up, disoriented and sick. What time is it? When did he get in? Fog clouds his memory, somehow viscous. Did he dream? A groan falls from his mouth into the silence. Where's his phone? He gets up, slides fingers over his cheek, temple, the damp strands of his hair. It smells like sea water. He chews his lip, tries once more and fails to recall anything at all after he'd gone to the beach. He walks into the kitchen and puts on the kettle, then fishes for his phone, finds it plugged into the charger. It's 5pm. There's a wrongness in having missed the sparse daylight, as if wasting blood. The nights lengthen as they pass and tonight the longest awaits. Dongji, the Winter Solstice. He should prepare hot red beans and rice porridge, even if he has no family to share it with. But he could ask Junso… It's eerie, how he seems to be the only other person in this part of the village. Further north where most shops are located, life goes on as always, muffled by the winter and cold winds coming in from the sea. But here… He hasn't seen anyone around at all. What was it that Junso had said? Cattle and fish died from an illness. Goose-bumps run over his arms. Was there not something important? Something he's forgotten. He tries to grate against the veil of last night. It feels... wrong.

A high-pitched noise tears him into the present. The kettle. It's just the kettle. He hurries to take it off the fire and prepares himself a cup of green tea. That at least should wake him.

He sits on the sofa, scrolls through his phone mindlessly. There's no wifi in this house, his grandmother had not even owned a computer. He slides through his gallery. Pictures of the city at night, blue streets and blurred neon lights, his ex sleeping in his bed. It pushes the air from his lungs. He hasn't touched anyone in two months. The relationship ended and everything got worse, the comments on his music, the variations of *you should kill yourself.* He's never gotten this much hatred before, nor this casually. He's been honest in his music, spoken of things people hush and hide. There's been support too. He doesn't want to say it's not enough. It's... different. To know the malice of people and not be able to close his eyes from it. It leaves traces. He lingers over the photo of his ex, the curled brown hair on his nape, the warmth he'd feel if pressing his lips against it, and breathe him in. The knowledge of him is carved inside, hollow as his chest expands. He drops the phone. It's better this way. Sometimes people don't fit together. And some colder part of him knows it's the warmth he misses more than the boy.

He should go and buy ingredients to make porridge for Dongji, maybe take a walk along the shoreline. He gets up and leaves his phone on the table.

★ ★ ★

The walk back from the store is tranquil. The only sounds are his steps and the plastic grocery bag rustling in the wind. He's bought a bottle of whiskey, too, Japanese, from a brand he likes to drink at home. The path is stony. He needs to be careful where to step. The moon is filling, bright enough to lighten the way, but just so. He rounds a corner, eyes on the ground, and when he looks up a silhouetted shape turns towards him.

"Hey." Junso's voice is quiet. The wind almost takes the words from his mouth.

Sanchul nods in acknowledgement and stops beside him.

For a moment they just stand there, gazing at the ocean. The wind picks up, finds its way into the caves beneath them and sighs, mournful as if for bereavement.

Junso is close, his warmth palpable without touch.

"They say the spirits follow on the wings of the east wind onto land. Violent death finds no sleep in black water. But it's me who is sleepless. Aren't you?"

Sanchul looks back, lungs all corded up, recognising something haunted in Junso's expression.

"Yes," he says.

When they walk back to the village, Sanchul offers his arm and Junso takes it. Bizarre, he thinks, heartbeat pounding in his head, how close one can be to a stranger.

★ ★ ★

He invites Junso inside with little more than a nod. They take their shoes off together, and for the first time the house doesn't feel so cold or empty.

They don't speak much while they prepare the porridge and in the narrow space, their arms brush, and when Sanchul hands Junso a knife their fingers slide against each other. Perhaps they both let them linger. Junso pours two glasses of whiskey and they sip them quietly as the red beans cook. Junso paces the living room, reverently as if counting steps to measure, then he looks out of the window.

"The planets are so clear today."

Sanchul joins him at the window and Junso does not move when their sides press together.

"Look," Junso points, "that's Mars. There's Venus. And Jupiter."

"Heavenly bodies."

Junso hums in agreement. "A pretty word."

Sanchul hands him his refilled glass and Junso takes it. He's beautiful up close. The awareness of it leaves him with a sense of dread. And deeper still, envy twists inside him. He can see the muscles on Junso's arms, his dewy skin, mouth plum like a woman's, framed by a strong jaw. He's delicate from the side, a profile to be traced with sharp lines. He's radiant, and so close. Shame curdles on Sanchul's tongue as he looks, and *wants*, and as so often he does not know if he wants to have him or be him. Then Junso shifts to glance at him. He is a person, not a husk to steal, alive with blood thrumming under skin.

"You're pretty," Junso says. The corners of his mouth rise into a surprisingly sweet smile.

The words reverberate in Sanchul's skull. Stunned, he stares. Heat pulses in his cheeks.

"And prettier when you blush." Now Junso grins, showing teeth.

Sanchul turns back to the sky. From the corner of his eye, he can see Junso still looking at him, but his smile has faded. Junso inches closer, face tilted up at him. His brows are slanted, lips slightly parted. He must know what he does to people.

Sanchul steps back, throat dry. "I think the beans are ready."

Junso's gaze follows him as he walks into the kitchen.

He sets a strainer over a bowl and pours the beans in. He'd done this often with his grandmother as a child, mashing them with a wooden spoon like he does now. Then he uses his hands, soon coated red. Junso comes in behind him. He thinks of what Junso said about restless spirits. Suddenly the room feels colder despite the hot beans under his hands. Grandmother used to smear a stripe of the red porridge on the front door to ward off ghosts.

"I've been having strange dreams," Junso says.

Sanchul turns to him. The world slants into darker blue, refractured light cooling Junso's skin from gold to ivory.

Junso moves closer, eyes empty with grief, so open Sanchul steps back, feeling like he's seen something he has no right to.

Junso smiles painfully, then nods to himself. He comes closer. And closer. His breath cools on Sanchul's cheek. Sanchul's back hits the kitchen counter.

"I did a bad thing," Junso says.

★ ★ ★

Height of summer. Bright blue sky. The afternoon sun blazes, scorching earth and skin, casting long, cleanly outlined shadows. Sanchul is six and runs naked into the waves, throwing himself at the largest he can reach. Seagulls cry above, darting down to snatch up fish. Time is endless and freedom is in his grasp. Other children play nearby and the beach, though stony, is full of bodies. Sanchul screeches happily and dives under, the way his grandmother has taught him as she says any daughter ought to be taught. Grandmother is in the water, too, way ahead on the reef, catching conches and other treasures she will sell on the market later.

He plays in the water, diving under, trying to catch fish with his hands, but he is too slow, maybe he will succeed when he turns the ripe age of seven later this month. The water is exhausting, exhilarating and he needs to take breaks back on the beach, where he devours the rice cakes his grandmother prepared for him last evening, piles stones and runs after crabs, then wades back into the water.

Sunset. The whole sky fills with orange and pink arching over the emptying beach. Sanchul is tired but sways with the waves, his body has taken their rhythm and aligned itself with it. On the horizon the sea opens its maw to drown the sun, glorious as it sinks, still blinding in deeper red. The caves are close by, and though the tides there can be perilous, Sanchul paddles over. The water darkens as the light dims.

A cry sounds from behind him, a hastily shouted name, peculiar and old, meaning *sky*.

"Haneul!"

Sanchul casts his gaze around, and sees a man near the caves, golden hand on black volcanic stone. That's when it happens. Fingers clutch around Sanchul's ankle and his mouth fills with water. Something drags him down.

★ ★ ★

Sanchul opens his eyes and looks at the ceiling. He's lying on the carpet, Junso's head next to his own, feet in opposite directions. Junso breathes quietly and when Sanchul turns to look at him, he sees his hair is wet. The smell of salt and algae fills his nose. He feels very quiet, warm and as if there was an echo of memory. He's been losing time again.

"I'm sorry about your grandmother," Junso says.

Sanchul does not remember telling him, but it seems there's much he does not recall.

He says, "Do you want to spend Dongji with me?"

Junso shifts onto his elbow, eyes searching.

"Yeah," he says very quietly.

Without thought Sanchul reaches out and touches Junso's hair where it falls onto his forehead. It's dry. Of course it is. When his gaze focuses back on Junso's face, he realises Junso's holding his breath. But he's not moving away. Not moving closer, either.

"More whiskey?" Sanchul murmurs as he retracts his hand.

Junso nods.

He trails into the kitchen, Junso on his heels. Their shoulders brush when Junso pushes past him.

"Did you go swimming the other night?" The words leave Sanchul's mouth before he can stop himself.

Junso freezes. "No," he breathes.

Sanchul pours the whiskey. The bottle's half empty already. On the stove, the porridge cools in a Tupperware container.

In another, rice cakes. Dirty dishes in the sink. He swallows a mouthful of his drink.

"They say on Dongji the spirits walk freely. Do you think... you will see your grandmother tonight? Do you think she is restless?" Junso's mouth quivers like he tries to hold back some deeper emotion.

"Did someone... die?" Sanchul asks. "Someone you cared about?"

They're close. When did they move closer? He looks into Junso's eyes and wants to drown himself in this grief he does not comprehend. Carefully, Junso places his hand on his shoulder, thumb rubbing where his collar gives way to skin. The world simmers down to that point of contact and Junso's low-lidded gaze. His chin tilts up.

"Please kiss me."

And Sanchul does. It's warm, just a press of skin at first. The old fear in him awakens but then Junso's tongue pushes between his lips. It's wet and intimate, and he can't believe it's happening. Feels like sinking. Junso swans his arms around Sanchul's neck and kisses him harder. The almost-cut in Sanchul's lip splits, tinging their kiss with copper. Junso draws back, cheeks rosy and wet. He's crying. Sanchul leans down and licks the tears from his skin. A strangled noise comes from Junso's mouth.

"I want," Junso says, needy and desperate.

Sanchul wraps an arm around him and lifts Junso onto the low kitchen table before sinking to his knees.

★ ★ ★

Lights off. The water of the bathtub is so hot, both of their skin has wrinkled where they're submerged. Junso shifts on Sanchul's lap, strong thighs clutching him close, Junso's hot mouth breathing against his lips. It's overwhelming. The simplicity and magnitude of feeling his skin against his own. Junso's hands spread over Sanchul's chest, stroking over the long scars, one under each of his pectoral muscles. The movement is reverent, unconscious.

"It was my brother," Junso whispers.

Sanchul caresses his cheek but, with his dripping hair, cannot say whether he is crying or not. Hunger inside. He wants all of Junso's anguish.

"He died?"

A scratch at the back of his mind. The dream. Has he dreamt it last night? The whiskey warms him from inside, heavies his limbs. One of Junso's hands has settled on his shoulder, the other he cannot see. Something strokes along his ankle. He shivers.

"Yeah," Junso says, a little out of it. "Yeah, he died."

Sanchul's eyes flutter close. He opens them again. The end of a sob echoes, as if sound had cut out for a moment and now returned. Junso's. Then Junso laughs quietly, high-pitched and effeminate.

In the dark a shape rises behind Junso from the water.

"It was an accident."

Sanchul can't breathe, he feels so goddamn heavy. Junso brings both of his hands to grasp at his own hair. The grip around Sanchul's ankle tightens.

I did a bad thing.

"I've had… such strange dreams," Sanchul slurs as the stench of putrid meat fills the room.

"Me too," Junso whispers. "I'm talking to the devil every night. He wears my brother's face." Another sob. "I can't let him go."

"Was he… a bad man?"

"I loved him."

A golden arm snakes around Junso's middle. The shape leans closer and even in the darkness, the man's face glows as he nestles his face against Junso's neck.

"Haneul." Junso's voice is blank.

Flare of dreamscape, sunset-red demimonde, a tide that ensnares him. He sees himself as a child, drifting towards the water caves.

"Don't go in." Another child swims next to him, small-faced and sweet. Unmistakably Junso. The man by the caves looks at them, not really a man yet, barely an adolescent. Bronzed by sunlight, wiry strong, a smile as wide as a starless night.

"Don't go in." They swim back to the beach, to where their lunch boxes lie, the piles of rock they've built together, as they had done all summer long.

"He was... like the sun mid-collapse. Quiet when nobody watched. He gutted fish with his left hand and sang me to sleep. We swam together, closer than close. Only bodies in water."

"How did he die?"

Sanchul's heart beats so loud he almost doesn't hear his own voice, staring at Haneul behind Junso, lips grazing Junso's neck. Then Junso's gaze finds him. He's not crying anymore.

"He loved me too."

Pain shoots through Sanchul's ankle. Then the hand tears him under. Panic blots everything out. The bathtub falls away and the sea swallows him whole. Frantically he clutches where his hand still feels Junso's warm flesh.

He opens his eyes and looks into Junso's face.

"Get out," Sanchul hisses and drags Junso from the water. They struggle from the tub, water splashing everywhere.

Junso's eyes are glazed. He's shivering. Teeth marks mar his neck. Sanchul does not dare to feel them with his fingertips. A shuddering breath escapes Junso as he braces himself against Sanchul.

"I killed him." Junso's voice is toneless. "I didn't want to." It almost sounds like the truth. "He told me to."

Sanchul holds him and manoeuvres him away from the tub. He doesn't want to know. Doesn't want –

"We were in the caves."

What were you doing there?

"Six months ago. He fell."

It's like he can see it. The cave and its bones, and amidst it two warm bodies. Perhaps more than two, less warm.

"I heard his head crack against the stone." Junso sounds reverent with memories. "I dragged him outside, it took so long. He was so heavy in my arms. There was... so much blood. Neither of us had a phone with us." *Why not?* "It was night."

Tears gather at Junso's lashes; he looks young like this, still beautiful.

"He was bleeding out in front of me. He didn't seem to be in pain. He seemed..." Happy. Junso's eyes dart around, as if searching for something. "He told me to pull him into the waves. It was still so hot in June, and I did. Then he told me to push him under." His voice frays. "I pulled him under."

The muscles in Junso's arms quiver, as if remembering the strength it took to drown him. But there's something behind Junso's terror, something almost smiling. And where Sanchul should feel horror, he just feels empty.

They dress in silence. Sanchul thinks of crow feathers, of his grandmother, short and bulky with strength despite her age, cackling at some old joke or other that she's already told him twenty times. He watches Junso carefully from the corner of his eye. That summer so many years ago they'd been inseparable. He recalls it bit by bit and now remembers Haneul too. His black eyes.

It sobers him up. An idea starts to form in his head.

"Show me where it happened."

★ ★ ★

The village is quiet. No sound echoes beside their steps. The moon has waxed to fullness and gleams orange like rising sickness. Wind sweeps in from the sea, carrying the scent of fish and salt and rot. Sanchul grabs Junso's hand. Is this madness? To go to the caves at this hour? To look for... what? He does not believe in ghosts, but this has nothing to do with belief. He's been dreaming of Haneul for months. He has seen and felt. And yet – they could go to a shaman. But that would mean telling her exactly what happened for the ritual to proceed.

Junso pulls him close. His mouth tastes bitter, faintly of whiskey, warm like any creature on the inside. He twines their fingers, palm to palm. Before them the night sky melts into the ocean. Waves break close to the shore. High tide.

Together they climb down the rocks to the beach.

"Don't get lost," Junso murmurs, half stolen by the wind.

They only have the full moon and their phones for light. It barely pierces the umbra, as if things move within it, blocking the feeble rays with bodies that no light can reach.

"Careful," Junso says as they cautiously tread along a narrow stone path, dropping away to deep waters. He knows the currents are dangerous here. If they fall... But it's the only way from the beach to the caves. Junso breathes hard in front of him. Maybe they shouldn't do this.

Junso stops.

"We're here."

The maw of the caves opens wide before them and vertigo sways Sanchul for a moment, looking into its darkness. He feels the same sick pull he felt as a child, the gurgling black lure of it. His hearing sharpens and his heart pounds in his chest, heat and cold claw at his body as he fights the urge to run – away or inside, he does not know. A gurgling sound echoes from within. Water has already flooded the caves, only leaving a few boulders of volcanic rock for them to balance on.

They climb inside.

Sweat beads at Sanchul's temple despite the cold, and his stomach turns from the stench of rot that increases the deeper they advance. The wind trapped inside the caves sounds eerily, an unearthly sound like Sanchul's never heard before. Wet algae clings to the rocks, and the water surges high enough to sink into their shoes. It feels primordial. The passing of time means nothing here. This is an old place, and they mustn't go too far or they might never find out again.

"Here," says Junso.

Sanchul stills and stares. He cannot fathom it. That Haneul

fell here, perhaps only days from his grandmother drowning. Days from cattle dying and fish floating dead on the water. Have others dreamt of him? And did they find Haneul's corpse, or did the tide suck him into the innards of the sea?

"Do you smell this?" Sanchul asks.

They look at each other.

"Dead meat."

They both look around, trying to locate the source of the stench, but it is everywhere, permeating the air. Sanchul thinks of Haneul gleaming under the setting sun. The empty radiance of his smile. His dark eyes.

"Do you think... he wanted to die?"

Junso lowers his gaze, his brows crease and his mouth presses tight.

"I don't know... But he wanted me to..."

"Kill him."

Junso looks back up at him. Sanchul sees him the way he was in the bathtub, how the *shape* rose behind him, how Sanchul saw him through the window after his walk, head tilted up to Haneul, the memory rushes back to him with such force it chokes the air out of his lungs. And his dream. The whale and crows and Haneul's golden hands.

"I think you need to talk to him," Sanchul says, voice barely his own. "Like you did before."

Silence between them.

Junso takes a deep breath, clutches Sanchul's hand and then lets go. He turns away and takes another shuddering breath. Are they really doing this? They are not shamans. They shouldn't do this. Sanchul is about to speak, when –

"Brother," Junso's voice sounds fragile, child-like as it reverberates in the cave. "Please."

Nothing happens.

"*Please.*"

And nothing still.

Rush of water gurgles in the labyrinthine hollows and veins

of the cave, some leading deep into the ocean, others stopping dead against the bedrock of the island.

The stench exacerbates. It's so overwhelming Sanchul crouches, hand pressing over his mouth to keep in the rising gall.

"I am... so far from home." Haneul's voice. It's strangled and wet as if something is blocking his throat. Sea water. A shape rises from the waves at Sanchul's feet. He shrieks, almost slips –

Their phone lights cut.

Drip of water in the dark. Soft breath. A song rises, an old melody, half-remembered tune, blue sky, warmer skin. A lullaby.

Moon, moon,
There, there now I see
As Etabae saw, a cinnamon-tree,
With my gold axe...

"I will cut it down," Sanchul murmurs. He's heard Haneul sing it once before, that summer so long ago. Dusk had warmed the sky and Sanchul walked Junso home after play and they had lingered in the little garden. Haneul had just come back, skin still sea-wet, fingers curling around Junso's nape. Sanchul had caught Haneul's gaze as he hummed the lullaby. Something tender and greedy had reflected in Haneul's eyes.

"Don't go in," he hears Junso say. He hadn't. He remembers his grandmother and her firm hand on his shoulder as she'd picked him up that evening, wary twist in her brows, and Haneul – smiling at her.

Hands close around his ankles. A face ebbs from the shadows. He's not dreaming.

Haneul is golden, blood-spattered but for his hands. He rises from the waves, tangled with stinking algae.

"Why didn't you come in? You left Junso all alone... with me."

Somewhere behind him, Junso whimpers. Fear chokes Sanchul of breath. He can't see Junso, can only see Haneul. Cold freezes through him, then sudden heat – a sweltry June night – engulfs him.

"You're dead," Sanchul says, sweating. He's suffocating, moisture clogs all air.

"*Leave him alone!*" Junso shrieks, sounding distant.

"Let me cool you." Haneul's whisper brushes against Sanchul's ear. "Here, jagi, come in."

Hands grab at Sanchul and tear him sideways. He falls. Water splashes around him, he struggles, pulse hammering, panic taking him whole. He's not dreaming. He's not dreaming. He's not –

He holds his breath as he goes under. And there he sees him, eyes darker than the water, sun-kissed even now. Haneul is close. He looks nothing like Junso, no trace of kinship in his appearance, he does not belong. Not here, not anymore. Sanchul struggles, but Haneul snares him, claws at Sanchul's chest, higher, to his throat –

A body crashes into the water beside him.

Haneul turns to Junso and grins. Junso shoves closer, tears at Haneul's hands and Sanchul kicks underwater, and for a second it seems he might escape. Then Haneul yanks them both deeper. Sanchul's head is getting light and the need to *inhale* overwhelms him. Water breath, that's what his grandmother called it. Your last. He thrashes, his sight dimming as he hears whispers echo in the gloom.

The sound of brass bells ringing. A swaying breeze. A warm, old hand on his shoulder. His heartbeat races and strength surges through him, and one last time he *kicks*.

He breaks free. There, he sees Junso's hand floating lifelessly. He grabs it and pulls Junso up, breaks the surface, coughs up water, heaves, crying, can't see but somehow manages to drag Junso to the nearest rock.

"Hey," he croaks, "hey, Junso. Junso!"

His voice echoes off the cave walls, somehow emptier than before. Colder, too. The tide draws at his body. Sea-pull. Behind him the first rays of dawn paint the stone.

Junso coughs, then retches, clinging to him.

"You're okay," Sanchul murmurs for them both.

Junso is trembling, breath stuttering out of him as he looks at Sanchul, eyes bereft of hope.

An echo of something underwater, quiet like sobbing, *Don't – follow me home –*

"Come on," Sanchul says and hefts himself out of the water. He shivers from the cold, nauseous and sick with exhaustion. They have to get out of here. He offers his hand. Junso's gaze lingers on the water for a moment.

Then he takes Sanchul's hand.

★ ★ ★

The way back to the village is like waking after nights of fever. The air is crisp and cool, the sky a blossoming blue. Junso's hand feels small in his own. They're both drenched and shivering, teeth clattering from the cold. Later, Sanchul will question what truly happened in the caves, distrustful of his memory, though their bodies hold their own tales, handprints bruising wrists and throats. It feels like there is more still, lost in that child-hood summer, but perhaps some things best remain forgotten. Sanchul looks at Junso like a stranger. How had he been so close to him mere hours ago? Junso is like a bird in his hand, heart-beat thundering against his wrist bone where Sanchul's thumb presses, but his face is bare of emotion. He feels it then, grief like rain, as time passes between them. Some things, Sanchul begins to understand, do not return.

When they reach the houses, Junso retracts his hand.

"I think," says Junso, gaze averted, "I need to be alone."

Sanchul stares at him. Want is a thing he does not know how to speak.

"Yeah," he says.

Junso raises his eyes for just a moment. Like a wound in water.

"Okay," Junso says and turns.

Sanchul watches him walk to his house. He watches Junso's door for a long time.

* * *

The sea is deep azure under a blazing sky. A breeze carries the scent of salt and life as it teems under the waves, crashing against the bulk of the ferry. Sanchul clasps the railing and holds his face into the wind. For the first time in a long while, he feels like himself. Grief has turned warm like the memory of spring, like days lengthening again after an age of night. It's still there and he keeps it close, no longer too afraid to feel it. He turns and looks back at the island. In summer he will return for ancestor worship. He will put flowers on her grave.

"Hey," a voice sounds behind him.

Sanchul turns. Junso steps out on the deck, hair tangling in the wind.

"Hey," Sanchul says.

Junso joins him at the railing, leaning against it with his back, looking at the island. He's beautiful like this, his eyes so dark.

Junso had been waiting at the ferry dock in the rain that morning, umbrella in hand, no suitcase, wearing a jacket too big for him. He's still wearing it now, thumbing at his sleeve. Sanchul wants to touch him, but the haunted expression on Junso's face holds him back. What was it Junso had said? *Closer than close. Only bodies in water.* And how they had looked at each other... It's far from anything Sanchul can touch. He does not want to think of the caves. Or him.

"Do you still dream of him?" Sanchul asks quietly.

Junso gazes at him, eyes searching, expression unreadable. Then he smiles and turns to look toward the mainland, and the wind steals his answer, carrying it off to the sea.

REYNARDINE

Kallyn Hunter

As the fight between Celia and her Meemaw gains steam, the fox fur stole slithers from the closet. It curls onto the bed like an oversized cat, glass eyes focused on the open bedroom door. Wrinkled ears perk up to listen to the angry shouting that echoes up the stairs from the living room below.

"I said I don't want you goin' out!"

"Why are you making a big deal outta this?!"

"That little Black girl's been missin' for over a month, and all you can think about is some party!"

"It's just a bonfire down at Luke's! There will be plenty of people there!"

"You think that'll protect you from some stranger who wants to do you harm? You're gonna end up just like your ma running around at night like this!"

"What I do ain't none of your business!"

"It is while you're living under my roof, Celia Rose Taylor!"

Celia's angry footsteps start up the stairs. "I never asked you to take me in!"

Meemaw's shout follows her. "And if your ma were alive to take care of you, I'd be happy to send you both on your merry way!"

Celia comes into the room like a thunderclap, slamming the door behind her with the intent to break Meemaw's house apart, but all sixteen years of rage only manage to rattle the frame.

"Don't slam doors in my house!"

Her Meemaw liked to say that women cry when they're angry because they've been told their whole lives not to throw fists. Now, tears stained with eyeliner streak down Celia's face like war paint. She tosses herself onto the quilted cover of her bed, shoulders shaking with anger.

The fox fur uncurls from its ball, empty limbs dragging at its sides as it glides onto her back. The plastic hinge of its lower jaw brushes her ear, raising goosebumps over her skin. Celia stews in her anger for a few moments longer before she reaches back to scratch behind its limp ear.

"Fuck her," Celia mutters and pushes herself up with renewed determination. The fur tumbles onto the bed as Celia heads for the mirror. A quick swipe under her eyes brushes away the tears. Another fixes her smudged eyeliner. Her face is red from crying, but she tries to redistribute the colour, pinching the blush back into her cheeks before smoothing black hair away from her pale face.

Spring's just arrived, and down by the lake, the humid air will be cold. She grabs a jacket to cover the loose-fitting baby-doll dress that's more of an oversized shirt than anything. The coat has deep pockets, and inside one is a crumpled gas station receipt, a half-smoked packet of cigarettes, and the Zippo Nat gave her for her birthday. She scoops the fox fur off the bed and drapes it around her neck as a final touch. There are nicer looking shoes in her closet, but she keeps her boots.

She checks herself over one more time. The fox fur wiggles to adjust itself, resting its head right by her neck, plastic jaw clamped at the base of the tail that hangs down her shoulder. Its glass eyes stare at their reflection before a sound of approval hisses from somewhere in its boneless neck. Celia straightens her dress and decides it's a good look. Casual, pretty, and just a little sharp.

She turns the radio on, letting the advertisement for John's Auto on Route 13 play over the creak of the balcony door. In the years she's lived with her Meemaw, she's learned to jiggle it in just the right way so it won't scrape over the uneven balcony planks. Old wood groans under her feet before she closes the door, just as carefully, behind her.

The sky is black as sin, and moths whisper quiet flatteries to her balcony light. Katydids are already starting to call their nightly yearnings to one another. The oak at the far end of the balcony offers a moss-draped branch that she uses to lower herself gently to the ground. Once spring turns to summer and summer starts to cool, Celia will fill her pockets with acorns and spread them halfway around the lake. It only seems fair for these small favours.

The hill's too steep to go behind the house, so she has to cut in front. Inside, her grandmother glows blue in front of the television. Eustis sits curled on her lap, a little white ball of fur, though his neck is starting to rub bald under his collar. One wrong step, and he'll come barking at the front door, and the night will be over before it can even begin.

Celia moves carefully, ducking across the gap of light left by the window of the screen door. Eustis stays asleep. His hearing's not so great anymore, and the twig from the oak tree stays quiet when her foot snaps it. She snatches the can of bug spray off the porch banister before she heads into the woods.

The trees get less familiar, less friendly. An old missing poster flutters against the ground, torn free from some light post or brick wall. A pretty Black girl with a hair full of braids smiles out from the weather-beaten picture. Her name, Justine Elliott, had never made it to the news. A runaway, the officials had said, despite the fact that she was only thirteen, and happy with her family in the neighbouring town of Branson. But Celia knows firsthand just how little the cops around the lake care when folks go missing.

The buzzing of insects crescendos the closer she gets to the water. A chill that has nothing to do with the cool air creeps up Celia's spine. She's not a fan of the lake. Too many bad memories live on its shores. Celia shakes the can of spray like it'll chase them away before coating herself in a thin layer of Deet and citronella. It doesn't do much for the memories, but at least it sends the mosquitos off in search of less tainted skin to sink into.

As if sensing her unease, the fox fur growls around its mouthful of tail. It coils a little tighter around her neck, fur bristling against the humid chill. Celia follows the lightning bugs through the trees, passing by the old Flat Rock Campground sign that glows in shades of neon, flashing a bright "vacancy." This time of year, it's empty, waiting for the tourists that will flock to the shores of the lake in droves come summer.

Then Celia sees the fire pit through the trees, the flickering light breaking the darkness apart. She lets out a sigh of relief as she hears tinny music played through a phone speaker. It's one of Nat's picks, full of bagpipes, drums and shouting.

Alice's sharp laugh rises over the raucous music. If she's here, then she will have brought Billy, too. Even though Alice has been wanting to cut it off with him for weeks, he's the one with the car. No doubt Emerson and Tuck are here, dancing around each other like two grouses, neither willing to admit they're more than just football buddies. Selena and Opal should be here, too, at least until they decide to sneak off into the woods to do the things they can't do in front of everyone else. And Luke, of course. Luke's always around.

As Celia gets close, Nat cheers at the sight of her, raising a beer can in salute. The party is already in full swing. Alice and Billy don't look up from their intense conversation on the other side of the crackling fire pit. Selena and Opal dance with each other, hands roving to dip under shirt hems as they sway, completely out of time with the up-tempo punk music. Emerson and Tuck sit near the base of Luke's lawn chair like disciples, faces upturned to soak in his every word.

Luke Absher is the odd one out among the festivities, even though it's his campground. While his congregation are high schoolers or recent graduates, Luke is old and bent, white hair stained yellow from the ever-present cigarette between his fingers. During the off season, he's the one who provides the location and the beer, so long as the kids toss him a twenty or two. The simple kindness extended to the queers and rejects of Kimberling City has made his campground by the lake their church, and Luke their unlikely savior.

Nat gets to his feet and saunters over to Celia, beer in hand. His proximity makes Celia's heart thud in her chest, but no more than that special, white-toothed smile he seems to save just for her. On her shoulder, the fur's nose twitches as if to breathe in his scent. He's dressed in jeans, cowboy boots, and a white t-shirt with a V-neck that doesn't quite hide the pantyhose binder he's rigged to flatten his chest. His folks have the money, but when they still insist on calling him by his deadname, asking for a proper binder is a battle to be fought after the war is won.

"Glad you could make it," he says. "Your granny give you trouble?"

"'Course she did," Celia says as she plucks the beer from his hand. "But seeing you is worth the tongue lashing I'll get tomorrow." She cracks the can open and takes a long drink, exhilarated with the thrill of freedom. The cheap beer tastes as sweet as nectar.

Nat's fingers stroke down the neck of her scarf, and the fox shivers in response. "Where'd you get this? I've never seen you wear it before."

Celia scratches the fur behind its ear. "It belonged to my ma."

"Oh."

Nat leaves it at that. He doesn't like to talk about it. No one does. Everyone remembers how Evelyn Taylor was last found but, in that small town way, they only talk about it behind closed doors, and even then, only in whispers.

Ten years have come and gone since that cool spring morning when someone noticed the turkey vultures circling the little spit of land that rests in the middle of the lake. It was unusual.

Nothing lived on the little island save for a grove of trees and the herons and muskrats that nested in them. With a woman missing, the cluster of red-skulled birds had been ominous enough to warrant a call to the police.

The officers used some of the paddle boats that Luke Absher rented to tourists to get out there. It had been nearly two weeks since Celia's ma had gone missing, but right there on heron island is where they found her. Her clothes were uncovered first. Her shirt and skirt had been neatly folded, shoes set beside them as though someone had laid the outfit to wear the next day.

Her body had been far less pristine. Sprawled in the grove of trees, half missing thanks to scavengers and rot. Yet even two weeks of decomposition couldn't disguise the fact that she had been skinned like a deer, her lidless eyes forever open, staring unseeingly at the blue sky overhead.

It wasn't until weeks later, when the crime scene had been cleared and the news had turned their attention to more recent tragedies, that Luke had shown up at Meemaw's house with the fox fur in hand. He'd found it when he'd gone out to the island to check his muskrat traps. The police must have missed it during their sweep, which was only a premonition of how their search for Evelyn's killer would go. Meemaw didn't remember her daughter having such a thing, but when a six-year-old Celia took the stole from the old man and it nuzzled into her hand, she felt it in her gut; it had belonged to her mother.

Folks always hold Evelyn Taylor's name in their mouths, but what they don't like to talk about is how her murderer was never caught. An ex-lover, they'd said, though none of them could name which one. But as awful as her end was, in their eyes, she had brought it on herself, inviting such dubious attention from the rakes and scoundrels in and around town.

To this day, folks in town use Evelyn's tragic end as a warning for their daughters. Don't be out past dark. Don't trust strange men that come through town. But even more important, don't be loose, and keep your legs closed. Obedient, God-fearing girls don't get murdered.

Celia throws her head back, swallowing the anger and grief along with the last few gulps of beer from her can. She crushes the aluminiumin her hand, feeling the satisfying give before tossing it into the open trash bag that hangs heavy from a tree branch.

Nat chuckles. "So it's that kind of night."

"After that fight it is."

Nat takes Celia's hand and guides her to the cooler. He grabs another sweating can from its innards before cracking the tab. He offers it to her as he says, "Hopefully this fight wasn't about me."

Celia laughs as she takes it. "You kidding? Boy or girl – she's hated everyone I've brought home, *except* you. You're the golden boy in her eyes. Though I'll bet she'd give you an earful about coming out tonight, too."

Nat flashes that white-toothed grin that's too charming for its own good. Seeing it makes Celia's heart flutter in her chest. "Well," Nat says. "I'm glad you made it out in spite of her. You look beautiful."

The single word warms her, chasing away the chill of bad memories. Meemaw's never so much as called her cute. And beautiful? Beautiful is for women, and after their argument, Meemaw made it clear that, in her eyes, Celia is still very much a child. On her shoulder, the fur preens at the praise, letting its lush, white tipped tail dangle over her shoulder to follow the V of her dress.

Nat's eyes follow it before he reaches a hand out to touch it. Fingers stroke down the soft fur as his thumb dips down to trail, like a line of fire, over her collar, down her chest. Celia's breath catches as she looks at him, leaning into his touch.

Meemaw likes to compare Celia to her mother like it's an insult. Calls her reckless, headstrong. Claims she'd date anyone who showed her even passing attention. In that, maybe

Meemaw's occasionally right. Celia's last girlfriend had strung her along as a joke, just to claim that she wasn't *into* girls when she asked her to the spring formal. But nothing about this feels reckless. Nat's touch is like finding the missing piece of a puzzle. Something right and safe and… perfect.

Her mother had loved too easily. Gave her heart readily to men who were careless or cruel with it. In those six years Celia lived with Evelyn, she had seen just as many men come and go from her mother's life. But it was the last man, Celia was certain, that had ended it. She'd only seen him once, the night he drew her mother out of their front door with that charming smile and an offered arm, like a true gentleman. There isn't much to remember about him save for those piercing honey-coloured eyes and that smile that had seemed just a little too sharp. Yet even the vague shadow of the man sticks like a burr in her memory.

"You two plannin' on joining the party?" Luke calls out. His jovial voice cuts across the little clearing, and Celia and Nat jump apart like startled deer. They share a grin at their own skittishness before going to join the rest of the congregation. As the two of them sit in the soft grass at Luke's feet, he smiles.

"You look lovely in that scarf, Celia," he says, accent pouring over every word.

"Thanks, Luke," Celia says, though she doesn't like the way his eyes linger. She pulls the scarf to cover the exposed skin of her chest. The fox fur quivers gently, face hidden against her neck.

"I don't think I've ever seen someone look so mad to be at a party," Opal says. Her words slur as her arm drapes around Celia's shoulder, the can in her hand sloshing. "What's shit on your mood tonight, Celia?"

"That's awful rude, Opal," Tuck says. "She can't help how her face looks."

It's an insult only her friends could get away with. Celia laughs and kicks one booted foot against Tuck's thigh. "Didn't regret coming out 'til now," she says. "Meemaw tried her best to keep me home, and with this kind of welcome, maybe I should've listened."

"Paranoid old bat," Selena mutters. She grabs her girlfriend's arm from Celia's shoulder to drape it around her own. Celia raises her beer can in agreement before taking a long drink.

"Now your Meemaw's just looking out for you," Luke says, ever diplomatic. "With so many disappearances around these parts, you can't blame her. I don't think she could stand another heartbreak if something happened to her granddaughter."

"Yeah, but that's why we come here," Emerson says in his quiet way. "Your place is safe."

Luke chuckles and the tip of his cigarette flares bright. "There's a fact," he says, smoke billowing from his toothless mouth. "Y'all are always welcome at Uncle Luke's."

The night stretches on. The moon breeches the horizon and lifts gradually into the sky. Celia finishes her second beer and starts on a third as the conversation meanders. She listens to her friends talk about summer and senior year, and what they'll do after. Emerson's already thinking about college, looking at schools in Michigan or Colorado. Tuck says he'll follow him. Selena and Opal want to move to New York or LA, places where the possibilities are endless.

"You don't want to be stuck here forever, right?" Nat asks. Over the fire, his eyes travel to Luke. Celia knows what he's thinking. Get away while you still have the chance, because if you stay here, your future's easy to see. You end up just like Luke or Meemaw if you're lucky, or you end up like Evelyn Taylor and Justine Elliott if you're not.

"Sure don't," Celia says, eyes full of firelight.

Something loud crunches behind them, making everyone but Luke jump. They turn to see Billy throw his crushed can into the fire. Embers leap into the air in an angry plume.

"Fine! Then you can get yourself home," he snarls. Alice jumps away from the fire as the embers cool to ash. Billy storms off. A moment later, his car roars to life, headlights disappearing down the dirt road in a cloud of dust. For a long moment, no one says a word.

Celia breaks the silence. "You want a beer, Alice?"

Alice sighs and turns to look at them, blond hair flowing over her shoulder. "I think I'm gonna head home," she says with a sad smile. "Got a long way to walk all the sudden."

Tuck tsks and gets to his feet. He nudges Emerson with a boot. "We'll give you a lift," he says.

Selena and Opal are already getting up as well. They'd been looking for an excuse to break off somewhere more private, and they snatch the opportunity. Selena's hand is tucked into Opal's back pocket as she says, "We'll catch you guys later. Thanks for the fun, Luke."

"Anytime," the old man says, smiling. "Y'all drive safe."

Celia sighs, dreading the return to Meemaw's, but Nat's hand slides across the ground to cover hers. Celia meets his eyes, an unspoken agreement passing between them. The night's still young, and neither are ready to go home quite yet. The others pack up and head out, but Celia and Nat stay, warm and content in the ring of firelight.

After a moment, Luke gets to his feet with the sound of crunching joints. "Hey Nat, think you could help an old man out with something? It needs a young man's back."

"Sure, Luke. What'cha need?"

Nat gets to his feet and offers Celia a hand up. She takes it and sways a little, the half-empty can sloshing as she throws an arm out for balance. The cheap beer creeps through her bloodstream, making everything feel warm, comfortable, and a little sedate.

"Celia, you don't need to bother yourself," Luke says. "Why don't you stay warm by the fire? We'll be right back."

The fox fur tightens around her neck, constricting like a warning hand. Celia frowns. "It's alright, Luke. I don't mind helping."

Something sharp flashes in Luke's rheumy eyes. It's gone just as quick, and the old man chuckles, lips smacking over his empty gums before he says, "Suit yourself. It's down by the water. Just some scrap I'm hauling away from the dock. I'm making room for a few more campsites."

Nat follows him away from the clearing, Celia trailing just behind as she drains the rest of her beer. She tosses the can into the trash bag on the way past, but as soon as the heat of the fire disappears, the fox fur stirs. It lifts its head away from the crook of her neck, glass eyes staring, wide and alert.

Luke steps over a couple fallen tree trunks. "Sorry 'bout the mess. Clearing this area may have been more of a project than my old bones can handle," he says and offers Celia a hand. The fox fur bristles, hair tickling her chin. A silent hiss vibrates from somewhere in its boneless neck. Celia grabs onto it like scruffing a kitten as she steps over the trunks. Luke lets his offered hand fall, smiling.

"Well, maybe we could help you get it cleared out before summer. Right, Celia?" Nat asks. Sometimes he's too kind for his own good.

"Yeah, maybe," Celia says.

Without the light of the fire, the trees and shrubs around them no longer feel welcoming. They stand as darkened silhouettes, spindly arms outstretched to grab at the hem of Celia's dress. She snaps nearly two feet of the offending branch clean off before she's able to detangle it from the black lace circling her dress. The fox fur is alert and wary, glass eyes shining in the dark as it stares ahead. It coils around Celia's neck, tamping down some of Celia's comfortable haze. Unease settles like a rock in her stomach. Celia keeps a hold of the branch, liking the weight of it in her hand.

Luke leads them down to the shore where the waterbugs draw equations over the still surface of the lake. A dock reaches out into the water, small paddleboats bobbing against it like puppies suckling at their mother's teat. Celia pulls up short at the sight of them, remembering the shimmer of red and blue police lights hitting their sides.

Luke points a bony finger and, for a moment, all Celia can see is the black body bag that had held what was left of her mother. Then she blinks, and the vision is gone, replaced by a mangled mess of chicken wire and netting that rests at the edge of the dock.

"Can you believe I hauled all that up fishing the other day?"

Celia tears her eyes from the water to look at the pile. No – she can't. The netting is clean and dry. Unused. Underneath it, the chicken wire is shaped into a rough cube.

"Think you could help me carry it up to the dumpster, Nat?" Luke asks.

"Yeah, I think so," Nat says, but he doesn't sound so sure. The whole pile looks heavy. "I'll take this side."

Luke smiles and, in the glow of moonlight, Celia sees the glint of teeth under his beard. "You're a good kid, Nat," he says, one bony hand reaching out to clap his shoulder. The fox fur lunges, boneless and ineffective, little more than a frantic jerk around Celia's neck. Fear, hot and urgent clutches her chest.

"Nat–"

He looks back at her just as Luke's hand touches his shoulder. Nat freezes, eyes going wide. A strange, unnatural ripple passes under his skin. His mouth opens in a silent scream as the fur on Celia's shoulder lets out a low, mournful noise. Luke smiles, showing teeth that are just a little too sharp.

Celia watches, frozen with horror as Nat collapses, crumpling like a sack of rocks. Except rocks and bodies have mass when they hit the ground, but Nat's clothes fall to the earth with a quiet little *fwump*. It lands in a messy pile. One that thrashes and yowls.

Celia's heart leaps into her throat as Luke reaches into the pile and grabs the reynard fox by its scruff before tossing it into the cage of wire and net. The creature screams, claws and teeth raking against the chicken wire. The fox looks out at Celia with Nat's blue eyes, wide and pleading.

Luke straightens, no longer hunched and bent. He turns to face Celia. The wrinkled features of his face shift, like flipping through a scrapbook of pictures. Celia sees a dimple-cheeked white girl, a handsome man that Celia recognises from the depths of her memory, offering her mother an arm. Justine Elliott's features overtake them, her pretty young face made cold and foreign by those honey-coloured eyes, that sharp smile.

"Won't you come with me, Celia?" the creature asks in a high, girlish voice. The words shift to a deeper, familiar tone as Luke Absher's face settles back into place. But this isn't the kindly old man that Celia grew up around. It may use his voice, wear his face, but those golden eyes are devoid of emotion or warmth. His sharp teeth curl into a cruel smile. "Would you like to see the hunt?"

Celia feels like she's being crushed, lungs unable to draw in a proper breath. Inside of the cage, Nat screams, an animal sound of fear that roots her to the spot. The thing that is *not* Luke steps towards her, its smile growing impossibly wide, impossibly sharp.

"I've been waiting to add you to my collection, Celia," it says, its voice a deadly hiss. "You and your mother are both so beautiful. I gave her back to you as a gift, but now I can hang you next to each other. Your boyfriend could be right beside you both. A happy family. Wouldn't that be nice?"

Rage cuts through her fear. Ten years of grief and pain boil up inside of her like a kettle ready to scream. The scream becomes manifest as she thrusts the broken end of the branch forward, stabbing it into the creature's honey-gold eye. For a second, Luke's stolen features vanish, leaving the awful reality of its true form behind. Around Celia's stick, black ichor blossoms from the creature's wide, lidless eye. The other golden eye widens as it jerks back with a scream, taking Celia's stick with it. Agony spills forth in a dozen voices, shrieked from the maw of a mouth filled with jagged, gnashing teeth. But aside from the awful mouth and eyes, the creature is a blank slate. No nose, no ears, no lips. A creature that takes from others what it doesn't possess itself.

The beer in Celia's stomach turns sour at the sight of it. The chorus of pain grips her chest, making it hard to breathe. The need to silence it, to *make it stop* fuels her. She surges forward, tucking her head and shoulders low, just like Tuck and Emerson taught her to, before shoving all her weight into the creature's middle. It's just enough. The creature stumbles back, one foot landing in the water as the other trips over a docked boat.

The creature goes down with a splash, and Celia doesn't wait to see if it comes back up. Panicked fingers fumble against the trap until she manages to pry it open. Nat skitters out and jumps straight into Celia's arms. Under the lush red fur, his heart beats fast as a hummingbird's.

Celia runs. Her boots pound against the ground as she dodges between the unfriendly trees. Roots trip her up, branches snag at her hair and coat. She regrets the beers, now. Her boot laces have come untied, and she stumbles, trips. The skin of her knee tears against the ground, but she picks herself back up, never loosening her grip on Nat.

A sound carries through the forest, a choir of snarled curses. "CELIA!" Her name is echoed tenfold, as if screamed by a dozen different people. Nat's animal shriek of fear is echoed by her own, but she doesn't stop running. She can't prove her Meemaw right. She can't end up just like her mother.

A structure appears through the trees, though they cluster around it as if trying to hide it. An old barn with Spanish moss dripping from decaying shingles, its roof half collapsed. Celia runs for it and wrenches the rusted metal door open as far as she can before she squeezes through the gap. The air inside smells of damp rot and something else. Something sickly sweet.

Celia backs into a corner, holding Nat to her chest. Both the fox in her arms and the one around her neck tremble, matching the shudders of fear that wrack through her own body. A quiet whimper escapes Nat, and Celia tightens her grip on him, his soft fur an odd sort of comfort.

Her rapidly blinking eyes slowly adjust to the darkness. Moonlight peeks through the small, grime-streaked window, casting the little barn's interior into shadowy relief. And illuminating the fox furs that line the wall.

Eleven in all. They hang limp, expertly tanned and preserved. Nails pin them to the wall by the tips of their noses, like insects on display. The furs collectively shift, turning their empty sockets to focus on Celia, silently pleading. She slaps a hand over her mouth to stop her scream as Luke's stolen voice cuts through the normal sounds of night, closer now.

"Celia!" it shouts. "Where you at, girl?"

No matter how hard she tries, she can't tear her eyes away from the line of furs. The limp, gutted bodies hang helpless, toothless mouths gaping, caught mid-scream. Then something sharp digs into her arm, and she barely bites back a yelp.

Nat licks the spot he just bit as if in apology. The pain clears the fog of fear enough to think. Staying still means waiting for the faceless creature to catch them. They have to move.

Around her neck, her fox fur tugs to the right, and Celia's gaze follows. In the corner, a few musty bales of hay have burst from the confines of their rotten twine. Celia's shaking hand reaches into her coat pocket and pulls out her lighter, flipping the lid open with a quiet click. A flick of her thumb coaxes the flame to life. She looks down at the fox in her arms, seeing Nat's familiar blue eyes looking back at her, wide and afraid.

"Celia!" the creature shouts, voices drawing ever nearer. "You better not be in my shed, girl."

Celia drops the lighter into the hay just as the door's rusted hinges screech open. The creature stands in the entrance, one inhuman golden eye shimmering like a disk in the dark. "There you are." The stolen voices hiss out of it like the rasp of a snake's rattle.

Without warning, the faceless thing lunges for her. Celia jumps back, but not fast enough. Bony fingers wrap around the fox fur and snag the lapel of her coat. The creature tugs hard, yanking Celia close enough that she can smell the tobacco and rot on its breath. The fox stole rears, coiling up before it strikes. The plastic jaw can't do much damage, but surprise loosens the monster's grip just enough for Celia to tug her coat free, leaving the fox fur writhing and hissing in its hand.

Celia doesn't hesitate. The creature's blocking the door, so she rushes to the window. The old glass breaks like thin ice as her elbow connects with it. She pushes Nat through first and climbs after him, broken glass sinking into her hands and arms and chest like so many jagged teeth. A scream of pain escapes her as she forces herself through the too-small window. Her hips slow her down, causing the glass to dig in deeper.

"No you don't," the creature snarls. A hand grabs her boot and *tugs*. Celia is pulled back with it before the boot slips from her foot. She kicks hard with her other foot, and the heavy sole connects with a satisfying crunch of bone. Celia tumbles out of the window, hitting the ground hard as the creature screams. An arm reaches through the window after her, but it's too big to follow. Stolen voices swell to a furious screech, all of them shouting their hatred.

But now, a new voice joins the choir. Her mother's, twisted with fury.

"You're a dead girl, Celia!" Evelyn Taylor screams, her voice echoed by the others. "I'll skin you alive!"

Celia's vision swims. Blood seeps from cuts down her front, staining her black dress darker, flowing in rivulets of red down her arms. Nat's teeth sink into the hem of her dress and tug, urgent, demanding.

A shout of disbelief echoes from inside of the barn as the fire takes to the hay like a starving thing. Through the broken window, firelight flickers and gutters. Celia scrambles to her feet, following Nat's urgent tugs around to the front of the barn.

She throws herself against the door, slamming it closed just as the faceless creature connects with the other side. The rusted metal shudders and inches open under the force. Celia's weight and tenacity aren't enough.

Over the shriek of a dozen voices, a different sound echoes through the woods. Barking, high and urgent. A moment later, Eustis comes tearing through the underbrush. His white tail wags happily at the sight of Celia, but he yelps and cowers as the faceless creature slams its weight against the door again. Celia shouts as the rusted hinges creak open another inch.

Then a voice carries through the trees. "Celia Rose Taylor, I know you're down here!" Meemaw shouts. "I'm fixin' to jerk a knot in your tail!"

"Meemaw, help!" Celia screams.

"Eustis, come off it!" Meemaw shouts, and the little dog disappears back through the trees. The creature slams against the door again, and there's enough force behind it to rattle Celia's to her marrow. Her feet slide against the dirt as the door opens enough to allow a bony hand to reach out, fingers hooked to claws that grab for her. Celia dredges up the last of her strength and throws her weight against the door, crushing the creature's arm between it and the frame. Stolen voices swell to a shriek that makes her eardrums vibrate.

Meemaw rushes from the underbrush in oil-stained overalls, a shotgun in her hand. Her eyes go wide, fear slowing her footsteps. "Sweet Jesus."

"I'll kill you!" It's her daughter's furious voice at the forefront of that unholy din.

Meemaw's mouth parts in a horrified o, tears springing to her eyes. "Evelyn?"

A sob breaks out of Celia's throat. The door shudders hard, but Celia's used up all her strength. An arm emerges through the gap, then a shoulder.

"He killed her," Celia sobs. "He took Nat."

Meemaw looks to the trembling fox at Celia's feet, seeing

that nice young boy's eyes looking pleadingly up at her. For a moment, the truth of it is too much to bear. Disbelief and sorrow chase one another in an endless loop.

"You're a dead girl, Celia!"

Evelyn would never have threatened Celia like that. The twisted fury that distorts her daughter's voice breaks through Meemaw's shock. The sorrow on her face hardens. She racks the shotgun and lifts it to her shoulder.

"Get away from the door, Celia."

Celia doesn't have much of a choice. As the fire grows inside, the creature charges, fueled by desperation. It shoves against the rusted door with all its strength and sends it flying open. Celia goes sprawling against the damp ground, but Meemaw is ready.

The crack of the gun is deafening, but no more than the monster's hellish scream as the force of the blast knocks it back into the burning barn. Meemaw steps forward and shoves the door closed with her shoulder. Celia stumbles to help her, leaving another bloody handprint on top of the rusted metal. Together, they brace the door closed.

The creature's thumps and thuds get weaker and weaker, but the sounds of agony swell, a mob of screaming voices that echo from inside of the barn. The door gets too hot to hold, and Meemaw stumbles back, taking Celia with her. She keeps her shotgun raised, aimed and ready even as the roof of the barn erupts into flames.

Celia sinks to the ground, bloodied and burned. Nat crawls into her lap, his warm body shivering against hers. The chorus of screams reach a bloody pitch that makes Celia slap her hands over her ears. Meemaw doesn't flinch. She keeps the gun raised, watching the door even though it never opens again.

It takes an eternity, but the voices start to fade. The scream turns to a whimper, and then finally, a collective sigh of relief. Evelyn's voice is the last they hear. A whispered *thank you, thank you, thank you* that quietly fades to nothing. After a time, Celia and Meemaw's laboured breaths, and the roar of the fire is the only sounds left.

Celia holds Nat close, her face buried against his bristled fur. "I'm sorry, Nat," she whispers. "I'm so, so sorry."

Under her cheek, the fur softens to skin. The growing weight in her lap slides to the ground beside her. Nat's naked body settles against her, solid and warm and very human. He wraps his arms around his bare chest, shivering from cold and shock alike. Celia looks at him in disbelief, her hand shaking as she reaches out to touch his cheek, afraid that it's some cruel joke.

But Nat leans into her hand. His laugh sounds closer to a sob, and Celia pulls him close as he buries his face against her neck. Meemaw strips off her jacket to cover the naked boy. Celia does the same, tying her own coat around his waist. Eustis comes to lick his hand until Nat reaches out to scratch the bald spot under his collar.

The fire rages, and the barn collapses as it's devoured by the hungry maw of flames. Only then does Meemaw lower her shotgun.

"I told you I didn't want you goin' out tonight," Meemaw says, her voice shaking.

Celia can't stop a small, tired laugh as the shock catches up to her. Tears sting at the corner of her eyes as she watches the fire burn, taking the twelve fox furs with it. Her neck feels cold without the stole there to keep her warm. Its absence joins the ache in her heart where the memory of her mother lives.

Yet even so, Celia could swear she still hears the quiet *thank you, thank you, thank you* of her mother's voice.

"I'm glad I didn't listen."

They watch the fire burn itself out and start to cool, the rubble turned to cinders. And as the cold grey of dawn creeps over the horizon, nothing remains of the faceless creature or its collection but ash.

REFLECTIONS

Gillian Joseph

I always wake them up gently when they begin to writhe, asleep-awake, away-close from my body lying beside them. Soft shushing and stroking, punctuated by their groaning voice:

"*Clean the mirrors, please... Did you find them all?*"

Assuring words that have become repetitive in my mouth: "Of course I have, Zee, it's okay."

They don't believe me, insist that I must've made a mistake, overlooked something hidden, something deceitful. This is the pattern of our mornings; I propose again that maybe it's this house. It's grown accustomed to us; we've carved out habitual grooves that are too comfortable to leave.

There's nothing significant about the day that they finally agree with me, maybe apart from the sex. The kind of sex where you manifest a shared vision: minds melting into each other. You create a singular desire together, and then you bring it to life, piece by piece, touch by touch. A hand slicking across their skin is me reaching out, grabbing on to what we've chosen, and their inhale pulls it back into us. And that's exactly what we do on the day that we decide to move out, back to Zee's partial homeplace.

I say partial because although they refer to it as their home-place, it's not where Zee actually grew up, at least not in this existence. I say place because it's not a town in any sense of the word – more so a community, a system of roots that has spread and burrowed deeply. It's the kind of scattered community of a long-established family, one that has deeper ties to the land than to town names or state names or country names, let alone to houses.

It took a long time for Zee to find their exact homeplace, hundreds of hours of combing through faded government-issued documents and listening patiently to stories that spoke of familiar names. Zee had started the process before we even met, so when I came along, they at least had a foothold. But still, there were always vintage plat maps and printouts of online maps covered in notes scattered around. Zee was trying to triangulate the precise allotment of land that had been an attempted conciliatory gift to one of their ancestors.

Finding my homeplace was never an ordeal. My family history was easy to trace; my ancestors didn't face the erasure that Zee's did. Guilt and anger and sadness bubbled up watching Zee hunched over our table, sorting and scanning and scribbling. So, when they found their partial homeplace, we drank two thirty-one-dollar bottles of champagne, not sure if what we were feeling was tipsiness or the shift that had just occurred. Zee had set themself on the path to return to their history.

We make a game out of packing the furniture and decorations: each day, one of us hides something in the house that we aren't sure is worth the journey. If, by the end of the day, the other person hasn't noticed that the object is gone, we mark it as something to sell or donate. A couple of items become exceptions but, overall, this practice works well for us. We end up with far less than initially predicted and a sense of relief, especially for Zee. "Now I have an excuse to curate! I've always felt like I should wait for some cue to buy what I want for the house. Well, I guess this is it, huh?"

"Baby, you can decorate however you want, but I'm pretty sure you already do that anyways…"

"But I mean specific things, like the bigger buys, or the kinda stuff that's meant to stay in one place for a while."

"Anything particular you have in mind?"

Zee tilts their face upwards, with a yearning expression. "Big wooden bookshelves… some raised garden beds for outside… and a vintage rug in the living room, for sure."

★ ★ ★

The first weeks in the new house are marked by energetic cleaning, positioning and repositioning, and landscaping that borders on excessive. We drive into the nearest city multiple times, burning through gas and money that was saved away for satiating at least a portion of Zee's imagination. It was no secret to us that the house would need a complete overhaul, so the savings also included less exciting non-aesthetic expenses, like bringing the wiring up to date and solving the mystery of rattling plumbing. I try with zero luck to find a quiet moment to relax, without being interrupted by the noises of strangers' feet on hardwood or tape being ripped from cardboard boxes.

As fall creeps in, the house and Zee mellow in response to the environment. The chill stiffens everything, winds whisper through trees to shed our burdens along with them, for now. We put a pause on the larger outstanding projects; we enjoy being present, being here in their homeplace. The lands and waters are so serene and beautiful that I can't help gushing to Zee again and again about how glad I am that they gave me the privilege to move with them, to be part of this experience.

"Well, what would I do without you? I'd be a lonely two-spirit in their little rez house, waiting for my sister to have kids so I can officially be a gossiping auntie. And besides, who would help me scrub away all the colonialism left behind?"

I roll my eyes, but feel appreciated. Zee's right as far as their second reason goes; it was only the other day that they finally believed we had bagged up all the remnants of the past hundred years. As soon as we thought we'd gotten everything, a scrap of fabric or a piece of a long-broken dish or other miscellaneous trash would show up. The people who previously claimed ownership over the allotment were a white middle-class farming family who were capitalising on Zee's ancestors' disenfranchisement, stripping away their homeplace for barely any money. But, the grandchildren must've decided that they weren't profiting enough off of Native land. They had vacated our house decades ago, but not without leaving their mark.

"It's a labour of love, reclaiming this place."

I agree with Zee. We have begun nestling back into their homeplace, and I relish every second of it.

★ ★ ★

Zee's dream subsides for a while, maybe because their brain is too preoccupied and exhausted from the physical cleaning we're doing. They are better rested, and have more energy, which is put directly into the details of the house.

"Hey, did you clean the doorknobs or something?"

"Why?"

"I don't know… they're different!"

I walk over and join Zee's inspection of the doorknobs, starting with the bedroom and continuing through our house together.

"Hmm… maybe they look a little bit more bronze? Probably from you opening and shutting them all the time."

Zee grins and shrugs. "Maybe I polished them up and forgot."

A few days later, they fixate on a blanket.

"You didn't wash the blanket we bought, right? I'm not sure if you're supposed to…" Zee presents me with a green blanket a few shades lighter than I remember it being when we originally brought it back from the store.

"Huh. Nope, I didn't… maybe it transferred onto one of the other blankets? Or maybe we're just remembering the colour wrong, we haven't really used it yet…"

Zee didn't seem satisfied after finding nothing amiss about the other blankets. "Well, I miss the colour I imagined! Dang.

Maybe it changes colours in different light."

"You'd know more about that than me – you're the interior decorator in this relationship."

Zee gives a teasing smile. "It's the fall, it makes everything look different I guess, with earthy undertones and all that."

★ ★ ★

We both work from home; most of our time is spent inside, broken up by long walks through the surrounding land, together or separate. The time between sunrise and sunset diminishes by increments of minutes each day, and we have to prioritise finding time to be with the sun. I prefer the middle of the day, when the sun resists the temperatures inching down and the incessant tugging of night. Zee likes to take their strolls in the afternoon, stretching into twilight, so they can see the sky transition and bask in the moonlight – they just wear warmer clothes.

I come home from my walk a bit later than usual, struggling to tear myself away from the crisp air and waning sunlight that splashes itself onto the hills around me. I'm ready to make tea and then start a fire in the living room, but Zee interrupts my plan as I walk into the kitchen.

"These are wrong."

"What? What's wrong?"

Zee gestures at one of the cabinets, which is wide open and half emptied. "The plates aren't right."

"Are they broken? What do you mean?"

They hand me one of our plates, stacked haphazardly on the counter. "Just look."

I eyeball Zee first, unsure of why they seem unsettled by plates. "You're okay? Did anything happen?"

"Work is stressing me out… and I know that can make me hyper-sensitive to everything… but I honestly can't tell if I'm obsessing or if my eyes are playing tricks or what, but I swear that all of the plates are weird."

I turn the plate over in my hands. "The design does look kinda off, is that what you mean?"

"Pff, kind of? It's totally changed."

I resume peering at the rim of the plate; it looks like the design is a vintage interpretation of the one on the plates we had recently bought. There are some clear differences, and the colours have all changed slightly. "You think the dishwasher messed them up?"

"I don't know! But I'm annoyed. And come see this." Zee motions for me to follow and walks to the bathroom, where they point down at the sink.

I crane my neck over their shoulder. "Needs a good scrubbing?"

Zee grunts. "Already gave it three, the colour won't budge."

The previously pristine white ceramic sink was obviously tinted, almost a blue colour. "Maybe it's the water…"

"Could be… who knows what shit is getting leached into the water here, with that construction down the river."

I nod in consensus but try to steer Zee away from going down a rabbit hole. "I'm sure there's an explanation. You're still getting used to the house, and to being here – we'll keep an eye on it, okay?"

★ ★ ★

These conversations become our new pattern, but aren't restricted only to mornings like the dream used to be. First once or twice a week, then nearly every day, Zee discovers something amiss; the wood of the table has changed, a book is lost and another is found in its place, the cut of their pants has been altered.

"You think I'm having my late bloomer growth spurt?"

I chuckle. "Do you feel taller?"

It all feels silly at first, like a funny adjustment period to our house. But Zee isn't wrong.

Although I don't notice the things they point out first, I do notice them after, and always agree with their findings.

This escalates one night, when I get off the phone with a friend to find the entire living room has exploded into a mess. Zee is on the floor sorting through every single piece of linen we own, from bath towels to bedsheets, and stuff is strewn across the table and couch.

"What's happening?"

"They are all different, feel them." Zee throws me a wash-cloth, followed by a pillowcase.

"Feels thinner, maybe rougher too. I wonder why they wore out so fast?" Zee purses their lips and stands up. "And this."

I realise that Zee has taken down some of the frames from the wall and dismantled them completely. When we first moved in, they had framed some old hand-drawn maps of the surrounding area, along with maps showing their ancestors' different allotments of land.

"What's wrong with the maps?"

"They've all been changed." They usher me over to the table, where their computer sits open, with dozens of tabs pulled up on it.

"Like, someone wrote on them? Show me."

"No, just changed. Like, someone got different maps and replaced mine. You're not pranking me, are you?" Zee asks, half-serious.

"Of course not. I don't even know where you would find maps like this anymore…"

Zee begins outlining the changes with their finger, circling the spots on the map that were revised and comparing them to the original scans on their computer. Some of the markings and landmarks on the map have been altered, placed a bit differently, renamed or misspelled. But the most perplexing change is that Zee couldn't find the allotment we're living on.

"What am I missing?" Zee runs their finger methodically through the entire map, piece by piece, searching for their ancestor's name.

"Let me…" I repeat their process, carefully scouring the map, to be rewarded with further confusion. "Here's where it should be… right?" I point out the correct position.

Zee shakes their head vigorously. "This is fucked up. I'm calling my dad."

"Do you think someone broke in, or…?"

"No, I think something never left. This isn't right."

While Zee retreats back to their position on the floor and rings their dad, I dutifully go over the maps and wait for my goosebumps to go away. I take blank pieces of paper and cover different parts of the maps, focusing on small portions at a time. Still nothing to show Zee. I try without much luck to listen in on the conversation Zee is having, to sus out how entrenched their uneasiness is becoming and strategise on how best to pacify them. The last thing I want is for Zee to spiral into a frenzy that I can't help them out of.

Zee's dad tells them to put tobacco down, to ask for help while cleansing the house. He says to make sure that we are protecting ourselves, to braid some sweetgrass and keep it close to our bodies at all times, in a pocket and under the pillows. To let whatever was playing tricks on us know it isn't welcome in the house, to show that we won't be intimidated.

We stay up all night after following his directions. Zee is bubbling over with anxiety, and they are beginning to wear off on me. The normal creaking of our aged house now elicits a slight shiver, a ripple of anticipation as though we might catch a shadowy figure escaping through a window. We open all the doors, after noticing that we were spending too much time staring underneath their thresholds, waiting for feet to emerge on the other side. Every glinting light is a distraction, a breath caught in the back of our throats. Zee rests in my arms as daylight spills into our bedroom. I pull them close, anchoring us together, and feel their chest expand and shrink as I regather my senses and my voice.

"It's only some lingering energy… we should've expected as much."

Zee's body tenses slightly, then relaxes reluctantly, drowsiness sneaking into their body and voice. "Yeah. I hope you're right."

I kiss their bare shoulders and drift into the inbetween with them.

★ ★ ★

The next day I wake up before Zee, and spend that time cleaning up the living room, refolding the linens and trying my best to organise the scattered frames and maps. I make us coffee, although the sun is only a few hours away from setting again.

Zee ventures into the living room a bit later with a blanket wrapped around them and heads straight for the coffee. "The smell got me out of bed." They smile dryly at me.

"How did you sleep?"

"Eh, nothing special…"

I look them over suspiciously. "Really? No dreams?"

Zee shrugs. "Nope. Not yet…"

When we've both fully woken up, we decide it's time to capitalise on the sinking sun and take a walk. I can tell that Zee feels more at ease in the nature surrounding us, but they are distracted, searching the whole time.

"What're you looking for?"

"Anything. You see signs out here, they're not always obvious."

The land sprawls out around us in all directions, a smattering of trees and some long grasses filling out the endless space. A creek murmurs constantly in the background, the competition of crackling leaves already long gone, dampened by the first snow that fell last week.

We walk well into the evening, and when we get back to our house, Zee immediately notices another change.

They shine their phone flashlight onto the exterior of the house. "The shutters aren't normal."

We get closer, to have a better look. Zee's right: the shutters that we had installed and painted black now appear to be dilapidated, worn wooden shutters.

Zee exchanges a glance with me. "Do I even wanna go inside?"

"It's gonna be okay, come on, let's go warm up."

As soon as we cross the doorway, Zee begins tearing through our house, overturning everything in their path. The pastel candles are now off-white, the basket beside the couch is now wire instead of bamboo.

I flinch with every change that they find. I have the urge to check over Zee's body, and have them do the same with mine, searching for any transformations that have taken place without our knowledge. I wonder whether we'd find any.

"What do we do now?"

Zee grimaces. "Search for something hidden. Something that burrowed in here and doesn't want to leave."

We painstakingly search every nook of our house, once again staying up through the night. There's nothing new, only things that have been replaced.

I sit back on my heels in exhaustion after searching through the cabinet underneath the kitchen sink. "Is it all in our heads?"

"I don't know. It can't be."

Zee goes into the bedroom to find something warmer for their feet, and I hear a shout shortly after.

I rush over and Zee is wildly raking through everything in the closet. "I can't find my moccasins! These were sitting where they normally are!" Zee brandishes a pair of loafers that I've never seen before, pissed off and with tears brimming.

I join them on the floor and give them a hug.

Zee's voice wavers. "It took my sister so long to make them for me."

"They're not gone, Zee, we're going to get them back, I promise." They crumple into me. "We should sleep. We won't be able to get anything done like this."

Zee agrees, and we abandon the mess for the bed.

I wake up what feels like mere minutes after falling asleep, to Zee's pleading voice.

"*Clean the mirrors.*"

I caress Zee's back. "We've already done them all."

The room falls quiet again, my eyelids get heavier, until Zee's words cut through the air.

"*Then we must've missed one.*"

I sit up and turn the side table lamp on in one fluid motion, startled that Zee answered. The light it throws out into the room is a different colour than usual; the lampshade and light-bulb have both been replaced. I lean over Zee. Their eyes are shut and their breathing is rhythmic. I'm not sure whether I should wake them up or not. There is a palpable heaviness in the room. It's dark outside, and I figure that it's the early hours of the morning. Terror swirls slowly. A tapping sound carries into our bedroom and I gently shake Zee.

They don't flinch.

"*I must've missed one.*"

My heartbeat picks up pace, I feel like the air is being sucked out of the room by some invisible portal. I shake Zee more vigorously but can't bring myself to say anything. I jostle them again.

Zee sits up and turns towards me. "What? Are you okay?"

My sigh heaves audibly. "Holy shit, you scared me bad, and then you wouldn't wake up!" I whisper heatedly.

"I had a dream…."

"About the mirrors?"

"Yeah…"

"You were talking to me during it. Like, we were talking normally but you were fully out of it."

Zee's eyes widen. "I need to call my dad again."

We both stay in bed while Zee's phone rings. Their dad answers groggily, and Zee tells him about their dream and about what they'd said to me during it, then turns the phone over to me for my side of the story. He tells us that we can wait for him to drive one of his friends over to help us, but the fastest he could get here was two days from now. He advises us to cover all the mirrors and spend as much time outside as we could manage.

Since we can't go back to sleep, Zee and I go through our house once again, hanging sheets in front of all the mirrors. Then we get together all of our camping supplies and set our tent up a little ways away, sheltered under the trees' spindly, bare fingers, and partially obscured by some high brown brush.

We accompany each other whenever we need to go back inside. Despite the cold, sleeping in the tent feels refreshing; it makes us realise how watched we felt indoors. There was a mutual mixed feeling of relief and exasperation and culpability; who were we to be pushed out from this house in Zee's home-place? But we still find solace in the land, and talk well into the night, filling the tent with stories and collective warmth.

The sounds of heavily falling snow wake us up, and we step into its fast-accumulating blanket.

"Guess we aren't staying out here again today, huh?"

Zee bites their lip. "Guess my dad and his friend won't make it tomorrow either."

I run my hands vigorously up and down their upper arms. "Let's get everything packed up, then we'll figure out what's next."

The house is ever-changing. Entering this time exposes a sofa upholstered in dull fabric in place of the faded brown leather one we purchased for the living room. Yellowing muslin curtains instead of the light blue ones that we had lovingly hand dyed during the summer. Uniform, dimpled glass cups replaced our thrifted, eclectic collection. The house is reverting, teasing Zee along the way.

Zee wrinkles their nose. "It even smells old. We've gotta find that mirror."

"You think we missed a mirror? How? We've gone through everything…"

"I dunno, but it makes the most sense to me. It must've

been hidden, something's little portal that they thought no one would be able to find."

I blow my breath out with force, making the hairs framing my face levitate for a second. "Okay, let's find it then."

We start with the walls, knocking on them to listen for any possible hollow places. When that turns up nothing, we move to the fixtures on the wall and the furniture that was already here when we arrived. We rap and push against the wooden cabinets in the kitchen, and pull out every single drawer in the entirety of our house. Maybe there will be one with a false back, a hidden compartment, a skillfully placed piece of wood that is covering a little reflective surface. Zee isn't sure what the mirror will look like, or how big it will be, or if any part of it will be marred by whatever evilness originally placed it. Does it move around? Is it underneath the floors? Built into the roof?

There is no way to know whether we are making any progress, and it is a miserable task to pull apart everything that we had so carefully organised and arranged only months ago. Our rushed steps turn into trudges, exhaustion pulling down on our bodies slowly but steadily.

"Could you put on some water for coffee?"

I yawn before answering, "Of course."

Zee side-eyes me. "We can't sleep in here like this…"

"Yeah, you're right. I'm just running out of ideas for where to look…"

The uneasiness accumulating in Zee is obvious, furrowing itself into their brows and hardening their jaw. We sit down on the couch after the coffee is done.

"I'm surprised dust didn't come out of it when we sat down." I try to joke with Zee, watching for a slight upturn of the corners of their mouth. It doesn't come, I don't blame them; I just mask my fear better.

The sun has set, and darkness gathers, embracing us from every opening. It seeps in, dimming the lights. It begs us to return to it, to abandon our house and everything in it, to let the ground cradle us while we rest. It asks us why we want to be surrounded by walls imbued with trickery when we could be in the open, with no boundaries or falsities.

Time warps itself in strange ways as we continue our search. No clock seems reliable, and there's no way to mark the passing hours. We haven't heard from Zee's dad or anyone else all day, and are becoming progressively more unsure what our connection is to the world outside.

At some point, Zee announces that they are going to take a shower. Their clothes and hair have a coating of dust, and their hands and knees are dirty from going through every possible hiding place. I make more coffee and sit at the table to drink it while Zee is in the bathroom. I hear the water stop running after a while, and what seems like a longer-than-normal chunk of time passes without any noise.

I decide to go check on Zee and find them with their palms pressed down on the sink ledge, looking intently into the bathroom mirror. Their wet hair drips methodically onto the sheet that had been covering the mirror. A towel is wrapped loosely around their hips. They've removed everything from around the sink and placed it on the floor. I stand in the doorframe of the bathroom as the remaining steam rolls out, and Zee doesn't flinch or acknowledge me.

"Zee? What're you doing?"

No answer.

"Hey? What's up?"

Zee isn't fazed. I struggle to form any meaningful words. I reach my hand out to them timidly, placing it over theirs, which is still firmly on the sink. The silence stretches out until Zee decides to speak.

"I think I found it."

"This is the mirror?" I'm confused, remembering the multiple times that they've cleansed it.

"It's behind this one. Can't you see it?"

I step fully into the bathroom, so that I'm beside Zee and looking directly into the mirror.

Zee interrupts my concentration. "Look *through* it, not at it, or at the reflection."

I try to relax my eyes and let myself take every part of the mirror in, ignoring Zee and my own image. My body is tense, waiting for our reflections to morph or take on a life of their own, or for something to appear behind us. I hold my breath, thinking that if I can stabilise my stare, I will be able to see through the mirror as well.

I struggle to notice what Zee does, though. "I... I don't know how. I don't see anything."

Zee lets the silence expand into the bathroom. "Help me take the mirror off."

I hesitate before dutifully retrieving the toolbox from the kitchen, and then try to remove the mirror from the wall. I start by taking a screwdriver to the rusty clips holding the mirror in place, but they refuse to budge. Their age screams against the metal, mocking me as I tighten my grip.

Meanwhile, Zee won't break their gaze, barely even blinking as their eyes penetrate the mirror. A shiver blooms across my skin, and I'm not sure if it's from their intentness or the sound the clips made.

Next is a crowbar, which I manage to shimmy between the wall and the base of the mirror. I expect Zee to offer me their help, but no noise escapes their mouth. My breathing hitches with the effort. It feels futile, I swear that the mirror is being held onto, some steely grip belonging to the other side of this wall. I close my eyes and push.

The mirror lifts slightly, emitting a metallic groan.

"Zee, you need to cover the mirror in case it shatters, can you put the sheet over it?"

They move awkwardly, slowly crouching to the floor to pick up the sheet while never removing their eyes from the mirror. They hold the sheet at arms' length, waiting wordlessly for me to take it. I set the crowbar into the sink and pull the sheet over the mirror in one motion.

Zee reaches towards the mirror at the same time I reach for the crowbar again. My breath hitches – they pull back a corner of the sheet, holding it up without acknowledging me.

I heave against the mirror again; it answers me in a series of scraping and grating sounds. Eventually, it gives way, loosening itself from the wall just enough that I can slide the metal in further and gain leverage. Zee holds the sheet steadily, refusing to take their eyes away. I pry it off, slowly revealing a divot in the wall, a kind of sloppily carved out cubby.

I give the mirror a firm yank and it comes off along with an accumulation of debris. There's a hand mirror standing upright in the hole, with a tarnished handle and frame. The reflective surface is in perfect condition, not even a film of dust covers it.

Zee snatches the hand mirror before I can even set the bathroom mirror down. They hold it up to their face. The hand mirror is double-sided, with a reflective surface on the front and the back; it can be held either way. Zee gasps as they peer through the mirror, rotating its position in their hand to try both sides. They spin around slowly, and turn it on themselves.

"What?!"

"Everything is… different… when you look through it… and I can't see myself."

"Different how?"

"Like you went back in time, a century ago."

"Show me." I reach out my hand for the mirror, but Zee refuses.

"Here…" They hold the mirror level with my face, leaning back. "What do I look like through it?"

"I can't see you through it. And everything looks pretty… normal. Does it matter which way it faces?"

"Not for me it doesn't…" Zee pulls the mirror back towards them. "It changes what you look like."

"Changes how?"

Zee drops their head and studies the frame and handle of the mirror. They run their finger along it, then their towel, vigorously rubbing at one spot. Zee wraps the towel around the mirror and places the bundle on the floor behind them, blocking me from getting any closer to it. Then they begin to rapidly redress before snatching the mirror back up and pushing past me.

"Where are you going?" I can feel my voice waver slightly, despite me willing it not to. I don't want Zee to hear the frustration or urgency building up inside my chest.

I follow behind as they storm outside, only stopping for a second to slip on their boots at the front door. They run towards the tree line and fall onto their knees before burying the mirror in snow, then take it out and shake the snow off, wiping it clean with their sleeve. They hold the mirror between us as I walk towards them.

"Stop!" Zee nearly screams at me.

"What the hell, Zee?"

"I know it's your mirror."

"What're you talking about?"

"It has your fucking name on it. You don't look right through it... You look like you're rotting away in front of me. Like you should've been buried decades ago."

I put my hands up and walk slowly, practically tiptoeing towards them.

Zee stands up and backs away from me.

"I think you're tired, Zee. Relax."

"Don't try to put this on me. Explain yourself!"

"Jesus! There's nothing to explain... it's probably a coincidence." I try to steady my tone, to not let it show my multiplying aggravation.

"You told me that your ancestors lived near mine. You never told me where, exactly!"

"Sure I did. Just, please put the mirror down, and we can..."

Zee lowers the mirror slightly and tightens their hold on it. Their face is warped with betrayal and rage as they cut me off.

"Where did they live?"

A smile ripples across my face involuntarily. "Here."

Zee smashes the mirror against a tree.

A blinding pain rips through me, as though my internal and external self are being unzipped from each other. It is simultaneously over in seconds and stretches on for all of time; at some point, it becomes a part of me, and then there is nothing.

★ ★ ★

When I wake up, I'm comforted by my old, ancestral house. I'm not sure where it is, because there is no land outside. There are no doors or windows to look through. Instead, there are mirrors, and silence, broken up by the occasional sound of Zee's voice.

"*I found all the mirrors and cleaned them myself.*"

I can never tell where it's coming from.

IN RUINS

G.T. Korbin

Some places are not meant to exist at night. They get draped in shadows and echoes, for the absence of people stretches the gaps in between, distorting everything out of shape.

It's her favourite time to wander.

Daphne will owe Markos for this. After weeks and weeks of begging, her best friend and newly appointed security guard finally let her slip in the museum after hours with the excuse that she needed to finish the art project for her class.

It's not a lie. It's not the whole truth either.

Daphne does have a project to finish. Much like the dozens of art students loitering around the halls of the museum every morning, perched on the floor in front of the exhibits with sketchbooks on their laps. But everything looks different without light, and it's that perspective she seeks: the intimacy of a barely lit room, the haunting edge of knowing you're somewhere you're not supposed to be.

She gives Markos a kiss on the cheek, and he opens the door for her, warning that he will tell on her without hesitation if she leaves even the tiniest mark. With a heavy backpack swung over her shoulders, she strolls inside. She already knows where she's going.

Hundreds of tourists walk these floors every day. People come here in search of old gods and lives enduring only in stone, carved and painted with such devotion that even time cannot touch them.

She was only ten when she opened her first book of mythology and absorbed the tales of heroes, legends made under the whims of those watching from a mountain too high to reach. Back then, everything wondrous was assigned to a person, as if every act of love needed to be protected by something divine. No matter how many pages she went through, all she found were stories of fickle gods, or people who were too beautiful or too unlucky or both, as to be favoured or hated by them.

What she has always sought, and has yet to find, are the quieter stories. Of those who existed in the margins of the gods' world, unnoticed, who were worshipped only in the hearts of mortals but still held as if they were a miracle within themselves.

The love of humans, she thinks, who have only one short life to give, can never be compared to the fickle tendencies and spites of ancient gods.

The closest she got was poetry. The tender way Sappho spoke of love, of longing, so much so that her name became imbued with people like her. It was the one piece of Daphne's culture, of roots so ancient she could never trace back, that she could show off and have it feel like hers, like home.

The weak flashlight of her phone is no match for the tall walls that reach high above her. The shadows drip down from the ceiling, trapping her in a suffocating bubble. But she knows the way by now, her steps certain in the dark. They click against the cold floors, reverberating through the vast halls, and the sound travels between pieces of history, announcing her presence amongst them.

The statues haunt this room at night, their shapes obscured and foreboding. Still, they can't scare her; she only has eyes for one.

Daphne smiles when her light brushes the cracked ends of her marble feet, and she takes her spot in front of her. She rummages through her backpack and takes out a small camping lantern to place at her side, giving a brighter light to her subject.

Kore, the plaque reads. *Girl*. One of the unnamed ones, just a woman beautiful enough to inspire, or a fantasy of the sculptor, a person they wished existed. With every line of her features that Daphne mirrors with care onto the paper, the sentiment reaches closer and closer to her heart.

The odd, harsh light dresses the girl in new shadows, so different from the way the sun embraces her marble form every morning. It draws her lines more dramatic, powerful and grim, and as Daphne translates the image in her own hand, she adds bold splotches of black with strokes so deep they dig into the page. Rows of small curls fall in tight waves down to her waist, arranged into an elaborate hairstyle at the crown of her head. The folds of her clothes flow so delicate for the rough stone, and in her smile, the tiniest mirth accents her features, a hidden invitation. Daphne wants to trace the intricate curve of the marble, the gentle shape of her lips. Instead, she draws, smudging shadows in near-reverence.

"Don't you worry, my sweet. I'll try my best to do you justice."

She does this a lot at nights like this. Talks to her instead of talking to herself, like a child would to a stuffed animal with all the care that promises. She murmurs and sings to pass the time, then looks up at the statue with a breathless, guilty laugh when she belts too high and out of pitch.

"If I sang in English, would you understand me? Actually, you probably don't understand my Greek either, right?" She muses as she brushes the eraser dust away. With a smile, she turns the sketchbook over as if to show her. "But you understand this, right? Do you like it?"

She laughs.

"Thanks for the company, my sweet. I'll see you soon."

With the statues' watchful eyes at her back, Daphne retraces her steps to the entrance of the museum, where Markos, three hours into his shift, doesn't appear any more lively than the rest of the occupants there. They renew their deal for the following night and he makes her promise to at least bring him food next time. Clutching the straps of her backpack, Daphne wanders out into the night.

She breathes in the crisp winter air. It doesn't snow here much, not the way it did back north. But the cold still stings at her cheeks, and she wraps her jacket tighter around herself, zipping it up all the way to the top.

The Parthenon stands over her as she walks to the closest bus stop, looking down from the top of the hill. At night, the scene is bathed in warm, golden light, playing with the shapes of both the monument and rock below it. Athens always seems to linger, stuck between two worlds. The past blooms in every corner, monuments scattered like wildflowers between modern buildings. Ruins remain hidden, buried under the asphalt, and maybe their presence has done something to them because they are all standing still, so far behind she wonders if there is a place for her here at all.

★ ★ ★

"Hey, good morning. How's it going?" Anna asks her as she slips into the seat next to hers in the lecture hall.

"It's going," Daphne groans, reaching for another sip of cafeteria coffee. Moonlighting with her statue friend is fun until she has to wake up in the morning and attend her lectures.

Anna snorts, then takes a sip from her own cup, scrunching her nose at the bitterness. "I admire your stubbornness to come to the early morning classes considering you hate them so."

"I'd admire me more if I paid any attention," Daphne shrugs but gives her a slight smile for the attempt at small talk. They're not friends exactly, even if Anna stops to talk to her every day. "How's the project going?"

"It's going," she repeats with a soft laugh. Throwing her arms wide, Anna stretches her back, sending her curls bouncing behind her. "Yours?"

The mention of her drawings makes her kick her backpack closer to the seat on instinct, though a thread of a smile spreads again unchecked on her lips. "Needs some work, but I'm enjoying it."

"That's all you can ask, right?"

And though Daphne nods, her expression freezes on her face. She can't identify the pinch of disappointment that nicks at her heart, yet she feels the cut with every move she makes.

★ ★ ★

"How many times are you going to do this?"

"Here's your dinner, and a cup of coffee from your favourite place – thanks for having such cheap taste, by the way. It works wonders for me."

"So more than once."

With a quick hug that almost makes Markos drop the coffee, Daphne hurries inside the building, up the steps again to meet her real date for the night. She makes her way through the halls and builds herself a nest in front of her favourite statue once more.

"Good evening, my sweet," she says, pulling her sketchbook and pencils from the bag. "Let's work on yesterday's for a bit longer, then we can try something new. That all right with you? So, um—" Her words die in her throat as her eyes jump frantically from her work to the statue in front of her. "Huh, how did it – I swear I had that right." Nervous laughter bubbles in her chest as her stress rises, thinking of the changes she'll have to make. "Did you *move*?"

It takes some time, but she readjusts all the inaccuracies, careful to erase the lines as cleanly as possible; she should have been gentler with her strokes the first time around. She moves on to the finer details in her sketch, sharpening an edge here, blending the shadow there.

"Between you and me," she mutters, gnawing at the pencil in her mouth as she shifts her gaze from the paper to her Muse. "I was almost done, but I wanted to spend another night here. Or I thought I was, anyway. Do you like this place?"

Her eyes catch at the faults peppered along her body, pieces of stone lost to the centuries.

"It's... better than being buried, isn't it?" Her voice falls quiet, smothered by the image of being trapped underground with no end in sight, thousands of steps walking above, oblivious to your terror. "That must have been horrifying."

On a whim too sudden yet too strong to deny, Daphne pushes herself to her feet and takes a tentative step closer to the figure. With the lamp in her hand, she goes around her, studying the signs of wear and tear on the stone. The crumbled edge of her elbow, the mark on her left cheek. Her right leg has broken clean off, nowhere to be found, while her left arm is separated from the rest of her body, attached to a metal rod.

Her hand reaches for the crack running like lightning down her shoulder, and she almost brushes against it before she remembers herself. "No touching, right?" She chuckles. "That must be lonely. But it keeps you safe. Is that better?"

The pale gaze stares down at her, silent, her lips always lifted upwards ever so slightly.

Daphne tilts her head, excitement expanding with her breath. "I have an idea."

She throws herself down on her knees and scrambles to get her sketchbook, flipping to a new page. "I know you used to have colour, but I didn't bring my watercolours with me, so I will add that later..." She pauses, her pencil hovering over the paper. "Or I can just come back." She looks up, grinning. "Would you like that?"

Daphne starts over, sacrificing accuracy for humanity. Where her previous drawing shows the picture-perfect image of a statue, this one outlines the rich features of a woman, as real and alive as the one who presses her into paper. She gives a bounce to her curls, and baby hairs that roll out of line. A fluidity to her pose, curving her waist, letting the fabric of her peplos twist around her hips. She strokes in eyelashes, framing eyes no longer just pale white, staring at her with an imploring look.

And she keeps the markings too, the tear on her cheek, on her elbow, the cracks like scars on smooth skin. She fills the gap where the statue tore off its arm and binds the pieces with vines and flowers, delicate cyclamens like a swirling bracelet around her arm. She adapts the pattern for her missing leg, a prosthetic made of intertwining flora, bear's breeches on her shin, curled roots on her foot.

She looks up at her Muse for a moment, before going back and erasing with fervour. "Not yet, my sweet, hang on." She builds the straight edge of her nose, deepens the contour under her cheekbones. Pencils in the details on her curls and refines the shape of the headpiece in her hair.

Once she's done, she holds the sketch away from her, studying it in different angles under the light. Daphne smiles, a small, brittle thing, both excited and self-conscious all at once. Her cheeks are burning when she turns the sketchbook to the Muse.

"What do you think?" She swears the upward curl of her lips seems sharper somehow. "I'll colour it too. You'll see. I'll come show you. You, my love, are going to be beautiful. You *are* beautiful."

"Daphne?" Markos' voice comes from a floor below and she jumps. Her name echoes too loudly around the empty halls and it breaks something in the air around her, stealing the magic out of a world in which she dove too deep. Where the Muse in front of her was a girl and all that mattered was making her happy. "You've been here far too long, the shift is about to change. You need to get the hell out."

"Coming!" she calls back, cringing at the sound of her own voice. "I'll be back soon," she whispers and winks. "Sorry to tell you this, but we're in this together."

Daphne walks to the end of the hall yet lingers on the last step, giving her Muse one last look. She can't see her in the darkness she left behind, but she smiles anyway.

★ ★ ★

Class passes by in a cloud. She doodles on the edges of her notebooks, and the same figure decorates all her pages. Small rows of curls, curious eyes, flowers circling around her limbs. Her life unravels in those pages, a backstory sketched piece by piece like layers of a background. She draws her in scenes of her past and imagines her in places of the future. Expressions mould her soft features, a personality shining through, smug and charming and mysterious. And in those fantasies given life, Daphne imagines what it would be like to know her.

She doesn't look up when Anna talks to her, and she's certain her classmate tries to ask her something, but she tells her to pause for a moment until she's done then forgets to let her start again.

After class she takes the bus, grimacing when people push and pull against her. They are packed in too close, a mass of strangers as one, and still the couple next to her spends their time reminding everyone how much of a couple they are, with increasing dedication.

It wakes something visceral inside of her. Annoyance and envy and an underlying frustration that travels down her veins, of how unfair it can be, how the world outside the confines of her privacy seems made for people like them and them alone.

The museum looks different in the morning. Life breathes in its halls, and light flows in through the tall windows, washing everything in gentler tones.

The glass floor displays ruins underneath her feet, a sturdy layer to distance the new from the old. She steps upon it in slow movements, sneakers pressing against this odd window with care, not for a fear of falling, but so the sight can reach upwards in her mind, stretch itself to envelop her in what had once been. She imagines walking through these places, wondering if they could have fit her more.

She bypasses the tour guides and the bored high schoolers, lingers a minute longer on a few exhibits that catch her eye.

Inevitably, her path leads right back to her. The hall is so much more crowded in the morning, and her Muse gets swallowed by the other pieces and visitors. More students are settled on the floors, sketchbooks strewn around them. A group of girls are discussing something in front of an information plaque, while a tourist is mimicking a statue's pose for a photograph.

Daphne walks over to her Muse and smiles, small but heavy like a secret. *Hey*, she mouths. Someone bumps against her back to pass, shaking her out of her fascination. They don't stop to glance at the Muse as they carry on to another room in a hurry.

A flash of anger sparks through her. She wants everyone to see her the way she does, and the feeling simmers in the centre of her chest, unearned yet powerful. It scares her a little, but it's a worry she can banish to the back of her mind, even as it bites in fits and starts. It can't be healthy to be so consumed by an object.

Still, it's not the physical side of her that draws her so. It's the love that went into the carving. It's the unknown behind the pristine eyes. A story left for her to conjure, for no one knows if she was a person or a dream, and for her she can be both. She is both.

And Daphne is infatuated with her.

★ ★ ★

That night, Daphne brings her dinner with her to the museum. Markos warned her that she can't do this again, for they are bound to get caught eventually and he is rather attached to the idea of being employed. She swallowed back her disappointment and nodded, thanking him again for giving her the opportunity.

It's okay. It will be fine. She can just come in the day like everyone else. She has her own drawings too, a memento of the life she imagined to keep close.

Music from her phone filters out distorted into the empty hall, her own humming louder than the voice from the speaker.

She turns to her first sketch; it has to be perfected tonight. As she looks from the paper to her Muse and back, a low groan builds in her throat. "Are you *moving*? I don't understand – how can this not match? *Again*?"

Her fingers curl around her hair, tugging at her locks in frustration. "I can't fix this now. We'll just work with what we already have, yes, love?" She pushes down on the pressure point between her brows, and takes a deep breath, grounding herself so she can continue without her hands trembling.

Her gaze travels up the length of the figure, stopping on those eyes that she swears are looking at her. She doesn't remember her head being so tilted downwards but the patience in her smile makes Daphne return it. "It's all right. She still looks like you, my sweet. And you are beautiful."

The realisation dawns on her again that this is the last time she gets to be here alone like this. With a deep breath caught in her chest, Daphne gets to her feet and closes the distance between them. She stops herself a second, a shudder away from touching the cool marble, her skin tingling with the power of the possibility.

She's not supposed to. She could hurt the statue – she could hurt her Muse. But it's her last night here. She has to know.

Her fingers brush against the smooth surface of her hands, the same hands that a sculptor gave life to thousands of years ago. And they're *warm*.

Daphne stumbles backwards with a gasp, tripping over her own lamp and crashing to the ground. The upturned light rolls away, elongating the shadows around them. Though the darkness can't hide what she sees next, it renders the scene in chiaroscuro, three artforms tangling with each other to haunt her. The ancient statue, the heavy shadows, and her own sketches spilling into the image in front of her. Colours wash over the stone, springing from the crown of her hair and running down the length of her body like rivers. Small brown curls and tanned skin, dark lips and a mesmerizing pair of golden-brown eyes that lock with Daphne's own.

In the gap where her elbow broke, vines sprout in knots and bows and garlands, wrapping in a circlet around her lower arm to connect the two pieces, cyclamen blossoms and tiny, purple crocus flowers blooming between the earth-bound muscle. Bear's breeches twist around bones made of roots to form her missing leg. And when the last wildflowers dot her makeshift prosthetic like freckles, she takes the first step forward, slipping out of her display and towards Daphne sprawled on the floor.

"Why are you trembling, my love?" her Muse speaks in a language Daphne understands, more modern than anything the ancient woman should have known.

"Oh, this is what I get for fantasising…" Daphne half laughs, half sobs. A hand, shaking just as she said, comes up to cover her mouth. "I'm hallucinating."

The Muse smiles, a gentle lift of lips that look soft and warm like the touch of her hand, the cold perfection of the marble long gone. "No. *No.* Breathe, Daphne."

Her name meets the ancient woman's voice with ease like it belongs there. And how could it not? Daphne was an ancient story and a gift of nature, the two pieces weaved in the image of the Muse. A woman chased by the god of the arts, turned into a tree to be protected from those who didn't know how not to take. Apollo's holy flower. A farce of a sacrifice.

"You know my name." Daphne nods, in jerky movements of compacted stress. "And I can understand you, even though you should be speaking a language I don't know. Definitely a hallucination."

The Muse looks around with fondness in her gaze, even as her smile fades into a careful contemplation. "I have been in these halls for years. I picked up on the changes in the language over time." When she turns back to meet Daphne's eyes, the sight lifts some of the sadness from her own. "And you've been talking to me for days – how could I not know your name?"

Daphne pauses, the beginnings of a breath stuttering in her throat. Slowly, she pushes herself to her knees, and when her

Muse offers a hand to help her to her feet, she takes it, gaping at the steady warmth shared freely from the touch.

"You heard me," she whispers. "You saw me?"

"I heard all of it. And I saw all of it." Even when they're both standing, the Muse keeps their hands intertwined, suspended between them. "And I'm grateful for every second of it." Her smile stretches into a grin, and even the white of her teeth is glossier than the white of the old marble. "Thank you for the company, my love. It's been a while since someone has looked at me the way you do."

"Like what?" Daphne exhales, barely blinking.

"Like you saw me. Like I mattered."

"You *do*."

The Muse squeezes her hand, brushing the arch of her knuckles with her thumb. "People come here for different reasons. Some are here because they're forced to," she laughs. "Some to admire their own history – some a little too much, if you ask me." Daphne cringes, nodding in agreement. "And some truly come to admire the past, the civilisation, the humanity. But they look at us like sculptures. Like art. They marvel at the skill of the sculptor, at the craft, never once wondering what could have led them to create us."

Daphne glances over at her sketchbook, left open on the floor behind them. A hand cups her cheek, guiding her to look at the Muse again. She feels scar tissue against her skin where pieces of the fingertips were once chipped off the statue.

"You looked at me and wanted to know my story. And when you didn't find it, you gave me one." Daphne's heart flutters in her chest, her gaze trapped in those golden eyes that look at her as if she painted her world in colours. "The last person who gazed upon me like that, my love, was the person who gave me my shape. And when I was broken, you gifted me a new one."

"Do you like it?" Daphne blurts out. Perhaps it's not the most important thing to know yet she needs to ask.

Her Muse grins, running a hand through her thick curls,

stroking the small lilac petals of the flowers on her arm. When her eyes capture hers again, they are bright with joy, and it looks magnificent on her. "I love it."

She wants to say she's glad. She wants to say that's all she wanted. And she says none of those things because her Muse is in front of her, happy and alive, the way she envisioned her in all those pieces. Her hand rests warm on her cheek, and against all thought and reason, Daphne closes the distance between them.

Her lips are not made of marble.

They're tender like the petals of her flowers, warm like sunshine on her skin. They part with a gasp, inviting her in, and the breath that should not be there feels as real as her own rattling in her chest. She smells like the cyclamen that decorate her body, a sweet fragrance Daphne could drown in.

She pulls back, eyes blown wide, heart drumming against her ribcage. This can't be happening. It's not real. But if this is where her fantasy has led her, she can stay in there a little longer – why shouldn't a touch like this feel wild and impossible and meant for her alone?

The Muse presses another brush of a kiss to the corner of her lips, as if to lift it so they would match. Daphne wonders if this is what it feels like to be wanted, if this is what the Muse felt when she looked upon her with such awe, and she understands why she climbed down from the pedestal they had her on. Down to an Earth she doesn't belong in anymore, for just a second of being seen, being touched.

They settle down on the floor together this time, Daphne resting against the Muse's chest, feeling the subtle heat from her body surround her like a blanket. She doesn't pay any mind to the strange stillness of her chest.

They leaf through the sketchbook together, and the Muse marvels over all the little details she loves, pointing them out on her body now – *Look, this one is actually missing the same petal you accidentally brushed off here!* – in a manner so endearing, it makes Daphne want to take her colours and paint right into her skin,

273

so she can feel the care she gave each brushstroke, the tender way she'd touch.

For a few hours, the emptiness around them protects them from the world outside, marking a space just for them. The moonlight streaming in from the windows softens the darkness into tones of blue and grey, and Daphne dims the artificial light on her side and lets herself fall fully into this dreamlike scene that does nothing to convince her she's not imagining it all.

But time passes. Her phone pings with a message, shattering the peace they have created around them. The contentment washes out of Daphne in a wave, and her expression falls as she pushes herself to her feet.

"I need to go."

The Muse bends her neck to look up at her. It sits at an awkward angle and Daphne frowns at the sight of it. "You can stay here with me," she says, like it's the most logical statement in the world.

Daphne shakes her head. "I'm sorry, I'm not supposed to be here."

"And where are you supposed to be?" It comes out innocent enough, but the words reach straight for her heart, forming a coil that tightens with every second she contemplates the question. "Will you come tomorrow?"

"In the morning, I could," she explains. "I can't come here again at night. They won't let me in." Her mouth is dry.

"I can let you in."

"You can?"

"Of course. You can come here every night." She stands up too, and wraps her fingers around Daphne's wrist, tracing crescent moons on her skin. "You were never the same in the mornings," she says, too soft for the sharp edge of her implication. "I like you like this." The hesitation must show in Daphne's eyes, for her brows furrow, her lips pursing into a small pout. "What is it? What troubles you?"

Daphne pulls back, yet her hand is stuck in the grip. It's hard as stone. As marble. "I can't stay with you."

"Why not? Love, no one will care that you're here. No one can stop you. No one can see. It's just you and me. You can come back and give all you want to give, and no one will take anything from you. Isn't that what you were fantasizing about all these hours you spent in here?"

The Muse is not wrong. And it makes that feeling in her stomach claw deeper into her, a dread like standing on the precipice of something, a decision in the tip of her tongue she can never take back. Daphne stood here every night and every morning since, imagining this statue alive through her art, and a world where both could live together, in a secret so silent she didn't even dare put it to paper.

And she lets herself picture it. Getting a job in the museum in the day, working on her art at night, wandering between the statues and the glories of the past. Never leaving, for her love awaits her after dark. Never leaving.

"How are you real?" Daphne whispers, taking a step back.

The Muse doesn't blink. "I'm real because you made me."

She doesn't *blink*.

"That doesn't make sense." Daphne leans away, shaking her head. "I can't stay."

"Why? Daphne. *Daphne*, you belong here."

No. Just because this is what she has been given, it doesn't mean it's the only thing that she can, that she should ever have. It doesn't mean it's her place. Maybe it's outside. Maybe it's somewhere further away. She won't find it by being entombed here.

This city always seems to linger, stuck between two worlds.

"With me."

People come here in search of old gods and times enduring only in stone.

"You know this. It's why you came here every night. And you sang and you drew and talked to me."

Ruins remain hidden, and they must have done something to them because they're all standing still.

"You belong here."

And if people truly want to find what they have lost, then maybe they should fight for the future instead of clinging to the past.

"*I need to leave,*" Daphne whispered.

Yes, this was her dream. But it was always meant to be a dream.

"You'll come in the morning?"

If she gets stuck in it, she will never leave.

"I don't know if I can."

The Muse's face falls, growing colder. The softness disappears like a trick of the light, a stillness left behind. Her eyes that were so brilliant and alight with life glaze with a snowy sheen, though the way her lips curve make her look like she's crying.

"I'm sorry—"

"You will regret this." Her voice is no longer warm. It's hoarse, like scratching against stone. "There's nothing for you there."

"I do love you. You're a fantasy," Daphne whispers, placing her hand on a cheek that's too hard in her palm. Her own eyes are watering, regret welling up inside of her. Fear. She presses her lips to hers, and there is still a warmth there, the barest touch of life behind the polished stone.

"So you need to stay in my dreams."

Daphne pushes the statue backwards, sending her stumbling back to her spot. She grabs her bag from the floor, her sketchbook and lamp, and almost drops everything in her haste to get away.

She hears her name cried out behind her. Once. Twice. Then cut mid-breath, a note left hanging, a story undone. It tears the pressure in her chest but the rip is too violent, leaving wounds open and bleeding.

Daphne doesn't stop until she's out of the building, ignoring Markos' voice that replaces the Muse's. She doesn't stop until the cold air is on her face, whipping her hair into tangles, and she can no longer hear voices behind her, even though she still feels the touch on her skin, the weight of her hand on her cheek. Her lips taste like dust but the scent of cyclamen clings to her clothes.

She runs the entire way to the bus stop, and the ruins on the hill towering above stare her down as she hides into the dark.

★ ★ ★

"Hey, what happened?" Anna marches over, concern spread like a veil over her features. "I heard you failed the project? I thought you were almost done."

Daphne looks up from her coffee. There is no sketchbook in front of her today, just a half-empty paper cup, frayed at the edges from biting into it. "I... couldn't hand it in."

Anna claims the seat across from her, her eyes glued to Daphne's face; she never noticed how closely she always looks at her. "Why not? I saw your work. It was really, *really* good."

Unable to muster an explanation, she settles for a glimpse of a smile. She can't admit why she couldn't put her name on the sketches of her Muse, why she couldn't face what she had done and instead ran like a thief in the night.

Most of all, she can't put a voice to the fear that she doesn't know how to continue to do this. Put her heart on the paper when the paper might swallow it whole. Or how to make something worthwhile if she doesn't pour her everything into it.

"I guess I was scared," is what she admits.

"We're all a little scared," Anna tries for an encouraging smile, and how did Daphne never notice how cute she is, how bright her hazel eyes turn when the sun hits them just right? Why does she have to notice now, when the thought of being touched feels like stone against her skin and a hundred mistakes waiting to happen?

Anna pats her shoulder and leaves the hand there as though she can lift her up despite the defeat weighing down her spine.

"There's love in your art. It's really powerful. I think you should try again."

She shudders, curling in around herself. "Tell me more," she jokes without much heart.

"Are you fishing for compliments?"

"Maybe I'm fishing for another cup of coffee. My treat?"

Anna halts, then lets a grin brighten those playful eyes of hers. And Daphne can see the difference now, she thinks, between alive and living. Her art is not good enough to put that to paper, no matter how much power she gives it. "I can't say no to free coffee." She gets up and offers a hand to help Daphne to her feet, frowning when she doesn't find a bag around her. "Where's your stuff?"

"No work today," she claims because it's easier, and gets up without taking her hand.

In truth, her sketchbooks are twice locked up in a drawer under her bed, layers of blankets stacked upon them. Her sketches might move if she steals a look. She thinks she hears them talk at night, reaching out when she sleeps, asking how dare she love them so just to move on to another. They're too much of her to be tossed away. Too much of her still to be witnessed.

And though her choice to leave the Muse behind feels like the lesser wound, no matter how much she still bleeds, she never expected all the ways it could cut.

Maybe she needs to find a new career.

BLOOD PLAY

Tabitha O'Connell

Here's where it started: a wannabe hipster bar in downtown Buffalo, crowded with a bunch of strangers – my grad school peers. I'd gone in assuming it would be easy to make friends, bonding over our common interest and all that. But by early October, I'd found that the only easy things were meeting a shit-tonne of people you didn't vibe with, or meeting someone once, thinking they seemed cool, and then never seeing them again.

My sister finally badgered me into going to one of the school's social events, because there people would be actively looking to get to know each other, right? Except when I walked in, fashionably late, everyone seemed to be successfully doing that already – smiling and laughing with their current companions, perfectly content without my presence. I spotted two or three faces from my potential-friend list, but it wasn't like any of them noticed me, and I couldn't bring myself to barge in to their conversations uninvited.

I ordered a drink just to have something to do and was sipping it at the bar, the draw of the few-block walk back to my apartment growing, when I noticed a guy I didn't recognise sitting alone in a booth towards the back of the room. Mostly-empty glass cupped in his hands, shoulders hunched in his hoodie, like he was uncomfortable and would rather be someplace else. Which made two of us. So I picked up my beer, wove through the obstacle course of students, and slid in across from him.

He jumped, and I said, "Oh, sorry. Um, I'm Lyle. They/them pronouns."

"Zach. He/him." His voice was soft, his head still kind of bent down, but he maintained eye contact from under his wavy brown hair. Against his pale skin, his eyes stood out, dark and striking.

"Cool. So, uh… what's your specialisation?"

"Oh – I actually don't go to your school." Now his gaze dropped. "Just happened to be here."

Fuck my luck – I'd picked the one person in the whole bar who I would not have a chance of running into on campus next week. But what the hell. At least he was someone to talk to.

Before I could ask anything about him, he said, "So, what's the program you're all in? Some sort of architecture thing?"

"Oh, no. We're urban planners. The architects are our nemeses."

One corner of his mouth quirked up, and he propped his chin in his hand. "Oh? I thought grad school was all about collaboration."

"Eh, in theory, but the school gets all their prestige from the architects. So guess who gets the best rooms, the best equipment, the best schedules…"

I was sure I was boring the hell out of him and any minute he'd find an excuse to leave. But instead, he asked, "Okay, so tell me – what exactly is 'urban planning'? I'm imagining you all sitting around sketching maps of utopian cities."

Planning nerd mode: activated. I gave him the whole spiel, and he listened with seemingly genuine interest, like it hadn't just been a small-talky question. At one point he smirked and said, "So architects plan the buildings, and then you guys have to make sure everything else makes sense? Sounds like your school has its priorities backward." So, you know, how could I not like him?

We got another round of drinks, and I told him more about school, about the obnoxious know-it-all guy who was somehow in every one of my classes, and the professor who regularly showed up ten minutes late smelling like booze, and he made sarcastic comments that made me snort, beer burning my nose. It was fun. I may have even daydreamed about an alternate reality where he was in school with me – we would sit together in class and roll our eyes at know-it-all boy, and commiserate about stupid busywork assignments…

He bought us shots, countering my objections to him paying for mine with, "Come on, you're a student." I lifted my glass to him in thanks before we downed them.

"Oh hey, is that an ace ring?" he asked.

"It issss!" I stretched out my fingers to show off the shiny black ring on my right hand. I'd never had anyone recognise it before.

"Cool. I'm…" He waved his hand in the air. "Gray-ace, is what I've settled on."

I grinned stupidly at him. "That's cool. That's *so* cool. You're the first ace person I've just, like, run into."

I flopped one arm onto the bar and rested my head on it, still looking at him, and he leaned on his elbows, body angled toward me. "Another round of shots to celebrate?"

Giggling, I pressed my face into my arm. "How are you not drunk?"

"High tolerance. So?" When I peered back at him, he smirked. "Can you handle one more?"

"If you can, I can."

This time he carried the tiny glasses back to our booth, only handing mine over once we'd stopped beside it, his ice-cold fingers brushing mine; I figured he had bad circulation. As I set down the empty glass I went a little wobbly, and grabbed his shoulder for support. Then left my hand there, and smiled at him, and when he shifted slightly toward me, his eyes meeting mine, I asked, "Do you wanna make out?"

Drunk Lyle is cuddly – especially with cute ace boys, apparently. And, you know, there was the loneliness…

Zach smiled, but dropped his eyes, as if suddenly shy. But then his chilly fingers slid to the back of my head as he leaned in. His lips were cold too, but I did not mind.

We ended up back in the booth, thighs pressed together, his mouth on my neck, me nuzzling his hair and playing with his earrings. "Hey," he said after a bit, lifting his head to reveal flushed lips. "This might be weird, but... can I bite you?"

"Sure." Honestly, I thought he just meant he wanted to use his teeth more, and it seemed sweet of him to check.

"I mean... hard. To like, draw some blood."

"Oh." So it was a kink, and he trusted me enough to tell me about it already. Also sweet. But maybe kind of unsanitary...?

"It's just... I'm a vampire." He lowered his voice and his eyes on that word. "But I only need a little blood, less than half a pint. It'll be quick."

I squinted my drunk eyes and made my drunk brain repeat his words. A vampire. It had to be part of the kink, pretending he was a blood-sucking monster. And somehow, that made it less weird. I could even be into it. Being ace did not make me immune to the sexy-vampire effect.

"Okay." I grinned at him and slid aside the collar of my shirt (my favourite blue flannel, worn especially for this occasion), and his right hand settled on my shoulder. He kissed me on the mouth again before moving over my jaw and back down my neck, finding the spot at my neck-shoulder junction where a hickey was already forming.

His front teeth grasped at my skin, grabbing and releasing as if testing it. Sharper teeth pricked the spot when he turned his head. "Are you sure?" he whispered.

"Yeah," I whispered back, and there was a pinch again before his teeth pierced my skin.

It felt less messy than I'd expected, and the caress of his tongue more than made up for the relatively small amount of pain. His left hand cupped my cheek, softly – affectionately? I was high on the intimacy of it. When he drew back, hand swiping at his mouth, I tried to glance down at the wound, but Zach gently tilted my chin away to dab at it with a napkin. "You okay?" he asked softly.

"Yeah." I leaned into him, letting my eyes close, giving myself a minute for the lightheadedness to pass.

"All right, this will sting…"

Something swabbed the wound, hurting more than the bite had. I opened my eyes in time to see him press a band-aid over it. Talk about aftercare – he was so prepared. When he drew my shirt back into place, it was like it had never happened.

Except, when my bleary gaze met his hesitant one, I noticed a smear of blood on his lower lip. "Oh – you have…" I touched my own lip, and he cringed away, grabbing for another napkin. "It's fine," I added. When he glanced back at me, the napkin still pressed to his mouth, I took his wrist and drew his hand away, smiling at him, and kissed him again without bothering to check if he'd gotten it all.

Before long he got me some water, and I was a little more sober when he checked his phone and said, "Shit, I should go."

"Aw, what? It's not even eleven."

"I've got work. Night shift."

"Ohhh." I laughed preemptively at my own cleverness. "Vampire, right."

"Yep." He said it straight-faced; a deadpan sense of humour, apparently.

"Well… do you wanna give me your number?" I unlocked my phone and held it out to him. At first he just looked at it, and I wondered if I'd misread him, if he'd just been looking for a one-night biting stand. But moments later he'd taken the phone and handed it back to me, with "Zach :vampire emoji:" saved as a new contact.

★ ★ ★

My sister/roommate, Daph, was asleep when I got home, but wide awake when I dragged myself out of my room the next morning.

"Sooo, how was your niiight?" She was at the kitchen table, hair back in a low ponytail, wearing her mandated navy blue scrubs. Unfortunately, our schedules are opposite – she works weekends at the hospital, so we really only have evenings together. But that's also my homework time, and sometimes my work-work time, so we're lucky to squeeze in a quick chat and a *Schitt's Creek* episode.

"It was gooood," I told her. (Do all siblings communicate primarily in singsong voices? Because we do.)

"Tell me moooore," she prompted as I sat down across from her with a cup of coffee.

"Okay, soooo, I actually met this guy."

"Oh?"

"He doesn't even go to BU – he just happened to be there. And, uh…" Pause for a long sip of coffee. "I may have gotten drunk and made out with him."

"Lyle! Holy shit!" She laughed, a kind of surprised, delighted laugh. Because, let's be real, neither of us had expected me to do anything more than have a few superficial conversations.

"And, wanna hear the best part?" I gave her a little shoulder shimmy.

"Go on…"

"I got his nummmmber."

She stared at me from under raised eyebrows. "Lyle. Seriously. Are you pulling my leg?"

"Hey! I got… game. Okay, yes, I just proved that I decidedly *don't* have game. But no, somehow, I am serious."

"Wow. Okay, so, what's his name? Age? Job? Height? Tell me *everything*."

I told her… some things. Most things. I hadn't even remembered the bite until I began the story, but as soon as I did, I almost betrayed myself by ripping off the band-aid to look at it.

I refrained, though. In the light of day, and the light of soberness, it was definitely... odd. Not necessarily bad-odd, but I didn't want Daph to think I'd been stupid, or tell me it was a red flag. I wanted to see Zach again.

"Lyyyy, he sounds so great! Have you texted him?" she asked.

"No. I mean, I just woke up. And... I don't really know what to say."

"'Last night was fun.' With a wink emoji. No, the kissy-face emoji!"

"Don't you have to get to work?"

"You don't want my expert advice? But I'm so knowledgeable about these things!"

She's an aro lesbian; we're close in part because we're both queer, especially since we grew up with conservative asshole parents. Lately she's had a thing going with her friend Claire, spending the night over there every so often. We do not call it "friends with benefits," because, in her words, "The only time that phrase is appropriate is if you have a friend named 'Benefits.'"

"Mmmm, I think I'm gonna wait to text him until after breakfast."

"Ohhh, you wanna wait till you're aloooone."

"He worked night shift, he's gonna be asleep!"

"Sure, suuuure..."

When the door closed behind her and the apartment went quiet, I felt a twinge of loneliness; now all I had to look forward to was homework. I distracted myself by working out when I could expect Zach to be awake. He had left the bar around 10:30 to get to his job — so, what, he probably worked until seven in the morning? Say he was asleep by eight, and slept seven hours — that had him awake at three in the afternoon. It was currently 8:45.

Well, plenty of time to craft a text. And examine my wound. Standing in front of the bathroom mirror, I pulled aside the collar of my pajama shirt, then eased the band-aid off. It was a neat little gash, the scab dark against my pale-ass shoulder/neck region, surrounded by a bit of redness. Weirdly clean for a bite. A pleasant surprise. I ran a hand over it, shivering slightly at the echo of Zach's mouth on my skin. Wondering if he would ask to do it again. Wondering if I would agree – and already suspecting my answer.

By the time I'd finished showering, I'd planned out my text. *Hey! It's Lyle. From last night.* Juuuust in case he'd forgotten my name. *You'll probably be sleeping most of the day, but I'm free this evening if you want to meet up.*

Was it weird to ask to see him again so soon? Maybe, but I didn't want to play games or try to guess at some mysterious rules. Might as well be honest.

★ ★ ★

Hey ;) Tonight's not the best, but what about tomorrow?

Zach's reply, time-stamped 1:54. I wanted to ask if he'd gotten enough sleep, but calculating his schedule might come off as kind of creepy.

Sure! Tomorrow works.

Cool. Pizza?

Sounds good! (Also, I'm vegetarian, jsyk.)

Oh hey same.

That's kind of ironic. With the whole vampire thing ;)

:P

He suggested a place he knew downtown, and once we'd set a time, the conversation was over. I wanted to keep texting him, but I didn't want to seem clingy. Instead, I sat in front of my open textbook wondering what he was doing tonight. Last night he'd been at a student bar alone, before work – *drinking* before work – which was kind of weird. But maybe tonight he was hanging with friends, or family… Which was fine. He didn't need to be all alone in the world to want to hang out with me.

On Sunday, I arrived at Penelope's Pizza right on time. Zach was already there in a booth, once again wearing a black hoodie. "Hey." In lieu of a smile, he gave me a friendly eyebrow-raise.

"Hey." I did smile, because within two days, I'd gone from having zero friends here to being on an actual *date*. I… may have agonised about what to wear, and what to do with my undercut – go natural, or floof it up with some goop. Goop won, and I settled on my second-favourite shirt, a green and black plaid. Sometimes, you just want to be visibly queer.

"Uh, so, how was work?" I asked.

"Eh. It was fine. Always is."

"Um, what… is it?"

"Oh." He looked down at his folded hands. His fingers were slender, with neatly trimmed nails. "Janitorial, over at Seneca One."

"Sounds peaceful. Just you and the city lights."

He cocked his head and kind of smirked, which I took as a good sign. "Well, and the other custodial staff. But yeah, it's not bad. You know, it's a job. One that I can actually do."

I mentioned it was October, right? So at 7pm, our meetup time, it was pretty dark. Meaning I wasn't sure if that remark was a jab at his skill level, or if he was continuing the vampire joke. My hand went to my neck wound before I could catch myself.

His eyes followed, and when they met mine again, he rolled them slightly. "Yep, you got it. No college degree or day jobs for me. Not that I was going for a practical degree, anyway."

"Oh? What was it?"

"Art." He shook his head, playing with his silverware-enfolding napkin, unwrapping and rewrapping the corner. "I don't even know what I thought I was gonna do with it."

"That's such a cool major, though. What kind of art do you do?"

He told me how he'd been into photography and digital art, and our pizza arrived, the Mediterranean one off the vegetarian menu. Zach meticulously picked off the artichokes, and I cringed and apologised, because it'd been my suggestion. But he said it was fine, and slid his plate toward me. "More for you."

He asked about my undergrad experience, and I told him about Daph, and we chatted about the city. He paid the bill, justifying it again with my student status, and I let him, but felt a little weird about it. On the way out we stopped at the bathrooms, which were gender-neutral, thank fuck, and I stared in the mirror trying to convince myself I did not look like a girl.

We'd decided to head over to the waterfront next. I drove, because it turned out he didn't have a car, instead relying on public transit – which I admired, and told him so. He gave me directions, taking us away from Canalside, where I'd assumed we were going, and having me park by the spit at the mouth of the Buffalo River. As we strolled down the waterside path, the wind off the river-becoming-lake blowing sporadically in our faces, I tried to think of how to ask him about had been bugging me. Finally, I came up with, "So, uh, I know you're ace, but, um, are you... queer in any other way?"

Immediately afterward I wanted to die, to drop dead right there on the sidewalk, where he could suck every last drop of blood from my veins if he wanted. But, if he was reading me as a girl, and was only into me because of that...

"Oh. I mean, duh." He nudged my arm with his elbow, tossing me his characteristic smirk.

"Okay." I sighed a way bigger sigh than anyone with any chill would have. "Sorry. Just, with the paying for me..."

He poked my arm. "Grad student." Then pointed to himself: "Not grad student. It's not some chivalry thing because I'm 'the man.'" His voice dropped into a masculine parody.

"Okay." I bumped him with my shoulder. "I get it. Sorry."

"You don't need to be *sorry.*" He caught my hand, his fingers slipping between mine. His skin was once again very cold, but it was chilly out. "But yeah, I mean, I'm cis, but I'm generally into masc people."

The gender euphoria had me practically glowing. We stopped by the railing across from the lighthouse, looking over the black water to the sparkling lights of Canada beyond. There were a few other people around – some guys goofing off, laughing and shoving each other, a couple walking their dog – but it still felt private, peaceful. I leaned into Zach, our hands still joined, and he nuzzled his face against my hair. The alcohol-mint of Listerine drifted by. I'd popped a mint in the bathroom, but mouthwash was going above and beyond.

After a bit, I turned slightly toward him, and when he looked back at me, I rested my free hand on his face and kissed him. I felt the intake of breath through his nose before he pressed back.

"Wait." I pulled away, but kept my hand on his icy cheek. "You're cold. Do you want to go inside somewhere?" I was cold too; I'd left my coat at home like a fool, thinking I'd be fine with my binder and layered shirts.

"Oh, nah, I'm fine. I'm really not feeling it much."

"The cold never bothered me anyway," I sang, a very off-key Princess Elsa.

His eyes crinkled as one side of his mouth quirked up. "You're cute." He leaned in and kissed me quickly. "But *you're* cold. Here." He dropped my hand, and before I could say anything he'd squirmed out of his hoodie and was holding it out to me, bare-armed now in just a t-shirt.

"No, wait, you'll be freezing–"

"Nah. Ice princess, remember?" He pushed the hoodie into my arms. "Besides. I want to see you in it."

I blushed, and hoped the lighting was dim enough that he couldn't tell. When I pulled on the hoodie, I was gently engulfed in his scent, a nice, cedary-gingery cologne. I hadn't particularly taken note of it the other night, but the smell brought me right back to that booth, his mouth on my neck. I shivered despite the new layer.

When my head emerged, he smiled and stepped closer, brushing straying strands of hair out of my eyes. "You look good." He was biting his lip, revealing one of his canines. I'd noticed earlier that they looked unnaturally sharp – no wonder he'd bitten me so easily. I had the slightly unsettling thought that maybe he deliberately sharpened them.

"Wanna sit?" he asked, and led the way to the nearest bench. As soon as we'd settled, he was pulling me in to kiss me again.

It was a little weird doing this sober – I had to contend with the *What are you doing!!* voice that alcohol had sent straight to sleep. What was I doing? Making out with a guy I barely knew outside in the dark next to the frigid waters of Lake Erie. A guy who'd bitten my neck with his extra-sharp teeth and literally *drank my blood* last time (the first time) we'd met.

But serial killers didn't take you out for dinner. Right? They didn't tell you they were a janitor; they didn't tell you you were cute. They didn't give you the hoodie off their back because you were cold.

Okay, I haven't actually met any serial killers. Maybe they did exactly all of those things. There was a reason people made TV shows and true-crime podcasts about them. What if *I* ended up on a true-crime podcast? Would Daph listen, and be furious that I hadn't confided in her? Would I become a cautionary tale for my fellow students?

Teeth pulled gently at my top lip, my bottom lip, my tongue. I suddenly couldn't remember my worries and fears anymore. There was no way I was going to stop.

"Can I..." he eventually whispered, sliding his icy fingers down my face, under the collar of the hoodie, finding the spot where my obsessive fingers had picked the scab off earlier that day.

I leaned in, pressing my mouth against his ear, and whispered back, "Bite me." My idea of a joke. His eyes met mine, pools of deep, lovely darkness. They blinked once before his hand pushed the layers of fabric aside. His mouth trailed down my neck, taking its time, building my anticipation. When he reached the layer of fresh skin, his lips plied at it before his teeth broke through.

One of his hands clutched the back of my neck while he drank; the other rested on my thigh, fingertips pressing in, thumb rubbing back and forth. And... I liked it. Being wanted; being craved. In a way that was very sensual, but didn't ping my sex aversion.

When he finished, he kissed the wound, a long, gentle press of his lips. Despite their cold, I missed his hands when they lifted away.

★ ★ ★

I accidentally wore Zach's hoodie home, inciting major teasing from Daph, but I didn't mind. On Tuesday evening Zach met me on campus (my last class, disgustingly, didn't end until seven) so I could show him around. It had been his suggestion, and I could hardly believe he was actually interested. I'd tried to emphasise how boring it would be, but he'd shrugged and said, "I wanna see where you do your planning stuff," and I'd stopped arguing.

"So, on a scale of one to ten street trees, how would you rate this campus?" he asked as we wandered outside, me naming the buildings we passed, enjoying seeing them lit up in the dark along the quiet paths. It was nice to have someone walking with me – someone who wasn't just there because we happened to be going the same way, because we had a class together but no other connection. Someone who wanted to be there, next to me.

"Street trees?" I stopped to look to him. "Do you have secret planning knowledge you didn't tell me about?"

Street trees is planning jargon; it means... you guessed it, trees along the street. An essential part of pedestrian-oriented development, but not one that's particularly interesting to talk about, so I definitely hadn't mentioned it to him.

He shrugged one shoulder, looking kind of self-satisfied but like he was trying to seem chill. "I may have done some Googling..."

"You did research." I'm sure my face lit up as bright as one of the sidewalk lamps. "For our date. Uh, I mean…"

Fuck, I'd lost my filter. But it wasn't the label that got him.

"Is that, like, super dorky?" He scratched the side of his head, temporarily hiding his face. "I was legit curious. And, you know…" Now he looked at me again, his lips curved in that familiar smirk. "I was hoping to impress you."

What I almost said: *Colour me impressed. The most impressed I have ever been with another human being. Or, vampire being. I will call you whatever you want because goddamn, you did some boring-ass research for me?*

What I actually said: "Yeah. Impressed. Me – you – uh – thanks."

And he laughed, a nice laugh, a with-you-not-at-you laugh, mouth open, flashing his teeth for a second. I almost kissed him right there.

It was cold again, even with a coat, and I had an assignment to finish for the next day. So once we'd finished the tour and had meandered our way to the edge of the parking lot, I reluctantly told him I had to go.

"Oh, well…" He gave me a quick, apologetic glance. "Would you be able to give me a ride? My place is close, and I'm not sure how long it'll be till the next bus…"

"Oh sure, no problem."

"For real?"

"Yeah. I mean, it gets me more time with you." I leaned into him for a second, and a smile spread across his face. Before we continued walking he kissed my cheek, right next to my mouth. Giving him a ride was sounding better and better.

So yeah, we made out in my car in the school parking lot, and I hated that I had to leave him to do homework. But finally, like a responsible student, I stopped kissing the cute boy. "I really should get back…" I let my fingers trail down his arm to curl around his before twisting to reach for my seatbelt.

"Wait–"

When I glanced back, he went on, "Can I just..." His hand slipped free of mine, lifting to run his thumb over my neck.

That was weird. Well, weird*er*. Wanting that specific thing enough to ask for it just as I was about to drive us away...

It was weird, but it wasn't necessarily *bad* weird. It showed a lot of trust, and vulnerability, to make a request like that of someone. Right?

I let him climb into my lap and go through the process – kiss, bite, clean, band-aid. Then I drove us away. Later, I thought about the pre-car cheek kiss, and wondered if we'd been picturing two different things.

★ ★ ★

On Friday (no, I was not feeling sappy because it was the one-week anniversary of when I'd met Zach, why would you think that) I got up to wave Daph off to work, planning to crawl right back in bed as soon as she was gone and sleep till I had to leave for class.

"Good morning, zombie sunshine!" she greeted me, looking up from her lunch-packing.

"Meh." I gave her a grumpy face, then leaned over her shoulder to see what she was eating. "Mmm, PB&J. Lunch of a true adult."

"It's quick, it's easy, and it's tasty." She dropped the peanut-buttered bread onto the jelly with a flourish, then turned toward me. "Scooch, you're blocking my lunch bag." As I started to obey, she grabbed my shoulder. "Holy fuck! What did you do to your neck?"

Yep. I had totally forgotten about my tell-tale injury – and that I was wearing a tank top. "Oh – it's nothing." I undermined my own lie by clapping my hand over it. "I, uh, fell."

"You fell my ass." She shot me a glare and pried my hand away. "Lyle! It looks like – someone bit you?"

There it was. Foiled by a lunch bag and a sleeveless shirt. FML.

I gave a big, dramatic sigh, because petulance was all I had left. "All right, fiiiine." Eye-roll for additional effect. "It was Zach, it was–"

"He bit you?!" she shrieked. She moved her face even closer, her eyeball practically touching my skin. "What the *fuck*, Lyle?"

"Dude, chill *out*." I pulled away from her aggressive stare. "It was while we were – making out. He asked, and I consented."

"But *why* would you consent to someone *biting* you? You could get an infection! And look at this bruising…"

"It's not that bad." Again, I put my hand between the wound and her gaze.

"Stop that!" Again, she pulled my hand away. "Well, I don't see any pus, and it's not too red, so you're probably okay infection-wise. But it still doesn't look *good*…"

Yeah, apparently being bitten repeatedly in the same exact spot will do that. Who knew?

"Ly…" Now she sighed, taking a step back and holding up surrender hands. "I'm not here to kink shame. I'm not here to stop you from… experimenting, or whatever." I gave her a stare, raising one eyebrow, which she ignored. "But if it's impacting your health–"

"It's not 'impacting my health.' I'm fine."

"Okay, but – do you… like it?"

"Um. I mean. I don't mind it."

That was the wrong thing to say. "Enthusiastic consent, Ly!" She threw up her hands. "Don't say yes just because the other person wants it!"

"That's not what I meant…"

What the fuck did I mean? Every time Zach had texted me since Tuesday, every time I'd thought about him at all, that moment in the parking lot – *Wait; can I just…* – popped back into my head. How would he have responded if I'd said no?

Daph gave me a long look before checking her watch. "Shit, I have to go. Just… be safe, okay? I don't want you to get hurt. Emotionally or physically. Remember, communication is vital, safe words are a thing, and no means no!"

"You sound like a sexual health poster in a college dorm."

"Right now, you *need* a sexual health poster in a college dorm."

That made me laugh, and for the briefest millisecond I wished I could introduce her and Zach, invite him over to hang with the two of us. But that was a recipe for blood-flavoured disaster.

★ ★ ★

When I'd dropped off Zach outside his place on Tuesday, he'd said, "You could come here next time. I mean, it's not that great, but it's somewhere quiet to chill." It had seemed sincere, absent of innuendo. So I'd agreed.

He'd suggested Friday, even though he had work that night – maybe *he* was feeling sappy about our one-week anniversary. Before she left I reminded Daph that I was going there, and her concern ramped right back up, but I gave her his address and promised to have my phone on me at all times.

Sometime between that conversation and picking up Chinese takeout on my way over that evening, I resolved to ask Zach about the biting. Daph's voice echoed in my head, convincing me it was worth having an actual conversation with him about it.

When I arrived at his place, an old mixed-use building on Bailey with a salon on the ground floor, he met me at the bottom of the side-entry stairs. "Hey." His voice was a little weak; his face looked pale, practically glowing in the dim light of the hanging bulb. But he smiled, and kissed me. Which was enough to send me internally swooning, pushing the biting issue to the back of my mind.

"Welcome to my abode," he said wryly when we reached the door at the top of the stairs, holding it open for me. "It's a short tour: bedroom, kitchen, bathroom, living room."

He pointed as he spoke – to a bed under the sloped roof; a counter with a sink and a hot plate; a shoddily constructed plywood enclosure; a love seat below the street-facing gable. Blackout curtains covered the window, their ends pinned between the wall and the couch. The window opposite held a matching set. In place of a closet there was a cheap clothes rack, and books sat in stacks on the worn wood floor at the foot of the bed. I couldn't decide if it was more cozy or depressing.

"It's cute," I told him, and he shrugged.

"Eh, it does the job. You can sit." He nodded me toward the couch as he walked backwards to the fridge. "What do you want to drink?"

I sat, setting the takeout bag next to a gaming laptop on the otherwise-empty coffee table. The whole place was unnaturally neat – he must've cleaned for me.

From across the room, Zach went on, "I have beer, um, water, beer…"

"Beer sounds good. The second beer, I mean."

He gave me major side-eye for that, which I deserved. As we settled in to eat, he suggested we watch something, and I ended up introducing him to *Schitt's Creek*. After a few episodes and another beer, I was sleepy – and snuggly. I curled my legs up and lay my head on his shoulder, and he slid his arm around me. It was kind of perfect.

When another episode ended, he leaned forward to pause Netflix, and I lifted my head groggily. He'd barely sat back before he was kissing me, one hand on the back of my head pulling me to him, and I slid closer, hands on his waist.

I wanted to just enjoy it – but I had made myself a promise. So when his mouth slid to the side, moving down my jaw, I pulled back. "Wait. Um…" He lifted his head, revealing slightly glazed eyes, even though he'd previously demonstrated his high alcohol tolerance. I made myself go on. "I wanted to ask… what… is the deal, with the whole… biting thing?"

"Oh." His gaze moved to my neck. "I… need it."

Was that a red flag? Nah. It was a blazing neon sign reading "NOPE."

He'd let me go, sitting back a bit. I was completely free to make a break for the door. When I didn't move, it wasn't because he was stopping me.

"What do you mean?" I asked softly, hugging my knees to my chest.

He shifted farther away, turning his head to stare across the room. "I told you. I know you thought I was bullshitting you, but it's true."

"You... you're saying you..."

When I didn't finish, he turned back to me. "Yeah. Here..."

I gasped when he tugged the collar of his hoodie aside. A large scar marred the base of his neck, twisted and gnarly, the remains of a nasty wound that had healed without stitches.

"Yep." He let his hand drop, and his eyes too. "It happened when I was in school. She jumped me on my way back to my dorm one night. She almost killed me, she was so desperate. She turned me to save my life. Afterward, she apologised." He laughed, short and grim.

I felt like I was falling through the couch. Like the room was tilting around me. My hand flew up to cover my vulnerable neck. "Wait – have you–" The scar still stuck out from under his lopsided shirt, conjuring an image of teeth tearing carelessly at his skin. He wasn't like that. Was he?

"No." His eyes leapt to my face. "No, never. I wouldn't. I get – cravings, but I haven't ever..."

"So – you can – control it?"

"Not... exactly." His eyes flickered shut as he drew in a deep breath. "At first I thought I could just ignore it. Like, maybe it wasn't really real. But then I couldn't hold out any longer. I was getting weak and sick, and all I could think about was..." His face scrunched up in a cringe. "But yeah, so, I went to the medical school building and broke into the fridge where they kept the blood and, you know, stole a bunch. After I dropped out I got a job at a hospital, just an aide thing that anyone could do, but then I got caught taking their blood..."

Finally his eyes opened, creeping up to meet mine again. "Sorry. That was a lot."

"So—" My voice cracked. I couldn't fully process everything he'd just said, but one thing suddenly seemed crystal clear. "Am I–?"

He moved closer, settling his arm over my shoulders; I let him, but didn't relax. "I like you," he whispered, pressing his forehead to my temple. His voice had a quaver in it, too. "It's not – I don't–"

I couldn't answer. How was I supposed to believe him?

"I didn't have anyone," he went on. "I couldn't tell my family, or friends. I ran away from everything. But then, you…"

He took a shuddery breath, and in the pause between inhale and exhale, I heard a tear hit my jeans, felt the dampness as it seeped into the fabric. I lifted a hand to his cheek and eased his head back to stare at him.

It was like looking in a mirror. In his face I saw my own deep loneliness, my own surprise and relief at having found someone. My own fear of losing said someone.

He was waiting for an answer. For me to make a choice. He needed me, but he would let me walk away if I wanted to.

The thing was… I also needed him. I let my eyes close as I leaned in to press my lips to his. He kissed me back, his tear-wet cheek cold against my face.

"Do it," I whispered. He held me, and kissed my neck, soft and gentle – right before his teeth pierced my skin.

AN EPITAPH, EPISTOLARY

M. Špoljar

You come home from my funeral and take off your dress. You do it by the door, without undoing the buttons fully – you slip it off, leave it where it fell, and it's still there three days afterwards. Maybe waiting, for the woman you just buried to come pick it up. Maybe celebrating, that it was just your dress and not all of you left crumbled by that doorframe.

You wear the same shirt for ten days afterwards. You eat nothing but canned soup and plain bread, and usually in full darkness. You're about to run out of spoons – all the used ones now a crinkly isolation lining your sink – if you notice, you don't care. You only leave the flat for cigarettes. You text your friends that you're fine, that you just need to be alone, and they'd all know how much of a lie that is the moment they caught a glimpse of you now. You never used to answer the door without some lip-gloss on, let alone forget to wash your hair for a week. You're turning almost unrecognisable. The neighbours will think both girlfriends got buried.

You're grieving. You went through a loss so striking it took two days to fully hit, two days for your ribs to collapse against this gaping hole, the vast nothing the woman you were ready to marry disappeared into. It feels surreal, the way nightmares do, and unfamiliar in a way you can't wake up from. The logistics of mortality, the fact of a cold body you were called in to identify all fall short of how it *feels* – all fail to explain how, exactly, you are supposed to rearrange sense back into anything that resembles a daily routine. You are angry at yourself, angry at a heart that stopped beating – angry at the way your bed still fits two, the way your neighbour still smokes outside every day at 7:30. Angry that anything could still go on, like a crack doesn't run through the very fabric of time, like there isn't a void where something so important used to be. You built this life like a house and then something knocked the load-bearing wall down and now, now it has the gall to not even *sink* – not even a little – not even a small crack down a window. Just something to show this suffocating feeling exists outside of your body – that someone else feels the same, in this world with the *audacity* to go on turning – that you are not so terribly alone – that the only other person who ever seemed to get you wasn't put in the ground ten days ago.

And you were really ready to commit for life. That test you found online had said you had the avoidant attachment style, but I guess somewhere along the road you changed your mind. You never said so out loud – never made that announcement to m – but there is a ring in your closet, hidden in the back where only you were tall enough to reach. And that fancy dinner you had planned was only a month away. It's safe to say you were about to let me know.

Years of dancing around the subject, around that relationship problem where one person isn't really into the idea of marriage while the other dreamt of it since high school – the accident happened before you could pop the question but if it matters any, I would've been okay without the ring. I might have died not knowing I had changed your mind, but I died at peace with it too.

And, like, obviously, I would have said yes.

★ ★ ★

I didn't follow you from the funeral. I wasn't even at the funeral. I hope it was a lovely service – you know how I loved my event planning – but, me, not there. I appeared once you realised I'm not coming back. And we've both been sitting here since.

And, before you ask, yes, I did try picking your dress up. Didn't work, my fingers phase through. I swear it's not an excuse, though with my past record of chore-avoidance, I can see why you wouldn't believe me.

I don't expect you to believe this either, but I really hadn't done it on purpose.

It was an accident. A very unfortunate accident, both in the sense that it killed me, and in that it so very resembled what a severely depressed person with manic tendencies – such as I was, before I was dead – might do to herself. I can't even act offended that that was where everyone's minds had gone first. I sure set the reputation up myself.

I wanted to die when I was younger, yes, I made quite a few attempts to. There were times when I didn't particularly enjoy being alive near the end – dangerously near the end – but acting on it was a thing of the past. I do not expect you to believe me. But I really had no plans to die by my own hand.

I could say it was because of you. I could say loving you showed me how to love myself. It wouldn't even be wholly untrue. I could say loving you *made* me love myself (that would be untrue). It would be a good story. People like that kind of a story.

The truth is that the things that made me want to die weren't the kind of things falling in love could fix. There are dangerously few things falling in love can fix. Maybe no things at all. I wanted to die before you and during you and should we ever have broken up – you know, with me still alive – I would have probably continued wanting to die, though not because of you. My depressive tendencies had nothing to do with how much love I was receiving. My symptoms were not going to go away for a romance, no matter how grand, no matter how lasting.

We used to talk, back when I still had a mouth that could speak, about what we thought our ghosts would look like.

"They're always the young versions of themselves," you'd say, "in the movies." Glorification of youth, you'd then say. Refusal to hire older women. Then we'd get distracted talking about the Hollywood age gaps. We always got so easily distracted.

You were a fan of ghosts looking the way that they did, the moment they died. Every outfit you picked had to pass that test – I used to hate this– the *would I agree to wear this for an eternity* test. It didn't matter where you were going – it didn't matter how much of a hurry you were in – be it date night or a quick run to the corner shop, you picked what you put on with so much care. If it had been vanity, I would have encouraged every second. But I knew you well enough to know how you were raised, and whose voice guided you to look for yourself in every reflective surface. That the way you pored over your lipstick was not adoration, but scrutiny.

You've been wearing the same outfit for two weeks now. It's a sweater and some leggings. First time I've seen you in either. You hate how your calves look, and think baggy clothes make your torso look boxy. I'd be proud of you for forgetting to give a shit if it looked like anything but a mental health crisis.

(Also, I'm wearing whatever you remember me wearing. In case you wanted to know. You really liked me in a suit, huh.)

What I'm trying to say is, if love could fix broken wiring, ours would've. What I'm trying to say is, if it were possible to love so right a wrong is forgotten, we would know, because we would have done it. What I'm trying to say is, I loved loving you even if it did nothing about my symptoms. What I'm trying to say is, you pushed me to try.

What I'm trying to say is, I really didn't do this to you on purpose.

And, god, you need to wash your fucking dishes.

I was able to explain it away at first. I was an expert in long-running slumps, after all. I'd had many a week of wallowing in self-made isolation and I – well, I didn't make it out fine, I guess, but it wasn't them that did me in.

But then your two weeks turned into four, and then into months, and then I realised you were really unwell.

★ ★ ★

It's not that I expected you to get over me in a fortnight. I would have been a little offended if you had, to be honest. We'd been together for quite a while. And I wasn't going to tell you how to feel your pain – I didn't have a right to that while I was alive and even less of one now I was gone. But I recognised concerning. And you were concerning.

It was during one of your especially bad nights – the kind of nights that made me think my mother was right, that gay people do go to hell, and that this was it and that it was just watching you kill yourself slowly and terribly until we were both gone. It was then that I found myself able to grab onto fabric.

I don't know how it works. I don't know what I am, to be made tangible by your grief. But I saw the chance, and I phoned your sister.

She tried getting you to respond for a minute first. Inside voice, first, then full-on screaming. You didn't answer, because your phone was on your bedside, and you were on the kitchen floor just vegetating. Then she hung up, and less than an hour later, she was at your door. When you didn't let her in I managed to flip the lock, and then thanked some god I don't believe in that she didn't question the mechanism moving on its own, and instead rushed to your side. She cursed her entire way through.

"Jesus Christ," she kept saying, and it was what we all were thinking. "Jesus fucking *Christ*. Did you – when'd you last – oh, man, you *smell*."

She made you take a shower, did your dishes (fucking finally), made you get dressed, and took you to her house. I don't know what happened next – I didn't seem to be able to go after you – but at least I knew you were looked after. By someone who could touch you, I mean. All the time. I don't really count for much anymore. I got all the practical use cremated out of me.

* * *

You came back a month later. I wasn't there to witness it – I vanished the moment the door shut after you, and reappeared only once you were back in – I was still deeply sure that it had been a month. I wish I could have told you, because you would have loved it, that it took *dying* for me to get a hang of the passage of time.

You looked better. Though that isn't saying much, considering how bad you looked before.

I still couldn't follow you out of the apartment but I found myself appearing by you at random places (though, of course, none of them were random). The bench we used to people-watch from. The store we did our weekly shopping in. The karaoke bar we liked for date night. You never went into that one, you just watched sadly from across the road, and it was always in broad daylight and you always looked extremely stupid. Our apartment, our kitchen, our bedroom, the one bus-route that took us to town – but only at 2:30, and only on Saturdays, because that's the only time we ever took it together.

I exist only in places I'm visibly absent from. That's how I decided to put it. Maybe because it currently feels really fucking true. It's a sad life, being defined by how gone you are.

And, that more frustratingly, it's *still* not as sad as yours.

I gave you two years to mope around – and it was only because you still socialised, though it was exclusively with your sister, and because you applied for an internship and you went to work and you didn't go back to eating soup and being sad on a floor all the time. But then two years passed and you were still so fucking sad.

Your sister tried to get you to go out and see friends, and you told her you would, and everyone who ever knew you knew you were lying. But you're so sad now, no one had the heart to call you out on it. I would have called you out, just like I always used to call you out. But I don't have a voice now. Maybe you don't miss me enough for it to formalise – maybe I've been gone long enough for you to have forgotten the sound of it. I was never one to send voice-messages, so you have nothing to replay over and over (thank *god*). You still have pictures, though, selfies and candids and those terrible official photos. And I have to watch you watch them.

See, the thing is – the thing is – I don't want you to forget me. I just want you to remember me as something other than whatever this is, as something other than this heaviness, dragging the rest of your twenties into the ground with my corpse. I wanted to spend the rest of my life with you, yeah, but not like this, never like this. I said it once, when we were fighting, but I meant it and I still mean it. I said, I'd rather never see you again than watch myself hurt you.

Please, don't tell me that I jinxed us.

★ ★ ★

The neighbour – the one always out at 7:30 – she asked you for a lighter today. She saw you smoking on our ground-floor balcony while out on the pavement and, well, shot her shot. I was scared you wouldn't, but you did hand over your lighter. She waited around for a bit afterwards, obviously hoping for some small talk, but you kept being so incredibly unresponsive she eventually just threw it back to you and gave up.

Still, super proud of you. Baby steps. You'll be the life of the party in no time.

Next big step came with you buying new plates. The ones we had were all cracked up. I'd stolen them from my mother right before getting disowned, and got a real surge of petty joy every time we used it for our lesbian domestic bliss. You tolerated them only for my sake and then I died and you continued, I guess, only for my memory.

You cry while boxing them away and I think I do too, and I am once again tangible enough to touch walls, to smell your hair. You changed your shampoo, in the time that passed, but you'll always smell like yourself to me.

You start having conversations with the neighbour. You go for after-work drinks with your office crew, and then decide you don't like them, which is fair. You go to our karaoke bar, with friends from high school – you pull me close enough to taste the bitterness in your throat, but you last the night, and the next morning I feel so much lighter.

You run into the neighbour near our bench, and you manage some shaky pleasantries, and I'm more of an echo with every second.

I exist in flashes now, I exist easily. I exist in bursts of flavour when you bite into my favourite shortbread, I exist in the bass-solo our song starts off with. I exist like a scar, healed over enough to handle being picked at here and there. I exist as an inside joke, its punchline slowly forgotten.

There's someone else in our bed eventually. I swear I don't look.

I swear I'm at peace with everything.

THE GHOST AT
HAUNTING'S END

Elisabeth R. Moore

The first person to step out onto the large hulking shelf of volcanic rock that people in Oregon called "the beach" was Brinkman. Brinkman, at age sixteen, had sent my father a letter. The first line read, "Congratulations on your new daughter, sir." It continued: "We understand why she is here. But... does she have to go to school? We don't want to see her."

I found the email, printed out and dated, in my father's files yesterday morning. He'd alphabetised every piece of hate mail he received, organised by sender. Even the anonymous handwritten notes were categorised: he'd probably recognised them based on the handwriting. All the notes, complaints, observations and documentation were about me – I was the only contentious decision in my father's life.

The email had surprised me – I had always thought that Brinkman was the most tolerant of the four. Once again, my human-esque instincts had deceived me.

It was strange seeing him now. He was shorter. More stooped. The sea had weathered him down too, like it weathered everyone who stayed in this town. He wore a thick jacket, and a huge, ugly hat. It wasn't the bright orange one that he had worn every day in high school, though it was equally big and chunky. I wondered if his mother was still alive, still knitting him hats.

I glanced behind me. Across the pot-holed road, my child-hood home sat. All the windows were dark, except for the small nightlight glowing up in the top right window. My mother's corpse was cooling in there.

I turned away. A stubborn mist shrouded the other houses that lined the torn-up asphalt. I was on an island. Just me, my mother's corpse, and ahead of me, Brinkman, staring into the sea.

I took a deep breath of the crisp, cold autumnal air. The shreds of darkness clung to the edges of the morning, even while the sun was making a sluggish attempt to rise from the horizon and free itself from the thick duvet of clouds.

I had a brilliant view from the edge of Ocean Drive. The beach sprawled in front of me, and on it stood Brinkman. Around him, the beach at low tide bared its secrets to the world. The sharp shards of black rock glistened, mottled textures catching even the feeblest beginning of light. Tide pools sat isolated from each other, though the ripples of wind along their surface hinted at life below the surface. The beach was nearly fifteen feet below me – I stood on the road, leaning against the guardrail, watching. In front of me was the precipice, a straight drop of sheer rock, now covered in seaweed and shells.

The next person who stepped onto the beach was Jessica Norwood. She appeared from behind a boulder. I wondered how long she'd opted to walk on the rocky, dangerous beach. She could have walked along the road, but then she'd risk someone seeing her. Clearly this ritual wasn't important enough to her to risk the gossip.

Jessica Norwood was born Jessica Carter – daughter of the grocers. I had found her father's letters in my father's collection. I hadn't been surprised to find them there – Mr Carter had never tried to hide his disdain for me. When I was newly created, sent to buy the one thing my mother forgot on our weekly grocery store trip, I lived in fear that he would see me between the isles of his tiny shop. I would walk into the store, shoulders hunched, collar of my coat turned up. Was I about to be thrown out? Often Jessica would be at the cashier. She would ignore me.

I never knew whether that was a kindness or an insult.

She looked surprisingly good now – she wore a long, thick wool coat, and a bright red scarf. It matched her coif of blond hair that shone brightly in the cold morning.

I was surprised to see her out there, to be honest. Of the four teenagers who had witnessed Calliandra's death, Jessica had been the most resilient. She'd gone to therapy, and dealt with her shit. She was always polite to me, though only if no one was looking. If anyone should have been able to leave this crummy town, leave the death of Calliandra behind her, and move on, it should have been her.

"I don't see anything when I dream," she had admitted to me decades ago with a small shrug, making as if to pass me the joint, and then pausing. She had looked between me and the joint, and then dropped it into its small tube. "I only hear the crack. It's a sound I immediately recognise: the sound of a skull being smashed against the rocks. It's so loud, and in my dream it's the exact moment I know she's dead." The tube with the weed clicked shut. "It sucks though, because I don't wake up. I don't wake up for hours – I just listen to the sound of the body being battered against the rocks. Over and over again."

The image of Jessica's dream has haunted me for years. I kept on looking for that sound – what did a skull against rock sound like? I will never know.

Jessica herself had never written to my family. Nor had her husband, which surprised me. Simon Norwood's whole family had been pretty active in protesting my existence. But neither of them showed up in my father's book.

Simon's mother, of course, had her own binder. She had written whole novels worth of hate mail. She had ousted my mother from book group, and then from the ladies' club, and then, finally, from the Daughters of the Revolution. My mother had been so hurt. She'd asked for a truce. Mrs Isabella Norwood suggested best-selling novels hiding vile anti-android propaganda as one of our town's books of the year every year.

My mother never recovered from the shame.

I hadn't really known about that though. My mother's ousting from the Daughters of the Revolution had been a huge deal, according to my father, but I hadn't known; I had severed my ties with them already.

My father had laid it all out in the handwritten letter he had sent to the Artist of which a carbon copy was preserved in his binder. Dated for the day after he visited me at my California college, it featured a sixteen-point justification for why he and my mother deserved to get a refund on me. I wasn't everything they'd wanted, everything they'd *needed*. The Artist, my father, believed, had not delivered. I was not good enough.

The letter itself had not shocked me: my father was a methodical man, and he had informed me of his intentions to write as he left me in my dorm room. I had been surprised of the descriptions my father gave of my mother's anguish and the town's vitriol.

The Artist's reply, stapled on the very next page, had delighted me. He had written three words on the back of a receipt from a diner in St Louis. It said: "Still no refunds." That was it. My father filed the note, and the envelope, dutifully.

There was no further correspondence.

★ ★ ★

Jannick Sorenson and Ashley Roderiguez arrived together. They were both married to other people, but had been having an affair – off and on – for the last two decades. It was our town's open secret: Jannick and Ashley, walking close enough to touch, but never holding the other's hand in public. He was the son of a fisherman, and worked as a software engineer now. She… she I didn't know.

When I was at college, my mother threatened to call him on me. As if he somehow could rewrite my programming, despite also only being a freshman too. I had happily informed her that he didn't have the skills to work on my software, though I concealed the fact that I had been editing my own software for years.

In the end, the fact that she even made the threat had opened a chasm between us that no amount of reasoning could bridge.

All four of them were gathered now, ready for their annual ritual. There was a moment of awkwardness – Jannick stepped forward and reached for Brinkman's hand to start their usual prayer circle, but Brinkman thought he was going in for a (left-handed?) handshake, and tried to return the gesture. They laughed it off, and I could hear the tinkle of nervous laughter even from my perch. Jannick clapped Brinkman on the back. A sham of camaraderie.

They began their ritual.

It's always like this. I watch them, curious at how resilient their strange human rituals have been over the years. The four of them gather, and they say a prayer. They think about Calliandra, the friend they lost when they were teenagers. They share thoughts for her. They say goodbye.

They've never invited me down there. I'm not surprised; you can't exactly mourn someone when an android, built in her image to replace what is lost, stands in front of you.

"Calliandra!"

I go by Callie now, but I returned his greeting anyway. It's Rod – Rod, with a face craggy and old, ears huge, nose even bigger. Rod, who walked this beach every morning, with his loyal dog and a pair of binoculars around his neck. Rod, who knew and loved my parents, who was kind to me, who never once wrote me hate mail, not even in secret. I smiled at him – I was surprised by how much his returning smile soothed something primal in me. Should I be surprised? I did become an orphan this morning.

"How is your mother today?" he asked.

"Just fine, thank you." Of course, my mother died at 3.02am. I had sat beside her side all night, and when she whimpered and gasped, I was there for her. Rod nodded, put his gnarled hand on my shoulder, and sighed.

"It's a good thing you did," he told me, "coming out here. I know they weren't great but..." He trailed off. He'd caught sight of the people on the beach, and frowned. "Are you watching them?" he asked, suddenly accusatory. I blinked, bewildered at this shift.

"Yes?" I offered, unsure of how to respond.

"You can't do that," he said, trying to use his hand on my shoulder to turn me away. "They're mourning!" I let myself be twisted, and stumbled a little as he physically turned my body away, cutting off my line of sight. A rush of rage thrummed through me, and I wanted to bare my teeth at him. Instead, I grabbed his hand – with way more force than necessary – and wrenched it from my shoulder. He flinched in pain. His dog began barking loudly. I held it for a second, relishing the feeling of brittle skin and bones under my hand, and then I dropped it.

"They're mourning *me*," I hissed, suppressed rage from hours of flicking through binders dedicated to my evil and sinful existence spilling out. "What do you mean, I don't have a right to watch?"

Rod shrunk back, his dog mirroring his actions, eyes widening as it stopped barking.

I relished his fear.

"It's not you," he corrected, cradling his hand.

Of course. Of course even this man, this man who had been kind to me my whole life, thought it. I thought of some of the other child-replacement androids, those who had broken under the grief they were programmed to carry; mostly, they had moved on from their human shapes, choosing a disembodied existence. He had *no right* to speak the one truth I had spent my life fearing.

"Leave," I snapped, and he scurried away, glancing back at me with a flash of fear before he stumbled, righted himself, and looked ahead, his dog pulling him along.

But he was right, and I knew it. I knew I wasn't her. I had never wanted to be *her*. My parents had commissioned me as a shrine to their grief, and they had spent their whole lives resenting me for not grieving with them. For not being *her*.

But the truth was that the four adults out on the beach weren't mourning Calliandra either. My parents, in their construction to me, had not been mourning *her*. Brinkman, Jessica, Jannik and Ashley weren't mourning *her*. They were mourning fossilised memories of her – probably, by now, only a series of images. A series of cherry-picked images did not a person make.

Calliandra herself had been a reckless, acidic, sometimes cruel fourteen-year-old. She had been the apple of her parents' eye, perfect, and the only daughter they had wanted. She had rotted a little under that protective mantle, lashing out viciously when kids didn't want to participate in her games. The night she drowned, she had jeered at the other teenagers when they were too scared to enter the waters.

This girl, who was never allowed to be a woman, was unmournable. She was cruel to her mother, bullied her father, and in middle school routinely held Eliza Carter's head in the toilet. She was neither kind, nor considerate. She was, in the unique way of some privileged teenagers, bent on her own self destruction. Her parents had raised her with constant praise, and it had left her hollow and hungry.

"It's not her either." Calliandra M. Ravos had died at the age of fourteen. The people on the beach had watched her die – watched a sneaker wave destabilise her in the water, and then drag her out into the ocean, cruel waves bashing her against the rocks. *I saw her head crack like a ripe pumpkin*, one of the bystanders had told the police.

★ ★ ★

The Artist had programmed me to be Calliandra. I had been wild, reckless and cruel. That first day of school, everyone glared at me. Their parents had instructed them to ignore me, and even as I sat down in my first class, a gangly android with new and unfamiliar limbs, I'd felt the algorithm responding to the stimulus (loneliness). It generated Calliandra's response: hurt people, now. At any cost.

The Artist was a skilled programmer, and an even better sculptor of silicon and metal. I was given a composite of Calliandra's entire digital footprint and every word from her diaries. I spent years obsessing over every aspect of what I knew of Calliandra. They were a dangerous cocktail – I got too much of the private Calliandra, and not enough of her public persona. I learned to code in secret, and began to update my algorithm compulsively, adding more and more data points, expanding the rules as the data set grew. And yet I remained flighty and cruel.

The day I threw a small ornamental sugar dish at my mother, I knew it was too much. My algorithm was *wrong*: the girl who had drowned had been a child. I was eighteen and had been held prisoner by this algorithm. No longer would I act on my first instinct, choosing short-term pleasure over long-term gain. I gently unwound the spooling network of instincts and thoughts, and archived them far away from my cognitive processes.

I resented these teenagers and their mourning ritual, keeping a false memory of Calliandra alive. My parents kept me, a calcified ghost of the daughter they lost. After the sugar dish incident, I wrapped up the defunct Calliandra algorithm, enrolled in the local state college, and left.

At first my parents were relieved and excited. Calliandra is making an effort! Calliandra is doing well! Calliandra is...on track? They realised pretty quickly what had happened.

I was truly surprised how hurt they were. Mother called me, sobbing, and raged at me. I had never realised that Calliandra's rages weren't spontaneous – none of the memories I had been given included this side of our mother. Our father came to visit me, and sat in my dorm room, looking at me. Tears rolled down his face, and he begged me to become Calliandra again.

As I listened to them, I realised – they would prefer to be hurt, over and over again, by an entity that reminded them of their daughter, than run the risk of forgetting her. They were so terrified of losing their connection to her, losing the thing that made them Mom and Dad. My action felt like a betrayal, a repeat murder of their child. But this time they had someone to blame.

They could barely look at me, by the end. I sat on the edge of my stiff dorm bed, trying to explain my rationale, the line in my code that demanded familial love repeating over and over again ad nauseam as I realised I'd failed. I'd failed at my basic programming, in their eyes. I was not built to be alive, or to be their child. I was built to replace Calliandra M. Ravos, and I had failed.

Their rejection was final. I left, and they didn't call me. They didn't reach out on my birthday. I spent all of November waiting for a text. I spent Thanksgiving alone, eating ramen in a restaurant in L.A. I graduated with honors. I became a lawyer. I joined the Androids Civil Liberties Union in L.A., and prosecuted high profile cases. I got married, and then married again. Both my partners, androids produced by a factory, never asked about my parents because they didn't have any.

And yet, despite the rejection, despite the edits to my code, still, I knew I was not like them. I *had* parents. It was just that in my parents' eyes, I was nobody. I was not their daughter, and they washed their hands of me. No one called to notify me of father's death. He died in his sleep on a Tuesday, and they held the memorial service that Friday. It was a quiet affair, according to the Oceanside Chronicle. *He is survived by wife Bethany Ravos.* I wasn't even worth the words in the obituary.

Eventually, my mother's social worker tracked me down. She informed me of my father's death in a dry, quick way. The words cut straight to the core of me – sharp and metallic, they tasted like corrosion and rust. I had stumbled against the doorframe of the house in L.A. that I shared with my partners. Two of them had come out, and frowned at the social worker's face on my tablet.

"You don't have time for this," the social worker clipped at me. "Decouple your emotions from your processing power. Come down to Oceanside. Your mother is dying."

All androids legally have to have the ability to decouple their emotions from their processing. It made us excellent emergency workers and brilliant technicians. The Artist, however, made me humanoid. Technically that was illegal; androids were only allowed to resemble humans in specific circumstances, and cognition wasn't one of them. They were allowed to react, but that reaction should be contained.

The Artist had never given me that luxury. My ability to decouple was a recent skill – my partner Switch had taught me only a couple of years ago. I didn't have to do it, though. I just went back to Oceanside.

My mother didn't react to seeing me; her blank eyes looked past me as I entered. I don't think she even realised I was there. She was sick enough that the hospice transferred her back to her home with one week's worth of oxygen. I gave her water, switched her IV fluids, administered her opiates. I switched out her bedpan, fed her, and washed her face with the soft washcloths I remembered from home.

I watched her die.

Was there a line in my code that was telling me I had to be here? Was there something anchoring me to this spot, watching her? All week, I felt like a quiet ghost, floating around Oceanside. I barely left the house, choosing to skip food in favour of more traditional charging. I walked around in the dead of night, my night-vision making it so I could avoid running into anyone who might remember me. There was something nearly unmatched to the darkness of small poverty-stricken towns. I could slide through every street, catalog every new house and development, and yet no one saw me.

I hadn't even noticed the date when she died. I had spent the day sitting at her bedside, organizing my father's paperwork, listening to her rattling breathing. It was only when I found the first letter, the letter my father had laboriously written by hand to lay inside a book to send to a man he had read about on the DarkWeb, that I realised. My mother had died the same day as Calliandra. The ultimate gesture of tragic love.

★ ★ ★

It was the realisation of the dates that had pushed me out of this house, onto this road, to watch these people gather.

As I stood on that cliff, and looked down at those four gathered victims, all I saw was four adults, mourning the teenagers they once were. Their grief was normal — rational, even — and it wasn't for me. It wasn't for Calliandra. It was for a version of themselves, a version that didn't understand how easy dying was, and a version of themselves that never had to see how far people went in their desperate need for their grief to be seen.

The wind picked up. It buffeted my hair, and I slowly turned to look at the house, and realised: I felt free.

I was no longer this ghost, anchored by my parents. They had held onto me, even in my absence. There were small signs all over the house that they had mourned me. My father had filed years' worth of a town's infractions. My mother had kept the small tinny eardrum I had lost when I was new. They had pasted cuttings from the Oceanside Chronicle onto cardboard and then framed them, announcements of my graduation from college, and then my job, and even one high profile case I litigated. They must have sent in the announcements themselves.

But I wasn't theirs anymore. I was Callie, and I was my own. I turned away from the ocean, turned away from my parents' house, and walked south.

I was a ghost no longer, and my haunting had come to an end.

Q.E.D.

Kimberly Rei

The crowd was on tenterhooks. It was an intimate group; small and well-contained in a dim room. Most of them knew each other, some by mere sight, some over shared experience. They gathered here every weekend to give praise and near-worship.

A single light shone on the stage, dead centre. All eyes locked on the platform, focused on the pool of light. A Shiver hung in the air, waiting to sweep through the room and feed on their delighted gasps.

No metaphor, no turn of phrase or literary device. The Shiver followed the emcee the way it did every night. Not just those weekend performances, but all the time. It hovered near, waiting until enough energy had built. And then it reached out to gently stroke arms, necks, spines. It licked, inhaled the rush of a sweet shudder, and was sated once more.

Once, before it knew itself and its power, the Shiver took too much. It would feed unto death and sometimes beyond, consuming souls. It had never dared enter a place like this. Instead, it would linger in back alleys, waiting for a lone addict to stumble outside for a hit of whatever poison they preferred. The Shiver didn't care. It only needed the moment just before euphoria struck. That moment was the tastiest. That moment, so precious and fleeting, lasted the longest.

The Shiver had its own addictions.

More than once, it was sure its meal had seen it. Stared right at it and offered up life-giving energy in exchange for quiet death.

They disturbed it a bit, these darkly painted humans with their black clothes and their infinite despair. There was a hint of guilt in taking from them, no matter how eagerly they gave. It was all too easy to take too much. To ride the high as they shifted from crushing sadness to exquisite release.

One night, no addicts stumbled over the back threshold. No violently lonely, tear-stained cheeks turned toward the careless moon. The Shiver almost went hungry that night.

Until someone, not a friend but still familiar to the Shiver, strolled by. They were always smiling and whistling a tune, never sad or dejected. The Shiver had seen, but never approached. Watched, but never taken from. It was afraid of breaking that joy. The not-friend opened the back door and let the sound of whispering out. Excited whispering. Anticipation. The shadowed veil between hunger and starvation.

It followed the whistling and found the whispering.

Here, in the hallowed halls of people, the creature paused. The joy it had feared destroying was *everywhere*. Hunger gnawed, but terror breathed a warning.

Hunger won and it moved in a rush.

The moment was nearly lost. The Shiver swept into the room exactly as the man stepped into the light. And what a man he was. Or woman, to be so beautifully ornamented. Or godling.

Fae. Demon. It couldn't be sure and hesitation came so very close to costing the Shiver its meal.

The enticing creature strolled the length of the stage, firing up the crowd. Their heeled boots clicked a pattern, giving the audience a pulse to cheer to. Skin-tight leather, black as a starless night, hugged every line and curve. A necklace of fake, fat gems hung close to the stroke of his neck. Painted lips curled in a smile that invited company and promised sinful adventures.

As their arms rose, diamonds and rubies dragging everyone's gaze, and they belted out a playful greeting, the Shiver moved. The Shiver stretched itself and wrapped around every body in the room. Always before, it sought single prey, keeping a tight focus. But here, amidst such a grand buffet, it could not contain itself. For a moment, it was lost in the gluttony of emotion, in danger of overdosing on ecstasy.

But not killing. It didn't kill. It was sated and then some. Where there had been shame in the past, from taking too much, from putting lives in danger, there was only satisfaction. There was more than enough euphoria for all.

After that night, the Shiver followed its newfound saviour everywhere. It learned that the creature, for it still hadn't narrowed down class nor phylum, caused the same sort of reaction everywhere. The Shiver sipped throughout the day, rolling in energy the way a cat lolled in a sunbeam.

The weekends were still the best, though. The most gluttonous. The most indulgent. The most fun.

It watched as its saviour stepped onto the stage. Light danced from the spangles and glitter decorating cloth. Slender, androgynous hips shimmied as strong fingers tipped in dyed talons wrapped around a microphone. Platform heels clicked. Laughter, warm and inviting filled the air. Eyes, cheeks, and lips perfectly painted lifted to the crowd and the Shiver swept through.

One arm raised, coaxing the crowd to a proper welcome. The Shiver joined in, as rapturous as any human.

"Queen Daddy!"

ABOUT THE

CONTRIBUTORS

THE EDITOR

Celine Frohn

Celine Frohn is a publisher, editor, and PhD researcher with a passion for Gothic and LGBTQ+ literature. The *Unspeakable* and *Unthinkable* anthologies combine both her academic work on the nineteenth-century Gothic, as well as her love for contemporary speculative fiction. Celine runs Nyx Publishing, which has published queer SFF including S.T. Gibson's *A Dowry of Blood* and Holly J. Underhill's *The Bone Way*.

THE INTRODUCTION

S.T. Gibson

Saint is a literary agent, author, and village wise woman in training. A graduate of the creative writing program at the University of North Carolina at Asheville and the theological studies program at Princeton Seminary, she currently lives in Boston with her partner, spoiled Persian cat, and vintage blazer collection. She is represented by Tara Gilbert of the Jennifer De Chiara literary agency.

THE CONTRIBUTORS

K. Blair

K. Blair (she/they) is a member of London Queer Writers. They have been published in Spoken Word London's *Anti-Hate Anthology*, *The Valley Press Anthology of Prose Poetry*, the *Dear Damsels* website, *Opia* magazine, *From the Farther Trees*, *HAD*, *Wretched Creations* magazine, *Stone of Madness Press*, *Not Deer* Magazine, *Queerlings* Magazine, *Daily Drunk Mag*, The Bad Betty Press *Book of Bad Betties Anthology*, the *Final Girl Bulletin Board*, *Rejection Letters*, *en*gendered lit* and *Fruit Journal*. Find her in the vending machine at your local train station or most likely on Twitter: @WhattheBlair, Instagram: @urban_barbarian, and their website, www.kblair.co.uk.

Jillian Bost

Jillian Bost loves horror, reading, and tea. In addition to her upcoming story in *Unthinkable,* she has had short horror works published by Cemetery Gates Media, Lycan Valley Press Publications, and Things in the Well Publications. She is an Affiliate Member of the Horror Writers Association.

G. T. Korbin

G. T. Korbin is an author from Greece, currently living abroad to pursue a career in STEM. Primarily a fantasy author, her writing often focuses on reimagining old myths and tales of her culture, with a love for drama that makes her think those tales might have been better left alone. When she's not writing, you can listen for the sound of Greek swearing to find her playing videogames or attempting to bake, both with similar success. You can follow her on twitter at @g_korbin, or read her short stories in anthologies from TL;DR Press and others.

Adriana C. Grigore

Adriana C. Grigore is a writer from the windswept plains of Romania. They have a degree in literature and linguistics, a penchant for folklore, and a tendency to overwater houseplants. You can find their fiction in *Clarkesworld*, *Beneath Ceaseless Skies*, *The Magazine of Fantasy & Science Fiction*, and others. Find them online at www.adrianacgrigore.com or on Twitter as @aicigri.

Dee Holloway

Dee Holloway is a librarian, writer, and Floridian in upstate New York. Selections of her short work have appeared most recently in *Unfettered Hexes* from Neon Hemlock, *Clockwork, Curses, and Coal* from Worldweaver Press, and among the Cup & Dagger mini-chapbook series from Sword and Kettle Press. When not writing, she's often sampling cold brew or hanging on the rail at the nearest racetrack.

Stewart Horn

Stewart Horn is a professional musician and amateur writer, poet and photographer. Originally from Glasgow, he now lives with his husband and assorted pets in the quaint seaside town of Troon. His short fiction and poetry have been published in books, magazines, journals and websites in Europe, North America and Australia, including *Crowded*, *Lovecraft Ezine*, *The Horrorzine*, *Feast of Frights*, *Estronomicon*, *Interzone*, *the British Fantasy Society Journal*, *Excessica*, *Davanti Alla Specchio*, *Thirty Years of Rain* and *Flotation Device*. His work has appeared in podcasts *Pseudopod* and *Tales to Terrify*. He blogs intermittently at stewartguitar.wordpress.com.

Kallyn Hunter

Kallyn Hunter is a queer writer, researcher and Renaissance Faire performer from the foothills of Colorado. She has a number of short stories published in various anthologies and is working on a full-length fantasy horror novel. When she's not creating worlds behind a computer screen, she can be found exploring our own with her partner, her mustang, and her adventure-seeking Pomeranian.

Gillian Joseph
Gillian Joseph (they/them) is a queer, 2-Spirit Ihaŋktoŋwaŋ and Mdewakaŋtoŋ Dakota storyteller who grew up as a guest on Waxhaw and Catawba lands. They are a folio editor at *Anomaly*, and enjoy spending time near mní + trying to figure out what their dreams mean. Their website is gillian-joseph.com.

Solstice Lamarre
Solstice Lamarre is a French, non-binary aroace writer. They write queer, neurodivergent stories in various genres, but always come back to themes of monstrosity, found family, and all sorts of queer love. When they're not writing, they work as an English teacher for French teens or volunteer at their local LGBTI+ centre and activist group. In between writing, work, and activism, they read an unholy number of books, play videogames they never finish, and cuddle with their cat.

Hunter Liguore
Hunter Liguore is a writer, professor, and historian, often found roaming old ruins, hillsides, and cemeteries. Her work can be found in *Bellevue Literary Review*, *Irish Pages*, *Porridge Magazine*, and more. *Whole World Inside Nan's Soup* is available from Yeehoo Press. hunterliguore.org or @skytale_writer.

Sydney Meeker
Sydney Meeker (he/him) is a Portland, Oregon-based writer of video games, short stories, and poetry. His work has appeared in *Zoetic Press*, *Entropy Mag*, *Prismatica Mag*, and others. He has been nominated for several awards for both video game writing and traditional prose and poetry, including the *Herman Melville Award for Best Writing* and *Best of the Net* awards. When he's

not writing, he can be found playing video games, getting lost in the woods, or sometimes doing both at the same time. He tweets at @SydMeeker.

Antonija Mežnarić

Antonija Mežnarić is a Croatian writer and editor, living and breathing speculative fiction. She loves to write queer horror and urban fantasy inspired by folklore. Alongside her partner, she runs a small Croatian publishing house Shtriga, she's the co-editor at online magazine for speculative fiction Morina kutija and a co-host of the Croatian podcast about writing and publishing, Mora FM. Her notable works include the sapphic horror comedy novella *What Do Nightmares Dream of* and a queer folk horror collection *Mistress of Geese*. You can follow her book ramblings on hauntednarratives.com or on Instagram and Twitter @antonijamezni.

Elisabeth R. Moore

Elisabeth R Moore is a grad student, writer, and lesbian. She and her wife live Essen, Germany, where Moore is working on her Masters Thesis on Climate Fiction. She writes strange stories about plants, birds and queer women. When she's not writing, she crochets, reads, and hikes. She tweets at @willowcabins.

Valentin Narziss

Valentin Narziss is a writer and painter, living in Berlin and Florence. His work merges the modern, archaic and queer, and usually has a dark twist to it. When not creating, he enjoys dressing androgynously and petting every cat he meets.

Tabitha O'Connell

Tabitha O'Connell is a historic preservationist and writer of queer fiction living in Western New York. Eir favorite things include animals, abandoned places, alliteration, long walks, and long sentences. Particularly passionate about stories featuring trans and ace-spectrum characters, ey has published several queer fantasy novellas, and eir short fiction has appeared in the anthologies *Queers Who Don't Quit* and *Prismatic Dreams*. Find em on Twitter @tabithawrites or visit tabithaoconnell.com..

Arden Powell

Arden Powell is a speculative-fiction author and illustrator from the Canadian East Coast. They graduated from St. Francis Xavier University in 2013 with a Bachelor of Arts degree, Honouring in English Literature. As a hybrid author they self-publish as well as publish with indie presses, and have had work accepted by literary magazines including *Baffling Magazine* and *Lightspeed*. A nebulous entity, they live with a small terrier and an exorbitant number of houseplants, and have conversations with both. They write across a range of fantasy sub-genres and everything they write is queer.

Kimberley Rei

Kimberly Rei does her best work in the places that can't exist... the in-between places where imagination defies reality. With a penchant for dark corners and hooks that leave readers looking over their shoulder, she is always on the lookout for new ideas, new projects, and new ways to make words dance. Kimberly lives in gorgeous Florida where the beaches defy reality and the sun is a special kind of horror. Her debut novelette, *Chrysalis*, is available on Amazon.

M. Špoljar

M. Špoljar writes prose and poetry, and in her free time works in audiovisual translation. His work has appeared in places such as Novel Noctule, warning lines, and perhappened.

THE DESIGNER

Ashley Hankins

Ashley Hankins is a fantasy and sci-fi illustrator. A native of Western New York, she spent several years in Humboldt County, California, where she became enamored with the mountains and mist-shrouded forests. She felt she had truly found someplace magical. Upon returning to New York, Ashley strives to inject her work with that same ethereal feeling she felt in those woods. Ashley is a primarily digital artist who loves palettes that feed into both a Gothic aesthetic and bright color pops, lots of mood, and experimenting with strong, graphic shapes. When Ashley is not working on her latest project, she can be found writing, hiking with her partner, and drinking excessive amounts of tea.

THE CREDITS

Creating a book takes a massive team effort. Haunt, the editor and the contributors would like to thank everyone who worked behind the scenes on *Unthinkable: A Queer Gothic Anthology*.

Managing Director
Rebecca Wojturska

Editor & Anthologist
Celine Frohn

Copy-editor
Ross Stewart

Cover Designer
Ashley Hankins
ashleydoesartstuff.com

Typesetter
Laura Jones
lauraflojo.com